WEE WILLIE WINKIE

Rudyard Joseph Kipling was born in Bombay in 1865. His father, John Lockwood Kipling, was the author and illustrator of *Beast and Man in India* and his mother, Alice, was the sister of Lady Burne-Jones. In 1871 Kipling was brought home from India and spent five unhappy years with a foster family in Southsea, an experience he later drew on in *The Light That Failed* (1890). The years he spent at the United Services College, a school for officers' children, are depicted in *Stalky and Co.* (1899) and the character of Beetle is something of a self-portrait. It was during his time at the college that he began writing poetry and *Schoolboy Lyrics* was published privately in 1881. In the following year he started work as a journalist in India, and while there produced a body of work, stories, sketches and poems – notably *Plain Tales from the Hills* (1888) – which made him an instant literary celebrity when he returned to England in 1889. *Barrack-Room Ballads* (1892) contains some of his most popular pieces, including 'Mandalay', 'Gunga Din' and 'Danny Deever'. In this collection Kipling experimented with form and dialect, notably the cockney accent of the soldier poems, but the influence of hymns, music-hall songs, ballads and public poetry can be found throughout his verse.

In 1892 he married an American, Caroline Balestier, and from 1892 to 1896 they lived in Vermont, where Kipling wrote *The Jungle Book*, published in 1894. In 1901 came *Kim* and in 1902 the *Just So Stories*. Tales of every kind – including historical and science fiction – continued to flow from his pen, but *Kim* is generally thought to be his greatest long work, putting him high among the chroniclers of British expansion.

From 1902 Kipling made his home in Sussex, but he continued to travel widely and caught his first glimpse of warfare in South Africa, where he wrote some excellent reportage on the Boer War. However, many of the views he expressed were rejected by anti-imperialists who accused him of jingoism and love of violence. Though rich and successful, he never again enjoyed the literary esteem of his early years. With the onset of the Great War his work became a great deal more sombre. The stories he subsequently wrote, *A Diversity of Creatures* (1917), *Debits and Credits* (1926) and *Limits and Renewals* (1932) are now thought by many to contain some of his finest writing. The death of his only son in 1915 also contributed to a new inwardness of vision.

Kipling refused the role of Poet Laureate and other civil honours, but he was the first English writer to be awarded the Nobel Prize, in 1907. He died in 1936 and his autobiographical fragment *Something of Myself* was published the following year.

•

Hugh Haughton was born in Cork in 1948. He studied English Literature at the University of Cambridge and was a Research Fellow of Merton College, Oxford. He is at present a lecturer in the Department of English and Related Literature at York University. Hugh Haughton has edited Gustav Janouch's *Conversations with Kafka* (Quartet) and he is currently editing *Alice in Wonderland* for Penguin Classics and an anthology of nonsense poetry.

Rudyard Kipling

WEE WILLIE
WINKIE

EDITED
WITH AN INTRODUCTION AND NOTES
BY HUGH HAUGHTON

PENGUIN BOOKS

PENGUIN BOOKS

Published by the Penguin Group
27 Wrights Lane, London w8 5TZ, England
Viking Penguin Inc., 40 West 23rd Street, New York, New York 10010, USA
Penguin Books Australia Ltd, Ringwood, Victoria, Australia
Penguin Books Canada Ltd, 2801 John Street, Markham, Ontario, Canada L3R 1B4
Penguin Books (NZ) Ltd, 182–190 Wairau Road, Auckland 10, New Zealand

Penguin Books Ltd, Registered Offices: Harmondsworth, Middlesex, England

First published by Macmillan and Co. Ltd 1895
Published in Penguin Classics 1988
Reprinted in Penguin Books 1989
1 3 5 7 9 10 8 6 4 2

Introduction and Notes copyright © Hugh Haughton, 1988
All rights reserved

Made and printed in Great Britain by
Richard Clay Ltd, Bungay, Suffolk
Filmset in 10/11 pt Monophoto Ehrhardt

Contents

Contents

Introduction

I

In the autobiographical story 'Baa Baa, Black Sheep', Kipling describes a small boy's excitement at reading his first story, a tale from an old children's magazine about a sheep being carried away by a griffin: '"This," said Punch, "means things, and now I will know all about everything in all the world." He read till the light failed, not understanding a tithe of the meaning, but tantalized by glimpses of new worlds hereafter to be revealed.' For Punch the thrill of fiction is allied to the fantasy of knowledge, of finding out about the 'new worlds' that make up 'the world'. Reading offers him the opportunity to know things, but makes him realize he has to know things in order to read. Understandably, he seeks to enlist help.

'What is a "falchion"? What is a "e-wee lamb"? What is a "base *us*urper"? What is a "verdant me-ad"?' he demanded with flushed cheeks, at bedtime, of the astonished Aunty Rosa.
'Say your prayers and go to sleep,' she replied, and that was all the help Punch then or afterwards found at her hands in the new and delightful exercise of reading.

Like all Kipling's best stories, Punch's history is both anecdotally specific and queerly archetypal. It is at the same time an episode from Kipling's autobiography and a fable of reading. It's a fable with a particularly ironic resonance for someone editing and introducing Kipling. Unlike Aunty Rosa, an editor has to answer the kinds of questions asked by Punch, like 'what is a "falchion"?' or 'base *us*urper', and to answer them without usurping upon the reader's own reading. In the end Punch enjoys his 'new and delightful exercise' without editorial assistance, as Kipling's readers can, but it is just because for Kipling storytelling and knowledge were so intimately allied that the problem of his reader's knowledge tends to come to the fore. What do they know of Kipling who only Kipling know?

Kipling is one of the few great storytellers in English who has the knack of giving the short story something of the grip of the first stories, like the one read by Punch. This is not only true of his children's books like the *Just So Stories* and *Jungle Books* but of his short stories first and last. During the years of his fame, during the last decade of the nineteenth century and the first of the twentieth, no author had a wider or deeper popular appeal. Yet the paradox remains; Kipling is also a dense and cryptic writer, drawing on often relatively local and arcane knowledge, and this is almost as true of the early Indian writings as of the notoriously enigmatic, highly wrought later stories like 'Mrs Bathurst' and 'The Church that was at Antioch'. Historical change and in particular the passing of the British Empire, has profoundly altered the nature of Kipling's work and it has also rendered many details of the stories more obscure than they were. Kipling had first-hand knowledge of an extraordinary range of countries, occupations, vocabularies and particular social codes, stretching across the British Empire and beyond, and he made his copious and diverse stories samples or maps that work like Punch's tale; they offer 'glimpses of new worlds hereafter to be revealed'. The individual stories are like entries in a mobile anthropological encyclopedia following in the wake of the British imperial administrative machine. Read carefully, they are a mine of cultural information but, like mines, they have to be worked.

An editor's work is to foreground what hidden backgrounds he can, and to clarify Punch's instinctive reflex: 'This means things.' In the case of *Wee Willie Winkie*, this has meant pointing out conventional textual and biographical information that has bearing on the stories, and documenting the densely allusive texture of the writing, with particular reference to the history of British India, social life in the army and Simla and such like. It has also meant revising the prevailing assumption that Kipling's early work is less complex, less masterfully *textual* than the work of his later years. *Wee Willie Winkie* is an uneven, experimental collection of stories, but it is the product of an absolutely crucial moment in his life, his last year in India, and it includes a handful of his most perfect and powerful stories, including 'Baa Baa, Black Sheep', 'The Strange Ride of Morrowbie Jukes' and the 'The Man who would be King'. Some understanding of the biographical context of this volume helps one to see the scale of the young Kipling's ambition at this time, and to estimate its place in his professional career. In the case of the best stories in the book, I have found my reading of them transformed by attending more closely than I had done to what Henry James called 'the figure in the carpet', the often highly idiosyncratic figurative design lurking in what had seemed plain tales or tall stories, and also by opening up the backgrounds to the narratives themselves by following on the tracks of Kipling's strange rides into the culture of British India. Ideally the Kipling reader should be equipped with a map and Murray's *Guide to India*, a biography of Kipling, a good history of India in the nineteenth century, a copy of *Hobson-Jobson* (the indispensable lexicon of Anglo-Indian and Hindustani phrases), and the imaginative equivalent of a powerful magnifying glass and telescope, to enable him or her to do justice to the writer's combination of disconcerting close-ups and long views. The more knowledge one gains of the British India in which Kipling's writing began, the more resonant the design of his stories becomes. Kipling as a writer nearly always has designs on his readers in terms of politics, plotting or play, but his best stories precisely through their grotesque interweaving of play, plotting and politics, acquire a complex, unstable figurative density that enables them to invoke forces which elude and undermine the writer's conscious designs. Kipling is a very intense case of Lawrence's dictum, 'Never trust the artist, trust the tale,' and his genius, as his first editor Henry James said, is 'in certain lights, so contradictory of itself'.[1] The more the reader opens out the stories and returns them to history, the more they come to life, both as journalistic reports from the British raj, and as grotesque fables of mastery and imagination.

9

Introduction

II

The stories collected in *Wee Willie Winkie* were first put together and published in 1888, a year that marked a watershed in Kipling's life. From autumn 1882 to autumn 1887 Kipling had worked as sub-editor, reporter and fiction-writer on the *Civil and Military Gazette*, based in Lahore. Then in autumn 1887 he was transferred to Allahabad to work on the *Civil and Military Gazette's* sister-paper the *Pioneer*, described by Kipling in his autobiography as 'India's greatest and most important paper'.[2] For the *Pioneer*, Kipling wrote up his travels in the native states of Rajputana, published much later in book form as *Letters of Marque*, and agreed to edit the newspaper's weekly supplement for 'home consumption' in Britain, the *Week's News*. Kipling had written his 'Plain Tales' as items to be crammed into a couple of columns of the *Civil and Military Gazette*, alongside official reports, local news, editorials and other standard journalistic material, but the *Week's News* offered him a more expansive format and a more extended audience. It gave the twenty-three-year-old story-writer a new stimulus, a chance to test himself on a bigger stage. *Something of Myself*, written half a century later, records the almost manic sense of opportunity he felt at the time:

My editing of the *Weekly* may have been a shade casual – it was but a re-hash of news and views after all. My head was full of, to me, infinitely more important material. Henceforth no mere twelve-hundred Plain Tales jammed into rigid frames, but three- or five-thousand-word cartoons once a week. So did young Lippo Lippi, whose child I was, look on the blank walls of his monastery when he was bidden decorate them! 'Twas 'ask and have, Choose for more's ready,' with a vengeance.[3]

Plain Tales from the Hills appeared in book form in January 1888, but it is in describing the stories written during his time at the *Pioneer* that Kipling first talks about himself as a conscious artist, a disciple of Robert Browning's rogue painter Fra Lippo Lippi. Oscar Wilde, who described reading the *Plain Tales* as like sitting under a palm tree 'reading life by superb flashes of vulgarity', asserted that 'the mere lack of style in the story-teller gives an odd journalistic realism to what he tells us'.[4] As if to rebut Wilde's paradoxical praise for his 'lack of style', the autobiography looks back at his work of the period in terms of almost Paterian aestheticism: 'Thus, then, I made my own experiments in the weights, colours, perfumes, and attributes of words in relation to other words, either as read aloud so that they may hold the ear, or, scattered over the page, draw the eye.' He portrays his time at the *Pioneer* as his self-conscious artistic apprenticeship, a moment of pioneering literary experimentalism which would prove him an artist as well as a journalist.

Kipling's *annus mirabilis* of 1888 had begun with the appearance of *Plain Tales* in January, and it ended with the publication of the works that made his name outside India, the booklets that now compose *Soldiers Three* and *Wee Willie Winkie*. In *Something of Myself* he records his personal and literary balance-sheet for the year with characteristic dryness, and more than a touch of pride:

On my side I was ripe for change and . . . had a notion now of where I was heading. My absorption in the *Pioneer Weekly* stories, which I wanted to finish, had put my plans to the back of my head, but when I came out of that furious spell of work towards the end of '88 I rearranged myself. I wanted money for the future. I counted my assets. They came to one book of verse; one ditto prose; and – thanks to the *Pioneer*'s permission – a set of six small paper-backed railway-bookstall volumes embodying most of my tales for the *Weekly* – copyright of which the *Pioneer* might well have claimed. The man who controlled the Indian railway bookstalls came of an imaginative race, used to taking chances. I sold him the six paper-backed books for £200 and a small royalty . . .

Fortified with this wealth, and six months' pay in lieu of notice, I left India for England by way of the Far East and the United States, after six and a half years of hard work and a reasonable amount of sickness.[5]

According to this gleefully businesslike account, and on the basis of this businesslike accounting, it was the money and intellectual confidence he earned during the 'furious burst' of work during his last year in India which enabled Kipling to retire from his journalistic career after his 'Seven Years' Hard', to leave India, effectively for good, in February 1889, and to pursue a full-time career as a writer. Kipling's artistic balance-sheet at the end of the *annus mirabilis* would have been remarkable for any writer, and is almost incredible for someone his age. On 30 December 1888, Kipling could celebrate more than his twenty-third birthday.

III

Wee Willie Winkie, like *Soldiers Three*, is the harvest of that year of 'furious' apprenticeship and rearrangement. Like *Soldiers Three*, which contains the first three of the 'set of six small paper-backed railway-bookstall volumes' Kipling refers to, *Wee Willie Winkie* is a composite work, neither a single coherent collection like *Plain Tales* nor a miscellaneous compilation of individual stories like *Life's Handicap*, but an Anglo-Indian triptych, made up of the last three volumes of Wheeler's Indian Railway Library set, *Under the Deodars*, *The Phantom Rickshaw* and *Wee Willie Winkie*. This means that the book is best approached as three distinct sequences within a double Anglo-Indian triptych, each sequence with its own title, and devoted to mapping a particular territory or exploring the possibilities of a particular genre or kind of voice. *Soldiers Three* offered the public a group of hard-boiled, eloquently colloquial stories from the British barrack-room: *The Story of the Gadsby's*, an officer-class novella in dramatic form and *In Black and White*, a series of exuberantly vocal Browning-style monologues and sketches of 'native' Indian life, mainly of a colourfully criminal kind. These were followed by an album of mordant vignettes of English men and women abroad in Simla and elsewhere (*Under the Deodars*), a highly strung quartet of colonial tales of mystery and imagination (*The Phantom Rickshaw*), and a mixed bag of four stories about the splendours and miseries of Anglo-Indian children (*Wee Willie Winkie*). In the Preface to *Under the Deodars* (reprinted in the notes) Kipling explains that the stories were arranged 'to be read in railway trains'. Yet if the series shows Kipling's commercial flair as a would-be popular author, it also shows something else, a combination of restless experimentalism and a quasi-systematic fantasy of knowledge. It is almost as if, before leaving for Europe, Kipling dreamed of constructing a representative cross-section map of British India, category by category, and at the same time displaying his mastery of the equally impressive House of Fiction, genre by genre and style by style.[6] He aspired to be as mobile as the railway trains.

It was presumably some perception of this combination of almost encyclopedic ambition and robust journalistic realism, that led Henry James to see Kipling as potentially 'an English Balzac'.[7] It may well be that in trying his hand at a variety of longer forms of short fiction, the young Kipling was preparing the ground for his future attempt to annex the terrain of the novel. The last of the *Plain Tales*, 'To be Filed for Reference', includes a tantalizing view of the 'Book of Mother Maturin', the never-published novel we know Kipling had been working on for some years, and the often scrupulously dull portraits of women and children in *Under the Deodars* and *Wee Willie Winkie*, as well as the unprecedented autobiographical account of his own Anglo-Indian childhood in 'Baa Baa, Black Sheep', point suggestively towards the Victorian domestic novel, as does *The Story of the Gadsby's*, with its study of marriage as a kind of failure of nerve. When he returned to England in 1889, Kipling did in fact have a go at a novel *The Light That Failed* but, like the wrecked master-portrait painted by its Hemingwayesque hero Dick Heldar, the attempt at a tragic work dissolves into a vacant pathos. The English domestic novel was to prove beyond even Kipling's confident virtuosity, and it is 'The Man who would be King', his experiment in the genre of exotic adventure-novel popularized by Rider Haggard, which was to prove the forerunner of Kipling's only successful large-scale fiction, *Kim* – a unique mixture of imperial picaresque, mythopeic travelogue and fable of split cultural identity.

If his new job at the *Pioneer* gave Kipling more space to develop individual stories than the *Plain Tales* had done, the Indian Railway Library encouraged him to think in terms of *sets* of tales – like *In Black and White* and *Under the Deodars*. In fact, of the thirty-six-odd items he wrote for the *Pioneer*, only 'A Wayside Comedy' and perhaps a couple of others are among his best works, as Angus Wilson pointed out.[8] Seven of the *Wee Willie Winkie* stories began in the columns of the *Pioneer*, but two of the outstanding ones, 'The Phantom Rickshaw' and 'The Strange Ride of Morrowbie Jukes', are among his very earliest work, dating back to the Christmas supplement of the *Civil and Military Gazette* for 1885, and four others, including 'Baa Baa, Black Sheep' and 'The Man who would be King', were written for the Indian Railway series.[9] Though he failed to develop as a novelist, Kipling's imagination was always *serial*. He was drawn to the idea of recurring characters favoured by novelists like Balzac and Zola – from the gabby-mouthed privates Mulvaney, Learoyd and Ortheris who, like Mrs Hauksbee, first saw the light of print in the *Plain Tales* but soldiered on through other collections, to Pyecroft, Stalky & Co., Mowgli and the jungle, Puck and kids, who travelled easily from story to story and book to book. Lucy Hauksbee began life in the *Plain Tales*, but it is in *Under the Deodars* that Kipling paints the fullest portrait of her and her Simla set. However, what I have called Kipling's serial imagination is most clearly seen in the conspicuously *designed* nature of his collections, starting with this Indian Railway series. Though all three sequences in *Wee Willie Winkie* contain the odd dud story, there is a lot to be said for reading them as clusters of related tales. *Under the Deodars* can be read as an account of the pressures on the seventh commandment registered by the British community in India, *Wee Willie Winkie* as a composite group portrait of Anglo-Indian children, all desperate for recognition by the group, and *The Phantom Rickshaw* as an exercise in imperial gothic, recounting the strange, potentially unhinging experiences of those who go beyond the boundaries of the known world of the ruling caste. All the stories are in some sense about crises of social solidarity, and they read best when read in their serial context, in their own fictional society, as it were. In September Kipling published the last of his regular stories for the *Pioneer* and signalled it as such by calling it 'The Last of the Stories' and making it a playful curtain-call of his fictional characters, with him as author taking centre stage. I have included it in an appendix, to illustrate both Kipling's self-consciousness about his fiction, and his strong sense of an ending at this time. When he had done with the *Pioneer* in September, Kipling obviously felt free to rearrange himself as he said, and also to set about rearranging his individual stories as sequences, and to write fresh ones which would get to the heart of his Indian experience and give his Indian survey a new kind of intensity and allegorical reach. As a result he wrote the three great culminatory fictions of his early period, 'On the City Wall' and 'The Man who would be King', intense and expansive fables about British rule in the Indian sub-continent, fraught with a sense of its history, and 'Baa Baa, Black Sheep', his autobiographical story about an Anglo-Indian childhood, which gets us as near as any other single story to the pre-history of Kipling's own view of the world.

The world viewed in the *Wee Willie Winkie* triptych is very much an Anglo-Indian one.[10] Unlike every other book Kipling wrote about India, this one contains no stories about Indians or about intimate relationships between Indians and their Anglo-Indian rulers. There are no stories like 'Lilith', 'Beyond the Pale', 'On the City Wall' or 'Without Benefit of Clergy', about inter-racial love-affairs or friendships, and there is scarcely a voice from the Indian sub-continent to be heard across these pages – certainly nothing like the rich vocal score for Indian speakers Kipling devised for *In Black and White* and *Kim*.[11] The one exception is Gunga Dass, the maliciously intelligent 'Babu' telegraph-officer who rebels against Morrowbie Jukes' authority during his 'Strange Ride'. In fact, with the exception of 'The Strange Ride' and 'The Man who would be King', which recount fantastic journeys beyond the pale of British rule, the dramatis personae of these stories are the ordinary, mainly middle-class personnel of the British stations, hill-resorts, barracks and newspaper-offices, who live in the tense, stratified ghetto of what is called in 'Wee Willie Winkie' 'the Dominant Race'.[12] In 'A Wayside Comedy', which gives a convincingly frayed picture of a hill-station called Kashima, the phrase 'all Kashima' is used to refer to its handful of British residents, and excludes the native population entirely. The story, an account of the incestuous amorous tensions that build up in this constricted community, depicts a claustrophobic world divided against itself and on the verge of complete disintegration. This is an extreme case of the book's real subject, the need to maintain or establish mastery in the face of near-intolerable pressures from within as well as without. 'The Drums of the Fore and Aft' is Kipling's one realistic record of border warfare on the North-West Frontier, and shows an entire British regiment panicking under stress, before reasserting control and winning a brutal victory over Pathan guerrillas. Both are about crises of group morale. 'The Strange Ride' on the other hand is a study of the colonial personality at a loss, confronted, in a squalid Hindu village, by a group to which he cannot imagine belonging. It's above all a story about the fear of losing face and thus losing caste. Perhaps this is also the deepest fear of the characters in *Under the Deodars*, fear of losing their status and membership within the privileged community of Anglo-Indian society. The bulk of the *Under the Deodars* stories deal with threats to the institution of marriage, and they turn upon the conflict between longing and belonging. Kipling's interest here is not, as one might perhaps expect in late-Victorian times, moralistic. His focus is not so much morals as morale, not the moral values of the enclosed British community but the mystique of status, the psychology of belonging and the fear of loss. This is one of the underlying threads that bind the three contrasted sets of stories in *Wee Willie Winkie* into some kind of unity: Kipling's interest in the moment when his sahibs and memsahibs come to the knowledge that they risk facing irreparable stigmatization through failing, falling or transgressing the boundaries of the known social code. At the crisis of nearly every story his characters, however conformist they are at heart, stare down into 'the pit's mouth', as in the story of that name, or into the 'Valley of Humiliation' known to Punch in 'Baa Baa, Black Sheep'.

IV

When he came to revise the early story called 'The Phantom Rickshaw' for the Indian Railway Library, Kipling added a brief Introduction, which makes the following remarkable claim:

One of the few advantages that India has over England is a great Knowability. After five years' service a man is directly or indirectly acquainted with the two or three hundred Civilians in his Province, all the Messes of ten or twelve Regiments and Batteries, and some fifteen hundred other people of the non-official caste. In ten years his knowledge should be doubled, and at the end of twenty he knows, or knows something about, every Englishman in the Empire.

It is not clear whether Kipling intends this characteristic assertion to be ironic or not, but its effect is to frame his magazine story about a private hallucination in Simla by invoking the shared imperialist phantom, the Phantom of Knowability. Significantly, the India that is at issue here is entirely European. It is knowable because it is envisaged as an extended colonial network of clubs, messes and civil servants, and because it excludes the vast majority of the native population. The knowable India is in fact precisely the audience for Kipling's Indian journalism, the readership of the *Civil and Military Gazette* and *Pioneer*, and what it knows, on this account, is itself. At the same time, however, it is confronted by the huge, unfamiliar and alien world of the Indian sub-continent and the many languages and beliefs of the population it is there to govern. As a journalist and fiction-writer Kipling was writing for an audience that he felt he knew inside out, the people he met every day at the club, the mess, the Masonic lodge or Simla parties, and he and his audience could share their special Hindustani-spattered dialect, their private jokes and slang and prejudices, in a way which would confirm the highly structured magical circle of rituals and allusions which ensured their own special status, against both the native Indians and the world of 'Home' in Britain. This gave Kipling something like the equivalent of a traditional storyteller's 'knowable community', though in a sophisticated, colonial context. This in turn may have encouraged the brassily 'knowing' tone of the early Kipling and the rhetoric of casually authoritative but scandalous 'knowledgeability' which character-ized the style of the *Plain Tales*. It also gives his tales something of the character of stories in an oral community, a strange, imperial mixture of the journalistic and the folkloric.

The 'Knowability' of Kashima in 'A Wayside Comedy' is a nightmare rather than a privilege, as is that of Simla to Jack Pansay in 'The Phantom Rickshaw' when he becomes wedded to his phantom lover. But Kipling is also aware that the ex-clusiveness of the Anglo-Indian community is also an ex-cludedness – thus its fascination with the world beyond its frontiers. This is the reason for the special appeal of the char-ismatic middlemen of Kipling's India: Strickland, the wizard policeman who is a master of disguise and native languages and acts on the theory that 'a Policeman in India should try to know as much about the natives as the natives themselves'; McIntosh Jellaludin, the scholar and gentleman who 'goes native', marries a Moslem girl and writes a book which gives the inside story on the exotically unknown world barred to Kipling himself; of officials like Muller in the first Mowgli story, 'In the Rukh', who recognizes Mowgli's potential value to the government; of Mowgli himself, the wolf-boy who moves between the human and feral worlds of the jungle; and, the greatest of all Kipling's mediators, Kim, who incarnates the fantasy of being both native and sahib, disciple of a holy man and spy of the British govern-ment, moving freely between the many worlds of India. Such charismatic spies and intermediaries represent privileged kinds of knowledge which transcend the 'Knowability' of British India, and embody a fantasy of total access to the attractive but threatening world of a largely unknown 'native' India. They represent Kipling's special version of the myth of orientalism unmasked by Edward Said in his *Orientalism*. In *Wee Willie Winkie*, however, only Morrowbie Jukes and the two adventurer-heroes of 'The Man who would be King' are allowed to gain access to that unknown world, and the superior Jukes is horribly humiliated, while Dan and Peachey, though they become kings in what was literally the *terra incognita* of Kafiristan, are ultimately destroyed by their own ignorance of the people they dream of subordinating.

Before going on to consider the three sequences in more detail, I would like to suggest that, though the quality of the stories in them is weirdly uneven, and they are mainly concerned with life inside the 'ghetto' of Anglo-Indian life, the best of them show Kipling at the height of his powers, mastering an impressively diverse set of worlds and genres in a way denied to his characters. 'A Wayside Story', 'At the Pit's Mouth', 'The Phantom Rickshaw', 'The Strange Ride', 'The Man who would be King' and the 'The Drums of the Fore and Aft' are in every way diverse: a tragi-comedy of manners, a macabre anecdote, a psychological ghost story, a nightmare report of a sahib's incarceration in a village of the dead, a swashbuckling adventure story about would-be empire builders, a study of a lonely childhood in England and a fictional war-report from a frontier war. Whether he was evoking a dreary hill-station or Simla's stuffy glamour, the Indian desert or the wilds of Kafiristan, a baking newspaper office or a Rocklington lodging-house, Kipling showed from the start an extraordinary knack of calling up an entire world, complete with its local dialect and codes of solidarity, and then going on to investigate the experience of those on or beyond its borders, in danger of losing their 'knowable' world.

Apart from his early childhood as a much-petted young sahib in Bombay, Kipling spent only six and a half years in India. Yet, though Kipling lived for almost half a century after taking his passage from India in 1889, he remained in some way an Anglo-Indian author all his long and prolific writing life. His vision of the world and stance as a writer were defined by his experience of India and shaped in the laboratory of his Anglo-Indian journalism and journalistic fiction. Those 'Seven Years' Hard', if they cannot be said to have made Kipling a writer, certainly helped to make him the writer he was – on the one hand a field-working imperialist, and on the other a poet and storyteller with an unparalleled sense of the anthropological and linguistic diversity of the world of his time – and of the English language. Despite, or perhaps because of, his belief in Britain's imperial role in India, Ireland, Africa and elsewhere, Kipling's work never suggests the easy authority of Matthew Arnold's 'tone of the centre', or some non-controversial 'natural' political order. If, as Randall Jarrell has said, 'Kipling's account is still unsettled', it is in part because his stories are always in some measure explicitly political or international, and suggest a drastically conflictual sense of social order and authority, born out of his profoundly self-contradictory knowledge of India.

V

Under the Deodars, despite its exotic travel-book title, offers a far from glamorous picture of life in Simla, the famous English hill-resort in the beautiful mountains of the eastern Punjab, which was the summer capital of the British raj. Simla had been the setting of many of the *Plain Tales* and *Departmental Ditties*, but it is in these stylized, jagged, tragi-comedies of manners that Kipling provides his most extended composite portrait of its lifestyle, and in particular of the claustrophobic life lived by British women, attached to husbands in the civil or military service, condemned to live in the alpine stuffiness of India's most mandarin hill-resort – a celestial Tunbridge Wells.

All the stories, with the exception of the last, 'Only a Sub-altern', portray a brittle, pretentious world of small-town intrigues and amateur theatricals, risqué conversations and more risky *liaisons dangereuses*. Kipling has kept the big social functions, balls and garden parties, off-stage, and likewise the male preserves of government and the club, concentrating instead on private conversations, secret plans and undercover romances taking place just out of earshot. 'I should like you better if you were not always looking into people's back-bedrooms,' says Mrs Mallowe to Mrs Hauksbee and, though we never actually enter anyone's bedroom, it's never far away. In his Preface, Kipling warns his readers that 'India is not entirely inhabited by men and women playing tennis with the Seventh Commandment', but five of the six stories in this sequence concern relationships which involve actual or potential adultery, small-scale border skirmishes on either side of the seventh commandment.[13] This should not surprise readers of *Plain Tales* which gives a comparably cynical picture of scandal and intrigue in the hills, but the overall effect of *Under the Deodars* is quite different to that of the short, sharp and often shocking anecdotes narrated in the earlier book. Instead of the flashy journalistic raconteur's voice of the *Plain Tales*, Kipling has chosen to dramatize most of these narratives in the form of close-up, conversational set-pieces, with a more artful eye to 'character' and an ear for the mannered small-talk of Simla's *grandes dames* and the faded clichés of its clubmen. You could say that the real subject of these tight little dramas of extra-marital flirtation and intrigue is the relation between private confidences and public confidence. Their natural form is a series of confidential conversations on the edge of the public arena – the Wildean bitching of Mrs Hauksbee and her confidante in her rooms overlooking the Mall, the graveyard 'trysting-place' where the almost anonymous lovers of 'At the Pit's Mouth' keep their rendezvous or the famous Simla bridleways where the illicit couple in 'The Hill of Illusion' whisper their sweet-and-sour nothings. There is no room for private passion in Kipling's Simla, and the language of personal ambition and desire is always trapped in the currency of social reputation, snobbery, gossip and innuendo. If 'A Wayside Comedy' is Kipling's most claustrophobic picture of sexual acrimony, with its close-up of a frustrated foursome in the dreary hill-station of Kashima, Simla is only Kashima writ large. Kipling treats the furtive excitements and silent inhibitions of adultery in the hills with chilling realism and candour – though his sympathies seem to lie with the absent husbands who pay the bills, and the public opinion which suppresses them. The women in *Under the Deodars* are caught between the tedium of respectability and the danger of scandal, between what Mrs Hauksbee calls the 'mob of Anglo-Indians' in the Mall and the 'pit' or cliff down which Frank falls in 'At the Pit's Mouth'. Though Kipling's overt ironies sound sourly conventional, with a whiff of misogynic disapproval, covertly the sequence reads as a perceptive account of the frustrations felt by spirited women denied any other opening for their wit or feelings than amateur theatricals and tea-parties and rickshaw rides under the deodars.

At the core of *Under the Deodars* are the three clipped, acid cameos of undercover adultery, 'At the Pit's Mouth', 'A Wayside Comedy' and 'The Hill of Illusion'. Kipling has framed them by two longish, society conversation-pieces about Mrs Hauksbee, his bravura personification of Simla Woman. These stories show Kipling trying to be brilliantly dull about the snobbish, gossipy world of 'the most dangerous woman in Simla' and her entourage. Though Mrs Hauksbee's malicious high-camp wit looks a bit faded now, and the stories are little more than elaborately studied anecdotes, they have some interest as accounts of the arid hothouse of British high society on the heights of the Himalayan foothills, where Lucy Hauksbee realizes the difficulties of setting up a salon or becoming 'an influence':

'Surely, twelve Simla seasons ought to have taught you that you can't focus anything in India; and a *salon*, to be any good at all, must be permanent. In two seasons your roomful would be scattered all over Asia. We are only little bits of dirt on the hillsides – here one day and blown down the *khud* the next. We have lost the art of talking – at least our men have. We have no cohesion –'

'George Eliot in the flesh,' interpolated Mrs Hauksbee wickedly.

'And collectively, my dear scoffer, we, men and women alike, have *no* influence. Come into the verandah and look at the Mall!'

The two looked down on the now rapidly filling road, for all Simla was abroad to steal a stroll between a shower and a fog.

Introduction

That pan from *salon* to dirt on the *khud* to 'all Simla' on the Mall, catches the social setting of the women's artful talk beautifully. Lucy Hauksbee's witty pretentiousness is a wilful triumph of style against the odds, among diplomatic bores like 'the Mussuck', 'dowds' like Mrs Delville and raw backwoods civil servants like Otis Yeere. Nevertheless, in both the stories in which she appears, Mrs Hauksbee's will to queen it has an unforeseen and humiliating outcome. 'The Education of Otis Yeere' describes her generous but ruthless attempt to groom a social nonentity from the wilds of Bengal into a social and professional success. It is a kind of inverted Pygmalion story, treated as an ironic comedy of manners, and it is the stagily sophisticated Mrs Hauksbee who is shown up as the *ingénue* when she completely misreads both the hapless Yeere ('this *Thing* I had picked out of his filthy paddy-fields') and herself ('Didn't I *create* that man? Doesn't he owe everything to me?'). In her grand ambition to become 'an Influence', she fails to recognize the sexual ambiguity in her plan to make Yeere her 'property' and the complicated mixture of love and personal ambition in his response. Her plan for Otis Yeere's cultural 'Education' turns out to be a painful Simla-style sentimental education for them both. 'A Supplementary Chapter', included in the appendix, is a comparable and complementary anecdote, which describes the equally humiliating outcome of her friend Polly Mallowe's dreams for her ambiguous protégé Trewinnard. It's another unsuccessful Pygmalian story about a woman who would be queen by proxy and kingmaker by way of an educational romance.

Ambiguities evaporate in the icy trilogy of stories about romantic adultery which lies at the heart of *Under the Deodars*. 'At the Pit's Mouth' was described by Randall Jarrell as 'one of the best and . . . decidedly the most unpleasant of all Kipling's stories of illicit affairs'.[14] Though it is set in the romantic landscape around Simla, Kipling refers to the two young lovers throughout as 'The Man's Wife' and 'The Tertium Quid', and treats them very much as if they were lab specimens or exhibits in a law-court. Though it is a story about private passions, the language of the narrative is rigorously public and external. From the word go, the young couple are located in terms of the hard currency of social approval and disapproval – and the text is peppered with terms like 'properly', 'naturally', 'official status' and 'sanctity of the marriage bond'. The girl is chided in a letter for 'allowing her name to be so generally coupled with the Tertium Quid's, as if the coupling of names were the real crime. In the cemetery which becomes their regular 'trysting-place', they speak a language to each other which is absolutely confined by the social conventions they defy. 'Frank, people say we are too much together,' she tells him, to which he replies that 'horrid people were unworthy of the consideration of nice people'. Denied any language of personal feeling or individual selfhood, they remain pawns in a language-game of public esteem or disapprobation. Even the minimal descriptive content of the narrative is unrelentingly external. They are always described from outside, as in a police report. He is first seen on horseback, hurtling 'downhill at fifteen miles an hour'; the Thibet road is six feet wide; the grave, we are told, has twelve, then eighteen inches of water in it; and he ends up 'underneath the mare, nine hundred feet below, spoiling a patch of Indian corn'. The couple are only allowed to acquire narrative vividness at the moment of catastrophe, when Kipling finally shows us their faces in grotesque close-up, as in a film, as they suddenly register what is happening to them. We see him at the moment he is about to fall over the cliff, 'glued to the saddle – his face blue and white' and his 'nervous grin still set on his face'; then we see her, 'with her eyes and mouth open, and her head like the head of a Medusa', while her hands lay 'picking at her riding-gloves'. In this sardonic *Liebestod*, the two lovers who had chosen the graveyard as their rendezvous are allowed a brief flare of life at the moment of his death.

The rigorous externality of the story might suggest it is just a macabre anecdote, but it is saved from superficiality by its peculiar brand of symbolic innuendo. It is built around the two central images: a man on horseback falling to his death, and a '*Sahib's* grave' filling with water in the cemetery where the lovers meet. There's a faintly perverse sexual charge associated with the man's relationship to the horse all through the tale (the only time he is seen off the horse's back, he's sharing his horse-blanket with the girl in the graveyard), which comes to a gruesome climax at the close. That climactic consummation also confirms the queer force of the 'pit' of the title, and seems to equate the open grave, the cliff below the crumbling mountain road, hell (the 'bottomless pit' of *Hamlet*) and the punitive sexual morality of the Old Testament, where in the Book of Proverbs it is written that: 'The mouth of strange women is a deep pit: he that is abhorred of the Lord shall fall therein.' It is also the only 'fine and private place' open to the lovers for their embraces, and the 'end of the world' invoked in the man's vacuously romantic last words. Characteristically, such symbolism is both crude and compelling, and makes this grotesque little fable a masterpiece of construction – as well as of constriction.

'A Wayside Comedy' is another triumph of formal construction and offers an even grimmer picture of social constriction, this time set in a small, remote hill-station with a view of 'a stretch of perfectly flat pasture', 'no amusements, except snipe and tiger shooting', and a handful of bored British residents locked into the station's 'immemorial' routines as if it were a prison. It seems to me to be one of Kipling's best stories, written with a psychological subtlety and abrupt poignancy more characteristic of Chekhov or D. H. Lawrence than a writer of Kipling's temperament and place. Charles Carrington calls it the kind of story that in Kipling's day was described as 'a shade too "French"', noting that 'in France it has always been much admired'. Randall Jarrell called it 'merciless and truthful', and 'the opposite of what one would expect of a Victorian, English story of a love affair'.[15] In fact, its plot is like a French farce with the comedy left out. By the end, the secret extramarital passions that bind the four main characters into an inextricable knot are all humiliatingly exposed to each other's eyes, though they have to be concealed from the innocent Major Vansuythen, for whom 'all Kashima' is still one 'happy family'.

Introduction

Mr and Mrs Boulte, Kurrell and the seductive Mrs Vansuythen are bound together by their knowledge of the tangle of illicit desire and jealousy which both divides and holds them stuck in an eternal stalemate. Kipling's brief but deadly group-portrait ends with a view of 'all Kashima' grouped round the happily oblivious Major with his 'burdensome geniality', locked into an excruciating travesty of propriety and community.

In his autobiography, Kipling says 'There was one . . . which . . . I handed up to the Mother, who abolished it and wrote me: *Never you do that again*. But I did and managed to pull off, not unhandily, a tale called "A Wayside Comedy", where I worked hard for a certain "economy of implication"'.[15] It is a convincing nightmare because of the way Kipling recreates the dull domestic rituals and habitual tones of voice of the five inmates of the station, with only a few, dry touches: Mrs Boulte in her *terai* hat going to borrow a copy of the latest *Queen*, Kurrell's style of manly banter with Mr Boulte ('Bad thing for a sober, married man, that. What will Mrs Boulte say?'), or the Major's thick-skinned *bonhomie* ('Sitting in the twilight! . . . That'll never do! Hang it all, we're one family here'). The story is unfolded through a series of harshly lit cameo scenes in which, with a kind of surgical insight, Kipling traces the workings of sexual jealousy and humiliation under the skin of the everyday formulas of domestic routine and polite social exchange.

It may be no coincidence that Mrs Boulte has the same Christian name as Emma Bovary.[17] Everything turns on the scene in which Emma Boulte, who is described as hating her husband 'with the hate of a woman who has met with nothing but kindness from her mate', is shown putting flowers in a vase ('There is a pretence of civilization even in Kashima,' as the narrator observes), just before she impulsively tells her husband of her longstanding secret affair with Kurrell:

She struck at Boulte's heart, because her own was sick with suspicion of Kurrell, and worn out with the long strain of watching alone through the Rains. There was no plan or purpose in her speaking. The sentences made themselves; and Boulte listened, leaning against the door-post

26

with his hands in his pockets. When all was over, and Mrs Boulte began to breathe through her nose before breaking out into tears, he laughed and stared straight in front of him at the Dosehri hills.

'Is that all?' he said. 'Thanks, I only wanted to know, you know.'

Though this is the moment she pulls her 'homestead about her own ears', Kipling presents the drama with a minimum of stage directions – his blank laugh or her breathing through her nose, his cool posture and polite response, and the sense behind the two of them, of the hills and the months of rains. The scene, like the story as a whole, seems intimate with the lack of intimacy between the characters, and with the economy of cruelty which makes her hurt her husband in response to the hurt from her lover. Something similar is found in the 'mirthless mirth' of the two men 'on the long white line of the Narkarra Road', and the raw exposure scene in the Vansuythen's house. The story leaves the characters trapped in their bare 'Knowability', in a present tense that envisages no exit in the foreseeable future. One critic has compared the effect to that of Sartre's *Huis Clos* – it might also be likened to an episode in Dante's *Divine Comedy*.[18] It is a colonial Wayside Inferno.

'The Hill of Illusion' is a slighter comedy of manners, in the form of an adulterous *pas de deux* in dialogue form. It is set on the slopes of Mount Jakko, the romantic peak above Simla, which had been the setting of an earlier satirical fantasy with the same title Kipling had contributed to the *Civil and Military Gazette*, on 28 September 1887, under the pseudonym of 'S.T.'. The earlier sketch spoofs the antics of Simla's scandalous lovers by disguising them as the great lovers of legend and romance, Dido and Aeneas, Tristram and Iseult, Lancelot and Guinevere and the like.[19] The 'hill of illusion' then is both Jakko and romantic adultery, and this dry little drama is another cynical exercise in exploding the myth of romantic love ('Even bearable! It'll be Paradise,' one lover assures his reluctant partner), as well as the couple's own cynicism about marriage ('"The holy state of matrimony!" Ha! ha! ha!'). Because of its dialogue form, it really does read as if the pair is playing tennis with the seventh commandment. *Blackwoods* in 1898 noted the extraordinary unevenness of Kipling's art, but picked this story as an example of his best work: 'Cheek by jowl with smart snip-snap you find something that probes the inmost recess of your soul. Only a few pages ... separate a specimen of flippant superficiality like "The Education of Otis Yeere" from a masterpiece of analysis and penetration like "The Hill of Illusion".' And Andrew Lang, who found *Under the Deodars* less to his taste than Kipling's 'native' stories, advised 'persons who wish to see the misery, the seamy, sorry side of irregular love-affairs' to turn to this one.

The last pair of stories in the set have openly deprecatory titles – 'A Second-Rate Woman' and 'Only a Subaltern' – but they seem designed to counteract the deprecatory view of Anglo-Indian society that prevails in the other stories. In the first story, a second-rate woman nicknamed 'the Dowd' by the snobbish Mrs Hauksbee turns up trumps in an emergency and is hailed as a 'Goddess from the Machine' for rescuing a sick baby's life. In the second, a sterling subaltern fresh from Sandhurst gives his life in the course of nursing his regiment through a cholera epidemic, and is hailed at the end by a loyal private as a '*Bloomin*' Hangel'. Kipling was always bad at heroics; certainly Mrs Delville's competence in a nursery crisis and Mrs Hauksbee's generosity to the sick child do little to dispel the atmosphere of Wildean bitching and seedy womanizing which characterizes the rest of Simla in the first of these stories. In some ways, 'Only a Subaltern', with its military setting, is a world apart from the round of hill-station flirtations and Anglo-Indian tragi-comedy explored in the other stories in *Under the Deodars*. Its military hero visits Simla on leave from the plains, and sees it in a very different light ('First-class place, Simla. Oh, ri-ipping!'). However, the portrait of the subaltern Bobby Wick lacks any touch of the harsh realism and vivid detail of life in the ranks evident in *Soldiers Three* and *Barrack-Room Ballads*. It is simply an officer-class regimental weepie. Bobby Wick *begins as a stock character, a standard product of his class and* training, and never graduates to anything else. 'They made

Bobby Wick pass an examination at Sandhurst,' runs the first sentence, and at the close Kipling makes him undergo a sentimental apotheosis on the plains of India. When the blushful male Florence Nightingale dies, Kipling pulls out all the stops: an unfinished love-letter to his fiancée, his mother's favourite waltz, his last words being 'Mummy dear', a tearful CO's letter home to Papa and his faithful Geordie subordinate's booming epitaph of *'Bloomin'* Hangel'. As a subaltern of 'the Line, the whole Line, and nothing but the Line', Bobby is nothing but a standard line himself, with little more free will or individuality than one of Pavlov's dogs.

The *Athenaeum*, which was generally dismayed by the cynical account of Anglo-Indian life in *Under the Deodars*, found this the one 'redeeming feature' of the volume, although modern readers are more likely to share Angus Wilson's view that the story is spoilt by its 'mawkish, Sunday-school-prize tone'.[20] Charles Carrington has argued that the portrait '. . . moulded a whole generation of young Englishmen into that type. They rose up in their thousands in 1914, and sacrificed themselves in the image that Kipling had created.'[21] This is a sobering thought, a reminder that lesser art may have a greater influence upon human action than the greatest. To my mind, 'Only a Subaltern' is a failure as a study in group morale because it is too patently designed to be a contribution to it. In the collected American edition of his works, Kipling replaced it as the finale to the sequence by 'Mrs Hauksbee Sits Out', a genial evocation of one of Simla's grand balls, portraying Mrs Hauksbee as a benign go-between in the ballroom of romance (originally printed in the *Illustrated London News*, Christmas number, December 1890). There is a case for Bobby Wick sitting out and Mrs Hauksbee sitting in, as the curtain falls on the Simla of *Under the Deodars*.

VI

The Phantom Rickshaw and Other Tales is an altogether more spectacular sequence, made up of two Anglo-Indian ghost stories and two fantastic histories of strange journeys beyond the frontiers of British India. They are tales of mystery and imagination, harking back to Poe and forward to Kafka, yet squarely anchored in the everyday realities of the imperial India they seem to undermine. Taken as a whole, the sequence can be read as a brilliant, dissonant exercise in colonial gothic, a kind of Anglo-Indian spook sonata, composed of case-studies of colonial man *in extremis* and Goyaesque fables of empire.

The original Preface set sensational terms like 'a wonderful fiction' and 'extraordinary account' beside evidential ones like 'a collection of facts', and Kipling works hard to set his extraordinary accounts in ordinary workaday settings. Jack Pansay in the title story is an overworked civilian in an undermanned commission, Morrowbie Jukes a hard-headed civil engineer, and the narrator of the other two stories is Kipling himself, very much the professional journalist on his travels in search of copy or sweating it out in the newspaper office described in 'The Man who would be King'. The phantom rickshaw appears in the familiar streets of Simla, while Jukes' ride and the travels of the would-be kings are carefully placed and documented, one in the Indian Desert and the other in the *terra incognita* of Kafiristan. Such documentation is a stock device of the tale of terror and enables the author to give the marvellous a sober alibi and the mystery ride a properly stamped entry visa. Yet in Kipling's tales it also enables him to represent what he calls 'the Dark World' as only just beyond the 'knowable' realities of his India. In that 'Dark World', fractured by powerful and alien-seeming forces beyond his control, the sahib loses his composure, and the fantasies behind his mask of ruling superiority take nightmare shape. 'From the horrible to the commonplace is but a step,' says Jack Pansay, misquoting Napoleon, and the converse is also true.

'He was in a high fever while he was writing, and the blood-and-thunder Magazine diction he adopted did not calm him,' observes the narrator apropos Jack Pansay's overwrought narrative in 'The Phantom Rickshaw'. This is a ruefully ironic joke at Kipling's own expense, but there is no doubt that behind his exercises in magazine fiction in these tales there lies an authentic experience of that 'Dark World' he described as coming through 'a crack in Pansay's head'. *Something of Myself* records his punishing regime of overwork on the newspaper during these years, often with a high fever and in overwhelming heat going on long into the night. It highlights one particular 'pivot' experience of acute mental crisis: 'It happened one hot-weather evening, in '86 or thereabouts, when I felt that I had come to the edge of all endurance. As I entered my empty house in the dusk there was no more in me except the horror of a great darkness, that I must have been fighting for some days. I came through that darkness alive, but how I do not know.'[22] The autobiography records cases of other men who broke down in these circumstances, but attributes Kipling's own survival to his 'capacity for being able to read, and the pleasure of writing what my head was filled with'. 'In The Matter of a Private' and 'At The End of the Passage' give memorable instances of hysterical breakdown due to similar pressures, while in writing the stories of 'The Phantom Rickshaw' Kipling's 'horror' of that 'great darkness' cannot have been far away.

Two of the stories, 'The Strange Ride' and the title story, were originally written for the special Christmas magazine *Quartette* in 1885, when Kipling was only nineteen, and are therefore two of his earliest published pieces of fiction. Initially they were straightforward first-person narratives in the manner of Poe, but when he revised them for the Railway Library in 1888 he added an introductory 'frame' for each of them, to set them in a quasi-normative context. In *Under the Deodars* Kipling tried out various devices for playing down the raconteur style of the *Plain Tales*, by giving more room to dramatized dialogue in particular, but here all four stories depend heavily upon first-person narration, now carefully framed by a larger context. They are therefore prototypes of some of Kipling's most remarkable later stories, such as 'On Greenhow Hill' (1891) and 'The Disturber of Traffic' (1893), with their interweaving of evocative setting and evoked internal narrative.

'The Phantom Rickshaw', however, occupies a very special

place in the development of Kipling's narrative art, as he explained at the end of his life, in *Something of Myself*, when discussing the creative role of the force he calls his 'Personal Daemon': 'Mine came to me early when I sat bewildered among other notions, and said: "Take this and no other." I obeyed, and was rewarded. It was a tale in the little Christmas magazine *Quartette* . . . and it was called "The Phantom Rickshaw". Some of it was weak, much was bad and out of key; but it was my first serious attempt to think another man's skin.'[23] To some extent, as is so often the way with Daemons, the other man's skin he actually enters in the story is another writer's, Edgar Allan Poe's in fact, though convincingly translated to the raj.[24] Jack Pansay describes himself as a 'well-educated Bengal Civilian', and, apart from his rash love-affair with Mrs Wessington, is clearly a blamelessly conservative clubman, yet, as a result of his encounter with his former mistress' phantom, he becomes increasingly estranged from the 'workaday Anglo-Indian world' of his acquaintances, and eventually a kind of semi-demented outcast, effectively wedded to his 'ghostly companion', and unable to 'return to the world as [he] used to know it'. Like Henry James' *The Turn of the Screw* or 'Jolly Corner', this is a psychological ghost story, for all its 'blood-and-thunder Magazine diction'. Framed as it is by Dr Heatherlegh's bluffly pragmatic diagnosis, Pansay's feverish but circumstantial record of his obsessive hallucinations during the 1885 season at Simla reads like something out of Freud's *Studies in Hysteria* of ten years later. For, like Freud's patients, what Pansay suffers from are unacknowledged memories – Hetherlegh calls them his 'queer reminiscences' – and repressed sexual guilt, associated with his illicit affair with Mrs Wessington, and remorse after her death. The persecutory phantom is a hallucinatory embodiment of his last sight of his rejected mistress, which is described as 'photographed on [his] memory', and its words are a nagging echo of her last words to him before her death. Significantly, it first appears when he buys an engagement ring for his fiancée Kitty Mannering as an 'outward and visible sign of her dignity as an engaged girl'; the phantom, like the monster which comes between Frankenstein and his bride in Mary Shelley's story, is an outward and visible sign to Pansay of his inner, unspoken disgrace. In time it leads Pansay to confess his hidden past, be rejected in his turn and withdraw into a psychotically self-punishing inner world where, as he says 'the rickshaw and I were the only realities in a world of shadows'.

The story works because Pansay's paranoid projections of his guilty inner shadows are anchored so firmly in the solid realities of Simla – the Mall, club, gossip and rickshaw rides, where the phantom of Pansay's past lover is superimposed over his present one. 'They're confoundedly particular about morality in these parts,' Pansay notes towards the end, and the combination of his own guilt and Simla's punitive conformism drive him into an irreparably estranged state based on a tie to the woman for whose death he feels responsible. It is in the confoundingly particular details, with their often cruelly perverse specificity, that the story strikes home, as when in the magnificently ambiguous revelation scene Kitty strikes him across the face with her riding-whip, leaving a 'livid blue wheal' upon it as her 'signature' – a gesture that reproduces the effect of his rejection of Mrs Wessington, which, he says, 'cut the dying woman before me like the blow of a whip'. Beneath its strained, gothic surface, the story touches a deeper strain in the values of 'Everyday, ordinary Simla', the structure of repression within the jovial 'Knowability' of Dr Heatherlegh's world.

'My Own True Ghost Story' is little more than a traveller's anecdote, and seems incongruously lightweight beside the other tales in the set. It has been described as an 'anti-ghost story', but might better be described as a shaggy ghost story, or a ghost story that got away. It opens with a list of British stations that 'bristle with haunted houses', which suggests something of the disorientation the British felt in the orient, despite the odd racist view that 'No native ghost has yet been authentically reported to have frightened an Englishman'. The curious currency of the supernatural in British India is confirmed by Sir Walter Lawrence in his memoirs, where he wrote: 'I have seen so much in India of what we in England would call the supernatural that I have an open mind, and I think that if we lived with the Hindus, apart from the influence of our people, we should soon in that land of enchantment find . . . there is indeed more than is dreamt of in our philosophy.'[25] The story itself is only notable for the mouldy historical atmosphere of the neglected *dak* bungalow it describes, and its undefined background sense of 'the real tragedy of our lives in India', the mildly paranoid sense of how isolated 'real Sahibs' felt in the vast subcontinent.

'The Strange Ride of Morrowbie Jukes', a tale which John Bayley calls 'one of the most memorable though least discussed of Kipling's oeuvre', is perhaps Kipling's most compelling account of a 'real Sahib' out of reach of the influence of his 'people'. Apparently based on an earlier traveller's report, it purports to be a factual, first-person account of a disastrous journey into the Indian desert made by a British civil engineer, who loses his way and gets trapped in a kind of concentration camp for Hindu survivors of the burning *ghats*, a nightmarish funeral colony from which there appears to be no escape. On one level this is simply an Anglo-Indian variant of Poe's 'The Pit and the Pendulum', a tale of horrific incarceration and miraculous rescue, but it also works as a grotesque political fable, fuelled by the ruling élite's fear of the subordinated native population, and haunted by memories of the Indian Mutiny twenty years earlier.[26] It is as if the Kafka of 'The Penal Settlement' and the Swift of *Gulliver's Travels* had collaborated to write an imperialist allegory of Hobbes' 'state of nature'.

The critic S. S. Husain has argued that Kipling's portrayal of native life is always 'intended primarily to underline the superiority of the white man over the Indian, and thus justify the former's right to govern India', and he picks out this story as a demonstration of 'Hinduism at its worst'.[27] On the face of it, Jukes' narrative, with its disgustingly detailed picture of the cruelty and squalour of life in the pit, and its portrayal of the Brahmin Gunga Dass as a treacherous killer, certainly does look like an unambiguous vision of the horrors of the Indian caste system and an implicit justification for British rule. That is certainly how Jukes sees it. To a modern reader on the other hand, how Jukes sees is as striking as what he sees, and his narrative of the ride shows up the strangeness of his own world view as much as anything in the Indian world he views.

On his own description, Jukes is 'a Civil Engineer, a man of thirteen years' standing in the Service, and, I trust, an average Englishman'. As a man 'with a head for plans and distances and things of that kind', he recounts his journey in the stiff British idiom of an official report. He describes the pit itself in terms of a professional survey ('a horseshoe shaped crater of sand with steeply-graded sand walls about thirty-five feet high'), gives a census of the number of inhabitants ('about forty men, twenty women, and one child'), an exact account of his finances ('Rs. 9-8-5') and a meticulous inventory of the contents of the dead Englishman's pockets ('Envelope, postmark undecipherable, bearing a Victorian stamp'). He is also a practitioner of the instant racial generalization no doubt current in official circles ('Hindus seldom laugh', 'a Briton's first impulse . . . is to guard the contents of his pockets'). Kipling's masterful impersonation of Jukes' language of colonial mastery is integral to the effect of his history of 'a Sahib, a representative of the dominant race', as Jukes represents himself, reduced to a state of being 'helpless as a child and completely at the mercy of his native neighbours'. At times he is like the incarnation of the language of British administration.

Yet under its mask of quasi-objective reportage, Jukes' narrative is riddled with an almost comic grotesquery and a vein of scarcely repressed hysteria. He sets out on his strange ride in a state of feverish delirium and rage, in pursuit of a 'huge black and white beast'; mounted on his polo saddle and brandishing his pig-sticking spear as emblems of his *pukka* status, while 'shouting challenges to the camelthorn bushes', he is like some absurd Sahib Quixote. Once in the pit, Jukes sees the pitiful natives as 'loathsome *fakirs*' and 'wild beasts' and is outraged by the 'disrespectful treatment' he receives from his 'inferiors' while there, and especially from Gunga Dass, a former civil servant. What Jukes finds terrible in his predicament is not the physical deprivation he shares with his neighbours, but his own social humiliation, the petty and terrible wounds to his sense of status. For it is Jukes who is most caste-conscious here, and Dass is a Hindu mirror to him: 'Once I was Brahmin and proud man, and now I eat crows.' Jukes is concerned when Dass stops calling him 'sir', but doesn't recognize the irony of being called 'Protector of the Poor' when the one time he shows the faintest twinge of compassion for his fellows is when he hears of a sahib who suffers a fate similar to his own. Everything Jukes does is designed to maintain his sense of social authority, and to re-establish mastery, in a place where 'every canon of the world' and every sign of British rule is negated in a terrible equality. The intelligent and mischievous Gunga Dass understands this very well, as is shown in their political confrontation while the Brahmin is about to share out Jukes' freshly killed horse:

Gunga Dass explained that horse was better than crow, and 'greatest good of greatest number is political maxim. We are now Republic, Mister Jukes, and you are entitled to a fair share of the beast. If you like, we will pass a vote of thanks. Shall I propose?'
  Yes, we were a Republic indeed! A Republic of wild beasts penned at the bottom of a pit, to eat and fight and sleep till we died.

It is an extraordinary tableau in which the ironic Brahmin confronts the outraged Jukes with a Grand Guignol parody of Indian democracy enacted over the sahib's dead horse. The Benthamite maxim Dass quotes might remind the reader of the contribution of utilitarianism to British government in India, both during the liberal reformist governorship of Bentinck and the more authoritarian regimes after the Mutiny.[28] Here Dass, as an educated Bengali telegraph-master, might almost be taken as a liberal spokesman for the Indian Congress Movement, while Jukes, who voices disapproval of local 'self-government' from the outset, clearly represents an authoritarian-style imperialism, rather on the lines of Kipling's own beliefs.[29] If Dass is an unsavoury representative of a possibly independent India, Jukes is like a caricature of the worst aspects of contemporary British rule. The 'fever' he speaks of at the outset speaks in his narrative the language of an imperious as well as imperialist paranoia.

VII

'If I want a crown I must go hunt it for myself,' says the narrator at the start of 'The Man who would be King', and the story he tells can be read as the crowning work of Kipling's Indian period.

It has always been one of Kipling's most popular stories, yet it is also a peculiarly packed and enigmatic one, drawing on a wide range of historical material and written with a complex figurative playfulness that makes it more like Melville's *Billy Budd* or Coleridge's *Ancient Mariner* than the swashbuckling travelogue it is often taken for. In 1891, J. M. Barrie called it 'our author's masterpiece', while the *National Observer* asserted that 'nothing he has ever written has the imaginative splendour of "The Man who would be King"', and prophesied its permanent place, with 'The Strange Ride', in the kingdom of English literature'. *Blackwoods* thought it his '*chef d'oeuvre* in prose' in 1898, and H. G. Wells, in *The Sleeper Wakes* of the same year, named it 'one of the best stories in the world'. More recently, Randall Jarrell dismissed it as a 'showy adventure story' that seemed to him 'romantic in the bad sense of the word', and Kingsley Amis declared it 'grossly overrated', intolerably garrulous' and full of 'cloudy importance'. Certainly it has a lot in common with popular imperial yarns like Rider Haggard's *King Solomon's Mines* and John Buchan's *Prester John*, a spectacular story of foolhardy explorers and fantastic kingdoms beyond the frontiers of the known world. But if it is a tall tale, which it is, it is also a deep one. In a letter, Kipling wrote that 'the tale is older than Plato by a few thousand years ... but men even lower than Peachey and Carnehan made themselves kings (and kept their kingdoms too) in India not 150 years ago. All "King" tales of that kind date back to the Tower of Babel,' but it is also given a very precise contemporary setting and frame of political

37

references, which enables it to tune into powerful political and historical ideas about empire. In its subject and intricately engineered narrative style, 'The Man who would be King' looks forward to Joseph Conrad's exploratory fable of African colonialism, *Heart of Darkness*, as well as back to Babel.

The opening 'frame' of the story is autobiographical and almost documentary, drawing upon Kipling's experience as a travelling correspondent in the native states of Rajputana for the *Pioneer* (thinly disguised as the *Backwoodsman*), and then sketching a brilliantly atmospheric picture of life behind the scenes in the newspaper offices Kipling worked in throughout his 'Seven Years' Hard' in India, as described in *Something of Myself*. 'All the queer outside world would drop into our workshop sooner or later,' he recollected there. 'One met men going up and down the ladder in every shape of misery and success.'[30] The story describes one sensational case-history of success and failure, and in it too the sweltering newspaper office is the theatre in which his two 'queer' heroes rehearse their ambitions and narrate their outcome. It is like the primal scene of Kipling's Indian period, the place where working journalist and extravagant oral storyteller meet. The germ of the tale was a real encounter during his Rajputana trip, recorded at length in a letter to Margaret Burne-Jones in January 1888, in which Kipling describes meeting a fellow-Mason on the borders of Bhilwarra and being given an unintelligible message to convey to another Mason in a train on the edge of the desert some time later, just as in the story. 'The Man who would be King' is in fact an elaborate fictional hypothesis to explain that bizarre meeting with two mysterious travelling Masons.[31] Kipling's close friend, Mrs Hill, has given an account of how they acquired their names:

When 'The Man who would be King' was germinating in R.K.'s mind he was lunching with us. Suddenly he demanded names for his characters. A. promptly said, 'Well the queerest name I ever heard was that of a missionary I met in the Himalayas ... Peachey Taliaferro Wilson.' Of course Rudyard seized on that at once. I could think of no name to give, so R. said, 'Well, who was the most prominent man in your home town?' ... I replied, 'Mr Dravo,' and sure enough he used these very names, adding a 't' to Dravo.

Perhaps because of that meeting in Bhilwarra, the tale is saturated with Masonic allusions; Freemasonry, declares one of its heroes, is the 'the key to the whole show'. This is explored in a suggestive but misleading article by Paul Fussell, 'Irony, Freemasonry and Humane Ethics in "The Man who would be King"'.[32] He interprets the tale as primarily a 'Masonic parable' about moral kingship, as well as a 'virtual parody' of biblical history, but Kipling has interwoven his Masonic plot with highly topical political material. Carnehan in the opening episode tells tales of 'out-of-the-way corners of the Empire' and talks 'politics' with the narrator, and Kipling's tale combines all three. As the text insists, Kipling was a journalist on the *Pioneer* as well as a Mason.

When Carnehan and Dravot, Kipling's rogue explorers, break into the journalistic routine of the newspaper office, they not only voice their wild aspirations to kingship and the conquest of Kafiristan over the frontier, but set about researching their trip much as Kipling would have done, by leafing through his reference books and maps, mining the *Encyclopaedia Britannica* and John Wood's classic travel book, *A Journey to the Source of the Oxus*, published in 1841, and glancing at specialist works by Surgeon-General H. W. Bellew, the contemporary expert on Afghanistan, who in 1880 had lectured in Simla on 'The New Afghan Question, or, Are the Afghans Israelites?' Kipling had obviously read the available literature on the unmapped and still largely unknown territory of Kafiristan, and the details of his fictional account are closely based on his miscellaneous reference books. Kafiristan, modern Nuristan, was completely unexplored at the time of the story, and it was not until just after that Sir George Robertson led an expedition there, enabling him to publish his *The Kafirs of the Hindu Kush* in 1895, the only complete picture of the pagan Kafirs before the bloody annexation and forcible conversion of the country by Abdur Rahman, the British-backed ruler of Afghanistan, in 1895.

Kipling's cockney adventurers are veterans of the Second Afghan War of 1878–80 as well as geographical pioneers, and their story takes them into an 'out-of-the-way corner' which was also one of the political hotspots of the time, given Afghanistan's strategic importance in the struggle between British and Russian interests in the Middle East. In the end, it was to be the Muhamaddan Abdur Rahman who was to be King of Kafiristan.

There was in fact one precedent for the duo's daredevil journey, and in composing the story I suspect that Kipling may have drawn upon the account of a visit to Kafiristan made by W. W. McNair, which was read to the Royal Geographical Society in December 1883.[33] McNair, an officer in the Indian Survey, disobeyed government orders forbidding Europeans to cross the frontier without permission, and made his way to Kafiristan disguised as a Muhammadan *hakim*, or native doctor, accompanied by a 'native explorer' and two Pathans, disguising his plane-table and other surveying instruments as books inscribed in Urdu. The president of the Society described McNair as the 'first European who had ever penetrated into Kafiristan' and Kafiristan, 'the country of infidels', as being 'surrounded by a sort of mystery'. It had been unconquered since the days of Alexander the Great and was inhabited by a people renowned for their 'European complexions', the beauty of their women, the potency of their wine and their ferocity in battle. This is very much the country of Kipling's megalomaniac adventurers, with their solemn 'Contrack' not to drink liquor or get involved with native women, and McNair's expedition provides a plausible model for their trek into the same territory, disguised as a *mullah* and his servant, smuggling their cargo of guns under piles of knick-knacks and whirligigs. But where McNair's account of his journey is modest and scientific, Kipling invents a mock-heroic, semi-crazed narrative style for the ancient mariner story poor Peachey Carnehan tells him over the office table. Kipling's art transforms the documentary material at his disposal into a dazzling fictional whirligig of his own.

Though Kipling's swaggering, half-baked amateur imperialists, Dan and Peachey, are fantastic figures in many ways,

Introduction

Kipling has also made them characteristic products of the British India of their time. They have been with General Roberts in the Afghan war, but also worked as 'Soldier, sailor, compositor, photographer, proof-reader, street-preacher, and correspondents of the *Backwoodsman*', quite apart from their careers in the expanding railways. Their impromptu curricula vitae are roll-calls of the petty skilled occupations demanded by the British imperial machine in north-west India. What gives them their larger-than-life swagger is their fantasy of kingship and military conquest, but that too is the product of their India, with its combination of militarism and the imperial idea. Dravot says that Kafiristan is the only place two men can 'Sar-a-*whack*', coining a word that puns on the word *sarwat*, meaning 'wealth', while calling up the triumphant career of Sir James Brooke who, on leaving the East India Company, became Rajah of Sarawak in 1841. When they become kings, Dan again recalls Brooke as their prototype, during his Falstaffian aria to Empire: '"I won't make a Nation," says he "I'll make an Empire! These men aren't niggers; they're English! ... They're the Lost Tribes, or something like it, and they've grown to be English ... They only want the rifles and a little drilling ... Peachey, man ... we shall be Emperors – Emperors of the Earth! Rajah Brooke will be a suckling to us ... Oh, it's big!"' Dravot has a big mouth, but his mixture of gargantuan imperialist rhetoric and brutal *realpolitik*, make him a mouthpiece, however burlesque, of powerful fantasies. He becomes a Gillray-like impersonation of the imperial idea, and a travesty of Kipling's vision of a responsible imperialism, since the pair are responsible to no one but themselves. Edmund Wilson described the story as a 'parable of what might happen to the English if they should forfeit their moral authority'.[34] Their story is like a mock-heroic Shakespearian double-plot within the serious historical drama of British imperialism. They conquer Kafiristan by ruthless military annexation, and, like the British in India, operate a policy of divide and rule, try to win over local chiefs, pretend to higher knowledge and put a ban on having affairs with native women (the cause of their eventual downfall). It is as if the two seedy railway-builders turned empire-builders were scripted to rerun a cartoon version of imperial history, but in their case ending in a violent and successful re-enactment of the Indian Mutiny of 1857. When the local population rebel, Peachey says 'there's no accounting for natives. This business is our Fifty-Seven.' Their adventure comes to a catastrophic end, a nightmare that can never have been far from the minds of the Anglo-Indian population of the raj.

Daniel Dravot's grandiose and farcical speech, like his story, has a way of calling up nineteenth-century power politics in queerly resonant ways, and 'The Man who would be King' is riddled with myths of kingdom, ancient and modern. It shows a particular interest in charismatic and archaic genealogies of power. The most prominent of these is Freemasonry, which is known to Masons as the 'royal art' and claims direct descent from the Craft used by the builders of Solomon's Temple in Jerusalem. In Kipling's story, Dravot and Carnehan acquire their kingship through their shaky exploitation of the Craft of Freemasonry, since it turns out that the Kafirs are Masons too and use the same secret marks, grips and rituals as European Masons like Dravot, who, by claiming to be a Master Mason, gives his mastery of his newly conquered people a mystique that military dictatorship of itself could not provide. The implausible idea of the ancient, secret and universal currency of Masonic ideas was widely accepted by Masons. The Afghans and the British also accepted two other ancient genealogical scenarios, one classical and one biblical, both of which play a part in the text. Dravot's claim to be 'the Son of Alexander' refers to the claim of many Afghan rulers to royal descent from Alexander the Great and his Greek colony in the region, while his reference to his people as 'the Lost Tribes, or something like it', makes use of the generally current idea that the Pathans of the North-West Frontier were the descendants of the Jewish tribes who failed to return from Babylon. This was, according to Lewis Wurgaft, 'something of an *idée fixe* among the British along the entire length of the frontier'. In *The North-West Frontier*,[35] C. C. Davies notes that the Afghans themselves regularly claim they are direct descendants of Saul, first king of Israel. During their military takeover of Kafiristan, the Bible is much in the mind of the two Masons, who play fast and loose with garbled Scripture, as when Peachey recalls annexing a remote village: 'So we took that village too, and I gives the Chief a rang from my coat and says, "Occupy till I come"; which was scriptural.' Scriptural it may have been, but it is a grotesque application of Christ's words in the parable of the talents. At the beginning of their occupation of Kafiristan, Dan as grotesquely appropriates God's commands in Genesis when he orders his people to 'Go and dig the land, and be fruitful and multiply.' At its end, Peachey becomes a twisted biblical allusion in himself when he is crucified by the Kafirs and is later found crawling in the street singing the Anglo-Indian Bishop Heber's hymn, 'The Son of Man goes forth to war,/A golden crown to gain,' a humiliating travesty of the crucified king of the New Testament. In his broken state he misquotes the hymn's second line, which should read 'a kingly crown to gain' – he is no longer a man who would be kingly.

I have tried to show how the two crackpot imperialists of the story exploit Freemasonry, Old and New Testament scripture and prestigious classical and biblical theories of descent, in order to establish credentials for their mercenary venture. I have also to suggest that in having Dan equate the Kafirs with the English Kipling is bringing into play one of the more bizarre political ideas of the time, 'the marvellous story of the British and the Lost Tribes of Israel being one and the same people'. The words are quoted from a pamphlet of 1878 called 'The Answer to the Eastern Question', which uses that 'marvellous story' to justify the 'white governing race' in India and the worldwide domination of the 'Anglo-Saxon race' over 'millions of dark-skinned heathens'. There was an English periodical called the *Banner of Israel*, devoted to publicizing the theory and proving it by procrustean philological and biblical scholarship, culminating in the triumphalist equation of the stone kingdom promised in the book of Daniel with the British Empire, the Jewish Disraeli as a sort of imperialist Moses, Queen Victoria as

43

the descendant of Solomon and the worldwide domination of the British as the real 'chosen people' with the will of God. A Colonel J. C. Gawlor, writing as 'Keeper of the Crown Jewels' at the Tower of London, wrote a series of pamphlets, such as *Dan the Pioneer of Israel*, which proved that the Anglo-Saxons were descendants of the Scythians who were in turn descendants of the tribe of Dan, and, in 1879, went so far as to assert that on both 'strategic' and 'scriptural' grounds, 'the British Empire stands or falls with the Anglo-Israel theory'. Though 'The Man who would be King' makes no explicit reference to this influential lunatic fringe of imperialist theory, Kipling has engineered it to plug into comparable archaic webs, and it may be no coincidence that his pioneering would-be king is called Dan and wishes to found a stone kingdom in central Asia that is related to Solomon's Masonic kingdom. Certainly Daniel Dravot's heated mock-heroic rhetoric sounds at times like a parody of the batty imperialism of philo-Israel and the *Banner*, and, in a late Stalky story, Kipling refers to a cranky 'Colonel-bird who believed that the English were the lost Tribes of Israel'.[36] When Dan proclaims, 'we shall be Emperors – Emperors of the Earth,' and offers to hand over his kingdom to Queen Victoria, Kipling seems to be burlesquing all such pretentious claims to empire, even as he recognizes their charismatic appeal.

As Conrad was to frame his tale of colonial breakdown in the African 'heart of darkness' on the darkened Thames in the imperial capital, so Kipling sets his tale of colonial catastrophe over the North-West Frontier within the sweltering confines of an Indian newspaper office, preoccupied both with local news of obituaries and 'amusements in the hill-stations' and the wider theatre where kings are killed on the Continent' and Mr Gladstone is 'calling down brimstone upon the British Dominions'. Much of the peculiar power of the story comes from Peachey's slightly unhinged survivor's eloquence – 'Keep looking at me,' he pleads, 'or maybe my words will go all to pieces' – and the way he switches back and forward between first and third person narrative – 'There was a party called

Peachey Taliaferro Carnehan that was with Dravot.' There is a grim humour about the narrative idiom, something like that generated by Mulvaney's theatrical blarney in *Soldiers Three*: it is partly a result of the mock-heroic plot and play with grandiose biblical and imperial images, but also an effect of the grotesque authenticating details with which it is studded – Carnehan's hand, 'twisted like a bird's claw', or his body falling, 'turning and twisting in the air like a penny whirligig'. His whole speech is 'twisted', like everything else in this whirligig of a story, most vividly at the close, where he is allowed to invent a kind of lunatic poetry to capture his terrible sense of dislocation on his way to the asylum – 'The mountains they danced at night', though 'He never let go of Dan's hand, and he never let go of Dan's head.' In the end it is the narrative bravura Kipling devises for his broken empire-builder which makes this one of his best tales. Narrative mastery survives the traumatic collapse of the imperial dream. The real Masonic pact that binds the two men in the office is that between Anglo–Indian journalist and pioneering storyteller.

VIII

In the original Preface to the last book in the Indian Library series, *Wee Willie Winkie and Other Child Stories*, Kipling wrote that 'Only women understand children thoroughly', and that 'even after patient investigation and the condescension of the nursery, it is hard to draw babies correctly'.[37] Kipling is one of the great children's writers in English and in *Kim*, the *Jungle Books*, *Puck of Pook's Hill* and *Rewards and Fairies*, he gave fiction for children a new and intense mobility in time and space and across cultures that opened up worlds of enthralling *difference*. The *Wee Willie Winkie* stories represent Kipling's first concerted attempt to gain access to the world of childhood in his fiction yet, as a group, they tend to confirm the truth of J. I. M. Stewart's judgement that 'Kipling was to write with genius for children, not invariably with genius about them'.[38]

Introduction

There is an unnerving streak of sentimentality running through these stories of Anglo-Indian childhood, and only the autobiographical 'Baa Baa, Black Sheep' can be numbered among Kipling's best works. The Preface reveals Kipling's usual obsession with the link between telling and being in the know, suggesting perhaps that where children were concerned he could never acquire the necessary inside knowledge through observation ('patient investigation'), only through impassioned identification with a child's own need to explore and know – the real creative impulse behind his stories for children. It is that identification which makes the autobiographical account, in 'Baa Baa, Black Sheep', of the typical Anglo-Indian child sent 'Home' to England to be educated – just 'one case among hundreds', as the story says – one of the classic portraits of an unhappy nineteenth-century boyhood, like Dickens' *David Copperfield*, Samuel Butler's *The Way of All Flesh* and Kipling's friend Edmund Gosse's *Father and Son*.

'Wee Willie Winkie' and its companion-piece, 'His Majesty the King', are very much in the mould of his first real child story, 'Tods' Amendment', from *Plain Tales*, calculatedly winning genre studies of six-year-old children of senior British personnel in India, here the sons of a commander-in-chief and high-ranking civil servant respectively. With their excruciating baby-talk and corny endings, they have a look of commissioned studio portraits about them, providing just the right degree of individual pathos in the details of the young sahib's features, and crowned in the end by a triumphant personal recognition and cheerful reaffirmation of social solidarity within the Regiment and Family. Charles Carrington has called the stories 'conventional tales in a genre which delighted our grandparents' during the heyday of *Little Lord Fauntleroy*.[39] As a result, perhaps, they cast a certain light on the conventions of Anglo-Indian society as well as of popular fiction. Even Kipling's most sentimental stories have a certain grim realism about them and, as accounts of the formation of a conventional sahib, they have their own sad interest.

Wee Willie Winkie is like several other Kipling characters in acquiring his nickname from a nursery book, but he derives his real sense of identity from being the son of 'the Colonel of the 195th', brought up under 'Military Discipline'. Though he is idolized by all the regiment as a sweet little tearaway, he is defined to a pathetic degree by the regimented language of army life, good-conduct medals and 'regimental penalties'. He calls his nursery his 'quarters', and his house the 'barracks', and strictly adheres to his father's view that it is 'un-man-ly' to kiss girls. The unfortunately named Wee Willie is particularly impressed by his favourite subaltern's shaving brush, or 'sputter-brush', and regards the same subaltern's fiancée 'with as much respect as Coppy's big sword or shiny pistol', that is, as just another phallic attribute of the military world. The story tells how little Willie breaks out of his enforced confinement to barracks and rides off over the forbidden North-West Frontier to rescue Coppy's fiancée, who has imprudently ventured beyond the jurisdiction of the raj. Its climax is the bizarre confrontation between 'Wee Willie Winkie, child of the Dominant Race, aged six and three-quarters' and a threatening bunch of Afghan 'natives' approaching the wounded memsahib. 'I am the Colonel Sahib's son,' he announces, 'and my order is that you go at once. You black men are frightening the Miss Sahib.' In this characteristic story of confinements and frontiers, Willie identifies the border of 'British India' with 'the end of all the Earth', which makes his plucky impersonation of his father's imperial style of command rather grandly absurd. In leaving the cantonment against orders, Willie is described as feeling 'guilty of mutiny', but the real test of his 'training' comes when he has to prevent himself from crying when laughed at by the natives – 'an infamy greater than any mutiny.' In the end, of course, the miniature St George rescuing Miss Allardyce from the natives is himself rescued by the regiment and hailed by Coppy as a '*pukka* hero'.

One interesting feature of this unlikely *pukka* fairy story is its own reference to George MacDonald's fairy story, *The Princess and the Goblin*, added when Kipling revised the piece for the Indian Railway Library. Kipling has Willie map his colonial world on the frontier of Afghanistan in terms borrowed from George MacDonald – that 'wonderful tale of a land where the Goblins were always warring with the children of men until they were defeated by one Curdie', first published in 1871, when Kipling was Willie's age. For Willie, 'the purple hills across the river were inhabited by Goblins', so that his adventure among the Afghans is a re-enactment of Curdie's fight against 'warring' Goblins – a telling imperial translation of MacDonald's supernatural fable. It's a shrewd psychological touch, but unfortunately Kipling's little study in a regimental childhood makes 'the future Colonel of the 195th' the object as well as the subject of fairy-tale wishfulness.

As Willie internalizes the world of the British army, the neglected little nursery 'King' who is the subject of 'His Majesty the King' internalizes the frigidly formal social world of his parents, 'the empire of his father and mother'. In the nursery, tended only by the underprivileged Miss Biddums from Calcutta, the boy is absolute monarch, but 'At the door of the nursery his authority stopped' and he passes 'the frontier of his own dominions', to find himself overshadowed by his father in his wilderness of pigeon-holes and by his remote but wonderful mother 'who was always getting into or stepping out of the big carriage'. That language of territory and authority, derived from his father's civil-service world, regulates the entire story, and when the boy steals the star meant for his mother and appropriates it as his own ''parkle crown' he feels so guilty that he falls ill and imagines himself as one of the Indian thieves incarcerated by his father's administration in the 'Central Jail'. The story touches here on vulnerable psychological territory, but the fairy-tale transformation of his awful parents at the end offers a mawkishly wishful resolution to the story of the Boy who would be King and who wins his parents' affection by stealing his mother's 'crown'. His Majesty is only a watery reflection of Punch in 'Baa Baa, Black Sheep', a story which undermines the credibility of the other two portraits of six-year-olds.

The fourth story of the set, 'The Drums of the Fore and

Aft', is a grisly account of a frontier battle, and deals with a very different social world of childhood, and a much more ambiguous kind of youthful 'heroism'. Charles Carrington finds this the only really convincing account of an actual battle among Kipling's stories about the Indian army, and shows that it is largely a mosaic made up from the disaster at Maiwand and the fight at Ahmed Khel in 1880, towards the end of the Second Afghan War.[40] The germ of the story, however, goes back much further in time, to an episode in the British siege of Masulipatam in 1759. In *Military Transactions of the British Nation in Indostan*,[41] R. Orme describes the retreat of British troops in panic after the discovery of a supposed mine, all except 'Captain Yorke, who marched at the head . . . left alone with only two drummers, who were black boys, beating the grenadier march, which they continued, but in vain, for none rejoined.' Though Captain Yorke managed to recall some of the troops to the attack, he was shot, 'and each of the black drummers was killed dead at his side'. Kipling transfers this incident from the eighteenth century to the Afghan War of his own time, makes his two drummers hard-boiled English squaddies rather than native Indians, and transforms what is simply a picturesque incident in a long campaign into a decisive, morale-boosting event that turns near-defeat into British victory over Pathan guerrilla fighters.

Yet this is neither a romantic battle story nor a celebration of schoolboy heroics. Unlike 'Only a Subaltern'. 'The Drums of the Fore and Aft' gives a harshly unidealized picture of officers and troops, this time undergoing a crisis of morale and leadership in a bloody border skirmish. The story opens with a journalistic essay on Kipling's theories of army training, in the course of which he gives his characteristically thick-skinned definition of his ideal professional army: 'blackguards commanded by gentlemen, to do butcher's work with efficiency and despatch.' The narrative that follows describes a cheerfully inexperienced, badly led regiment of 'drafts from an over-populated manufacturing district', demoralized and over-whelmed by their first experience of actual warfare under

guerrilla conditions. The shadow of the British defeat at Maiwand lies over these pages. Though in Kipling's story the regiment's shambolic retreat is converted into victory at the crucial
moment, this only occurs due to the shame-inducing, drink-
induced gesture of the two desperate drummer-boys who strike
up the 'old tune of the Old Line', the heroic, patriotic ballad of
the 'British Grenadiers'. Like the 'Old Flag', the corny tune
and the boys' absurd heroics transform morale in the dispersed
troops and unite them in a vengeful *ésprit de corps* which helps
to salvage their battered self-esteem. There is no success in
Kipling like the knowledge of failure.

It's an uncomfortable story, strangely out of place in *Wee
Willie Winkie*, with its vivid reminder of the realities of war,
and the premature militarization and death of the two young
Tommies. In fact it starts out as a pragmatic essay on military
policy in the 80s in the wake of Gladstone's reforms of the army
which had involved the introduction of a new territorial army
based on the idea of linked home and overseas battalions, with
short-term troops in place of life-long professionals, and with
officers selected by public examination.

The Second Afghan War had finished a couple of years before
Kipling arrived in India in 1882, and Kipling himself, despite
his fascination with the army, was not to have first hand experience of warfare until 1900 during the Boer War, yet 'The Drums
of the Fore and Aft' is a surprisingly convincing recreation of
the experience of battle. At the end of the story a newspaper
correspondent who has arrived on the scene too late to give an
eyewitness report on the fighting asks participants for 'the details somehow – as full as ever you can, please'. Kipling, who
had been too late too, provides them, with something like Ste-
phen Crane's sharpness of focus: the handsome Lew on the
parade-ground 'like a Seraph in red worsted embellishments',
the hopelessly congested supply lines where 'Commissariat
officers swore from dawn till far into the night amid the wind-
driven chaff of the fodder-bales', a bullet that 'flicked out the
brains of a private seated by the fire', the Colonel blenching
before the hospital sheets and his men before the 'dark stale

blood that makes afraid', and finally 'the big ditch-grave for the dead under the heights of Jagai'. But though the story is studded with such details, it is the study of group feeling among the troops which makes it so raw and alive – the aggro, the endemic racism, the smart of shame, the big talk, the fear, the rivalry between regiments, the desire for revenge and the sense of general confusion. Without the vocal bravura of the *Soldiers Three* stories, it offers an unpalatable inside-view of the British army in action, highlighting Kipling's underlying interest not in group morals but in group morale.

'As often in Kipling, what may at first seem very crude is in fact rather subtle,' J. I. M. Stewart observes of this story, and it has won many admirers, from Angus Wilson who noted that, 'characteristically, the finest battle scene in Kipling is not a victory but a near-disaster,'[42] to Henry James, who confessed in 1891: 'one might as well admit . . . that one has wept profusely over "The Drums of the Fore and Aft", the history of the "dutch courage" of two dreadful little boys.' Reading this story, one readily understands the admiration the great Russian short-story writer, Isaac Babel, author of *Red Cavalry*, felt for Kipling's work. Like Babel's, Kipling's fiction has the disquieting virtue of making his own causes as unenchanting as those he opposes.[43]

IX

'Baa Baa, Black Sheep' is unique in Kipling's *oeuvre* in being directly autobiographical in inspiration. His friend Edmonia Hill was with him when he was writing it in December 1888, and found it 'pitiful' to see him reliving his early experiences as he told what she calls 'a true story of his early life. When he was writing it he was a sorry guest, as he was in a towering rage at the recollection of those days.'[44]

Kipling gives the two children in the story the palpably archetypal names of Punch and Judy, so that the personal nature of their history was not apparent until *Something of Myself* was

Introduction

published posthumously in 1937. Kipling's biographer Charles Carrington is sceptical about many features of this harrowing tale of childhood persecution, but it bears a remarkably close resemblance to the broad outlines and specific details of the account of his childhood in Bombay and England Kipling gave when he came to write *Something of Myself* some forty years later.[45] It is also corroborated by his sister's memoir reprinted in *Kipling: Interviews and Recollections*[46] and Kipling ascribes a very similar childhood to Dick Heldar, the hero of his first novel, *The Light that Failed*, largely written in 1890 on his return from India to England. Writing about the *Wee Willie Winkie* volume in the *Athenaeum* in December 1890 Kipling characteristically picked out this one story as 'not true to life', but as the notes to this edition show, it is remarkably true to his life story as he came to record it in his magnificently artful late autobiography.

Whatever its factual verisimilitude, 'Baa Baa, Black Sheep' is unlikely to be forgotten by any of its readers, as a story of traumatic separation and persecution anxiety. It is one of the most memorably unforgiving first-hand accounts of childhood in literature, and the intensity of its self-dramatizing exploration of the psychology of rejection and compensation make it central not only to our understanding of Kipling's world, but to the psychology of childhood in general. Edmund Wilson called it 'one of the most powerful things he wrote', and gave it a significant place in defining the nature of Kipling's character and achievement. Though some critics have objected to his naïve use of the story as a kind of psychoanalytic key to Kipling's life, the story itself opens up a territory later explored by the pioneers of child-psychoanalysis, Anna Freud, Melanie Klein and D. W. Winnicott.[47] In digging up the traumas he underwent on being sent away to England for his education, Kipling is not primarily interested in either psychology or self-analysis – he had little interest in such things at the best of times – but he clearly needed to exorcize or master his shaping experiences of loss and guilty self-assertion, and he did so by telling a story which is above all a story about the redemptive power of stories.

Introduction

In September 1888 Kipling had published 'The Last of the Stories'; 'Baa Baa, Black Sheep' is in a sense the first of the stories, a story at any rate about the roots of fiction and the need for stories. It is that as much as anything which makes it more than a self-pitying document of Kipling's sense of childhood persecution or a means of revenge upon the fairy-tale stepmother figure of the evangelical Aunty Rosa, who acts as the children's guardian in England. Like most of Kipling's fiction, it is an extremist tale in which the underlying scenario concerns the fear of not belonging and loss of the world, here rooted in the primal human terror of separation from the mother and the paranoid fear of total rejection. In leaving behind what is called 'his world' in his parents' home in Bombay, a place where he had been 'unquestioned despot', Punch finds himself in an alien world like the 'House of Desolation' of Kipling's childhood in Southsea, no longer a petted sahib surrounded by affectionate parents and servants but a 'Black Sheep', made to feel guilty and unwanted, trapped in the 'Valley of Humiliation'. In that predicament Punch's only means of survival, apart from some baffled fellow-feeling from his younger sister Judy, is narrative. As a 'Black Sheep' Punch is trapped in an unacceptable narrative that won't accept him, woven by his 'Aunt' and her son Harry, with the help of their evangelical reading of the Good Book. To escape it, and to compensate for the loss of the primary world of his family in India, Punch hungers for his own stories to resist and master the unacceptable in the alien Rocklington world. As a result, the narrative is a kind of archaic triumph of reading.

When we first see Punch he is clamouring for 'the story about the Ranee that was turned into a tiger' in the friendly atmosphere of his Indian nursery on the day he hears the news of his departure for England. Once in the stuffy, moralistic domesticity of Aunty Rosa's lodging house, Punch finds himself forbidden to 'explain his ideas about the manufacture of this world', and lectured on Christian morals about 'an abstraction called God' out of a 'dirty brown book filled with unintelligible dots and marks'. Kipling, like Punch, was a late reader. In her reminiscences of their childhood, Kipling's sister records that 'it was strange, but Ruddy only learned to read with the greatest difficulty'; when four years old – and more than two years younger than he – she was 'promoted to reading [her] verse of the psalms at family prayers while Ruddy was still spelling letters into syllables'. 'I was probably crowing over him,' she writes, 'and he said, "No, Trix, you're too little, you see; you haven't the brains to understand the hard things about reading. *I* want to know *why* 't' with 'hat' after it should be 'that'."'[48] When Punch eventually learns to read 'the Cat lay on the Mat', though a more serious matter than the creed, this accomplishment seems barren enough to him until he stumbles across an old children's magazine where he finds a story about a griffin carrying off a sheep – he is a Black Sheep himself – and it comes to him as a revelation: '"This," said Punch, "means things, and now I will know all about everything in all the world." He read till the light failed, not understanding a tithe of the meaning, but tantalized by glimpses of new worlds hereafter to be revealed.' With the same fantastic sense of new power he writes to his father for 'all the books in all the world', and finds Grimm's *Fairy Tales* and Hans Andersen 'enough', opening up a 'land of his own, beyond reach of Aunty Rosa and her God'. Thereafter, the rest of Punch's history is a desperate struggle between Punch's stories and his aunt's prohibition upon them.

The newly arrived sahib began by scandalizing his pious guardian by mixing up the biblical story of Genesis with 'his Indian fairy tales', his first 'sin'. He is then told off for telling 'tales' (in the sense of lies), for spinning Judy 'interminable tales', and then, having been forbidden to read at all, for secretly reading while 'acting a lie'. From then on his consolation is to 'string himself tales of travel and adventure', or invent 'horrible punishments' for his hated rival Harry – two genres in which Kipling himself was to excel. Driven by his aunt's accusations of deception and guilt, Punch's eventual triumph is to plot a 'tangled web of deception' by telling her deliberate lies about his progress at school – a strategy which enables him to pay her 'back full tale' (the pun on the two meanings of tale here, meaning 'sum' and 'story', tells its own tale). In his autobiography Kipling commented dryly on this aspect of his own childhood response to comparable Christian bullying: 'it made me give attention to the lies I soon found it necessary to tell: and this, I presume, is the foundation of literary effort.' In a sense, 'Baa Baa, Black Sheep' is a kind of founding story of his own literary vocation.

Punch too is most interested in stories of first and last things – from fairy tales to Genesis. 'Baa Baa, Black Sheep' is itself something like a Grimms' tale of the Hansel-and-Gretel type, describing the two children's efforts to survive the catastrophic separation from their parents and to learn autonomy. Like the Grimms' tale, it sees the world in terms of extreme oppositions and archetypal distinctions: black sheep and white sheep, wicked step-relations and true parents, heaven and hell. In part due to the narrow biblical fundamentalism of Aunty Rosa (for whom Punch coins the aptly archetypal name of Anti-Rosa), Punch's experience is mediated through quasi-theological terms. The child's world is eschatological, and in fact the word 'world' is crucial to it – it occurs seventeen times in the story, supported by terms like 'the earth', 'the Universe', Heaven and Hell. In England we see the sprawling little Punch explaining his 'ideas about the manufacture of this world', welding 'the story of the Creation on to what he could remember of his Indian fairy tales'. When the children are left behind by their parents, the narrator says, 'Punch and Judy, through no fault of their own, had lost all their world.' The story is strung between the 'manufacture' and 'loss' of the world. The 'First Bag' ends with the children on the beach at Rocklington, undergoing a loss of faith comparable to that described by Matthew Arnold in his elegy upon Christian faith, 'Dover Beach'. The second 'Bag' quotes Clough's 'Easter Day', another great Victorian poem about lost belief, and the last 'Bag' ends with an ambiguous affirmation of stoically repaired 'Faith', a faith now darkened by 'Knowledge'. It is another story of the Fall, of course, rewritten as a child's experience, but in Punch's case thirst for knowledge succeeds the fall, it does not cause it. When he learns to read he expresses his characteristically Kiplingesque wish to 'know all about everything in all the world'. In Genesis man lost Paradise because of his wish to know, in the Kipling story Punch needs to know because he has experienced that loss already, and forgotten 'what manner of life he had led in the beginning of things'. There are other echoes of Genesis. When at school Punch is incited by Harry to live up to his name and punches another boy, 'meaning honestly to slay him', he is accused of 'the offence of Cain' – Cain, the first Black Sheep of all. Soon afterwards, he tries to commit suicide and chooses the bizarrely apt method of sucking paint off the animals from a 'disused' toy Noah's Ark in the nursery, licking 'Noah's Dove clean'. Thereafter, terrorized by the family and 'God and Hell', Punch retreats into a shadowy, neurotic existence, where it is found that he is going blind, perhaps as a result of the very reading that has enabled him to glimpse new worlds.

The story ends with the return of his mother, and Punch's return to something like the 'better place' of the opening, the world of maternal recognition and acceptance. This is comparable to the fairy-tale endings of 'Wee Willie Winkie' and 'His Majesty the King', and perhaps their unconvincingly faked conclusions are best seen in the light of Punch's 'darkened eyes'. Punch was an 'unquestioned despot' at Bombay, just as 'His Majesty' was in the nursery and aspired to be outside it, and as the baby Winkie was 'idolized' by the regiment. Kipling might have assented to D. W. Winnicott's remark that infancy is the 'age of natural dictatorship'.[49] 'Baa Baa, Black Sheep' is a study of a paranoid childhood where due to premature separation, the boy's natural need for special status in his mother's eyes is thwarted and he is left with a world of absolute divisions, between belonging and not belonging, being a black sheep or part of the fold, being an outcast or king. The strained extremism of the story has made it seem unbalanced to some readers – to Charles Carrington in the article quoted, to Kingsley Amis in his book on Kipling (he describes the story as the 'only sorry result of Kipling's childhood experiences') – but it reflects something inherent in Kipling's whole outlook. Punch, on being sent to school, is outraged to find himself among tradespeople's sons, Jews, and even a negro, – whom he calls a *hubshi*, using his privileged Anglo-Indian caste word to distance himself from those of lower caste. The 'Black Sheep', though stigmatized himself, or *through* being stigmatized himself, adopts all the conventional stigmatizing prejudices of his background. In the early days of his time in England, Punch is much concerned with 'be-membering' both his Mother and his Indian past, and his child's word intimately allies being, memory, re-membering (as after a dis-membering) and membership of the family group. In remembering his own childhood in December 1888, Kipling created a memorable account of the forces at work behind the 'manufacture' of the Kipling world.

X

Wee Willie Winkie maps out many worlds in often grotesque detail, with Kipling's characteristic appetite for colonizing new fictional territories. In the light of his founding story, 'Baa Baa, Black Sheep', it can be seen that the best stories in all three series are in some way concerned with the extremes faced by Punch: the fear of loss of the world, and the urge to establish mastery over it. Unlike most writers, Kipling has little interest in moral rebels and outsiders, misfits or nonconformists. His stories follow the careers of marginal representatives of the ruling caste, people who identify with social authority and give allegiance to some hard-boiled, stoic version of the governing imperial morality, but are in danger of losing it, of being cast out or marginalized, and losing their selves as they lose their 'world'. Time and again the characters in these stories are faced with an alternative between high status or pariah-hood, being king or worse than nothing. Mrs Hauksbee seeks to 'create' Yeere as some civil-service star, but nearly ruins her reputation in doing so. The lovers in 'The Hill of Illusion' and 'At the Pit's Mouth' are threatened by the loss of both reputation and 'the world'. Morrowbie Jukes in his pit among the Hindu outcasts feels he has 'left the world for centuries' and Jack Pansay in 'The Phantom Rickshaw', robbed of his dreamed-of status as a respectably married pillar of society, implores heaven to let him return to the world as [he] used to know it'. Peachey and Dan get to be Kings of Kafiristan and dream of being 'Emperors of the Earth', but end up as pitiable outcasts, one beheaded and the other in the madhouse. The drummer-boys of 'The Drums of the Fore and Aft' aspire to be heroes, become so only through dutch courage and end up in 'the big ditch-grave for the dead under the heights of Jagai'. Behind Kipling's densely imagined social worlds one can see versions of the same extremist scenario framed by Punch's story. It was their Anglo-India which enabled Kipling to weld together his peculiar combination of studied social realism and mythopeic storytelling, the combination which makes him the great short-storywriter he is.

With the publication of the six sets of stories collected in *Soldiers Three* and *Wee Willie Winkie*, Kipling must have felt he had put his House of Fiction in some kind of order. More than the *Plain Tales*, they represent his conscious, experimental period of literary apprenticeship as a storyteller. In 'The Last of the Stories', published in the *Pioneer* in September 1888, the devil introduces the young Kipling to his literary master François Rabelais as 'An Entered Apprentice in difficulties with his rough ashlar', combining architectural, literary and Masonic ideas in one. It's a light-hearted self-reflexive allegory about the shadowy afterlife of fictional characters, his own and those of his contemporaries, but it shows the seriousness of Kipling's literary ambition and a certain self-mocking pleasure in his achievement to date. The story is an eclectic compendium of the popular fiction of the late nineteenth century, from Rider Haggard and Mark Twain to Zola and Balzac, and provides a final frame-story for the fiction he wrote in India. In Pirandello fashion, Kipling is confronted by the varied dramatis personae of his prodigious journalistic output, including most of the personnel of *Wee Willie Winkie*: Mrs Hauksbee and 'the actors in the Wayside Comedy', Bobby Wick and the Haeley Boy, Wee

Introduction

Willie and the entire regiment of 'The Drums of the Fore and Aft' who, in typically colonial style, are deployed to keep the shady French cast of Zola's novels in proper order. Kipling is doing more than mustering a roll-call of his 150 created characters in this playfully eschatological fiction, he is summing up his career and achievement at this moment of watershed during the close of 1888. Punch in 'Baa Baa, Black Sheep' looks to literature to 'know all about everything in all the world', requesting his father to send him 'all the books in all the world'. In 'The Last of the Stories', Kipling's version of the *Divine Comedy*, Rabelais presides over the characters from all those books, including Kipling's own, who accuse their 'puppet-master' of not knowing or understanding enough. At climax, Kipling, Rabelais and the devil have the following Dantesque dialogue about the relation between fiction and life:

'By the Great Bells of Notre Dame, you are in the flesh – the warm flesh! – the flesh I quitted so long – ah, so long! And you fret and behave unseemly because of those shadows! Listen now! I, even I, would give my Three, Panurge, Gargantua and Pantagruel, for one little hour of the life that is in you. And *I* am the Master!'

But the words gave me no comfort. I could hear Mrs Mallowe's joints cracking – or it might have been merely her stays.

'Worshipful Sir, he will not believe that,' said the devil. 'Who live by shadows lust for shadows. Tell him something more to his need.'

The Master grunted contemptuously: 'And he is flesh and blood! Know this, then. The First Law is to make them stand upon their feet, and the Second is to make them stand upon their feet, and the Third is to make them stand upon their feet. But, for all that, Trajan is a fisher of frogs.' He passed on, and I could hear him say to himself; 'One hour – one minute – of life in the flesh, and I would sell the Great Perhaps thrice over!'

Acknowledgements

I would like to thank the following for their help: John Birtwhistle, Judith Flanders, Tim Gates, Paul Keegan, Hermione Lee, Sean Ryan, Fiona Shaw, Timothy Webb and the librarian and staff of Sussex University Library. I owe a special debt to Adam Phillips for his unscholarly, intellectual encouragement throughout.

Further Reading

Allen, Charles, *Plain Tales from the Raj: images of British India in the twentieth century*, London, Futura Publications, 1979.

Amis, Kingsley, *Rudyard Kipling and his World*, London, Thames and Hudson, 1975.

Bayley, John, 'The Puzzles of Kipling', *The Uses of Division*, London, Chatto and Windus, 1976.

Birkenhead, Lord, *Rudyard Kipling*, London, Weidenfeld & Nicolson, 1978.

Buck, Sir Edward, *Simla, Past and Present*, Bombay, Times Press, 1925.

Carrington, Charles, *Rudyard Kipling, His Life and Work*, Harmondsworth, Penguin Books, 1970, 1986.

Cornell, Louis, *Kipling in India*, London, Macmillan, 1966.

Gilbert, Elliott L., ed., *Kipling and the Critics*, London, Peter Owen, 1966.

Green, R. L., ed., *Kipling: The Critical Heritage*, London, Routledge & Kegan Paul, 1971.

Gross, John, ed., *Rudyard Kipling: The man, his work and his world*, London, Weidenfeld & Nicolson, 1972.

Howard, J. E., *Memoir of W. W. McNair, the first European explorer of Kafiristan*, London, Keyser & Co., 1889.

Hutchins, Francis, *The Illusion of Permanence: British Imperialism in India*, Princeton, NJ, Princeton University Press, 1967.

Jarrell, Randall, *Kipling, Auden & Co*, Manchester, Carcanet Press, 1981.

Orel, Harold, ed., *Rudyard Kipling: Interviews and Recollections* (2 vols). London, Macmillan, 1983.

Page, Norman, ed., *A Kipling Companion*, London, Macmillan, 1984.

Pinney, Thomas, ed., *Kipling's India: Uncollected Sketches 1884–88*, London, Macmillan, 1986.

Further Reading

Rutherford, Andrew, ed., *Kipling's Mind and Art*, London, Oliver & Boyd, 1964.

Stewart, J. I. M., *Eight Modern Writers*, Oxford, Clarendon Press, 1963.

Tompkins, J. M. S., *The Art of Rudyard Kipling*, London, Methuen, 1959.

Wilson, Angus, *The Strange Ride of Rudyard Kipling*, London, Secker & Warburg, 1977.

Wilson, Edmund, 'The Kipling that Nobody Read', *The Wound and the Bow*, Cambridge, Mass., Houghton Mifflin Co., 1941.

Woodruff, Philip (Philip Mason), *The Men Who Ruled India*, Vol. 1: 'The Founders', Vol. 2: 'The Guardians', London, Jonathan Cape, 1953, 1954.

Yule, Henry and Burnell, A. L., eds., *Hobson-Jobson: being a glossary of Anglo-Indian colloquial words and phrases*, London, John Murray, 1886 (2nd ed., William Cooke, ed., 1903. New edition, with a forward by Anthony Burgess, London, Routledge & Kegan Paul, 1985).

Note on the Text

Wee Willie Winkie comprises numbers 4, 5 and 6 of Wheeler's Indian Railway Library, published by Messrs. A. H. Wheeler & Co., Allahabad, in 1888. The three booklets, *Under the Deodars*, *The Phantom Rickshaw* and *Wee Willie Winkie* were first published together in one volume with the title *Wee Willie Winkie* in 1892, published by Wheeler in India and by Messrs. Marston, Searle & Rivington Ltd. in London. In 1895, Macmillan & Co. took over copyright and published a revised text, which after 1899 was that used in the Uniform Edition. This is the text used here.

A high proportion of the stories were originally published in Indian periodicals: *Quartette*, the *Civil and Military Gazette*, and the *Week's News* of the *Pioneer*. Details of original publication and significant textual revisions are to be found in the notes to the stories.

The three stories in the appendix have never formed part of the standard English editions of Kipling. The text of 'A Supplementary Chapter' and 'The Last of the Stories' comes from *Abaft the Funnel* (1909), and 'Mrs Hauksbee Sits Out' from the American edition of *Under the Deodars*, published as part of Scribners' standard Kipling edition.

UNDER THE DEODARS[1]

And since he cannot spend nor use aright
   The little time here given him in trust,
But wasteth it in weary undelight
   Of foolish toil and trouble, strife and lust,
He naturally clamours to inherit
The Everlasting Future that his merit
   May have full scope – as surely is most just.
                The City of Dreadful Night[2]

﹛ The Education of Otis Yeere [1] ﹜

I

In the pleasant orchard-closes
'God bless all our gains,' say we;
But 'May God bless all our losses,'
Better suits with our degree. [2]
The Lost Bower

This is the history of a failure; but the woman who failed said that it might be an instructive tale to put into print for the benefit of the younger generation. The younger generation does not want instruction, being perfectly willing to instruct if any one will listen to it. None the less, here begins the story where every right-minded story should begin, that is to say at Simla, where all things begin and many come to an evil end.

The mistake was due to a very clever woman making a blunder and not retrieving it. Men are licensed to stumble, but a clever woman's mistake is outside the regular course of Nature and Providence; since all good people know that a woman is the only infallible thing in this world, except Government Paper of the '79 issue, bearing interest at four and a half per cent. Yet, we have to remember that six consecutive days of rehearsing the leading part of *The Fallen Angel*, at the New Gaiety Theatre [3] where the plaster is not yet properly dry, might have brought about an unhingement of spirits which, again, might have led to eccentricities.

Mrs Hauksbee [4] came to 'The Foundry' to tiffin with Mrs Mallowe, her one bosom friend, for she was in no sense 'a woman's woman'. And it was a woman's tiffin, [5] the door shut to all the world; and they both talked *chiffons*, [6] which is French for Mysteries.

'I've enjoyed an interval of sanity,' Mrs Hauksbee announced, after tiffin was over and the two were comfortably settled in the little writing-room that opened out of Mrs Mallowe's bedroom.

'My dear girl, what has *he* done?' said Mrs Mallowe sweetly. It is noticeable that ladies of a certain age call each other 'dear girl', just as commissioners of twenty-eight years' standing address their equals in the Civil List as 'my boy'.

'There's no *he* in the case. Who am I that an imaginary man should be always credited to me? Am I an Apache?'

'No, dear, but somebody's scalp is generally drying at your wigwam-door. Soaking rather.'

This was an allusion to the Hawley Boy,[7] who was in the habit of riding all across Simla in the Rains, to call on Mrs Hauksbee. That lady laughed.

'For my sins, the Aide at Tyrconnel[8] last night told me off to The Mussuck.[9] Hsh! Don't laugh. One of my most devoted admirers. When the duff[10] came – some one really ought to teach them to make puddings at Tyrconnel – The Mussuck was at liberty to attend to me.'

'Sweet soul! I know his appetite,' said Mrs Mallowe. 'Did he, oh *did* he, begin his wooing?'

'By a special mercy of Providence, *no*. He explained his importance as a Pillar of the Empire. I didn't laugh.'

'Lucy, I don't believe you.'

'Ask Captain Sangar; he was on the other side. Well, as I was saying, The Mussuck dilated.'

'I think I can see him doing it,' said Mrs Mallowe pensively, scratching her fox-terrier's ears.

'I was properly impressed. Most properly. I yawned openly. "Strict supervision, and play them off one against the other," said The Mussuck, shovelling down his ice by *tureenfuls*, I assure you. "*That*, Mrs Hauksbee, is the secret of our Government."'

Mrs Mallowe laughed long and merrily. 'And what did you say?'

'Did you ever know me at loss for an answer yet? I said: "So I have observed in my dealings with you." The Mussuck swelled with pride. He is coming to call on me tomorrow. The Hawley Boy is coming too.'

68

'"Strict supervision and play them off one against the other. *That*, Mrs Hauksbee, is the secret of *our* Government." And I daresay if we could get to The Mussuck's heart, we should find that he considers himself a man of the world.'

'As he is of the other two things.[11] I like The Mussuck, and I won't have you call him names. He amuses me.'

'He has reformed you, too, by what appears. Explain the interval of sanity, and hit Tim on the nose with the paper-cutter, please. That dog is too fond of sugar. Do you take milk in yours?'

'No, thanks. Polly, I'm wearied of this life. It's hollow.'

'Turn religious, then. I always said that Rome[12] would be your fate.'

'Only exchanging half-a-dozen *attachés* in red for one in black, and if I fasted, the wrinkles would come, and never, *never* go. Has it ever struck you, dear, that I'm getting old?'

'Thanks for your courtesy. I'll return it. Ye-es, we are both not exactly – how shall I put it?'

'What we have been. "I feel it in my bones," as Mrs Crossley says. Polly, I've wasted my life.'

'As how?'

'Never mind how. I feel it. I want to be a Power before I die.'

'Be a Power then. You've wits enough for anything – and beauty!'

Mrs Hauksbee pointed a teaspoon straight at her hostess. 'Polly, if you heap compliments on me like this, I shall cease to believe that you're a woman. Tell me how I am to be a Power.'[13]

'Inform The Mussuck that he is the most fascinating and slimmest man in Asia, and he'll tell you anything and everything you please.'

'Bother The Mussuck! I mean an intellectual Power – not a gas-power. Polly, I'm going to start a *salon*.'

Mrs Mallowe turned lazily on the sofa and rested her head on her hand. 'Hear the words of the Preacher, the son of Baruch,'[14] she said.

'*Will* you talk sensibly?'

'I will, dear, for I see that you are going to make a mistake.'

'I never made a mistake in my life – at least, never one that I couldn't explain away afterwards.'

'Going to make a mistake,' went on Mrs Mallowe composedly. 'It is impossible to start a *salon* in Simla. A bar would be much more to the point.'

'Perhaps, but why? It seems so easy.'

'Just what makes it so difficult. How many clever women are there in Simla?'

'Myself and yourself,' said Mrs Hauksbee, without a moment's hesitation.

'Modest woman! Mrs Feardon would thank you for that. And how many clever men?'

'Oh – er – hundreds,' said Mrs Hauksbee vaguely.

'What a fatal blunder! Not one. They are all bespoke by the Government. Take my husband, for instance. Jack *was* a clever man, though I say so who shouldn't. Government has eaten him up. All his ideas and powers of conversation – he really used to be a good talker, even to his wife, in the old days – are taken from him by this – this kitchen-sink of a Government. That's the case with every man up here who is at work. I don't suppose a Russian convict under the knout is able to amuse the rest of his gang; and all our men-folk here are gilded convicts.' [15]

'But there are scores –'

'I know what you're going to say. Scores of idle men up on leave. I admit it, but they are all of two objectionable sets. The Civilian who'd be delightful if he had the military man's knowledge of the world and style, and the military man who'd be adorable if he had the Civilian's culture.'

'Detestable word! [16] *Have* Civilians culchaw? I never studied the breed deeply.'

'Don't make fun of Jack's Service. Yes. They're like the teapoys [17] in the Lakka Bazar – good material but not polished. They can't help themselves, poor dears. A Civilian only begins to be tolerable after he has knocked about the world for fifteen years.'

'And a military man?'

70

'When he has had the same amount of service. The young of both species are horrible. You would have scores of them in your *salon*.'

'I would *not*!' said Mrs Hauksbee fiercely. 'I would tell the bearer to *darwaza band*[18] them. I'd put their own colonels and commissioners at the door to turn them away. I'd give them to the Topsham Girl to play with.'

'The Topsham Girl would be grateful for the gift. But to go back to the *salon*. Allowing that you had gathered all your men and women together, what would you do with them? Make them talk? They would all with one accord begin to flirt. Your *salon* would become a glorified Peliti's[19] – a "Scandal Point" by lamplight.'

'There's a certain amount of wisdom in that view.'

'There's all the wisdom in the world in it. Surely, twelve Simla seasons ought to have taught you that you can't focus anything in India; and a *salon*, to be any good at all, must be permanent. In two seasons your roomful would be scattered all over Asia. We are only little bits of dirt on the hillsides – here one day and blown down the *khud*[20] the next. We have lost the art of talking – at least our men have. We have no cohesion –'

'George Eliot in the flesh,' interpolated Mrs Hauksbee wickedly.

'And collectively, my dear scoffer, we, men and women alike, have *no* influence. Come into the verandah and look at the Mall!'

The two looked down on the now rapidly filling road, for all Simla was abroad to steal a stroll between a shower and a fog.

'How do you propose to fix that river? Look! There's The Mussuck – head of goodness knows what. He is a power in the land, though he *does* eat like a costermonger. There's Colonel Blone, and General Grucher, and Sir Dugald Delane, and Sir Henry Haughton, and Mr Jellalatty. All Heads of Departments, and all powerful.'

'And all my fervent admirers,' said Mrs Hauksbee piously. 'Sir Henry Haughton raves about me. But go on.'

'One by one, these men are worth something. Collectively,

they're just a mob of Anglo-Indians. Who cares for what Anglo-Indians say? Your *salon* won't weld the Departments together and make you mistress of India, dear. And these creatures won't talk administrative "shop" in a crowd – your *salon* – because they are so afraid of the men in the lower ranks overhearing it. They have forgotten what of Literature and Art they ever knew, and the women –'

'Can't talk about anything except the last Gymkhana, or the sins of their last nurse. I was calling on Mrs Derwills this morning.'

'You admit that? They can talk to the subalterns though, and the subalterns can talk to them. Your *salon* would suit their views admirably, if you respected the religious prejudices of the country and provided plenty of *kala juggahs*.' [21]

'Plenty of *kala juggahs*. Oh my poor little idea! *Kala juggahs* in a *salon!* But who made you so awfully clever?'

'Perhaps I've tried myself; or perhaps I know a woman who has. I have preached and expounded the whole matter and the conclusion thereof [22] –'

'You needn't go on. "Is Vanity". Polly, I thank you. These vermin' – Mrs Hauksbee waved her hand from the verandah to two men in the crowd below who had raised their hats to her – 'these vermin shall not rejoice in a new Scandal Point or an extra Peliti's. I will abandon the notion of a *salon*. It did seem so tempting, though. But what shall I do? I must do something.'

'Why? Are not Abana and Pharpar [23] –'

'Jack has made you nearly as bad as himself! I want to, of course. I'm tired of everything and everybody, from a moonlight picnic at Seepee [24] to the blandishments of The Mussuck.'

'Yes – that comes, too, sooner or later. Have you nerve enough to make your bow yet?'

Mrs Hauksbee's mouth shut grimly. Then she laughed. 'I think I see myself doing it. Big pink placards on the Mall: "Mrs Hauksbee! Positively her last appearance on *any* stage! This is to give notice!" No more dances; no more rides; no more luncheons; no more theatricals with supper to follow; no more

sparring with one's dearest, dearest friend; no more fencing
with an inconvenient man who hasn't wit enough to clothe what
he's pleased to call his sentiments in passable speech; no more
parading of The Mussuck while Mrs Tarkass calls all round
Simla, spreading horrible stories about me! No more of anything
that is thoroughly wearying, abominable, and detestable, but,
all the same, makes life worth the having. Yes! I see it all! Don't
interrupt, Polly, I'm inspired. A mauve and white striped
"cloud" round my excellent shoulders, a seat in the fifth row of
the Gaiety, and *both* horses cold. Delightful vision! A comfortable arm-chair, situated in three different draughts, at every
ball-room; and nice, large, sensible shoes for all the couples to
stumble over as they go into the verandah! Then at supper.
Can't you imagine the scene? The greedy mob gone away.
Reluctant subaltern, pink all over like a newly-powdered baby –
they really ought to *tan* subalterns before they are exported,
Polly – sent back by the hostess to do his duty. Slouches up to
me across the room, tugging at a glove two sizes too large for
him – I *hate* a man who wears gloves like overcoats – and trying
to look as if he'd thought of it from the first. "May I ah-have
the pleasure 'f takin' you 'nt' supper?" Then I get up with a
hungry smile. Just like this.'

'Lucy, how *can* you be so absurd?'

'And sweep out on his arm. So! After supper I shall go away
early, you know, because I shall be afraid of catching cold. No
one will look for my rickshaw. *Mine*, so please you! I shall
stand, always with that mauve and white "cloud" over my
head, while the wet soaks into my dear, old, venerable feet, and
Tom swears and shouts for the *mem-sahib's gharri*.[25] Then home
to bed at half-past eleven! Truly excellent life – helped out by
the visits of the *Padri*,[26] just fresh from burying somebody
down below there.' She pointed through the pines toward the
Cemetery, and continued with vigorous dramatic gesture –

'Listen! I see it all – down, down even to the stays! *Such*
stays! Six-eight[27] a pair, Polly, with red flannel – or list, is it? –
that they put into the tops of those fearful things. I can draw
you a picture of them.'

'Lucy, for Heaven's sake, don't go waving your arms about in that idiotic manner! Recollect every one can see you from the Mall.'

'Let them see! They'll think I am rehearsing for *The Fallen Angel*. Look! There's the Mussuck. How badly he rides. There!'

She blew a kiss to the venerable Indian administrator with infinite grace.

'Now,' she continued, 'he'll be chaffed about that at the Club in the delicate manner those brutes of men affect, and the Hawley Boy will tell me all about it – softening the details for fear of shocking me. That boy is too good to live, Polly. I've serious thoughts of recommending him to throw up his commission and go into the Church. In his present frame of mind he would obey me. Happy, happy child!'

'Never again,' said Mrs Mallowe, with an affectation of indignation, 'shall you tiffin here! "Lucindy your behaviour is scand'lus."'

'All your fault,' retorted Mrs Hauksbee, 'for suggesting such a thing as my abdication. No! *jamais!* nevaire! I will act, dance, ride, frivol, talk scandal, dine out, and appropriate the legitimate captives of any woman I choose, until I d-r-r-rop, or a better woman than I puts me to shame before all Simla – and it's dust and ashes in my mouth while I'm doing it!'

She swept into the drawing-room. Mrs Mallowe followed and put an arm round her waist.

'I'm *not*!' said Mrs Hauksbee defiantly, rummaging for her handkerchief. 'I've been dining out the last ten nights, and rehearsing in the afternoon. You'd be tired yourself. It's only because I'm tired.'

Mrs Mallowe did not offer Mrs Hauksbee any pity or ask her to lie down, but gave her another cup of tea, and went on with the talk.

'I've been through that too, dear,' she said.

'I remember,' said Mrs Hauksbee, a gleam of fun on her face. 'In '84, wasn't it? You went out a great deal less next season.'

Mrs Mallowe smiled in a superior and Sphinx-like fashion.

'I became an Influence,' said she.

'Good gracious, child, you didn't join the Theosophists [28] and kiss Buddha's big toe, did you? I tried to get into their set once, but they cast me out for a sceptic – without a chance of improving my poor little mind, too.'

'No, I didn't Theosophilander. Jack says –'

'Never mind Jack. What a husband says is known before. What did you do?'

'I made a lasting impression.'

'So have I – for four months. But that didn't console me in the least. I hated the man. *Will* you stop smiling in that inscrutable way and tell me what you mean?'

Mrs Mallowe told.

'And – you – mean – to – say that it is absolutely Platonic on both sides?'

'Absolutely, or I should never have taken it up.'

'And his last promotion was due to you?'

Mrs Mallowe nodded.

'And you warned him against the Topsham Girl?'

Another nod.

'And told him of Sir Dugald Delane's private memo about him?'

A third nod.

'*Why?*'

'What a question to ask a woman! Because it amused me at first. I am proud of my property now. If I live, he shall continue to be successful. Yes, I will put him upon the straight road to Knighthood, and everything else that a man values. The rest depends upon himself.'

'Polly, you are a most extraordinary woman.'

'Not in the least. I'm concentrated, that's all. You diffuse yourself, dear; and though all Simla knows your skill in managing a team –'

'Can't you choose a prettier word?'

'*Team*, of half-a-dozen, from The Mussuck to the Hawley Boy, you gain nothing by it. Not even amusement.'

75

'And you?'

'Try my recipe. Take a man, not a boy, mind, but an almost mature, unattached man, and be his guide, philosopher, and friend.[29] You'll find it *the* most interesting occupation that you ever embarked on. It can be done —you needn't look like that — because I've done it.'

'There's an element of risk about it that makes the notion attractive. I'll get such a man and say to him, "Now, understand that there must be no flirtation. Do exactly what I tell you, profit by my instruction and counsels, and all will yet be well." Is that the idea?'

'More or less,' said Mrs Mallowe, with an unfathomable smile. 'But be sure he understands.'

II

> Dribble-dribble – trickle-trickle –
> What a lot of raw dust!
> My dollie's had an accident
> And out came all the sawdust!
> *Nursery Rhyme*[30]

So Mrs Hauksbee, in 'The Foundry' which overlooks Simla Mall, sat at the feet of Mrs Mallowe and gathered wisdom. The end of the Conference was the Great Idea upon which Mrs Hauksbee so plumed herself.

'I warn you,' said Mrs Mallowe, beginning to repent of her suggestion, 'that the matter is not half so easy as it looks. Any woman – even the Topsham Girl – can catch a man, but very, *very* few know how to manage him when caught.'

'My child,' was the answer, 'I've been a female St Simon Stylites[31] looking down upon men for these – these years past. Ask The Mussuck whether I can manage them.'

Mrs Hauksbee departed humming, '*I'll go to him and say to him in manner most ironical.*'[32] Mrs Mallowe laughed to herself. Then she grew suddenly sober. 'I wonder whether I've done well in advising that amusement? Lucy's a clever woman, but a thought too careless.'

A week later the two met at a Monday Pop.[33] 'Well?' said Mrs Mallowe.

'I've caught him!' said Mrs Hauksbee: her eyes were dancing with merriment.

'Who is it, mad woman? I'm sorry I never spoke to you about it.'

'Look between the pillars. In the third row; fourth from the end. You can see his face now. Look!'

'Otis Yeere! Of *all* the improbable and impossible people! I don't believe you.'

'Hsh! Wait till Mrs Tarkass begins murdering Milton Wellings;[34] and I'll tell you all about it. *S-s-ss!* That woman's voice always reminds me of an Underground train coming into Earl's Court with the brakes on. Now listen. It is *really* Otis Yeere.'

'So I see, but does it follow that he is your property!'

'He *is!* By right of trove. I found him, lonely and un-befriended, the very next night after our talk, at the Dugald Delanes' *burra-khana*.[35] I liked his eyes, and I talked to him. Next day he called. Next day we went for a ride together, and today he's tied to my rickshaw-wheels hand and foot. You'll see when the concert's over. He doesn't know I'm here yet.'

'Thank goodness you haven't chosen a boy. What are you going to do with him, assuming that you've got him?'

'Assuming, indeed! Does a woman – do *I* – ever make a mistake in that sort of thing? First' – Mrs Hauksbee ticked off the items ostentatiously on her little gloved fingers – 'First, my dear, I shall dress him properly. At present his raiment is a disgrace, and he wears a dress-shirt like a crumpled sheet of the *Pioneer*. Secondly, after I have made him presentable, I shall form his manners – his morals are above reproach.'

'You seem to have discovered a great deal about him consider-ing the shortness of your acquaintance.'

'Surely *you* ought to know that the first proof a man gives of his interest in a woman is by talking to her about his own sweet

77

self. If the woman listens without yawning, he begins to like
her. If she flatters the animal's vanity, he ends by adoring her.'

'In some cases.'

'Never mind the exceptions. I know which one you are thinking of. Thirdly, and lastly, after he is polished and made pretty,
I shall, as you said, be his guide, philosopher, and friend, and
he shall become a success – as great a success as your friend. I
always wondered how that man got on. *Did* The Mussuck come
to you with the Civil List and, dropping on one knee – no, two
knees, *à la Gibbon*[36] – hand it to you and say, "Adorable angel,
choose your friend's appointment"?'

'Lucy, your long experiences of the Military Department
have demoralized you. One doesn't do that sort of thing on the
Civil Side.'

'No disrespect meant to Jack's Service, my dear. I only asked
for information. Give me three months, and see what changes I
shall work in my prey.'

'Go your own way since you must. But I'm sorry that I was
weak enough to suggest the amusement.'

'"I am all discretion, and may be trusted to an in-fin-ite
extent,"' quoted Mrs Hauksbee from *The Fallen Angel*; and the
conversation ceased with Mrs Tarkass's last, long-drawn war-
whoop.

Her bitterest enemies – and she had many – could hardly
accuse Mrs Hauksbee of wasting her time. Otis Yeere was one
of those wandering 'dumb' characters, foredoomed through life
to be nobody's property. Ten years in Her Majesty's Bengal
Civil Service, spent, for the most part, in undesirable Districts,
had given him little to be proud of, and nothing to bring confidence. Old enough to have lost the first fine careless rapture[37]
that showers on the immature 'Stunt[38] imaginary Com-
missionerships and Stars,[39] and sends him into the collar with
coltish earnestness and abandon; too young to be yet able to
look back upon the progress he had made, and thank Providence
that under the conditions of the day he had come even so far, he
stood upon the dead-centre of his career. And when a man
stands still he feels the slightest impulse from without. Fortune

had ruled that Otis Yeere should be, for the first part of his
service, one of the rank and file who are ground up in the
wheels of the Administration; losing heart and soul, and mind
and strength, in the process. Until steam replaces manual power
in the working of the Empire, there must always be this percentage – must always be the men who are used up, expended, in
the mere mechanical routine. For these promotion is far off and
the mill-grind of every day very instant. The Secretariats know
them only by name; they are not the picked men of the Districts
with Divisions and Collectorates awaiting them. They are
simply the rank and file – the food for fever – sharing with the
ryot[40] and the plough-bullock the honour of being the plinth
on which the State rests. The older ones have lost their aspirations; the younger putting theirs aside with a sigh. Both learn to
endure patiently until the end of the day. Twelve years in the
rank and file, men say, will sap the hearts of the bravest and
dull the wits of the most keen.

Out of this life Otis Yeere had fled for a few months; drifting,
in the hope of a little masculine society, into Simla. When his
leave was over he would return to his swampy, sour-green,
under-manned Bengal district; to the native Assistant, the native
Doctor, the native Magistrate, the steaming, sweltering Station,
the ill-kempt City, and the undisguised insolence of the Municipality that babbled away the lives of men. Life was cheap,
however. The soil spawned humanity, as it bred frogs in the
Rains, and the gap of the sickness of one season was filled to
overflowing by the fecundity of the next. Otis was unfeignedly
thankful to lay down his work for a little while and escape from
the seething, whining, weakly hive, impotent to help itself, but
strong in its power to cripple, thwart, and annoy the sunken-
eyed man who, by official irony, was said to be 'in charge' of it.

'I knew there were women–dowdies in Bengal. They come up here
sometimes. But I didn't know that there were men–dowds, too.'

Then, for the first time, it occurred to Otis Yeere that his
clothes wore rather the mark of the ages. It will be seen that his
friendship with Mrs Hauksbee had made great strides.

As that lady truthfully says, a man is never so happy as when he is talking about himself. From Otis Yeere's lips Mrs Hauksbee, before long, learned everything that she wished to know about the subject of her experiment: learned what manner of life he had led in what she vaguely called 'those awful cholera districts'; learned, too, but this knowledge came later, what manner of life he had purposed to lead and what dreams he had dreamed in the year of grace '77, before the reality had knocked the heart out of him. Very pleasant are the shady bridle-paths round Prospect Hill for the telling of such confidences.

'Not yet,' said Mrs Hauksbee to Mrs Mallowe. 'Not yet. I must wait until the man is properly dressed, at least. Great heavens, is it possible that he doesn't know what an honour it is to be taken up by *Me!*'

Mrs Hauksbee did not reckon false modesty as one of her failings.

'Always with Mrs Hauksbee!' murmured Mrs Mallowe, with her sweetest smile, to Otis. 'Oh you men, you men! Here are our Punjabis [41] growling because you've monopolized the nicest woman in Simla. They'll tear you to pieces on the Mall, some day, Mr Yeere.'

Mrs Mallowe rattled downhill, having satisfied herself, by a glance through the fringe of her sunshade, of the effect of her words.

The shot went home. Of a surety Otis Yeere was somebody in this bewildering whirl of Simla – had monopolized the nicest woman in it, and the Punjabis were growling. The notion justified a mild glow of vanity. He had never looked upon his acquaintance with Mrs Hauksbee as a matter for general interest.

The knowledge of envy was a pleasant feeling to the man of no account. It was intensified later in the day when a luncher at the Club said spitefully, 'Well, for a debilitated Ditcher, [42] Yeere, you *are* going it. Hasn't any kind friend told you that she's the most dangerous woman in Simla?'

Yeere chuckled and passed out. When, oh, when would his

new clothes be ready? He descended into the Mall to inquire; and Mrs Hauksbee, coming over the Church Ridge in her rickshaw, looked down upon him approvingly. 'He's learning to carry himself as if he were a man, instead of a piece of furniture – and,' she screwed up her eyes to see the better through the sunlight – 'he *is* a man when he holds himself like that. O blessed Conceit, what should we be without you?'

With the new clothes came a new stock of self-confidence. Otis Yeere discovered that he could enter a room without breaking into a gentle perspiration – could cross one, even to talk to Mrs Hauksbee, as though rooms were meant to be crossed. He was for the first time in nine years proud of himself, and contented with his life, satisfied with his new clothes, and rejoicing in the friendship of Mrs Hauksbee.

'Conceit is what the poor fellow wants,' she said in confidence to Mrs Mallowe. 'I believe they must use Civilians[43] to plough the fields with in Lower Bengal. You see I have to begin from the very beginning – haven't I? But you'll admit, won't you, dear, that he is immensely improved since I took him in hand. Only give me a little more time and he won't know himself.'

Indeed, Yeere was rapidly beginning to forget what he had been. One of his own rank and file put the matter brutally when he asked Yeere, in reference to nothing, 'And who has been making *you* a Member of Council,[44] lately? You carry the side of half-a-dozen of 'em.'

'I – I'm awf'ly sorry. I didn't mean it, you know,' said Yeere apologetically.

'There'll be no holding you,' continued the old stager grimly. 'Climb down, Otis – climb down, and get all that beastly affection knocked out of you with fever! Three thousand a month wouldn't support it.'

Yeere repeated the incident to Mrs Hauksbee. He had come to look upon her as his Mother Confessor.

'And you apologized!' she said. 'Oh, shame! I *hate* a man who apologizes. Never apologize for what your friend called "side". *Never!* It's a man's business to be insolent and overbearing until he meets with a stronger. Now, you bad boy, listen to me.'

Simply and straightforwardly, as the rickshaw loitered round Jakko, Mrs Hauksbee preached to Otis Yeere the Great Gospel of Conceit, illustrating it with living pictures encountered during their Sunday afternoon stroll.

'Good gracious!' she ended with the personal argument, 'you'll apologize next for being my *attaché*!'

'Never!' said Otis Yeere. 'That's another thing altogether. I shall always be –'

'What's coming?' thought Mrs Hauksbee.

'Proud of that,' said Otis.

'Safe for the present,' she said to herself.

'But I'm afraid I have grown conceited. Like Jeshurun,[45] you know. When he waxed fat, then he kicked. It's the having no worry on one's mind and the Hill air, I suppose.'

'Hill air, indeed!' said Mrs Hauksbee to herself. 'He'd have been hiding in the Club till the last day of his leave, if I hadn't discovered him.' And aloud –

'Why shouldn't you be? You have every right to.'

'I! Why?'

'Oh, hundreds of things. I'm not going to waste this lovely afternoon by explaining; but I know you have. What was that heap of manuscript you showed me about the grammar of the aboriginal – what's their names?'

'*Gullals*. A piece of nonsense. I've far too much work to do to bother over *Gullals* now. You should see my District. Come down with your husband some day and I'll show you round. Such a lovely place in the Rains! A sheet of water with the railway-embankment and the snakes sticking out, and, in the summer, green flies and green squash. The people would die of fear if you shook a dogwhip at 'em. But they know you're forbidden to do that, so they conspire to make your life a burden to you. My District's worked by some man at Darjiling, on the strength of a native pleader's[46] false reports. Oh, it's a heavenly place!'

Otis Yeere laughed bitterly.

'There's not the least necessity that you should stay in it. Why do you?'

'Because I must. How'm I to get out of it?'

'How! In a hundred and fifty ways. If there weren't so many people on the road I'd like to box your ears. Ask, my dear boy, *ask!* Look! There is young Hexarly with six years' service and half your talents. He asked for what he wanted, and he got it. See, down by the Convent! There's McArthurson, who has come to his present position by asking – sheer, downright asking – after he had pushed himself out of the rank and file. One man is as good as another in your service – believe me. I've seen Simla for more seasons than I care to think about. Do you suppose men are chosen for appointments because of their special fitness *beforehand?* You have all passed a high test – what do you call it? – in the beginning, and, except for the few who have gone altogether to the bad, you can all work hard. Asking does the rest. Call it cheek, call it insolence, call it anything you like, but *ask!* Men argue – yes, I know what men say – that a man, by the mere audacity of his request, *must* have some good in him. A weak man doesn't say: "Give me this and that." He whines: "Why haven't I been given this and that?" If you were in the Army, I should say learn to spin plates or play a tambourine with your toes. As it is – *ask!* You belong to a Service that ought to be able to command the Channel Fleet, or set a leg at twenty minutes' notice, and *yet* you hesitate over asking to escape from a squashy green district where you *admit* you are not master. Drop the Bengal Government altogether. Even Darjiling is a little out-of-the-way hole. I was there once, and the rents were extortionate. Assert yourself. Get the Government of India to take you over. Try to get on the Frontier, where *every* man has a grand chance if he can trust himself. *Go* somewhere! *Do* something! You have twice the wits and three times the presence of the men up here, and, and' – Mrs Hauksbee paused for breath; then continued – 'and in *any* way you look at it, you *ought* to. *You* who could go so far!'

'I don't know,' said Yeere, rather taken aback by the unexpected eloquence. 'I haven't such a good opinion of myself.'

It was not strictly Platonic, but it was Policy. Mrs Hauksbee laid her hand lightly upon the ungloved paw that rested on the

83

turned-back rickshaw hood, and, looking the man full in the face, said tenderly, almost too tenderly, '*I* believe in you if you mistrust yourself. Is that enough, my friend?'

'It is enough,' answered Otis very solemnly.

He was silent for a long time, redreaming the dreams that he had dreamed eight years ago, but through them all ran, as sheet-lightning through golden cloud, the light of Mrs Hauksbee's violet eyes.

Curious and impenetrable are the mazes of Simla life – the only existence in this desolate land worth the living. Gradually it went abroad among men and women, in the pauses between dance, play, and Gymkhana,[47] that Otis Yeere, the man with the newly-lit light of self-confidence in his eyes, had 'done something decent' in the wilds whence he came. He had brought an erring Municipality to reason, appropriated the funds on his own responsibility, and saved the lives of hundreds. He knew more about the *Gullals* than any living man. Had a vast knowledge of the aboriginal tribes; was, in spite of his juniority, the greatest authority on the aboriginal *Gullals*. No one quite knew who or what the *Gullals* were till The Mussuck, who had been calling on Mrs Hauksbee, and prided himself upon picking people's brains, explained they were a tribe of ferocious hillmen, somewhere near Sikkim, whose friendship even the Great Indian Empire would find it worth her while to secure. Now we know that Otis Yeere had showed Mrs Hauksbee his M S. notes of six years' standing on these same *Gullals*. He had told her, too, how, sick and shaken with the fever their negligence had bred, crippled by the loss of his pet clerk, and savagely angry at the desolation in his charge, he had once damned the collective eyes of his 'intelligent local board' for a set of *haramzadas*.[48] Which act of 'brutal and tyrannous oppression' won him a Reprimand Royal from the Bengal Government; but in the anecdote as amended for Northern consumption we find no record of this. Hence we are forced to conclude that Mrs Hauksbee edited his reminiscences before sowing them in idle ears, ready, as she well knew, to exaggerate good or evil. And Otis Yeere bore himself as befitted the hero of many tales.

'You can talk to *me* when you don't fall into a brown study. Talk now, and talk your brightest and best,' said Mrs Hauksbee.

Otis needed no spur. Look to a man who has the counsel of a woman of or above the world to back him. So long as he keeps his head, he can meet both sexes on equal ground – an advantage never intended by Providence,[49] who fashioned Man on one day and Woman on another, in sign that neither should know more than a very little of the other's life. Such a man goes far, or, the counsel being withdrawn, collapses suddenly while his world seeks the reason.

Generalled by Mrs Hauksbee, who, again, had all Mrs Mallowe's wisdom at her disposal, proud of himself and, in the end, believing in himself because he was believed in, Otis Yeere stood ready for any fortune that might befall, certain that it would be good. He would fight for his own hand, and intended that this second struggle should lead to better issue than the first helpless surrender of the bewildered 'Stunt.

What might have happened it is impossible to say. This lamentable thing befell, bred directly by a statement of Mrs Hauksbee that she would spend the next season in Darjiling.

'Are you certain of that?' said Otis Yeere.

'Quite. We're writing about a house now.'

Otis Yeere 'stopped dead', as Mrs Hauksbee put it in discussing the relapse with Mrs Mallowe.

'He has behaved,' she said angrily, 'just like Captain Kerrington's pony – only Otis is a donkey – at the last Gymkhana. Planted his forefeet and refused to go on another step. Polly, my man's going to disappoint me. What shall I do?'

As a rule, Mrs Mallowe does not approve of staring, but on this occasion she opened her eyes to the utmost.

'You have managed cleverly so far,' she said. 'Speak to him, and ask him what he means.'

'I will – at tonight's dance.'

'No—o, not at a dance,' said Mrs Mallowe cautiously. 'Men are never themselves quite at dances. Better wait till tomorrow morning.'

'Nonsense. If he's going to 'vert in this insane way there isn't a day to lose. Are you going? No? Then sit up for me, there's a dear. I shan't stay longer than supper under any circumstances.'

Mrs Mallowe waited through the evening, looking long and earnestly into the fire, and sometimes smiling to herself.

'Oh! oh! oh! The man's an idiot! A raving, positive idiot! I'm sorry I ever saw him!'

Mrs Hauksbee burst into Mrs Mallowe's house, at midnight, almost in tears.

'What in the world has happened?' said Mrs Mallowe, but her eyes showed that she had guessed an answer.

'Happened! Everything has happened! He was there. I went to him and said, "Now, what does this nonsense mean?" Don't laugh, dear, I can't bear it. But you know what I mean I said. Then it was a square, and I sat it out with him and wanted an explanation, and *he* said – Oh! I haven't patience with such idiots! You know what I said about going to Darjiling next year? It doesn't matter to me *where* I go. I'd have changed the Station and lost the rent to have saved this. He said, in so many words, that he wasn't going to try to work up any more, because – because he would be shifted into a province away from Darjiling, and his own District, where these creatures are, is within a day's journey –'

'Ah—hh!' said Mrs Mallowe, in a tone of one who has successfully tracked an obscure word through a large dictionary.

'Did you ever *hear* of anything so mad – so absurd? And he had the ball at his feet. He had only to kick it! I would have made him *anything!* Anything in the wide world. He could have gone to the world's end. I would have helped him. I made him, didn't I, Polly? Didn't I *create* that man? Doesn't he owe everything to me? And to reward me, just when everything was nicely arranged, by this lunacy that spoilt everything!'

'Very few men understand your devotion thoroughly.'

'Oh, Polly, *don't* laugh at me! I give men up from this hour. I could have killed him then and there. What *right* had this man –

this *Thing* I had picked out of his filthy paddy-fields – to make love to me?'

'He did that, did he?'

'He did. I don't remember half he said, I was so angry. Oh, but such a funny thing happened! I can't help laughing at it now, though I felt nearly ready to cry with rage. He raved and I stormed – I'm afraid we must have made an awful noise in our *kala juggah*. Protect my character, dear, if it's all over Simla by tomorrow – and then he bobbed forward in the middle of this insanity – I *firmly* believe the man's demented and kissed me.'

'Morals above reproach,' purred Mrs Mallowe.

'So they were – so they are! It was the most absurd kiss. I don't believe he'd ever kissed a woman in his life before. I threw my head back, and it was a sort of slidy, pecking dab, just on the end of the chin – here.' Mrs Hauksbee tapped her masculine little chin with her fan. 'Then, of course, I was *furiously* angry, and told him that he was no gentleman, and I was sorry I'd ever met him, and so on. He was crushed so easily then I couldn't be *very* angry. Then I came away straight to you.'

'Was this before or after supper?'

'Oh! before – oceans before. Isn't it perfectly disgusting?'

'Let me think. I withhold judgment till tomorrow. Morning brings counsel.'

But morning brought only a servant with a dainty bouquet of Annandale[50] roses for Mrs Hauksbee to wear at the dance at Viceregal Lodge that night.

'He doesn't seem to be very penitent,' said Mrs Mallowe. 'What's the *billet-doux* in the centre?'

Mrs Hauksbee opened the neatly-folded note, – another accomplishment that she had taught Otis – read it, and groaned tragically.

'Last wreck of a feeble intellect! Poetry! Is it his own, do you think? Oh, that I ever built my hopes on such a maudlin idiot!'

'No. It's a quotation from Mrs Browning,[51] and in view of the facts of the case, as Jack says, uncommonly well chosen. Listen –

Wee Willie Winkie

Sweet, thou hast trod on a heart,
  Pass! There's a world full of men;
And women as fair as thou art
  Must do such things now and then.

Thou only hast stepped unaware –
  Malice not one can impute;
And why should a heart have been there,
  In the way of a fair woman's foot?

'I didn't – I didn't – I didn't!' – said Mrs Hauksbee angrily, her eyes filling with tears; 'there was no malice at all. Oh, it's *too* vexatious!'

'You've misunderstood the compliment,' said Mrs Mallowe. 'He clears you completely and – ahem – I should think by this, that *he* has cleared completely too. My experience of men is that when they begin to quote poetry they are going to flit. Like swans singing before they die, you know.'

'Polly, you take my sorrows in a most unfeeling way.'

'Do I? Is that so terrible? If he's hurt your vanity, I should say that you've done a certain amount of damage to his heart.'

'Oh, you can never tell about a man!' said Mrs Hauksbee.

❴ At the Pit's Mouth [1] ❵

Men say it was a stolen tide –
 The Lord that sent it He knows all,
But in mine ear will aye abide
 The message that the bells let fall,
And awesome bells they were to me,
That in the dark rang, 'Enderby'. [2]
                                   Jean Ingelow

Once upon a time there was a Man and his Wife and a Tertium
Quid. [3]

All three were unwise, but the Wife was the unwisest. The
Man should have looked after his Wife, who should have avoided the Tertium Quid, who, again, should have married a wife
of his own, after clean and open flirtations, to which nobody
can possibly object, round Jakko or Observatory Hill. When
you see a young man with his pony in a white lather and his hat
on the back of his head, flying downhill at fifteen miles an hour
to meet a girl who will be properly surprised to meet him, you
naturally approve of that young man, and wish him Staff appointments, and take an interest in his welfare, and, as the
proper time comes, give them sugar-tongs or side-saddles according to your means and generosity.

The Tertium Quid flew downhill on horseback, but it was to
meet the Man's Wife; and when he flew uphill it was for the
same end. The Man was in the Plains, [4] earning money for his
Wife to spend on dresses and four-hundred-rupee bracelets,
and inexpensive luxuries of that kind. He worked very hard,
and sent her a letter or a post-card daily. She also wrote to him
daily, and said that she was longing for him to come up to
Simla. The Tertium Quid used to lean over her shoulder and

laugh as she wrote the notes. Then the two would ride to the Post-office together.

Now, Simla is a strange place and its customs are peculiar; nor is any man who has not spent at least ten seasons there qualified to pass judgment on circumstantial evidence, which is the most untrustworthy in the Courts. For these reasons, and for others which need not appear, I decline to state positively whether there was anything irretrievably wrong in the relations betwen the Man's Wife and the Tertium Quid. If there was, and hereon you must form you own opinion, it was the Man's Wife's fault. She was kittenish in her manners, wearing generally an air of soft and fluffy innocence. But she was deadlily learned and evil-instructed; and, now and again, when the mask dropped, men saw this, shuddered and – almost drew back. Men are occasionally particular, and the least particular men are always the most exacting.

Simla is eccentric in its fashion of treating friendships. Certain attachments which have set and crystallized through half-a-dozen seasons acquire almost the sanctity of the marriage bond, and are revered as such. Again, certain attachments equally old, and, to all appearance, equally venerable, never seem to win any recognized official status; while a chance-sprung acquaintance, not two months born, steps into the place which by right belongs to the senior. There is no law reducible to print which regulates these affairs.

Some people have a gift which secures them infinite toleration, and others have not. The Man's Wife had not. If she looked over the garden wall, for instance, women taxed her with stealing their husbands. She complained pathetically that she was not allowed to choose her own friends. When she put up her big white muff to her lips, and gazed over it and under her eyebrows at you as she said this thing, you felt that she had been infamously misjudged, and that all the other women's instincts were all wrong; which was absurd. She was not allowed to own the Tertium Quid in peace; and was so strangely constructed that she would not have enjoyed peace had she been so permitted. She preferred some semblance of intrigue to cloak even her most commonplace actions.

After two months of riding, first round Jakko, then Elysium, then Summer Hill, then Observatory Hill, then under Jutogh, and lastly up and down the Cart Road as far as the Tara Devi gap[5] in the dusk, she said to the Tertium Quid, 'Frank, people say we are too much together, and people are so horrid.'

The Tertium Quid pulled his moustache, and replied that horrid people were unworthy of the consideration of nice people.

'But they have done more than talk – they have written – written to my hubby I'm sure of it,' said the Man's Wife, and she pulled a letter from her husband out of her saddle-pocket and gave it to the Tertium Quid.

It was an honest letter, written by an honest man, then stewing in the Plains on two hundred rupees a month (for he allowed his wife eight hundred and fifty), and in a silk banian[6] and cotton trousers. It said that, perhaps, she had not thought of the unwisdom of allowing her name to be so generally coupled with the Tertium Quid's; that she was too much of a child to understand the dangers of that sort of thing; that he, her husband, was the last man in the world to interfere jealously with her little amusements and interests, but that it would be better were she to drop the Tertium Quid quietly and for her husband's sake. The letter was sweetened with many pretty little pet names, and it amused the Tertium Quid considerably. He and She laughed over it, so that you, fifty yards away, could see their shoulders shaking while the horses slouched along side by side.

Their conversation was not worth reporting. The upshot of it was that, next day, no one saw the Man's Wife and the Tertium Quid together. They had both gone down to the Cemetery, which, as a rule, is only visited officially by the inhabitants of Simla.

A Simla funeral with the clergyman riding, the mourners riding, and the coffin creaking as it swings between the bearers, is one of the most depressing things on this earth, particularly when the procession passes under the wet, dank dip beneath the Rockcliffe Hotel, where the sun is shut out, and all the hill streams are wailing and weeping together as they go down the valleys.

Occasionally folk tend the graves, but we in India shift and are transferred so often that, at the end of the second year, the Dead have no friends – only acquaintances who are far too busy amusing themselves up the hill to attend to old partners. The idea of using a Cemetery as a rendezvous is distinctly a feminine one. A man would have said simply, 'Let people talk. We'll go down the Mall.' A woman is made differently, especially if she be such a woman as the Man's Wife. She and the Tertium Quid enjoyed each other's society among the graves of men and women whom they had known and danced with aforetime.

They used to take a big horse-blanket and sit on the grass a little to the left of the lower end, where there is a dip in the ground, and where the occupied graves stop short and the ready-made ones are not ready. Each well-regulated Indian Cemetery keeps half-a-dozen graves permanently open for contingencies and incidental wear and tear. In the Hills these are more usually baby's size, because children who come up weakened and sick from the Plains often succumb to the effects of the Rains in the Hills or get pneumonia from their *ayahs* taking them through damp pine-woods after the sun has set. In Cantonments,[7] of course, the man's size is more in request; these arrangements varying with the climate and population.

One day when the Man's Wife and the Tertium Quid had just arrived in the Cemetery, they saw some coolies breaking ground. They had marked out a full size grave, and the Tertium Quid asked them whether any *Sahib* was sick. They said that they did not know; but it was an order that they should dig a *Sahib*'s grave.

'Work away,' said the Tertium Quid, 'and let's see how it's done.'

The coolies worked away, and the Man's Wife and the Tertium Quid watched and talked for a couple of hours while the grave was being deepened . Then a coolie, taking the earth in baskets as it was thrown up, jumped over the grave.

'That's queer,' said the Tertium Quid. 'Where's my ulster?'

'What's queer,' said the Man's Wife.

'I have got a chill down my back – just as if a goose had walked over my grave.'

'Why do you look at the thing, then?' said the Man's Wife. 'Let us go.'

The Tertium Quid stood at the head of the grave, and stared without answering for a space. Then he said, dropping a pebble down, 'It is nasty – and cold: horribly cold. I don't think I shall come to the Cemetery any more. I don't think grave-digging is cheerful.'

The two talked and agreed that the Cemetery was depressing. They also arranged for a ride next day out from the Cemetery through the Mashobra Tunnel up to Fagoo[8] and back, because all the world was going to a garden-party at Viceregal Lodge, and all the people of Mashobra would go too.

Coming up the Cemetery road, the Tertium Quid's horse tried to bolt uphill, being tired with standing so long, and managed to strain a back sinew.

'I shall have to take the mare tomorrow,' said the Tertium Quid, 'and she will stand nothing heavier than a snaffle.'

They made their arrangements to meet in the Cemetery, after allowing all the Mashobra people to pass into Simla. That night it rained heavily, and, next day, when the Tertium Quid came to the trysting-place, he saw that the new grave had a foot of water in it, the ground being a tough and sour clay.

''Jove! That looks beastly,' said the Tertuim Quid. 'Fancy being boarded up and dropped into that well!'

They then started off to Fagoo, the mare playing with the snaffle and picking her way as though she were shod with satin, and the sun shining divinely. The road below Mashobra to Fagoo is officially styled the Himalayan-Thibet road;[9] but in spite of its name it is not much more than six feet wide in most places, and the drop into the valley below may be anything between one and two thousand feet.

'Now we're going to Thibet,' said the Man's Wife merrily, as the horses drew near to Fagoo. She was riding on the cliff-side.

'Into Thibet,' said the Tertium Quid, 'ever so far from people who say horrid things, and hubbies who write stupid letters. With you – to the end of the world!'[10]

A coolie carrying a log of wood came round a corner, and the mare went wide to avoid him – forefeet in and haunches out, as a sensible mare should go.

'To the world's end,' said the Man's Wife, and looked unspeakable things over her near shoulder at the Tertium Quid.

He was smiling, but, while she looked, the smile froze stiff as it were on his face, and changed to a nervous grin – the sort of grin men wear when they are not quite easy in their saddles. The mare seemed to be sinking by the stern, and her nostrils cracked while she was trying to realize what was happening. The rain of the night before had rotted the drop-side of the Himalyan-Thibet Road, and it was giving way under her. 'What are you doing?' said the Man's Wife. The Tertium Quid gave no answer. He grinned nervously and set his spurs into the mare, who rapped with her forefeet on the road, and the struggle began. The Man's Wife screamed, 'Oh, Frank, get off!'

But the Tertium Quid was glued to the saddle – his face blue and white – and he looked into the Man's Wife's eyes. Then the Man's Wife clutched at the mare's head and caught her by the nose instead of the bridle. The brute threw up her head and went down with a scream, the Tertium Quid upon her, and the nervous grin still set on his face.

The Man's Wife heard the tinkle-tinkle of little stones and loose earth falling off the roadway, and the sliding roar of the man and horse going down. Then everything was quiet, and she called on Frank to leave his mare and walk up. But Frank did not answer. He was underneath the mare, nine hundred feet below,[11] spoiling a patch of Indian corn.

As the revellers came back from Viceregal Lodge in the mists of evening, they met a temporarily insane woman, on a temporarily mad horse, swinging round the corners, with her eyes and her mouth open, and her head like the head of a Medusa. She was stopped by a man at the risk of his life, and taken out of the saddle, a limp heap, and put on the bank to explain herself. This wasted twenty minutes, and then she was sent home in a lady's rickshaw, still with her mouth open and her hands picking at her riding-gloves.

She was in bed through the following three days, which were rainy; so she missed attending the funeral of the Tertium Quid, who was lowered into eighteen inches of water, instead of the twelve to which he had first objected.[12]

{ A Wayside Comedy¹ }

Because to every purpose there is time and judgment, therefore
the misery of man is great upon him.²

Eccles. viii. 6

Fate and the Government of India have turned the Station of
Kashima into a prison; and, because there is no help for the
poor souls who are now lying there in torment, I write this
story, praying the Government of India may be moved to scatter
the European population to the four winds.

Kashima is bounded on all sides by the rock-tipped circle of
the Dosehri hills. In Spring, it is ablaze with roses; in Summer,
the roses die and the hot winds blow from the hills; in Autumn,
the white mists from the *jhils*³ cover the place as with water,
and in Winter the frosts nip everything young and tender to
earth-level. There is but one view in Kashima – a stretch of
perfectly flat pasture and plough-land, running up to the grey-
blue scrub of the Dosehri hills.

There are no amusements, except snipe and tiger shooting; but
the tigers have been long since hunted from their lairs in the rock-
caves, and the snipe only come once a year. Narkarra – one
hundred and forty-three miles by road – is the nearest station to
Kashima. But Kashima never goes to Narkarra, where there are
at least twelve English people. It stays within the circle of the
Dosehri hills.

All Kashima acquits Mrs Vansuythen of any intention to do
harm; but all Kashima knows that she, and she alone, brought
about their pain.

Boulte, the Engineer, Mrs Boulte, and Captain Kurrell know
this. They are the English population of Kashima, if we except
Major Vansuythen, who is of no importance whatever, and Mrs
Vansuythen, who is the most important of all.

You must remember,[4] though you will not understand, that all laws weaken in a small and hidden community where there is no public opinion. When a man is absolutely alone in a Station he runs a certain risk of falling into evil ways. This risk is multiplied by every addition to the population up to twelve – the Jury-number. After that, fear and consequent restraint begin, and human action becomes less grotesquely jerky.

There was a deep peace in Kashima till Mrs Vansuythen arrived. She was a charming woman, everyone said so everywhere; and she charmed everyone. In spite of this, or, perhaps, because of this, since Fate is so perverse, she cared only for one man, and he was Major Vansuythen. Had she been plain or stupid, this matter would have been intelligible to Kashima. But she was a fair woman, with very still grey eyes, the colour of a lake just before the light of the sun touches it. No man who had seen those eyes could, later on, explain what fashion of woman she was to look upon. The eyes dazzled him. Her own sex said that she was 'not bad-looking, but spoilt by pretending to be so grave'. And yet her gravity was natural. It was not her habit to smile. She merely went through life, looking at those who passed; and the women objected while the men fell down and worshipped.

She knows and is deeply sorry for the evil she has done to Kashima; but Major Vansuythen cannot understand why Mrs Boulte does not drop in to afternoon tea at least three times a week. 'When there are only two women in one Station, they ought to see a great deal of each other,' says Major Vansuythen.

Long and long before ever Mrs Vansuythen came out of those far-away places where there is society and amusement, Kurrell had discovered that Mrs Boulte was the one woman in the world for him and – you dare not blame them. Kashima was as out of the world as Heaven or the Other Place, and the Dosehri hills kept their secret well. Boulte had no concern in the matter. He was in camp for a fortnight at a time. He was a hard, heavy man, and neither Mrs Boulte nor Kurrell pitied him. They had all Kashima and each other for their very, very own; and Kashima was the Garden of Eden in those days.

When Boulte returned from his wanderings he would slap Kurrell between the shoulders and call him 'old fellow', and the three of them would dine together. Kashima was happy then when the judgment of God seemed almost as distant as Narkarra or the railway that ran down to the sea. But the Government sent Major Vansuythen to Kashima, and with him came his wife.

The etiquette of Kashima is much the same as that of a desert island. When a stranger is cast away there, all hands go down to the shore to make him welcome. Kashima assembled at the masonry platform close to the Narkarra Road, and spread tea for the Vansuythens. That ceremony was reckoned a formal call, and made them free of the Station, its rights and privileges. When the Vansuythens settled down they gave a tiny housewarming to all Kashima; and that made Kashima free of their house, according to the immemorial usage[5] of the Station.

Then the Rains came, when no one could go into camp, and the Narkarra Road was washed away by the Kasun River, and in the cup-like pastures of Kashima the cattle waded knee-deep. The clouds dropped down from the Dosehri hills and covered everything.

At the end of the Rains Boulte's manner towards his wife changed and became demonstratively affectionate. They had been married twelve years, and the change startled Mrs Boulte, who hated her husband with the hate of a woman who has met with nothing but kindness from her mate, and, in the teeth of this kindness, has done him a great wrong. Moreover, she had her own trouble to fight with – her watch to keep over her own property, Kurrell. For two months the Rains had hidden the Dosehri hills and many other things besides; but, when they lifted, they showed Mrs Boulte that her man among men, her Ted – for she called him Ted in the old days when Boulte was out of earshot – was slipping the links of the allegiance.

'The Vansuythen Woman has taken him,' Mrs Boulte said to herself; and when Boulte was away, wept over her belief, in the face of the over-vehement blandishments of Ted. Sorrow in Kashima is as fortunate as Love because there is nothing to weaken it save the flight of Time. Mrs Boulte had never breathed her suspicion to Kurrell because she was not certain; and her nature led her to be very certain before she took steps in any direction. That is why she behaved as she did.

Boulte came into the house one evening, and leaned against the door-posts of the drawing-room, chewing his moustache. Mrs Boulte was putting some flowers into a vase. There is a pretence of civilization even in Kashima.

'Little woman,' said Boulte quietly, 'do you care for me?'

'Immensely,' said she, with a laugh. 'Can you ask it?'

'But I'm serious,' said Boulte. '*Do* you care for me?'

Mrs Boulte dropped the flowers, and turned round quickly. 'Do you want an honest answer?'

'Ye-es, I've asked for it.'

Mrs Boulte spoke in a low, even voice for five minutes, very distinctly, that there might be no misunderstanding her meaning. When Samson broke the pillars of Gaza, he did a little thing, and one not to be compared to the deliberate pulling down of a woman's homestead about her own ears. There was no wise female friend to advise Mrs Boulte, the singularly cautious wife, to hold her hand. She struck at Boulte's heart, because her own was sick with suspicion of Kurrell, and worn out with the long strain of watching alone through the Rains. There was no plan or purpose in her speaking. The sentences made themselves; and Boulte listened, leaning against the doorpost with his hands in his pockets. When all was over, and Mrs Boulte began to breathe through her nose before breaking out into tears, he laughed and stared straight in front of him at the Dosehri hills.

'Is that all?' he said. 'Thanks, I only wanted to know, you know.'

'What are you going to do?' said the woman between her sobs.

'Do! Nothing. What should I do? Kill Kurrell, or send you Home, or apply for leave to get a divorce? It's two days' *dâk*[6] into Narkarra.' He laughed again and went on: 'I'll tell you what *you* can do. You can ask Kurrell to dinner tomorrow – no, on Thursday, that will allow you time to pack – and you can bolt with him. I give you my word I won't follow.'

He took up his helmet and went out of the room, and Mrs Boulte sat till the moonlight streaked the floor, thinking and thinking and thinking. She had done her best upon the spur of the moment to pull the house down; but it would not fall. Moreover, she could not understand her husband, and she was afraid. Then the folly of her useless truthfulness struck her, and she was ashamed to write to Kurrell, saying, 'I have gone mad and told everything. My husband says that I am free to elope with you. Get a *dâk* for Thursday, and we will fly after dinner.' There was a cold-bloodedness about that procedure which did not appeal to her. So she sat still in her own house and thought.

At dinner-time Boulte came back from his walk, white and worn and haggard, and the woman was touched at his distress. As the evening wore on she muttered some expression of sorrow, something approaching to contrition. Boulte came out of a brown study and said, 'Oh, *that*! I wasn't thinking about that. By the way, what does Kurrell say to the elopement?'

'I haven't seen him,' said Mrs Boulte. 'Good God, is that all?'

But Boulte was not listening and her sentence ended in a gulp.

The next day brought no comfort to Mrs Boulte, for Kurrell did not appear, and the new life that she, in the five minutes' madness of the previous evening, had hoped to build out of the ruins of the old, seemed to be no nearer.

Boulte ate his breakfast, advised her to see her Arab pony fed in the verandah, and went out. The morning wore through, and at mid-day the tension became unendurable. Mrs Boulte could not cry. She had finished her crying in the night, and now she did not want to be left alone. Perhaps the Vansuythen Woman would talk to her; and, since talking opens the heart, perhaps there might be some comfort to be found in her company. She was the only other woman in the Station.

In Kashima there are no regular calling-hours. Every one can drop in upon every one else at pleasure. Mrs Boulte put on a big *terai*[7] hat, and walked across to the Vansuythens' house to borrow last week's *Queen*. The two compounds touched, and instead of going up the drive, she crossed through the gap in the cactus-hedge, entering the house from the back. As she passed through the dining-room, she heard, behind the *purdah*[8] that cloaked the drawing-room door, her husband's voice, saying –

'But on my Honour! On my Soul and Honour, I tell you she doesn't care for me. She told me so last night. I would have told you then if Vansuythen hadn't been with you. If it is for *her* sake that you'll have nothing to say to me, you can make your mind easy. It's Kurrell –'

'What?' said Mrs Vansuythen, with a hysterical little laugh. 'Kurrell! Oh, it can't be! You two must have made some horrible mistake. Perhaps you – you lost your temper, or misunderstood, or something. Things *can't* be as wrong as you say.'

Mrs Vansuythen had shifted her defence to avoid the man's pleading, and was desperately trying to keep him to a side-issue.

'There must be some mistake,' she insisted, 'and it can be all put right again.'

Boulte laughed grimly.

'It can't be Captain Kurrell! He told me that he had never taken the least – the least interest in your wife, Mr Boulte. Oh, *do* listen! He said he had not. He swore he had not,' said Mrs Vansuythen.

The *purdah* rustled, and the speech was cut short by the entry of a little thin woman, with big rings round her eyes. Mrs Vansuythen stood up with a gasp.

'What was that you said?' asked Mrs Boulte. 'Never mind that man. What did Ted say to you? What did he say to you? What did he say to you?'

Mrs Vansuythen sat down helplessly on the sofa, overborne by the trouble of her questioner.

'He said – I can't remember exactly what he said – but I understood him to say – that is – But, really, Mrs Boulte, isn't it rather a strange question?'

'*Will* you tell me what he said?' repeated Mrs Boulte. Even a tiger will fly before a bear robbed of her whelps, and Mrs Vansuythen was only an ordinarily good woman. She began in a sort of desperation: 'Well, he said that he never cared for you at all, and, of course, there was not the least reason why he should have, and – and – that was all.'

'You said he *swore* he had not cared for me. Was that true?'

'Yes,' said Mrs Vansuythen very softly.

Mrs Boulte wavered for an instant where she stood, and then fell forward fainting.

'What did I tell you?' said Boulte, as though the conversation had been unbroken. 'You can see for yourself. She cares for *him*.' The light began to break into his dull mind, and he went on – 'And he – what was *he* saying to you?'

But Mrs Vansuythen, with no heart for explanations or impassioned protestations, was kneeling over Mrs Boulte.

'Oh, you brute!' she cried. 'Are *all* men like this? Help me to get her into my room – and her face is cut against the table. Oh, *will* you be quiet, and help me to carry her? I hate you, and I hate Captain Kurrell. Lift her up carefully, and now – go! Go away!'

Boulte carried his wife into Mrs Vansuythen's bedroom, and departed before the storm of that lady's wrath and disgust, impenitent and burning with jealousy. Kurrell had been making love to Mrs Vansuythen – would do Vansuythen as great a wrong as he had done Boulte, who caught himself considering whether Mrs Vansuythen would faint if she discovered that the man she loved had forsworn her.

In the middle of these meditations, Kurrell came cantering along the road and pulled up with a cheery 'Good-mornin'. 'Been mashing⁹ Mrs Vansuythen as usual, eh? Bad thing for a sober, married man, that. What will Mrs Boulte say?'

Boulte raised his head and said slowly, 'Oh, you liar!' Kurrell's face changed. 'What's that?' he asked quickly.

'Nothing much,' said Boulte. 'Has my wife told you that you two are free to go off whenever you please? She has been good enough to explain the situation to me. You've been a true friend to me, Kurrell – old man – haven't you?'

Kurrell groaned, and tried to frame some sort of idiotic sentence about being willing to give 'satisfaction'. But his interest in the woman was dead, had died out in the Rains, and, mentally, he was abusing her for her amazing indiscretion. It would have been so easy to have broken off the thing gently and by degrees, and now he was saddled with — Boulte's voice recalled him.

'I don't think I should get any satisfaction from killing you, and I'm pretty sure you'd get none from killing me.'

Then in a querulous tone, ludicrously disproportioned to his wrongs, Boulte added —

''Seems rather a pity that you haven't the decency to keep to the woman, now you've got her. You've been a true friend to *her* too, haven't you?'

Kurrell stared long and gravely. The situation was getting beyond him.

'What do you mean?' he said.

Boulte answered, more to himself than the questioner: 'My wife came over to Mrs Vansuythen's just now; and it seems you'd been telling Mrs Vansuythen that you'd never cared for Emma. I suppose you lied, as usual. What had Mrs Vansuythen to do with you, or you with her? Try to speak the truth for once in a way.'

Kurrell took the double insult without wincing, and replied by another question: 'Go on. What happened?'

'Emma fainted,' said Boulte simply. 'But, look here, what had you been saying to Mrs Vansuythen?'

Kurrell laughed. Mrs Boulte had, with unbridled tongue, made havoc of his plans; and he could at least retaliate by hurting the man in whose eyes he was humiliated and shown dishonourable.

'Said to her? What *does* a man tell a lie like that for? I suppose I said pretty much what you've said, unless I'm a good deal mistaken.'

'I spoke the truth,' said Boulte, again more to himself than Kurrell. 'Emma told me she hated me. She has no right in me.'

'No! I suppose not. You're only her husband, y'know. And what did Mrs Vansuythen say after you had laid your disengaged heart at her feet?'

Kurrell felt almost virtuous as he put the question.

'I don't think that matters,' Boulte replied; 'and it doesn't concern you.'

'But it does! I tell you it does' – began Kurrell shamelessly.

The sentence was cut by a roar of laughter from Boulte's lips. Kurrell was silent for an instant, and then he, too, laughed – laughed long and loudly, rocking in his saddle. It was an unpleasant sound – the mirthless mirth of these men on the long white line of the Narkarra Road. There were no strangers in Kashima, or they might have thought that captivity within the Dosehri hills had driven half the European population mad. The laughter ended abruptly, and Kurrell was the first to speak.

'Well, what are you going to do?'

Boulte looked up the road, and at the hills. 'Nothing,' said he quietly; 'what's the use? It's too ghastly for anything. We must let the old life go on. I can only call you a hound and a liar, and I can't go on calling you names for ever. Besides which, I don't feel that I'm much better. We can't get out of this place. What *is* there to do?'

Kurrell looked round the rat-pit of Kashima and made no reply. The injured husband took up the wondrous tale.

'Ride on, and speak to Emma if you want to. God knows *I* don't care what you do.'

He walked forward, and left Kurrell gazing blankly after him. Kurrell did not ride on either to see Mrs Boulte or Mrs Vansuythen. He sat in his saddle and thought, while his pony grazed by the roadside.

The whir of approaching wheels roused him. Mrs Vansuythen was driving home Mrs Boulte, white and wan, with a cut on her forehead.

'Stop, please,' said Mrs Boulte, 'I want to speak to Ted.'

Mrs Vansuythen obeyed, but as Mrs Boulte leaned forward, putting her hand upon the splash-board of the dog-cart, Kurrell spoke.

'I've seen your husband, Mrs Boulte.'

There was no necessity for any further explanation. The

man's eyes were fixed, not upon Mrs Boulte, but her companion. Mrs Boulte saw the look.

'Speak to him!' she pleaded, turning to the woman at her side. 'Oh, speak to him! Tell him what you told me just now. Tell him you hate him. Tell him you hate him!'

She bent forward and wept bitterly, while the *sais*,[10] impassive, went forward to hold the horse. Mrs Vansuythen turned scarlet and dropped the reins. She wished to be no party to such unholy explanations.

'I've nothing to do with it,' she began coldly; but Mrs Boulte's sobs overcame her, and she addressed herself to the man. 'I don't know what I am to say, Captain Kurrell. I don't know what I can call you. I think you've – you've behaved abominably, and she has cut her forehead terribly against the table.'

'It doesn't hurt. It isn't anything,' said Mrs Boulte feebly. '*That* doesn't matter. Tell him what you told me. Say you don't care for him. Oh, Ted, *won't* you believe her?'

'Mrs Boulte has made me understand that you were – that you were fond of her once upon a time,' went on Mrs Vansuythen.

'Well!' said Kurrell brutally. 'It seems to me that Mrs Boulte had better be fond of her own husband first.'

'Stop!' said Mrs Vansuythen. 'Hear me first. I don't care – I don't want to know anything about you and Mrs Boulte; but I want *you* to know that I hate you, that I think you are a cur, and that I'll never, *never* speak to you again. Oh, I don't dare to say what I think of you, you — man!'

'I want to speak to Ted,' moaned Mrs Boulte, but the dogcart rattled on, and Kurrell was left on the road, shamed, and boiling with wrath against Mrs Boulte.

He waited till Mrs Vansuythen was driving back to her own house, and, she being freed from the embarrassment of Mrs Boulte's presence, learned for the second time her opinion of himself and his actions.

In the evenings it was the wont of all Kashima to meet at the platform on the Narkarra Road, to drink tea and discuss the trivialities of the day. Major Vansuythen and his wife found themselves alone at the gathering-place for almost the first time in their remembrance; and the cheery Major, in the teeth of his wife's remarkably reasonable suggestion that the rest of the Station might be sick, insisted upon driving round to the two bungalows and unearthing the population.

'Sitting in the twilight!' said he, with great indignation, to the Boultes. 'That'll never do! Hang it all, we're one family here! You *must* come out, and so must Kurrell. I'll make him bring his banjo.'

So great is the power of honest simplicity and a good digestion over guilty consciences that all Kashima did turn out, even down to the banjo; and the Major embraced the company in one expansive grin. As he grinned, Mrs Vansuythen raised her eyes for an instant and looked at all Kashima. Her meaning was clear. Major Vansuythen would never know anything. He was to be the outsider in that happy family whose cage was the Dosehri hills.

'You're singing villainously out of tune, Kurrell,' said the Major truthfully. 'Pass me that banjo.'

And he sang in excruciating-wise till the stars came out and all Kashima went to dinner.

That was the beginning of the New Life of Kashima – the life that Mrs Boulte made when her tongue was loosened in the twilight.

Mrs Vansuythen has never told the Major; and since he insists upon keeping up a burdensome geniality, she has been compelled to break her vow of not speaking to Kurrell. This speech, which must of necessity preserve the semblance of politeness and interest, serves admirably to keep alight the flame of jealousy and dull hatred in Boulte's bosom, as it awakens the same passions in his wife's heart. Mrs Boulte hates Mrs Vansuythen because she has taken Ted from her, and, in some curious fashion, hates her because Mrs Vansuythen – and here the wife's eyes see far more clearly than the husband's – detests Ted. And Ted – that gallant captain and honourable man – knows now that it is possible to hate a woman once loved, to the verge of wishing to silence her for ever with blows. Above all, is he shocked that Mrs Boulte cannot see the error of her ways.

Boulte and he go out tiger-shooting together in all friendship. Boulte has put their relationship on a most satisfactory footing.

'You're a blackguard,' he says to Kurrell, 'and I've lost any self-respect I may ever have had; but when you're with me, I can feel certain that you are not with Mrs Vansuythen, or making Emma miserable.'

Kurrell endures anything that Boulte may say to him. Sometimes they are away for three days together, and then the Major insists upon his wife going over to sit with Mrs Boulte; although Mrs Vansuythen has repeatedly declared that she prefers her husband's company to any in the world. From the way in which she clings to him, she would certainly seem to be speaking the truth.

But of course, as the Major says, 'in a little Station we must all be friendly'.

⨍ The Hill of Illusion[1] ⨍

What rendered vain their deep desire?
A God, a God their severance ruled,
And bade between their shores to be
The unplumbed, salt, estranging sea.[2]

Matthew Arnold

HE.[3] Tell your *jhampanies*[4] not to hurry so, dear. They forget I'm fresh from the Plains.

SHE. Sure proof that *I* have not been going out with anyone. Yes, they *are* an untrained crew. Where do we go?

HE. As usual – to the world's end. No, Jakko.

SHE. Have your pony led after you, then. It's a long round.

HE. And for the last time, thank Heaven!

SHE. Do you mean *that* still? I didn't dare to write to you about it – all these months.

HE. Mean it! I've been shaping my affairs to that end since Autumn. What makes you speak as though it had occurred to you for the first time?

SHE. I? Oh! I don't know. I've had long enough to think, too.

HE. And you've changed your mind?

SHE. No. You ought to know that I am a miracle of constancy. What are your – arrangements?

HE. *Ours*, Sweetheart, please.

SHE. Ours, be it then. My poor boy, how the prickly heat has marked your forehead! Have you ever tried sulphate of copper in water?

HE. It'll go away in a day or two up here. The arrangements are simple enough. Tonga[5] in the early morning – reach Kalka[6] at twelve – Umballa at seven – down, straight by night train, to

Bombay, and then the steamer of the 21st for Rome. That's my idea. The Continent and Sweden – a ten-week honeymoon.

SHE. Ssh! Don't talk of it in that way. It makes me afraid. Guy, how long have we two been insane?

HE. Seven months and fourteen days, I forget the odd hours exactly, but I'll think.

SHE. I only wanted to see if you remembered. Who are those two on the Blessington Road?

HE. Eabrey and the Penner Woman. What do they matter to *us*? Tell me everything that you've been doing and saying and thinking.

SHE. Doing little, saying less, and thinking a great deal. I've hardly been out at all.

HE. That was wrong of you. You haven't been moping?

SHE. Not very much. Can you wonder that I'm disinclined to amusement?

HE. Frankly, I do. Where was the difficulty?

SHE. In this only. The more people I know and the more I'm known here, the wider spread will be the news of the crash when it comes. I don't like that.

HE. Nonsense. We shall be out of it.

SHE. You think so?

HE. I'm sure of it, if there is any power in steam or horse-flesh to carry us away. Ha! ha!

SHE. And the *fun* of the situation comes in – where, my Lancelot?

HE. Nowhere, Guinevere. I was only thinking of something.

SHE. They say men have a keener sense of humour than women. Now *I* was thinking of the scandal.

HE. Don't think of anything so ugly. We shall be beyond it.

SHE. It will be there all the same – in the mouths of Simla – telegraphed over India, and talked of at dinners – and when He goes out they will stare at Him to see how he takes it. And we shall be dead, Guy dear – dead and cast into the outer darkness where there is –

HE. Love at least. Isn't that enough?

SHE. I have said so.

HE. And you think so still?

SHE. What do *you* think?

HE. What have I *done*? It means equal ruin to me, as the world reckons it – outcasting, the loss of my appointment, the breaking off my life's work. I pay my price.

SHE. And are you so much above the world that you can afford to pay it. Am I?

HE. My Divinity – what else?

SHE. A very ordinary woman, I'm afraid, but so far, respectable. How d'you do, Mrs Middleditch? Your husband? I think he's riding down to Annandale with Colonel Statters. Yes, isn't it divine after the rain? – Guy, how long am I to be allowed to bow to Mrs Middleditch? Till the 17th?

HE. Frowsy Scotchwoman! What is the use of bringing her into the discussion? You were saying?

SHE. Nothing. Have you ever seen a man hanged?

HE. Yes. Once.

SHE. What was it for?

HE. Murder, of course.

SHE. Murder. Is *that* so great a sin after all? I wonder how he felt before the drop fell.

HE. I don't think he felt much. What a gruesome little woman it is this evening! You're shivering. Put on your cape, dear.

SHE. I think I will. Oh! Look at the mist coming over Sanjaoli; and I thought we should have sunshine on the Ladies' Mile! Let's turn back.

HE. What's the good? There's a cloud on Elysium Hill, and that means it's foggy all down the Mall. We'll go on. It'll blow away before we get to the Convent, perhaps. 'Jove! It *is* chilly.

SHE. You feel it, fresh from below. Put on your ulster. What do you think of my cape?

HE. Never ask a man his opinion of a woman's dress when he is desperately and abjectly in love with the wearer. Let me look. Like everything else of yours it's perfect. Where did you get it from?

SHE. He gave it me, on Wednesday – our wedding-day, you know.

HE. The Deuce He did! He's growing generous in his old age. D'you like all that frilly, bunchy stuff at the throat? I don't.

SHE. Don't you?

> Kind Sir, o' your courtesy,
> As you go by the town, Sir,
> 'Pray you o' your love for me,
> Buy me a russet gown, Sir.[7]

HE. I won't say: 'Keek into the draw-well, Janet, Janet.'[8] Only wait a little, darling, and you shall be stocked with russet gowns and everything else.

SHE. And when the frocks wear out you'll get me new ones — and everything else?

HE. Assuredly.

SHE. I wonder!

HE. Look here, Sweetheart, I didn't spend two days and nights in the train to hear you wonder. I thought we'd settled all that at Shaifazehat.

SHE (*dreamily*). At Shaifazehat? Does the Station go on still? That was ages and *ages* ago. It must be crumbling to pieces. All except the Amirtollah *kutcha*[9] road. I don't believe *that* could crumble till the Day of Judgment.

HE. You think so? What *is* the mood now?

SHE. I can't tell. How cold it is! Let us get on quickly.

HE. 'Better walk a little. Stop your *jhampanies* and get out. What's the matter with you this evening, dear?

SHE. Nothing. You must grow accustomed to my ways. If I'm boring you I can go home. Here's Captain Congleton coming, I daresay he'll be willing to escort me.

HE. Goose! Between *us*, too! *Damn* Captain Congleton.

SHE. Chivalrous Knight. Is it your habit to swear much in talking? It jars a little, and you might swear at me.

HE. My angel! I didn't know what I was saying; and you changed so quickly that I couldn't follow. I'll apologize in dust and ashes.

SHE. There'll be enough of those later on — Good-night, Captain Congleton. Going to the singing-quadrilles already?

What dances am I giving you next week? No! You must have written them down wrong. Five and Seven, *I* said. If you've made a mistake, I certainly, don't intend to suffer for it. You must alter your programme.

HE. I thought you told me that you had not been going out much this season?

SHE. Quite true, but when I do I dance with Captain Congleton. He dances very nicely.

HE. And sit out with him, I suppose?

SHE. Yes. Have you any objection? Shall I stand under the chandelier in future?

HE. What does he talk to you about?

SHE. What do men talk about when they sit out?

HE. Ugh! Don't! Well, now I'm up, you must dispense with the fascinating Congleton for a while. I don't like him.

SHE (*after a pause*). Do you know what you have said?

HE. 'Can't say that I do exactly. I'm not in the best of tempers.

SHE. So I see – and feel. My true and faithful lover, where is your 'eternal constancy', 'unalterable trust', and 'reverent devotion'? I remember those phrases; you seem to have forgotten them. I mention a man's name –

HE. A good deal more than that.

SHE. Well, speak to him about a dance – perhaps the last dance that I shall ever dance in my life before I – before I go away; and you at once distrust and insult me.

HE. I never said a word.

SHE. How much did you imply? Guy, is *this* amount of confidence to be our stock to start the new life on?

HE. No, of course not. I didn't mean that. On my word and honour, I didn't. Let it pass, dear. Please let it pass.

SHE. This once – yes – and a second time, and again and again, all through the years when I shall be unable to resent it. You want too much, my Lancelot, and – you know too much.

HE. How do you mean?

SHE. That is a part of the punishment. There *cannot* be perfect trust between us.

HE. In Heaven's name, why not?

SHE. Hush! The Other Place is quite enough. Ask yourself.

HE. I don't follow.

SHE. You trust me so implicitly that when I look at another man — Never mind. Guy, have you ever made love to a girl – a *good* girl?

HE. Something of the sort. Centuries ago – in the Dark Ages, before I ever met you, dear.

SHE. Tell me what you said to her.

HE. What does a man say to a girl? I've forgotten.

SHE. *I* remember. He tells her that he trusts her and worships the ground she walks on, and that he'll love and honour and protect her till her dying day; and so she marries in that belief. At least, I speak of one girl who was *not* protected.

HE. Well, and then?

SHE. And then, Guy, and then, that girl needs *ten* times the love and trust and honour – yes, honour – that was enough when she was only a mere wife if – if – the other life she chooses to lead is to be made even bearable. Do you understand?

HE. Even bearable! It'll be Paradise.

SHE. Ah! Can you give me all I've asked for –not now, nor a few months later, but when you begin to think of what you might have done if you had kept your own appointment and your caste here – when you begin to look upon me as a drag and a burden? I shall want it most then, Guy, for there will be no one in the wide world but you.

HE. You're a little over-tired tonight, Sweetheart, and you're taking a stage view of the situation. After the necessary business in the Courts, the road is clear to –

SHE. 'The holy state of matrimony!' [10] Ha! ha! ha!

HE. Ssh! Don't laugh in that horrible way!

SHE. I – I – c-c-c-can't help it! Isn't it too absurd! Ah! Ha! ha! ha! Guy, stop me quick or I shall – l-l-laugh till we get to the Church.

HE. For goodness sake, stop! Don't make an exhibition of yourself. What *is* the matter with you?

SHE. N-nothing. I'm better now.

HE. That's all right. One moment, dear. There's a little wisp of hair got loose from behind your right ear and it's straggling over your cheek. So!

SHE. Thank'oo. I'm 'fraid my hat's on one side, too.

HE. What do you wear these huge dagger bonnet-skewers for? They're big enough to kill a man with.

SHE. Oh! don't kill *me*, though. You're sticking it into my head! Let *me* do it. You men are so clumsy.

HE. Have you had many opportunities of comparing us – in this sort of work?

SHE. Guy, what is my name?

HE. Eh! I don't follow.

SHE. Here's my card-case. Can you read?

HE. Yes. Well?

SHE. Well, that answers your question. You know the other man's name. Am I sufficiently humbled, or would you like to ask me if there is anyone else?

HE. I see now. My darling, I never meant that for an instant. I was only joking. There! Lucky there's no one on the road. They'd be scandalized.

SHE. They'll be more scandalized before the end.

HE. Do-on't! I don't like you to talk in that way.

SHE. Unreasonable man! Who asked me to face the situation and accept it? – Tell me, do I look like Mrs Penner? *Do* I look like a naughty woman! *Swear* I don't! Give me your word of honour, my *honourable* friend, that I'm not like Mrs Buzgago. That's the way she stands, with her hands clasped at the back of her head. D'you like that?

HE. Don't be affected.

SHE. I'm not. I'm Mrs Buzgago. Listen!

Pendant une anne' toute entière
Le régiment n'a pas r'paru.
Au Ministère de la Guerre
On le r'porta comme perdu.

On se r'noncait à r'trouver sa trace,
Quand un matin subitement,

The Hill of Illusion

On le vit r'paraître sur la place,
L'Colonel toujours en avant.[11]

That's the way she rolls her r's. *Am* I like her?

HE. No, but I object when you go on like an actress and sing stuff of that kind. Where in the world did you pick up the *Chanson du Colonel?* It isn't a drawing-room song. It isn't proper.

SHE. Mrs Buzgago taught it me. She is both drawing-room and proper, and in another month she'll shut her drawing-room to me, and, thank God, she isn't as improper as I am. Oh, Guy, Guy! I wish I was like some women and had no scruples about – What is it Keene [12] says? – 'Wearing a corpse's hair and being false to the bread they eat'.

HE. I am only a man of limited intelligence, and, just now, very bewildered. When you have *quite* finished flashing through all your moods tell me, and I'll try to understand the last one.

SHE. Moods, Guy! I haven't any. I'm sixteen years old and you're just twenty, and you've been waiting for two hours outside the school in the cold. And now I've met you, and now we're walking home together. Does *that* suit you, My Imperial Majesty?

HE. No. We aren't children. Why can't you be rational?

SHE. He asks me that when I'm going to commit suicide for his sake, and, and – I don't want to be French and rave about my mother, but have I ever told you that I have a mother, and a brother who was my pet before I married? He's married now. Can't you imagine the pleasure that the news of the elopement will give him? Have *you* any people at Home, Guy, to be pleased with your performances?

HE. One or two. One can't make omelets without breaking eggs.

SHE (*slowly*). I don't see the necessity –

HE. Hah! What do you mean?

SHE. Shall I speak the truth?

HE. Under the circumstances, perhaps it *would* be as well.

SHE. Guy, I'm afraid.

HE. I thought we'd settled all that. What of?

SHE. Of you.

HE. Oh, damn it all! The old business! This is *too* bad!

SHE. Of *you*.

HE. And what now?

SHE. What do you think of me?

HE. Beside the question altogether. What do you intend to do?

SHE. I daren't risk it. I'm afraid. If I could only cheat —

HE. *À la Buzgago?* No, *thanks*. That's the one point on which I have any notion of Honour. I won't eat his salt and steal too. I'll loot openly or not at all.

SHE. I never meant anything else.

HE. Then, why in the world do you pretend not to be willing to come?

SHE. It's *not* pretence, Guy. I *am* afraid.

HE. Please explain.

SHE. It can't last, Guy. It can't last. You'll get angry, and then you'll swear, and then you'll get jealous, and then you'll mistrust me — you do *now* — and you yourself will be the best reason for doubting. And I — what shall *I* do? I shall be no better than Mrs Buzgago found out — no better than any one. And you'll *know* that. Oh, Guy, can't you *see*?

HE. I see that you are desperately unreasonable, little woman.

SHE. There! The moment I begin to object, you get angry. What will you do when I am only your property – stolen property? It can't be, Guy. It can't be! I thought it could, but it *can't*. You'll get tired of me.

HE. I tell you I shall *not*. Won't anything make you understand that?

SHE. There, can't you see? If you speak to me like that now, you'll call me horrible names later, if I don't do everything as you like. And if you were cruel to me, Guy, where should I go? – where should I go? I can't trust you. Oh! I *can't* trust you!

HE. I suppose I ought to say that I *can* trust you. I've ample reason.

SHE. *Please* don't, dear. It hurts as much as if you hit me.

HE. It isn't exactly pleasant for *me*.

SHE. I can't help it. I wish I were dead! I can't trust you, and I don't trust myself. Oh, Guy, let it die away and be forgotten!

HE. Too late now. I don't understand you – I won't – and I can't trust myself to talk this evening. May I call tomorrow?

SHE. Yes. *No!* Oh, give me time! The day after. I get into my rickshaw here and meet Him at Peliti's. You ride.

HE. I'll go on to Peliti's too. I think I want a drink. My world's knocked about my ears and the stars are falling. Who are those brutes howling in the Old Library?

SHE. They're rehearsing the singing-quadrilles for the Fancy Ball. Can't you hear Mrs Buzgago's voice? She has a solo. It's quite a new idea. Listen!

MRS BUZGAGO (*in the Old Library, con. molt. exp.*).[13]

> See-saw! Margery Daw!
> Sold her bed to lie upon straw.
> Wasn't she a silly slut
> To sell her bed and lie upon dirt?

Captain Congleton, I'm going to alter that to 'flirt'. It sounds better.

HE. No, I've changed my mind about the drink. Good-night, little lady. I shall see you tomorrow?

SHE. Ye—es. Good-night, Guy. *Don't* be angry with me.

HE. Angry! You *know* I trust you absolutely. Good-night and – God bless you!

(*Three seconds later. Alone.*) Hmm! I'd give something to discover whether there's another man at the back of all this.

{ A Second-Rate Woman [1] }

Est fuga, volvitur rota,
   On we drift: where looms the dim port?
One Two Three Four Five contribute their quota:
   Something is gained if one caught but the import,
Show it us, Hugues of Saxe-Gotha.
                    Master Hugues of Saxe-Gotha [2]

'Dressed! Don't tell me that woman ever dressed in her life. She stood in the middle of the room while her *ayah* – no, her husband – it *must* have been a man – threw her clothes at her. She then did her hair with her fingers, and rubbed her bonnet in the flue under the bed. I *know* she did, as well as if I had assisted at the orgy. Who is she?' said Mrs Hauksbee.

'Don't!' said Mrs Mallowe feebly. 'You make my head ache. I'm miserable today. Stay me with *fondants*, comfort me with chocolates, for I am [3] – Did you bring anything from Peliti's?'

'Questions to begin with. You shall have the sweets when you have answered them. Who and what is the creature? There were at least half-a-dozen men round her, and she appeared to be going to sleep in their midst.'

'Delville,' said Mrs Mallowe, '"Shady" Delville, to distinguish her from Mrs Jim of that ilk. She dances as untidily as she dresses, I believe, and her husband is somewhere in Madras. Go and call, if you are so interested.'

'What have I to do with Shigramitish [4] women? She merely caught my attention for a minute, and I wondered at the attraction that a dowd has for a certain type of man. I expected to see her walk out of her clothes – until I looked at her eyes.'

'Hooks and eyes, surely,' drawled Mrs Mallowe.

'Don't be clever, Polly. You make my head ache. And round

this hayrick stood a crowd of men – a positive crowd!'

'Perhaps *they* also expected –'

'Polly, don't be Rabelaisian!'

Mrs Mallowe curled herself up comfortably on the sofa, and turned her attention to the sweets. She and Mrs Hauksbee shared the same house at Simla; and these things befell two seasons after the matter of Otis Yeere,[5] which has been already recorded.

Mrs Hauksbee stepped into the verandah and looked down upon the Mall, her forehead puckered with thought.

'Hah!' said Mrs Hauksbee shortly. 'Indeed!'

'What is it?' said Mrs Mallowe sleepily.

'That dowd and The Dancing Master – to whom I object.'

'Why to The Dancing Master? He is a middle-aged gentleman, of reprobate and romantic tendencies, and tries to be a friend of mine.'

'Then make up your mind to lose him. Dowds cling by nature, and I should imagine that this animal – how terrible her bonnet looks from above! – is specially clingsome.'

'She is welcome to The Dancing Master so far as I am concerned. I never could take an interest in a monotonous liar. The frustrated aim of his life is to persuade people that he is a bachelor.'

'O-oh! I think I've met that sort of man before. And isn't he?'

'No. He confided that to me a few days ago. Ugh! Some men ought to be killed.'

'What happened then?'

'He posed as the horror of horrors – a misunderstood man. Heaven knows the *femme incomprise*[6] is sad enough and bad enough – but the other thing!'

'And so fat too! *I* should have laughed in his face. Men seldom confide in me. How is it they come to you?'

'For the sake of impressing me with their careers in the past. Protect me from men with confidences!'

'And yet you encourage them?'

'What can I do? They talk, I listen, and they vow that I am

sympathetic. I know I always profess astonishment even when the plot is – of the most old possible.'

'Yes. Men are so unblushingly explicit if they are once allowed to talk, whereas women's confidences are full of reservations and fibs, except –'

'When they go mad and babble of the Unutterabilities after a week's acquaintance. Really, if you come to consider, we know a great deal more of men than of our own sex.'

'And the extraordinary thing is that men will never believe it. They say we are trying to hide something.'

'They are generally doing that on their own account. Alas! These chocolates pall upon me, and I haven't eaten more than a dozen. I think I shall go to sleep.'

'Then you'll get fat, dear. If you took more exercise and a more intelligent interest in your neighbours you would –'

'Be as much loved as Mrs Hauksbee. You're a darling in many ways, and I like you – you are not a woman's woman – but *why* do you trouble yourself about mere human beings?'

'Because in the absence of angels, who I am sure would be horribly dull, men and women are the most fascinating things in the whole wide world, lazy one. I am interested in The Dowd – I am interested in The Dancing Master – I am interested in the Hawley Boy – and I am interested in *you*.'

'Why couple me with the Hawley Boy? He is your property.'

'Yes, and in his own guileless speech, I'm making a good thing out of him. When he is slightly more reformed, and has passed his Higher Standard,[7] or whatever the authorities think fit to exact from him, I shall select a pretty little girl, the Holt girl, I think, and' – here she waved her hands airily – '"whom Mrs Hauksbee hath joined together let no man put asunder".[8] That's all.'

'And when you have yoked May Holt with the most notorious detrimental[9] in Simla, and earned the undying hatred of Mamma Holt, what will you do with me, Dispenser of the Destinies of the Universe?'

Mrs Hauksbee dropped into a low chair in front of the fire, and, chin in hand, gazed long and steadfastly at Mrs Mallowe.

'I do not know,' she said, shaking her head, '*what* I shall do with you, dear. It's obviously impossible to marry you to someone else – your husband would object and the experiment might not be successful after all. I think I shall begin by preventing you from – what is it? – "sleeping on ale-house benches and snoring in the sun".'[10]

'Don't! I don't like your quotations. They are so rude. Go to the Library and bring me new books.'

'While you sleep? *No!* If you don't come with me I shall spread your newest frock on my rickshaw-bow, and when any one asks me what I am doing, I shall say that I am going to Phelps's to get it let out. I shall take care that Mrs MacNamara sees me. Put your things on, there's a good girl.'

Mrs Mallowe groaned and obeyed, and the two went off to the Library, where they found Mrs Delville and the man who went by the nickname of The Dancing Master. By that time Mrs Mallowe was awake and eloquent.

'That is the Creature!' said Mrs Hauksbee, with the air of one pointing out a slug in the road.

'No,' said Mrs Mallowe. 'The man is the Creature. Ugh! Good-evening, Mr Bent. I thought you were coming to tea this evening.'

'Surely it was for tomorrow, was it not?' answered The Dancing Master. 'I understood . . . I fancied . . . I'm so sorry . . . How very unfortunate . . .!'

But Mrs Mallowe had passed on.

'For the practised equivocator you said he was,' murmured Mrs Hauksbee, 'he strikes *me* as a failure. Now wherefore should he have preferred a walk with The Dowd to tea with us? Elective affinities,[11] I suppose – both grubby. Polly, I'd never forgive that woman as long as the world rolls.'

'I forgive every woman everything,' said Mrs Mallowe. 'He will be a sufficient punishment for her. What a common voice she has!'

Mrs Delville's voice was not pretty, her carriage was even less lovely, and her raiment was strikingly neglected. All these things Mrs Mallowe noticed over the top of a magazine.

'Now *what* is there in her?' said Mrs Hauksbee. 'Do you see what I meant about the clothes falling off? If I were a man I would perish sooner than be seen with that rag-bag. And yet, she has good eyes, but – Oh!'

'What is it?'

'She doesn't know how to use them! On my honour, she does not. Look! Oh look! Untidiness I can endure, but ignorance never! The woman's a fool.'

'Hsh! She'll hear you.'

'All the women in Simla are fools. She'll think I mean some-one else. Now she's going out. What a thoroughly objectionable couple she and The Dancing Master make! Which reminds me. Do you suppose they'll ever dance together?'

'Wait and see. I don't envy her the conversation of The Dancing Master – loathly man! His wife ought to be up here before long.'

'Do you know anything about him?'

'Only what he told me. It may be all a fiction. He married a girl bred in the country,[12] I think, and, being an honourable, chivalrous soul, told me that he repented his bargain and sent her to her mother as often as possible – a person who has lived in the Doon since the memory of man and goes to Mussoorie when other people go Home. The wife is with her at present. So he says.'

'Babies?'

'One only, but he talks of his wife in a revolting way. I hated him for it. *He* thought he was being epigrammatic and brilli-ant.'

'That is a vice peculiar to men. I dislike him because he is generally in the wake of some girl, disappointing the Eligibles. He will persecute May Holt no more, unless I am much mis-taken.'

'No. I think Mrs Delville may occupy his attention for a while.'

'Do you suppose she knows that he is the head of a family?'

'Not from his lips. He swore me to eternal secrecy. Wherefore I tell you. Don't you know that type of man?'

'Not intimately, thank goodness! As a general rule, when a man begins to abuse his wife to me, I find that the Lord gives me wherewith to answer him according to his folly;[13] and we part with a coolness between us. I laugh.'

'I'm different. I've no sense of humour.'

'Cultivate it, then. It has been my mainstay for more years than I care to think about. A well-educated sense of humour will save a woman when Religion, Training, and Home influences fail; and we may all need salvation sometimes.'

'Do you suppose that the Delville woman has humour?'

'Her dress bewrays her.[14] How can a Thing who wears her *supplément*[15] under her left arm have any notion of the fitness of things – much less their folly? If she discards The Dancing Master after having once seen him dance, I may respect her. Otherwise –'

'But are we not both assuming a great deal too much, dear? You saw the woman at Peliti's – half an hour later you saw her walking with The Dancing Master – an hour later you met her here at the Library.'

'Still with The Dancing Master, remember.'

'Still with The Dancing Master, I admit, but why on the strength of that should you imagine –'

'I imagine nothing. I have no imagination. I am only convinced that The Dancing Master is attracted to The Dowd because he is objectionable in every way and she in every other. If I know the man as you have described him, he holds his wife in slavery at present.'

'She is twenty years younger than he.'

'Poor wretch! And, in the end, after he has posed and swaggered and lied – he has a mouth under that ragged moustache simply made for lies – he will be rewarded according to his merits.'

'I wonder what those really are,' said Mrs Mallowe.

But Mrs Hauksbee, her face close to the shelf of the new books, was humming softly: '*What shall he have who killed the Deer?*'[16] She was a lady of unfettered speech.

One month later she announced her intention of calling upon

Mrs Delville. Both Mrs Hauksbee and Mrs Mallowe were in morning wrappers, and there was a great peace in the land.

'I should go as I was,' said Mrs Mallowe. 'It would be a delicate compliment to her style.'

Mrs Hauksbee studied herself in the glass.

'Assuming for a moment that she ever darkened these doors, I should put on this robe, after all the others, to show her what a morning-wrapper ought to be. It might enliven her. As it is, I shall go in the dove-coloured – sweet emblem of youth and innocence – and shall put on my new gloves.'

'If you really are going, dirty tan would be too good; and you know that dove-colour spots with the rain.'

'I care not. I may make her envious. At least I shall try, though one cannot expect very much from a woman who puts a lace tucker into her habit.'

'Just Heavens! When did she do that?'

'Yesterday – riding with The Dancing Master. I met them at the back of Jakko, and the rain had made the lace lie down. To complete the effect, she was wearing an unclean *terai* with the elastic under her chin. I felt almost too well content to take the trouble to despise her.'

'The Hawley Boy was riding with you. What did he think?'

'Does a boy ever notice these things? Should I like him if he did? He stared in the rudest way, and just when I thought he had seen the elastic, he said, "There's something very taking about that face." I rebuked him on the spot. I don't approve of boys being taken by faces.'

'Other than your own. I shouldn't be in the least surprised if the Hawley Boy immediately went to call.'

'I forbade him. Let her be satisfied with The Dancing Master, and his wife when she comes up. I'm rather curious to see Mrs Bent and the Delville woman together.'

Mrs Hauksbee departed and, at the end of an hour, returned slightly flushed.

'There is no limit to the treachery of youth! I *ordered* the Hawley Boy, as he valued my patronage, not to call. The first person I stumble over – literally stumble over – in her poky, dark little drawing-room is, of course, the Hawley Boy. She kept us waiting ten minutes, and then emerged as though she had been tipped out of the dirty-clothes-basket. You know my way, dear, when I am at all put out. I was Superior, *crrrrushingly* Superior! 'Lifted my eyes to Heaven, and had heard of nothing – 'dropped my eyes on the carpet and "really didn't know" – 'played with my card-case and "supposed so". The Hawley Boy giggled like a girl, and I had to freeze him with scowls between the sentences.'

'And she?'

'She sat in a heap on the edge of a couch, and managed to convey the impression that she was suffering from stomach-ache, at the very least. It was all I could do not to ask after her symptoms. When I rose, she grunted just like a buffalo in the water – too lazy to move.'

'Are you certain? –'

'Am I blind, Polly? Laziness, sheer laziness, nothing else – or her garments were only constructed for sitting down in. I stayed for a quarter of an hour trying to penetrate the gloom, to guess what her surroundings were like, while she stuck out her tongue.'

'Lu – *cy!*'

'Well – I'll withdraw the tongue, though I'm sure if she didn't do it when I was in the room, she did the minute I was outside. At any rate, she lay in a lump and grunted. Ask the Hawley Boy, dear. I believe the grunts were meant for sentences, but she spoke so indistinctly that I can't swear to it.'

'You are incorrigible, simply.'

'I am *not!* Treat me civilly, give me peace with honour,[17] don't put the only available seat facing the window, and a child may eat jam in my lap before Church. But I resent being grunted at. Wouldn't you? Do you suppose that she communicates her views on life and love to The Dancing Master in a set of modulated "Grmphs"?'

'You attach too much importance to The Dancing Master.'

'He came as we went, and The Dowd grew almost cordial at the sight of him. He smiled greasily, and moved about that darkened dog-kennel in a suspiciously familiar way.'

'Don't be uncharitable. Any sin but that I'll forgive.'

'Listen to the voice of History. I am only describing what I saw. He entered, the heap on the sofa revived slightly, and the Hawley Boy and I came away together. *He* is disillusioned, but I felt it my duty to lecture him severely for going there. And that's all.'

'Now for Pity's sake leave the wretched creature and The Dancing Master alone. They never did you any harm.'

'No harm? To dress as an example and a stumbling-block for half Simla, and then to find this Person who is dressed by the hand of God – not that I wish to disparage *Him* for a moment, but you know the *tikka dhurzie*[18] way He attires those lilies of the field[19] – this Person draws the eyes of men – and some of them nice men? It's almost enough to make one discard clothing. I told the Hawley Boy so.'

'And what did that sweet youth do?'

'Turned shell-pink and looked across the far blue hills like a distressed cherub. *Am* I talking wildly, Polly? Let me say my say, and I shall be calm. Otherwise I may go abroad and disturb Simla with a few original reflections. Excepting always your own sweet self, there isn't a single woman in the land who understands me when I am – what's the word?'

'*Tête-fêlée*,'[20] suggested Mrs Mallowe.

'Exactly! And now let us have tiffin. The demands of Society are exhausting, and as Mrs Delville says –' Here Mrs Hauksbee, to the horror of the *khitmatgars*,[21] lapsed into a series of grunts, while Mrs Mallowe stared in lazy surprise.

'"God gie us a guid conceit of oorselves,"'[22] said Mrs Hauksbee piously, returning to her natural speech. 'Now, in any other woman that would have been vulgar. I am consumed with curiosity to see Mrs Bent. I expect complications.'

'Woman of one idea,' said Mrs Mallowe shortly; 'all complications are as old as the hills! I have lived through or near all – *all* – ALL!'

'And yet do not understand that men and women never behave twice alike. I am old who was young –if ever I put my head in your lap, you dear, big sceptic, you will learn that my parting is gauze – but never, no never, have I lost my interest in men and women. Polly, I shall see this business out to the bitter end.'

'I am going to sleep,' said Mrs Mallowe calmly. 'I never interfere with men or women unless I am compelled,' and she retired with dignity to her own room.

Mrs Hauksbee's curiosity was not long left ungratified, for Mrs Bent came up to Simla a few days after the conversation faithfully reported above, and pervaded the Mall by her husband's side.

'Behold!' said Mrs Hauksbee, thoughtfully rubbing her nose. 'That is the last link of the chain, if we omit the husband of the Delville, whoever he may be. Let me consider. The Bents and the Delvilles inhabit the same hotel; and the Delville is detested by the Waddy – do you know the Waddy? – who is almost as big a dowd. The Waddy also abominates the male Bent, for which, if her other sins do not weigh too heavily, she will eventually go to Heaven.'

'Don't be irreverent,' said Mrs Mallowe, 'I like Mrs Bent's face.'

'I am discussing the Waddy,' returned Mrs Hauksbee loftily. 'The Waddy will take the female Bent apart, after having borrowed – yes! – everything that she can, from hairpins to babies' bottles. Such, my dear, is life in a hotel. The Waddy will tell the female Bent facts and fictions about The Dancing Master and The Dowd.'

'Lucy, I should like you better if you were not always looking into people's back-bedrooms.'

'Anybody can look into their front drawing-rooms; and remember whatever I do, and whatever I look, I never talk – as the Waddy will. Let us hope that The Dancing Master's greasy smile and manner of the pedagogue will soften the heart of that cow, his wife. If mouths speak truth, I should think that little Mrs Bent could get very angry on occasion.'

'But what reason has she for being angry?'

'What reason! The Dancing Master in himself is a reason. How does it go? "If in his life some trivial errors fall, Look in his face and you'll believe them all."[23] I am prepared to credit *any* evil of The Dancing Master, because I hate him so. And The Dowd is so disgustingly badly dressed –'

'That she, too, is capable of every iniquity? I always prefer to believe the best of everybody. It saves so much trouble.'

'Very good. I prefer to believe the worst. It saves useless expenditure of sympathy. And you may be quite certain that the Waddy believes with me.'

Mrs Mallowe sighed and made no answer.

The conversation was holden after dinner while Mrs Hauksbee was dressing for a dance.

'I am too tired to go,' pleaded Mrs Mallowe, and Mrs Hauksbee left her in peace till two in the morning, when she was aware of emphatic knocking at her door.

'Don't be *very* angry, dear,' said Mrs Hauksbee. 'My idiot of an *ayah* has gone home, and, as I hope to sleep tonight, there isn't a soul in the place to unlace me.'

'Oh, this is too bad!' said Mrs Mallowe sulkily.

''Can't help it. I'm a lone, lorn grass-widow,[24] dear, but I will *not* sleep in my stays. And such news too! Oh, *do* unlace me, there's a darling! The Dowd – The Dancing Master – I and the Hawley Boy – You know the North verandah?'

'How can I do anything if you spin round like this?' protested Mrs Mallowe, fumbling with the knot of the laces.

'Oh, I forget. I must tell my tale without the aid of your eyes. Do you know you've lovely eyes, dear? Well, to begin with, I took the Hawley Boy to a *kala juggah*.'

'Did he want much taking?'

'Lots! There was an arrangement of loose-boxes in *kanats*,[25] and *she* was in the next one talking to *him*.'

'Which? How? Explain.'

'You know what I mean – The Dowd and The Dancing Master. We could hear every word, and we listened shamelessly – 'specially the Hawley Boy. Polly, I quite love that woman!'

'This is interesting. There! Now turn round. What happened?'

'One moment. Ah—h! Blessed relief. I've been looking for-

ward to taking them off for the last half-hour – which is ominous
at my time of life. But, as I was saying, we listened and heard
The Dowd drawl worse than ever. She drops her final g's like a
barmaid or a blue-blooded Aide-de-Camp. "Look he-ere, you're
gettin' too fond o' me," she said, and The Dancing Master
owned it was so in language that nearly made me ill. The Dowd
reflected for a while. Then we heard her say, "Look he-ere,
Mister Bent, why are you such an aw-ful liar?" I nearly exploded
while The Dancing Master denied the charge. It seems that he
never told her he was a married man.'

'I said he wouldn't.'

'And she had taken this to heart, on personal grounds, I
suppose. She drawled along for five minutes, reproaching him
with his perfidy, and grew quite motherly. "Now you've got a
nice little wife of your own – you have," she said. "She's ten
times too good for a fat old man like you, and, look he-ere, you
never told me a word about her, and I've been thinkin' about it
a good deal, and I think you're a liar." Wasn't that delicious?
The Dancing Master maundered and raved till the Hawley Boy
suggested that he should burst in and beat him. His voice runs
up into an impassioned squeak when he is afraid. The Dowd
must be an extraordinary woman. She explained that had he
been a bachelor she might not have objected to his devotion;
but since he was a married man and the father of a very nice
baby, she considered him a hypocrite, and this she repeated
twice. She wound up her drawl with: "An' I'm tellin' you this
because your wife is angry with me, an' I hate quarrellin' with
any other woman, an' I like your wife. You know how you have
behaved for the last six weeks. You shouldn't have done it,
indeed you shouldn't. You're too old an' too fat." Can't you
imagine how The Dancing Master would wince at that! "Now
go away," she said. "I don't want to tell you what I think of
you, because I think you are not nice. I'll stay he-ere till the
next dance begins." Did you think that the creature had so
much in her?'

'I never studied her as closely as you did. It sounds unnatural.
What happened?'

'The Dancing Master attempted blandishment, reproof, jocularity, and the style of the Lord High Warden, and I had almost to pinch the Hawley Boy to make him keep quiet. She grunted at the end of each sentence and, in the end, *he* went away swearing to himself, quite like a man in a novel. He looked more objectionable than ever. I laughed. I love that woman – in spite of her clothes. And now I'm going to bed. What do you think of it?'

'I shan't begin to think till the morning,' said Mrs Mallowe, yawning. 'Perhaps she spoke the truth. They do fly into it by accident sometimes.'

Mrs Hauksbee's account of her eavesdropping was an ornate one, but truthful in the main. For reasons best known to herself, Mrs 'Shady' Delville had turned upon Mr Bent and rent him limb from limb, casting him away limp and disconcerted ere she withdrew the light of her eyes from him permanently. Being a man of resource, and anything but pleased in that he had been called both old and fat, he gave Mrs Bent to understand that he had, during her absence in the Doon, been the victim of unceasing persecution at the hands of Mrs Delville, and he told the tale so often and with such eloquence that he ended in believing it, while his wife marvelled at the manners and customs of 'some women'. When the situation showed signs of languishing, Mrs Waddy was always on hand to wake the smouldering fires of suspicion in Mrs Bent's bosom and to contribute generally to the peace and comfort of the hotel. Mr Bent's life was not a happy one, for if Mrs Waddy's story were true, he was, argued his wife, untrustworthy to the last degree. If his own statement was true, his charms of manner and conversation were so great that he needed constant surveillance. And he received it, till he repented genuinely of his marriage and neglected his personal appearance. Mrs Delville alone in the hotel was unchanged. She removed her chair some six paces towards the head of the table, and occasionally in the twilight ventured on timid overtures of friendship to Mrs Bent, which were repulsed.

'She does it for my sake,' hinted the virtuous Bent.

'A dangerous and designing woman,' purred Mrs Waddy. Worst of all, every other hotel in Simla was full!

'Polly, are you afraid of diphtheria?'

'Of nothing in the world except small-pox. Diphtheria kills, but it doesn't disfigure. Why do you ask?'

'Because the Bent baby has got it, and the whole hotel is upside down in consequence. The Waddy has "set her five young on the rail" and fled. The Dancing Master fears for his precious throat, and that miserable little woman, his wife, has no notion of what ought to be done. She wanted to put it into a mustard bath – for croup!'

'Where did you learn all this?'

'Just now, on the Mall. Dr Howlen told me. The manager of the hotel is abusing the Bents, and the Bents are abusing the manager. They *are* a feckless couple.'

'Well. What's on your mind?'

'This; and I know it's a grave thing to ask. Would you seriously object to my bringing the child over here, with its mother?'

'On the most strict understanding that we see nothing of The Dancing Master.'

'He will be only too glad to stay away. Polly, you're an angel. The woman really is at her wits' end.'

'And you know nothing about her, careless, and would hold her up to public scorn if it gave you a minute's amusement. Therefore you risk your life for the sake of her brat. No, Loo, *I'm* not the angel. I shall keep to my rooms and avoid her. But do as you please – only tell me why you do it.'

Mrs Hauksbee's eyes softened; she looked out of the window and back into Mrs Mallowe's face.

'I don't know,' said Mrs Hauksbee simply.

'You dear!'

'Polly! – and for aught you knew you might have taken my fringe off. Never do that again without warning. Now we'll get the rooms ready. I don't suppose I shall be allowed to circulate in society for a month.'

'And I also. Thank goodness I shall at last get all the sleep I want.'

Much to Mrs Bent's surprise she and the baby were brought over to the house almost before she knew where she was. Bent was devoutly and undisguisedly thankful, for he was afraid of the infection, and also hoped that a few weeks in the hotel alone with Mrs Delville might lead to explanations. Mrs Bent had thrown her jealousy to the winds in her fear for her child's life.

'We can give you good milk,' said Mrs Hauksbee to her, 'and our house is much nearer to the Doctor's than the hotel, and you won't feel as though you were living in a hostile camp. Where is the dear Mrs Waddy? She seemed to be a particular friend of yours.'

'They've all left me,' said Mrs Bent bitterly. 'Mrs Waddy went first. She said I ought to be ashamed of myself for introducing diseases there, and I am *sure* it wasn't my fault that little Dora –'

'How nice!' cooed Mrs Hauksbee. 'The Waddy is an infectious disease herself – "more quickly caught than the plague and the taker runs presently mad".[26] I lived next door to her at the Elysium, three years ago. Now see, you won't give us the *least* trouble, and I've ornamented all the house with sheets soaked in carbolic. It smells comforting, doesn't it? Remember I'm always in call, and my *ayah*'s at your service when yours goes to her meals, and – and – if you cry I'll *never* forgive you.'

Dora Bent occupied her mother's unprofitable attention through the day and the night. The Doctor called thrice in the twenty-four hours, and the house reeked with the smell of the Condy's Fluid,[27] chlorine-water, and carbolic acid washes. Mrs Mallowe kept to her own rooms – she considered that she had made sufficient concessions in the cause of humanity – and Mrs Hauksbee was more esteemed by the Doctor as a help in the sick-room than the half-distraught mother.

'I know nothing of illness,' said Mrs Hauksbee to the Doctor. 'Only tell me what to do, and I'll do it.'

'Keep that crazy woman from kissing the child, and let her have as little to do with the nursing as you possibly can,' said the Doctor; 'I'd turn her out of the sick-room, but that I honestly believe she'd die of anxiety. She is less than no good, and I depend on you and the *ayahs*, remember.'

Mrs Hauksbee accepted the responsibility, though it painted olive hollows under her eyes and forced her to her oldest dresses. Mrs Bent clung to her with more than childlike faith.

'I *know* you'll make Dora well, won't you?' she said at least twenty times a day; and twenty times a day Mrs Hauksbee answered valiantly, 'Of course I will.'

But Dora did not improve, and the Doctor seemed to be always in the house.

'There's some danger of the thing taking a bad turn,' he said; 'I'll come over between three and four in the morning tomorrow.'

'Good gracious!' said Mrs Hauksbee. 'He never told me what the turn would be! My education has been horribly neglected; and I have only this foolish mother-woman to fall back upon.'

The night wore through slowly, and Mrs Hauksbee dozed in a chair by the fire. There was a dance at the Viceregal Lodge, and she dreamed of it till she was aware of Mrs Bent's anxious eyes staring into her own.

'Wake up! Wake up! Do something!' cried Mrs Bent piteously. 'Dora's choking to death! Do you mean to let her die?'

Mrs Hauksbee jumped to her feet and bent over the bed. The child was fighting for breath, while the mother wrung her hands despairingly.

'Oh, what can I do? What can you do? She won't stay still! I can't hold her. Why didn't the Doctor say this was coming?' screamed Mrs Bent. '*Won't* you help me? She's dying!'

'I – I've never seen a child die before!' stammered Mrs Hauksbee feebly, and then – let none blame her weakness after the strain of long watching – she broke down, and covered her face with her hands. The *ayahs* on the threshold snored peacefully.

There was a rattle of rickshaw wheels below, the clash of an opening door, a heavy step on the stairs, and Mrs Delville entered to find Mrs Bent screaming for the Doctor as she ran round the room. Mrs Hauksbee, her hands to her ears, and her face buried in the chintz of a chair, was quivering with pain at each cry from the bed, and murmuring, 'Thank God, I never bore a child! Oh! thank God, I never bore a child!'

Mrs Delville looked at the bed for an instant, took Mrs Bent by the shoulders, and said quietly, 'Get me some caustic. Be quick.'

The mother obeyed mechanically. Mrs Delville had thrown herself down by the side of the child and was opening its mouth.

'Oh, you're killing her!' cried Mrs Bent. 'Where's the Doctor? Leave her alone!'

Mrs Delville made no reply for a minute, but busied herself with the child.

'Now the caustic, and hold a lamp behind my shoulder. *Will* you do as you are told? The acid-bottle, if you don't know what I mean,' she said.

A second time Mrs Delville bent over the child. Mrs Hauksbee, her face still hidden, sobbed and shivered. One of the *ayahs* staggered sleepily into the room, yawning: '*Doctor Sahib* come.'

Mrs Delville turned her head.

'You're only just in time,' she said. 'It was chokin' her when I came, an' I've burnt it.'

'There was no sign of the membrane getting to the air-passages after the last steaming. It was the general weakness I feared,' said the Doctor half to himself, and he whispered as he looked, 'You've done what I should have been afraid to do without consultation.'

'She was dyin',' said Mrs Delville, under her breath. 'Can you do anythin'? What a mercy it was I went to the dance!'

Mrs Hauksbee raised her head.

'Is it all over?' she gasped. 'I'm useless – I'm worse than useless! What are *you* doing here?'

She stared at Mrs Delville, and Mrs Bent, realizing for the first time who was the Goddess from the Machine,[28] stared also.

Then Mrs Delville made explanation, putting on a dirty long glove and smoothing a crumpled and ill-fitting ball-dress.

'I was at the dance, an' the Doctor was tellin' me about your baby bein' so ill. So I came away early, an' your door was open, an' I – I – lost my boy this way six months ago, an' I've been tryin' to forget it ever since, an' I – I – I am very sorry for intrudin' an' anythin' that has happened.'

Mrs Bent was putting out the Doctor's eye with a lamp as he stooped over Dora.

'Take it away,' said the Doctor. 'I think the child will do, thanks to you, Mrs Delville. *I* should have come too late, but, I assure you' – he was addressing himself to Mrs Delville – 'I had not the faintest reason to expect *this*. The membrane must have grown like a mushroom. Will one of you help me, please?'

He had reason for the last sentence. Mrs Hauksbee had thrown herself into Mrs Delville's arms, where she was weeping bitterly, and Mrs Bent was unpicturesquely mixed up with both, while from the tangle came the sound of many sobs and much promiscuous kissing.

'Good gracious! I've spoilt all your beautiful roses!' said Mrs Hauksbee, lifting her head from the lump of crushed gum and calico atrocities on Mrs Delville's shoulder and hurrying to the Doctor.

Mrs Delville picked up her shawl, and slouched out of the room, mopping her eyes with the glove that she had not put on.

'I always said she was more than a woman,' sobbed Mrs Hauksbee hysterically, 'and *that* proves it!'

Six weeks later Mrs Bent and Dora had returned to the hotel. Mrs Hauksbee had come out of the Valley of Humiliation,[29] had ceased to reproach herself for her collapse in an hour of need, and was even beginning to direct the affairs of the world as before.

'So nobody died, and everything went off as it should, and I kissed The Dowd, Polly. I feel so old. Does it show in my face?'

'Kisses don't as a rule, do they? Of course you know what the result of The Dowd's providential arrival has been.'

'They ought to build her a statue – only no sculptor dare copy those skirts.'

'Ah!' said Mrs Mallowe quietly. 'She has found another reward. The Dancing Master has been smirking through Simla, giving everyone to understand that she came because of her undying love for him – for him – to save *his* child, and all Simla naturally believes this.'

'But Mrs Bent –'

'Mrs Bent believes it more than anyone else. She won't speak to The Dowd now. *Isn't* The Dancing Master an angel?'

Mrs Hauksbee lifted up her voice and raged till bed-time. The doors of the two rooms stood open.

'Polly,' said a voice from the darkness, 'what did that American-heiress-globe-trotter girl say last season when she was tipped out of her rickshaw turning a corner? Some absurd adjective that made the man who picked her up explode.'

'"Paltry,"'[30] said Mrs Mallowe. 'Through her nose – like this – 'Ha-ow pahltry it all is!'

'Which?'

'Everything. Babies, Diphtheria, Mrs Bent and The Dancing Master, I whooping in a chair, and The Dowd dropping in from the clouds. I wonder what the motive was – *all* the motives.'

'Um!'

'What do *you* think?'

'Don't ask me.[31] Go to sleep.'

{ Only a Subaltern [1] }

. . . Not only to enforce by command, but to encourage by example the energetic discharge of duty and the steady endurance of the difficulties and privations inseparable from Military Service.

Bengal Army Regulations

They made Bobby Wick pass an examination at Sandhurst. He was a gentleman before he was gazetted, so, when the Empress announced that 'Gentleman-Cadet Robert Hanna Wick' was posted as Second Lieutenant to the Tyneside Tail Twisters [2] at Krab Bokhar, [3] he became an officer *and* a gentleman, which is an enviable thing; and there was joy in the house of Wick where Mamma Wick and all the little Wicks fell upon their knees and offered incense to Bobby by virtue of his achievements.

Papa Wick had been a Commissioner in his day, holding authority over three millions of men in the Chota-Buldana Division, building great works for the good of the land, and doing his best to make two blades of grass grow where there was but one before. [4] Of course, nobody knew anything about this in the little English village where he was just 'old Mr Wick', and had forgotten that he was a Companion of the Order of the Star of India.

He patted Bobby on the shoulder and said: 'Well done, my boy!'

There followed, while the uniform was being prepared, an interval of pure delight, during which Bobby took brevet-rank as a 'man' at the women-swamped tennis-parties and tea-fights of the village, and I daresay, had his joining-time been extended, would have fallen in love with several girls at once. Little country villages at Home are very full of nice girls, because all the young men come out to India to make their fortunes.

'India,' said Papa Wick, 'is the place. I've had thirty years of it and, begad, I'd like to go back again. When you join the Tail Twisters you'll be among friends, if everyone hasn't forgotten Wick of Chota-Buldana, and a lot of people will be kind to you for our sakes. The mother will tell you more about outfit than I can; but remember this. Stick to your Regiment, Bobby – stick to your Regiment. You'll see men all round you going into the Staff Corps, and doing every possible sort of duty but regimental, and you may be tempted to follow suit. Now so long as you keep within your allowance, and I haven't stinted you there, stick to the Line, the whole Line, and nothing but the Line.[5] Be careful how you back another young fool's bill, and if you fall in love with a woman twenty years older than yourself, don't tell *me* about it, that's all.'

With these counsels, and many others equally valuable, did Papa Wick fortify Bobby ere that last awful night at Portsmouth when the Officers' Quarters held more inmates than were provided for by the Regulations, and the liberty-men[6] of the ships fell foul of the drafts for India, and the battle raged from the Dockyard Gates even to the slums of Longport, while the drabs of Fratton came down and scratched the faces of the Queen's Officers.

Bobby Wick, with an ugly bruise on his freckled nose, a sick and shaky detachment to manoeuvre inship, and the comfort of fifty scornful females to attend to, had no time to feel home-sick till the *Malabar* reached mid-Channel, when he doubled his emotions with a little guard-visiting and a great many other matters.

The Tail Twisters were a most particular Regiment. Those who knew them least said that they were eaten up with 'side'. But their reserve and their internal arrangements generally were merely protective diplomacy. Some five years before, the Colonel commanding had looked into the fourteen fearless eyes of seven plump and juicy subalterns who had all applied to enter the Staff Corps, and had asked them why the three stars should he, a colonel of the Line, command a dashed nursery for double-dashed[7] bottle-suckers who put on condemned tin spurs and rode qualified mokes at the hiatused heads of forsaken Black Regiments. He was a rude man and a terrible. Wherefore the remnant took measures (with the half-butt as an engine of public opinion) till the rumour went abroad that young men who used the Tail Twisters as a crutch to the Staff Corps had many and varied trials to endure. However, a regiment had just as much right to its own secrets as a woman.

When Bobby came up from Deolali and took his place among the Tail Twisters, it was gently but firmly borne in upon him that the Regiment was his father and his mother and his indissolubly wedded wife, and that there was no crime under the canopy of heaven blacker than that of bringing shame on the Regiment, which was the best-shooting, best-drilled, best-set-up, bravest, most illustrious, and in all respects most desirable Regiment within the compass of the Seven Seas. He was taught the legends of the Mess Plate, from the great grinning Golden Gods that had come out of the Summer Palace in Pekin to the silver-mounted markhor-horn snuff-mull [8] presented by the last C.O. (he who spake to the seven subalterns). And every one of those legends told him of battles fought at long odds, without fear as without support; of hospitality catholic as an Arab's; of friendships deep as the sea and steady as the fighting-line; of honour won by hard roads for honour's sake; and of instant and unquestioning devotion to the Regiment – the Regiment that claims the lives of all and lives for ever.

More than once, too, he came officially into contact with the Regimental colours, which looked like the lining of a bricklayer's hat on the end of a chewed stick. Bobby did not kneel and worship them, because British subalterns are not constructed in that manner. Indeed, he condemned them for their weight at the very moment that they were filling with awe and other more noble sentiments.

But best of all was the occasion when he moved with the Tail Twisters in review order at the breaking of a November day. Allowing for duty-men and sick, the Regiment was one thousand and eighty [9] strong, and Bobby belonged to them; for was he not a Subaltern of the Line – the whole Line, and nothing but the Line – as the tramp of two thousand one hundred and sixty sturdy ammunition boots attested? He would not have changed places with Deighton of the Horse Battery, whirling by in a pillar of cloud to a chorus of 'Strong right! Strong left!' or Hogan-Yale of the White Hussars, leading his squadron for all it was worth, with the price of horseshoes thrown in; or 'Tick' Boileau,[10] trying to live up to his fierce blue and gold turban while the wasps of the Bengal Cavalry stretched to a gallop in the wake of the long, lollopping Walers[11] of the White Hussars.

They fought through the clear cool day, and Bobby felt a little thrill run down his spine when he heard the *tinkle-tinkle-tinkle* of the empty cartridge-cases hopping from the breech-blocks after the roar of the volleys; for he knew that he should live to hear that sound in action. The review ended in a glorious chase across the plain – batteries thundering after cavalry to the huge disgust of the White Hussars, and the Tyneside Tail Twisters hunting a Sikh Regiment,[12] till the lean lathy Singhs panted with exhaustion. Bobby was dusty and dripping long before noon, but his enthusiasm was merely focused – not diminished.

He returned to sit at the feet of Revere, his 'skipper', that is to say, the Captain of his Company, and to be instructed in the dark art and mystery of managing men, which is a very large part of the Profession of Arms.

'If you haven't a taste that way,' said Revere between his puffs of his cheroot, 'you'll never be able to get the hang of it, but remember, Bobby, 't isn't the best drill, though drill is nearly everything, that hauls a Regiment through Hell and out on the other side. It's the man who knows how to handle men – goat-men, swine-men, dog-men, and so on.'

'Dormer, for instance,' said Bobby, 'I think he comes under the head of fool-men. He mopes like a sick owl.'

'That's where you make your mistake, my son. Dormer isn't a fool *yet*, but he's a dashed dirty soldier, and his room corporal makes fun of his socks before kit-inspection. Dormer, being two-thirds pure brute, goes into a corner and growls.'

'How do you know?' said Bobby admiringly.

'Because a Company commander has to know these things –
because, if he does *not* know, he may have crime – ay, murder –
brewing under his very nose and yet not see that it's there.
Dormer is being badgered out of his mind – big as he is – and he
hasn't intellect enough to resent it. He's taken to quiet boozing,
and, Bobby, when the butt of a room goes on the drink, or takes
to moping by himself, measures are necessary to pull him out of
himself.'

'What measures? 'Man can't run round coddling his men for
ever.'

'No. The men would precious soon show him that he was not
wanted. You've got to –'

Here the Colour-Sergeant entered with some papers; Bobby
reflected for a while as Revere looked through the Company
forms.

'Does Dormer do anything, Sergeant?' Bobby asked with the
air of one continuing an interrupted conversation.

'No, sir. Does 'is dooty like a hortomato,'[13] said the Sergeant,
who delighted in long words. 'A dirty soldier and 'e's under full
stoppages[14] for new kit. It's covered with scales, sir.'

'Scales? What scales?'

'Fish-scales, sir. 'E's always pokin' in the mud by the river
an' a-cleaning' them *muchly*-fish with 'is thumbs.' Revere was
still absorbed in the Company papers, and the Sergeant, who
was sternly fond of Bobby, continued – ''E generally goes
down there when 'e's got 'is skinful, beggin' your pardon, sir, an'
they *do* say that the more lush – in-*he*-briated 'e is, the more
fish 'e catches. They call 'im the Looney Fishmonger in the
Comp'ny, sir.'

Revere signed the last paper and the Sergeant retreated.

'It's a filthy amusement,' sighed Bobby to himself. Then
aloud to Revere: 'Are you really worried about Dormer?'

'A little. You see he's never mad enough to send to hospital,
or drunk enough to run in, but at any minute he may flare up,
brooding and sulking as he does. He resents any interest being
shown in him, and the only time I took him out shooting he all
but shot *me* by accident.'

'I fish,' said Bobby with a wry face. 'I hire a country-boat and go down the river from Thursday to Sunday, and the amiable Dormer goes with me – if you can spare us both.'

'You blazing young fool!' said Revere, but his heart was full of much more pleasant words.

Bobby, the Captain of a *dhoni*,[15] with Private Dormer for mate, dropped down the river on Thursday morning – the Private at the bow, the Subaltern at the helm. The Private glared uneasily at the Subaltern, who respected the reserve of the Private.

After six hours, Dormer paced to the stern, saluted, and said – 'Beg y' pardon, sir, but *was* you ever on the Durh'm Canal?'

'No,' said Bobby Wick. 'Come and have some tiffin.'

They ate in silence. As the evening fell, Private Dormer broke forth, speaking to himself –

'Hi was on the Durh'm Canal, jes' such a night, come next week twelve month, a-trailin' *of* my toes in the water.' He smoked and said no more till bedtime.

The witchery of the dawn turned the grey river-reaches to purple, gold, and opal; and it was as though the lumbering *dhoni* crept across the splendours of a new heaven.

Private Dormer popped his head out of his blanket and gazed at the glory below and around.

'Well – damn – my eyes!' said Private Dormer in an awed whisper. 'This 'ere is like a bloomin' gallantry-show!'[16] For the rest of the day he was dumb, but achieved an ensanguined filthiness through the cleaning of big fish.

The boat returned on Saturday evening. Dormer had been struggling with speech since noon. As the lines and luggage were being disembarked, he found tongue.

'Beg y' pardon, sir,' he said, 'but would you – would you min' shakin' 'ands with me, sir?'

'Of course not,' said Bobby, and he shook accordingly. Dormer returned to barracks and Bobby to mess.

'He wanted a little quiet and some fishing, I think,' said Bobby. 'My aunt, but he's a filthy sort of animal! Have you ever seen him clean "them *muchly*-fish with 'is thumbs"?'

'Anyhow,' said Revere three weeks later, 'he's doing his best to keep his things clean.'

When the spring died, Bobby joined in the general scramble for Hill leave, and to his surprise and delight secured three months.

'As good a boy as I want,' said Revere the admiring skipper.

'The best of the batch,' said the Adjutant to the Colonel. 'Keep back that young skrimshanker Porkiss, sir, and let Revere make him sit up.'

So Bobby departed joyously to Simla Pahar with a tin box of gorgeous raiment.

''Son of Wick – old Wick of Chota-Buldana? Ask him to dinner, dear,' said the aged men.

'What a nice boy!' said the matrons and the maids.

'First-class place, Simla. Oh, ri—ipping!' said Bobby Wick, and ordered new white cord breeches on the strength of it.

'We're in a bad way,' wrote Revere to Bobby at the end of two months. 'Since you left, the Regiment has taken to fever and is fairly rotten with it – two hundred in hospital, about a hundred in cells – drinking to keep off fever – and the Companies on parade fifteen file strong at the outside. There's rather more sickness in the out-villages than I care for, but then I'm so blistered with prickly-heat that I'm ready to hang myself. What's the yarn about your mashing a Miss Haverley up there? Not serious, I hope? You're over-young to hang millstones round your neck, and the Colonel will turf you out of that in double-quick time if you attempt it.'

It was not the Colonel that brought Bobby out of Simla, but a much-more-to-be-respected Commandant. The sickness in the out-villages spread, the Bazar was put out of bounds, and then came the news that the Tail Twisters must go into camp. The message flashed to the Hill stations – 'Cholera – Leave stopped – Officers recalled.' Alas for the white gloves in the neatly-soldered boxes, the rides and the dances and picnics that were to be, the loves half spoken, and the debts unpaid! Without demur and without question, fast as tonga could fly or pony gallop, back to their Regiments and their Batteries, as though they were hastening to their weddings, fled the subalterns.

Bobby received his orders on returning from a dance at Vice-regal Lodge where he had – But only the Haverley girl knows what Bobby had said, or how many waltzes he had claimed for the next ball. Six in the morning saw Bobby at the Tonga Office in the drenching rain, the whirl of the last waltz still in his ears, and an intoxication due neither to wine nor waltzing in his brain.

'Good man!' shouted Deighton of the Horse Battery through the mist. 'Whar you raise dat tonga? I'm coming with you. Ow! But I've a head and a half. *I* didn't sit out all night. They say the Battery's awful bad,' and he hummed dolorously –

> Leave the what at the what's-its-name,
> Leave the flock without shelter,
> Leave the corpse uninterred,
> Leave the bride at the altar! [17]

'My faith! It'll be more bally corpse than bride, though, this journey. Jump in, Bobby. Get on, *Coachwan!*'

On the Umballa platform waited a detachment of officers discussing the latest news from the stricken cantonment, and it was here that Bobby learned the real condition of the Tail Twisters.

'They went into camp,' said an elderly Major recalled from the whist-tables at Mussoorie to a sickly Native Regiment, 'they went into camp with two hundred and ten sick in carts. Two hundred and ten fever cases only, and the balance looking like so many ghosts with sore eyes. A Madras Regiment could have walked through 'em.'

'But they were as fit as be-damned when I left them!' said Bobby.

'Then you'd better make them as fit as be-damned when you rejoin,' said the Major brutally.

Bobby pressed his forehead against the rain-splashed window-pane as the train lumbered across the sodden Doab,[18] and prayed for the health of the Tyneside Tail Twisters. Naini Tal [19] had sent down her contingent with all speed; the lathering ponies of the Dalhousie Road staggered into Pathankot, taxed to the full stretch of their strength; while from cloudy Darjiling the Calcutta Mail whirled up the last straggler of the little army that was to fight a fight in which was neither medal nor honour for the winning, against an enemy none other than 'the sickness that destroyeth in the noonday'.[20]

And as each man reported himself, he said: 'This is a bad business,' and went about his own forthwith, for every Regiment and Battery in the cantonment was under canvas, the sickness bearing them company.

Bobby fought his way through the rain to the Tail Twisters' temporary mess, and Revere could have fallen on the boy's neck for the joy of seeing that ugly, wholesome phiz once more.

'Keep 'em amused and interested,' said Revere. 'They went on the drink, poor fools, after the first two cases, and there was no improvement. Oh, it's good to have you back, Bobby! Porkiss is a – never mind.'

Deighton came over from the Artillery camp to attend a dreary mess dinner, and contributed to the general gloom by nearly weeping over the condition of his beloved Battery. Porkiss so far forgot himself as to insinuate that the presence of the officers could do no earthly good, and that the best thing would be to send the entire Regiment into hospital and 'let the doctors look after them'. Porkiss was demoralized with fear, nor was his peace of mind restored when Revere said coldly: 'Oh! The sooner *you* go out the better, if that's your way of thinking. Any public school could send us fifty *good* men in your place, but it takes time, time, Porkiss, and money, and a certain amount of trouble, to make a Regiment. 'S'pose *you're* the person we go into camp for, eh?'

Whereupon Porkiss was overtaken with a great and chilly fear which a drenching in the rain did not allay, and, two days later, quitted this world for another where, men do fondly hope, allowances are made for the weaknesses of the flesh. The Regimental Sergeant-Major looked wearily across the Sergeants' Mess tent when the news was announced.

'There goes the worst of them,' he said. 'It'll take the best, and then, please God, it'll stop.' The Sergeants were silent till one said: 'It couldn't be *him!*' and all knew of whom Travis was thinking.

Bobby Wick stormed through the tents of his Company, rallying, rebuking mildly, as is consistent with the Regulations,[21] chaffing the faint-hearted; hailing the sound into the watery sunlight when there was a break in the weather, and bidding them be of good cheer for their trouble was nearly at an end; scuttling on his dun pony round the outskirts of the camp, and heading back men who, with the innate perversity of British soldiers, were always wandering into infected villages, or drinking deeply from rain-flooded marshes; comforting the panic-stricken with rude speech, and more than once tending the dying who had no friends – the men without 'townies'; organizing, with banjos and burnt cork, Sing-songs which should allow the talent of the Regiment full play; and generally, as he explained, 'playing the giddy garden-goat all round'.

'You're worth half-a-dozen of us, Bobby,' said Revere in a moment of enthusiasm. 'How the devil do you keep it up?'

Bobby made no answer, but had Revere looked into the breast-pocket of his coat he might have seen there a sheaf of badly-written letters which perhaps accounted for the power that possessed the boy. A letter came to Bobby every other day. The spelling was not above reproach, but the sentiments must have been most satisfactory, for on receipt Bobby's eyes softened marvellously, and he was wont to fall into a tender abstraction for a while ere, shaking his cropped head, he charged into his work.

By what power he drew after him the hearts of the roughest, and the Tail Twisters counted in their ranks some rough diamonds indeed, was a mystery to both skipper and C.O., who learned from the regimental chaplain that Bobby was considerably more in request in the hospital tents than the Reverend John Emery.

'The men seem fond of you. Are you in the hospitals much?' said the Colonel, who did his daily round and ordered the men to get well with a hardness that did not cover his bitter grief.

'A little, sir,' said Bobby.

''Shouldn't go there too o if I were you. They say it's not contagious, but there's no use in running unnecessary risks. We can't afford to have you down, y'know.'

Six days later, it was with the utmost difficulty that the post-runner plashed his way out to the camp with the mail-bags, for the rain was falling in torrents. Bobby received a letter, bore it off to his tent, and, the programme for the next week's Sing-song being satisfactorily disposed of, sat down to answer it. For an hour the unhandy pen toiled over the paper, and where sentiment rose to more than normal tide-level, Bobby Wick stuck out his tongue and breathed heavily. He was not used to letter-writing.

'Beg y' pardon, sir,' said a voice at the tent door; 'but Dormer's 'orrid bad, sir, an' they've taken him orf, sir.'

'Damn Private Dormer and you too!' said Bobby Wick, run-ning the blotter over the half-finished letter. 'Tell him I'll come in the morning.'

''E's awful bad, sir,' said the voice hesitatingly. There was an undecided squelching of heavy boots.

'Well?' said Bobby impatiently.

'Excusin' 'imself before'and for takin' the liberty, 'e says it would be a comfort for to assist 'im, sir, if —'

'*Tattoo lao!*[22] Get my pony! Here, come in out of the rain till I'm ready. What blasted nuisances you are! That's brandy. Drink some; you want it. Hang on to my stirrup and tell me if I go too fast.'

Strengthened by a four-finger 'nip' which he swallowed without a wink, the Hospital Orderly kept up with the slipping, mud-stained, and very disgusted pony as it shambled to the hospital tent.

Private Dormer was certainly ''orrid bad'. He had all but reached the stage of collapse and was not pleasant to look upon.

'What's this, Dormer?' said Bobby, bending over the man. 'You're not going out this time. You've got to come fishing with me once or twice more yet.'

The blue lips parted and in the ghost of a whisper said – 'Beg y' pardon, sir, disturbin' of you now, but would you min' 'oldin' my 'and, sir?'

Bobby sat on the side of the bed, and the icy cold hand closed on his own like a vice, forcing a lady's ring which was on the little finger deep into the flesh. Bobby set his lips and waited, the water dripping from the hem of his trousers. An hour passed and the grasp of the hand did not relax, nor did the expression of the drawn face change. Bobby with infinite craft lit himself a cheroot with the left hand, his right arm was numbed to the elbow, and resigned himself to a night of pain.

Dawn showed a very white-faced Subaltern sitting on the side of a sick man's cot, and a Doctor in the doorway using language unfit for publication.

'Have you been here all night, you young ass?' said the Doctor.

'There or thereabouts,' said Bobby ruefully. 'He's frozen on to me.'

Dormer's mouth shut with a click. He turned his head and sighed. The clinging hand opened, and Bobby's arm fell useless at his side.

'He'll do,' said the Doctor quietly. 'It must have been a toss-up all through the night. 'Think you're to be congratulated on this case.'

'Oh, bosh!' said Bobby. 'I thought the man had gone out long ago – only – only I didn't care to take my hand away. Rub my arm down, there's a good chap. What a grip the brute has! I'm chilled to the marrow!' He passed out of the tent shivering.

Private Dormer was allowed to celebrate his repulse of Death by strong waters. Four days later he sat on the side of his cot and said to the patients mildly: 'I'd 'a' liken to 'a' spoken to 'im – so I should.'

But at that time Bobby was reading yet another letter – he had the most persistent correspondent of any man in camp – and was even then about to write that the sickness had abated, and in another week at the outside would be gone. He did not intend to say that the chill of a sick man's hand seemed to have struck into the heart whose capacities for affection he dwelt on at such length. He did intend to enclose the illustrated programme of the forthcoming Sing-song whereof he was not a little proud. He also intended to write on many other matters which do not concern us, and doubtless would have done so but for the slight feverish headache which made him dull and unresponsive at mess.

'You are overdoing it, Bobby,' said his skipper. ''Might give the rest of us credit of doing a little work. You go on as if you were the whole Mess rolled into one. Take it easy.'

'I will,' said Bobby. 'I'm feeling done up, somehow.' Revere looked at him anxiously and said nothing.

There was a flickering of lanterns about the camp that night, and a rumour that brought men out of their cots to the tent doors, a paddling of the naked feet of doolie-bearers[23] and the rush of a galloping horse.

'Wot's up?' asked twenty tents; and through twenty tents ran the answer – 'Wick, 'e's down.'

They brought the news to Revere and he groaned. 'Any one but Bobby and I shouldn't have cared! The Sergeant-Major was right.'

'Not going out this journey,' gasped Bobby, as he was lifted from the doolie. 'Not going out this journey.' Then with an air of supreme conviction – 'I *can't*, you see.'

'Not if I can do anything!' said the Surgeon-Major, who had hastened over from the mess where he had been dining.

He and the Regimental Surgeon fought together with Death for the life of Bobby Wick. Their work was interrupted by a hairy apparition in a blue-grey dressing-gown who stared in horror at the bed and cried – 'Oh, my Gawd! It can't be *'im!'* until an indignant Hospital Orderly whisked him away.

If care of man and desire to live could have done aught, Bobby would have been saved. As it was, he made a fight of three days, and the Surgeon-Major's brow uncreased. 'We'll save him yet,' he said; and the Surgeon, who, though he ranked with the Captain, had a very youthful heart, went out upon the word and pranced joyously in the mud.

'Not going out this journey,' whispered Bobby Wick gallantly, at the end of the third day.

'Bravo!' said the Surgeon-Major. 'That's the way to look at it, Bobby.'

As evening fell a grey shade gathered round Bobby's mouth, and he turned his face to the tent wall wearily. The Surgeon-Major frowned.

'I'm awfully tired,' said Bobby, very faintly. 'What's the use of bothering me with medicine? I – don't – want – it. Let me alone.'

The desire for life had departed, and Bobby was content to drift away on the easy tide of Death.

'It's no good,' said the Surgeon-Major. 'He doesn't want to live. He's meeting it, poor child.' And he blew his nose.

Half a mile away the regimental band was playing the overture to the Sing-song, for the men had been told that Bobby was out of danger. The clash of the brass and the wail of the horns reached Bobby's ears.

> Is there a single joy or pain,
> That I should never kno—ow?
> You do not love me, 'tis in vain,
> Bid me good-bye and go! [24]

An expression of hopeless irritation crossed the boy's face, and he tried to shake his head.

The Surgeon-Major bent down – 'What is it, Bobby?' – 'Not that waltz,' muttered Bobby. 'That's our own – our very ownest own . . . Mummy dear.'

With this he sank into the stupor that gave place to death early next morning.

Revere, his eyes red at the rims and his nose very white, went into Bobby's tent to write a letter to Papa Wick which should bow the white head of the ex-Commissioner of Chota-Buldana in the keenest sorrow of his life. Bobby's little store of papers lay in confusion on the table and among them a half-finished letter. The last sentence ran: 'So you see, darling, there is really no fear, because as long as I know you care for me and I care for you, nothing can touch me.'

Revere stayed in the tent for an hour. When he came out his eyes were redder than ever.

*

Private Conklin sat on a turned-down bucket, and listened to a not unfamiliar tune.[25] Private Conklin was a convalescent and should have been tenderly treated.

'Ho!' said Private Conklin. 'There's another bloomin' orf'cer da—ed.'

The bucket shot from under him, and his eyes filled with a smithyful of sparks. A tall man in a blue-grey bedgown was regarding him with deep disfavour.

'You ought to take shame for yourself, Conky! Orf'cer? – Bloomin' orf'cer? I'll learn you to misname the likes of 'im. Hangel! *Bloomin'* Hangel! That's wot 'e is!'

And the Hospital Orderly was so satisfied with the justice of the punishment that he did not even order Private Dormer back to his cot.

THE PHANTOM RICKSHAW
AND OTHER TALES [1]

{ The Phantom Rickshaw[1] }

May no ill dreams disturb my rest,
Nor Powers of Darkness me molest.[2]
Evening Hymn

One of the few advantages that India has over England is a great Knowability. After five years' service a man is directly or indirectly acquainted with the two or three hundred Civilians in his Province, all the Messes of ten or twelve Regiments and Batteries, and some fifteen hundred other people of the non-official caste. In ten years his knowledge should be doubled, and at the end of twenty he knows, or knows something about, every Englishman in the Empire, and may travel anywhere and everywhere without paying hotel-bills.

Globe-trotters[3] who expect entertainment as a right, have, even within my memory, blunted this open-heartedness, but none the less today, if you belong to the Inner Circle and are neither a Bear nor a Black Sheep, all houses are open to you, and our small world is very, very kind and helpful.

Rickett of Kamartha stayed with Polder of Kumaon some fifteen years ago. He meant to stay two nights, but was knocked down by rheumatic fever, and for six weeks disorganized Polder's establishment, stopped Polder's work, and nearly died in Polder's bedroom. Polder behaves as though he had been placed under eternal obligation by Rickett, and yearly sends the little Ricketts a box of presents and toys. It is the same everywhere. The men who do not take the trouble to conceal from you their opinion that you are an incompetent ass, and the women who blacken your character and misunderstand your wife's amusements, will work themselves to the bone in your behalf if you fall sick or into serious trouble.

Heatherlegh, the Doctor, kept, in addition to his regular practice, a hospital on his private account – an arrangement of loose boxes for Incurables, his friend called it – but it was really a sort of fitting-up shed for craft that had been damaged by stress of weather. The weather in India is often sultry, and since the tale of bricks [4] is always a fixed quantity, and the only liberty allowed is permission to work overtime and get no thanks, men occasionally break down and become as mixed as the metaphors in this sentence.

Heatherlegh is the dearest doctor that ever was, and his invariable prescription to all patients is, 'Lie low, go slow, and keep cool.' He says that more men are killed by overwork than the importance of this world justifies. He maintains that overwork slew Pansay, who died under his hands about three years ago. He has, of course, the right to speak authoritatively, and he laughs at my theory that there was a crack in Pansay's head and a little bit of the Dark World came through and pressed him to death. 'Pansay went off the handle,' says Heatherlegh, 'after the stimulus of long leave at Home. He may or he may not have behaved like a blackguard to Mrs Keith-Wessington. My notion is that the work of the Katabundi Settlement ran him off his legs, and that he took to brooding and making much of an ordinary P. & O. flirtation. He certainly was engaged to Miss Mannering, and she certainly broke off the engagement. Then he took a feverish chill and all that nonsense about ghosts developed. Overwork started his illness, kept it alight, and killed him, poor devil. Write him off to the System that uses one man to do the work of two and a half men.'

I do not believe this. I used to sit up with Pansay sometimes when Heatherlegh was called out to patients and I happened to be within claim. The man would make me most unhappy by describing, in a low, even voice, the procession that was always passing at the bottom of his bed. He had a sick man's command of language. When he recovered I suggested that he should write out the whole affair from beginning to end, knowing that ink might assist him to ease his mind.

He was in a high fever while he was writing, and the blood-

and-thunder Magazine diction he adopted did not calm him. Two months afterwards he was reported fit for duty, but, in spite of the fact that he was urgently needed to help an under-manned Commission stagger through a deficit, he preferred to die; vowing at the last that he was hag-ridden. I got his manu-script before he died, and this is his version of the affair, dated 1885,[5] exactly as he wrote it:

My doctor tells me that I need rest and change of air. It is not improbable that I shall get both ere long – rest that neither the red-coated messenger nor the mid-day gun can break, and change of air far beyond that which any homeward-bound steamer can give me. In the meantime I am resolved to stay where I am; and, in flat defiance of my doctor's orders, to take all the world into my confidence. You shall learn for yourselves the precise nature of my malady, and shall, too, judge for yourselves whether any man born of woman [6] on this weary earth was ever so tormented as I.

Speaking now as a condemned criminal might speak ere the drop-bolts [7] are drawn, my story, wild and hideously improbable as it may appear, demands at least attention. That it will ever receive credence I utterly disbelieve. Two months ago I should have scouted as mad or drunk the man who had dared tell me the like. Two months ago I was the happiest man in India. To-day, from Peshawar to the sea,[8] there is no one more wretched. My doctor and I are the only two who know this. His ex-planation is, that my brain, digestion, and eyesight are all slightly affected; giving rise to my frequent and persistent 'de-lusions'. Delusions, indeed! I call him a fool; but he attends me still with the same unwearied smile, the same bland professional manner, the same neatly-trimmed red whiskers, till I begin to suspect that I am an ungrateful, evil-tempered invalid. But you shall judge for yourselves.

Three years ago it was my fortune – my great misfortune – to sail from Gravesend to Bombay, on return from long leave, with one Agnes Keith-Wessington, wife of an officer on the Bombay side. It does not in the least concern you to know what manner of woman she was. Be content with the knowledge that, ere the voyage had ended, both she and I were desperately and unreasoningly in love with one another. Heaven knows that I can make the admission now without one particle of vanity. In matters of this sort there is always one who gives and another who accepts. From the first day of our ill-omened attachment, I was conscious that Agnes's passion was a stronger, a more dominant, and – if I may use the expression – a purer sentiment than mine. Whether she recognized the fact then, I do not know. Afterwards it was bitterly plain to both of us.

Arrived at Bombay in the spring of the year, we went our respective ways, to meet no more for the next three or four months, when my leave and her love took us both to Simla. There we spent the season together; and there my fire of straw burnt itself out to a pitiful end with the closing year. I attempt no excuse. I make no apology. Mrs Wessington had given up much for my sake, and was prepared to give up all. From my own lips, in August 1882, she learnt that I was sick of her presence, tired of her company, and weary of the sound of her voice. Ninety-nine women out of a hundred would have wearied of me as I wearied of them; seventy-five of that number would have promptly avenged themselves by active and obtrusive flirtation with other men. Mrs Wessington was the hundredth. On her neither my openly-expressed aversion nor the cutting brutalities with which I garnished our interviews had the least effect.

'Jack, darling!' was her one eternal cuckoo cry: 'I'm sure it's all a mistake – a hideous mistake; and we'll be good friends again some day. *Please* forgive me, Jack, dear.'

I was the offender, and I knew it. That knowledge transformed my pity into passive endurance, and, eventually, into blind hate – the same instinct, I suppose, which prompts a man to savagely stamp on the spider he has but half killed. And with this hate in my bosom the season of 1882 came to an end.

Next year we met again at Simla – she with her monotonous face and timid attempts at reconciliation, and I with loathing of her in every fibre of my frame. Several times I could not avoid meeting her alone; and on each occasion her words were identically the same. Still the unreasoning wail that it was all a 'mistake'; and still the hope of eventually 'making friends'. I might have seen, had I cared to look, that that hope only was keeping her alive. She grew more wan and thin month by month. You will agree with me, at least, that such conduct would have driven anyone to despair. It was uncalled for; childish; unwomanly. I maintain that she was much to blame. And again, sometimes, in the black, fever-stricken night-watches, I have begun to think that I might have been a little kinder to her. But that really is a 'delusion'. I could not have continued pretending to love her when I didn't; could I? It would have been unfair to us both.

Last year we met again – on the same terms as before. The same weary appeals, and the same curt answers from my lips. At least I would make her see how wholly wrong and hopeless were her attempts at resuming the old relationship. As the season wore on, we fell apart – that is to say, she found it difficult to meet me, for I had other and more absorbing interests to attend to. When I think it over quietly in my sickroom, the season of 1884 seems a confused nightmare wherein light and shade were fantastically intermingled: my courtship of little Kitty Mannering; my hopes, doubts, and fears; our long rides together; my trembling avowal of attachment; her reply; and now and again a vision of a white face flitting by in the rickshaw with the black and white liveries I once watched for so earnestly; the wave of Mrs Wessington's gloved hand; and, when she met me alone, which was but seldom, the irksome monotony of her appeal. I loved Kitty Mannering; honestly, heartily loved her, and with my love for her grew my hatred for Agnes. In August Kitty and I were engaged. The next day I met those accursed 'magpie' *jhampanies* at the back of Jakko, and, moved by some passing sentiment of pity, stopped to tell Mrs Wessington everything. She knew it already.

'So I hear you're engaged, Jack, dear.' Then, without a moment's pause: 'I'm sure it's all a mistake – a hideous mistake. We shall be as good friends some day, Jack, as we ever were.'

My answer might have made even a man wince. It cut the

dying women before me like the blow of a whip. 'Please forgive me, Jack; I didn't mean to make you angry; but it's true, it's true!'

And Mrs Wessington broke down completely. I turned away and left her to finish her journey in peace, feeling, but only for a moment or two, that I had been an unutterably mean hound. I looked back, and saw that she had turned her rickshaw with the idea, I suppose, of overtaking me.

The scene and its surroundings were photographed on my memory. The rain-swept sky (we were at the end of the wet weather), the sodden, dingy pines, the muddy road, and the black powder-riven cliffs formed a gloomy background against which the black and white liveries of the *jhampanies*, the yellow-panelled rickshaw, and Mrs Wessington's down-bowed golden head stood out clearly. She was holding her handkerchief in her left hand and was leaning back exhausted against the rickshaw cushions. I turned my horse up a bypath near the Sanjowlie Reservoir and literally ran away. Once I fancied I heard a faint call of 'Jack!' This may have been imagination. I never stopped to verify it. Ten minutes later I came across Kitty on horseback; and, in the delight of a long ride with her, forgot all about the interview.

A week later Mrs Wessington died, and the inexpressible burden of her existence was removed from my life. I went Plainsward perfectly happy. Before three months were over I had forgotten all about her, except that at times the discovery of some of her old letters reminded me unpleasantly of our bygone relationship. By January I had disinterred what was left of our correspondence from among my scattered belongings and had burnt it. At the beginning of April of this year, 1885, I was at Simla – semi-deserted Simla – once more, and was deep in lover's talks and walks with Kitty. It was decided that we should be married at the end of June. You will understand, therefore, that loving Kitty as I did, I am not saying too much when I pronounce myself to have been, at that time, the happiest man in India.

Fourteen delightful days passed almost before I noticed their flight. Then, aroused to the sense of what was proper among mortals circumstanced as we were, I pointed out to Kitty that an engagement ring was the outward and visible sign[9] of her dignity as an engaged girl; and that she must forthwith come to Hamilton's to be measured for one. Up to that moment, I give you my word, we had completely forgotten so trivial a matter. To Hamilton's we accordingly went on the 15th of April 1885. Remember that – whatever my doctor may say to the contrary – I was then in perfect health, enjoying a well-balanced mind and an *absolutely* tranquil spirit. Kitty and I entered Hamilton's shop together, and there, regardless of the order of affairs, I measured Kitty for the ring in the presence of the amused assistant. The ring was a sapphire with two diamonds. We then rode out down the slope that leads to the Combermere Bridge and Peliti's shop.

While my Waler was cautiously feeling his way over the loose shale, and Kitty was laughing and chattering at my side – while all Simla, that is to say as much of it as had then come from the Plains, was grouped round the Reading-room and Peliti's verandah – I was aware that someone, apparently at a vast distance, was calling me by my Christian name. It struck me that I had heard the voice before, but when and where I could not at once determine. In the short space it took to cover the road between the path from Hamilton's shop and the first plank of the Combermere Bridge I had thought over half-a-dozen people who might have committed such a solecism, and had eventually decided that it must have been some singing in my ears. Immediately opposite Peliti's shop my eye was arrested by the sight of four *jhampanies* in 'magpie' livery, pulling a yellow-panelled, cheap, bazar rickshaw. In a moment my mind flew back to the previous season and Mrs Wessington with a sense of irritation and disgust. Was it not enough that the woman was dead and done with, without her black and white servitors reappearing to spoil the day's happiness? Whoever employed them now I thought I would call upon, and ask as a personal favour to change her *jhampanies'* livery. I would hire the men myself, and, if necessary, buy their coats from off their backs. It is impossible to say here what a flood of undesirable memories their presence evoked.

'Kitty,' I cried, 'there are poor Mrs Wessington's *jhampanies* turned up again! I wonder who has them now?'

Kitty had known Mrs Wessington slightly last season, and had always been interested in the sickly woman.

'What? Where?' she asked. 'I can't see them anywhere.'

Even as she spoke, her horse, swerving from a laden mule, threw himself directly in front of the advancing rickshaw. I had scarcely time to utter a word of warning when, to my unutterable horror, horse and rider passed *through* men and carriage as if they had been thin air.

'What's the matter?' cried Kitty; 'what made you call out so foolishly, Jack? If I *am* engaged I don't want all creation to know about it. There was lots of space between the mule and the verandah; and, if you think I can't ride – There!'

Whereupon wilful Kitty set off, her dainty little head in the air, at a hand-gallop in the direction of the Band-stand; fully expecting, as she herself afterwards told me, that I should follow her. What was the matter? Nothing indeed. Either that I was mad or drunk, or that Simla was haunted with devils. I reined in my impatient cob, and turned round. The rickshaw had turned too, and now stood immediately facing me, near the left railing of the Combermere Bridge.

'Jack! Jack, darling!' (There was no mistake about the words this time: they rang through my brain as if they had been shouted in my ear.) 'It's some hideous mistake, I'm sure. *Please* forgive me, Jack, and let's be friends again.'

The rickshaw-hood had fallen back, and inside, as I hope and pray daily for the death I dread by night, sat Mrs Keith-Wessington, handkerchief in hand, and golden head bowed on her breast.

How long I stared motionless I do not know. Finally, I was aroused by my syce [10] taking the Waler's bridle and asking whether I was ill. From the horrible to the commonplace is but a step. [11] I tumbled off my horse and dashed, half fainting, into Peliti's for a glass of cherry-brandy. There two or three couples were gathered round the coffee-tables discussing the gossip of the day. Their trivialities were more comforting to me just then than the consolations of religion could have been. I plunged into the midst of the conversation at once; chatted, laughed, and jested with a face (when I caught a glimpse of it in a mirror) as white and drawn as that of a corpse. Three or four men noticed my condition; and, evidently setting it down to the results of over-many pegs,[12] charitably endeavoured to draw me apart from the rest of the loungers. But I refused to be led away. I wanted the company of my kind – as a child rushes into the midst of the dinner-party after a fright in the dark. I must have talked for about ten minutes or so, though it seemed an eternity to me, when I heard Kitty's clear voice outside inquiring for me. In another minute she had entered the shop, prepared to upbraid me for failing so signally in my duties. Something in my face stoped her.

'Why, Jack,' she cried, 'what *have* you been doing? What *has* happened? Are you ill?' Thus driven into a direct lie, I said that the sun had been a little too much for me. It was close upon five o'clock of a cloudy April afternoon, and the sun had been hidden all day. I saw my mistake as soon as the words were out of my mouth; attempted to recover it; blundered hopelessly, and followed Kitty in a regal rage out of doors, amid the smiles of my acquaintances. I made some excuse (I have forgotten what) on the score of my feeling faint; and cantered away to my hotel, leaving Kitty to finish the ride by herself.

In my room I sat down and tried calmly to reason out the matter. Here was I, Theobald Jack Pansay, a well-educated Bengal Civilian in the year of grace 1885, presumably sane, certainly healthy, driven in terror from my sweetheart's side by the apparition of a woman who had been dead and buried eight months ago. These were facts that I could not blink. Nothing was farther from my thought than any memory of Mrs Wessington when Kitty and I left Hamilton's shop. Nothing was more utterly commonplace than the stretch of wall opposite Peliti's. It was broad daylight. The road was full of people; and yet here, look you, in defiance of every law of probability, in direct outrage of Nature's ordinance, there had appeared to me a face from the grave.

Kitty's Arab had gone *through* the rickshaw: so that my first hope that some woman marvellously like Mrs Wessington had hired the carriage and the coolies with their old livery was lost. Again and again I went round this treadmill of thought; and again and again gave up baffled and in despair. The voice was as inexplicable as the apparition. I had originally some wild notion of confiding it all to Kitty; of begging her to marry me at once, and in her arms defying the ghostly occupant of the rickshaw. 'After all,' I argued, 'the presence of the rickshaw is in itself enough to prove the existence of a spectral illusion. One may see ghosts of men and women, but surely never coolies and carriages. The whole thing is absurd. Fancy the ghost of a hill-man!'

Next morning I sent a penitent note to Kitty, imploring her to overlook my strange conduct of the previous afternoon. My Divinity was still very wroth, and a personal apology was necessary. I explained, with a personal apology born of night-long pondering over a falsehood, that I had been attacked with a sudden palpitation of the heart – the result of indigestion. This eminently practical solution had its effect; and Kitty and I rode out that afternoon with the shadow of my first lie dividing us.

Nothing would please her save a canter round Jakko. With my nerves still unstrung from the previous night I feebly protested against the notion, suggesting Observatory Hill, Jutogh, the Boileaugunge road – anything rather than the Jakko round. Kitty was angry and a little hurt; so I yielded from fear of provoking further misunderstanding, and we set out together towards Chota Simla. We walked a greater part of the way, and according to our custom, cantered from a mile or so below the Convent to the stretch of level road by the Sanjowlie Reservoir. The wretched horses appeared to fly, and my heart beat quicker and quicker as we neared the crest of the ascent. My mind had been full of Mrs Wessington all the afternoon; and every inch of the Jakko road bore witness to our old-time walks and talks. The boulders were full of it; the pines sang it aloud overhead;

the rain-fed torrents giggled and chuckled unseen over the shameful story; and the wind in my ears chanted the iniquity aloud.

As a fitting climax, in the middle of the level men call the Ladies' Mile the Horror was awaiting me. No other rickshaw was in sight – only the four black and white *jhampanies*, the yellow-panelled carriage, and the golden head of the woman within – all apparently just as I had left them eight months and one fortnight ago! For an instant I fancied that Kitty *must* see what I saw – we were so marvellously sympathetic in all things. Her next words undeceived me – 'Not a soul in sight! Come along, Jack, and I'll race you to the Reservoir buildings!' Her wiry little Arab was off like a bird, my Waler following close behind, and in this order we dashed under the cliffs. Half a minute brought us within fifty yards of the rickshaw. I pulled my Waler and fell back a little. The rickshaw was directly in the middle of the road; and once more the Arab passed through it, my horse following. 'Jack! Jack dear! *Please* forgive me,' rang with a wail in my ears, and, after an interval: 'It's all a mistake, a hideous mistake!'

I spurred my horse like a man possessed. When I turned my head at the Reservoir works the black and white liveries were still waiting – patiently waiting – under the grey hillside, and the wind brought me the mocking echo of the words I had just heard. Kitty bantered me a good deal on my silence throughout the remainder of the ride. I had been talking up till then wildly and at random. To save my life I could not speak afterwards naturally, and from Sanjowlie to the Church wisely held my tongue.

I was to dine with the Mannerings that night, and had barely time to canter home to dress. On the road to Elysium Hill I overheard two men talking together in the dusk – 'It's a curious thing,' said one, 'how completely all trace of it disappeared. You know my wife was insanely fond of the woman ('never could see anything in her myself), and wanted me to pick up her old rickshaw and coolies if they were to be got for love or money. Morbid sort of fancy I call it; but I've got to do what the *Memsahib* tells me. Would you believe that the man she hired it from tells me that all four of the men – they were brothers – died of cholera on the way to Hardwar, poor devils; and the rickshaw has been broken up by the man himself. 'Told me he never used a dead *Memsahib*'s rickshaw. 'Spoilt his luck. Queer notion, wasn't it? Fancy poor little Mrs Wessington spoiling anyone's luck except her own!' I laughed aloud at this point; and my laugh jarred on me as I uttered it. So there *were* ghosts of rickshaws after all, and ghostly employments in the other world! How much did Mrs Wessington give her men? What were their hours? Where did they go?

And for visible answer to my last question I saw the infernal Thing blocking my path in the twilight. The dead travel fast, and by short cuts unknown to ordinary coolies. I laughed aloud a second time and checked my laughter suddenly, for I was afraid I was going mad. Mad to a certain extent I must have been, for I recollect that I reined in my horse at the head of the rickshaw, and politely wished Mrs Wessington 'Good-evening'. Her answer was one I knew only too well. I listened to the end; and replied that I had heard it all before, but should be delighted if she had anything further to say. Some malignant devil stronger than I must have entered into me that evening, for I have a dim recollection of talking the commonplaces of the day for five minutes to the Thing in front of me.

'Mad as a hatter, poor devil – or drunk. Max, try and get him to come home.'

Surely *that* was not Mrs Wessington's voice! The two men had overhead me speaking to the empty air, and had returned to look after me. They were very kind and considerate, and from their words evidently gathered that I was extremely drunk. I thanked them confusedly and cantered away to my hotel, there changed, and arrived at the Mannerings' ten minutes late. I pleaded the darkness of the night as an excuse; was rebuked by Kitty for my unlover-like tardiness; and sat down.

The conversation had already become general; and, under cover of it, I was addressing some tender small talk to my sweetheart when I was aware that at the farther end of the table a short, red-whiskered man was describing, with much embroidery, his encounter with a mad unknown that evening.

A few sentences convinced me that he was repeating the incident of half an hour ago. In the middle of the story he looked round for applause, as professional story-tellers do, caught my eye, and straightway collapsed. There was a moment's awkward silence, and the red-whiskered man muttered something to the effect that he had 'forgotten the rest', thereby sacrificing a reputation as a good story-teller which he had built up for six seasons past. I blessed him from the bottom of my heart, and – went on with my fish.

In the fulness of time that dinner came to an end; and with genuine regret I tore myself away from Kitty – as certain as I was of my own existence that It would be waiting for me outside the door. The red-whiskered man, who had been introduced to me as Dr Heatherlegh of Simla, volunteered to bear me company as far as our roads lay together. I accepted his offer with gratitude.

My instinct had not deceived me. It lay in readiness in the Mall, and, in what seemed devilish mockery of our ways, with a lighted head-lamp. The red-whiskered man went to the point at once, in a manner that showed he had been thinking over it all dinner-time.

'I say, Pansay, what the deuce was the matter with you this evening on the Elysium Road?' The suddenness of the question wrenched an answer from me before I was aware.

'That!' said I, pointing to It.

'*That* may be either D.T. or Eyes for aught I know. Now you don't liquor. I saw as much at dinner, so it can't be D.T. There's nothing whatever where you're pointing, though you're sweating and trembling with fright like a scared pony. Therefore, I conclude that it's Eyes. And I ought to understand all about them. Come along home with me. I'm on the Blessington lower road.'

To my intense delight the rickshaw, instead of waiting for us kept about twenty yards ahead – and this, too, whether we walked, trotted, or cantered. In the course of that long night ride I had told my companion almost as much as I have told you here.

'Well, you've spoilt one of the best tales I've ever laid tongue to,' said he, 'but I'll forgive you for the sake of what you've gone through. Now come home and do what I tell you; and when I've cured you, young man, let this be a lesson to you to steer clear of women and indigestible food till the day of your death.'

The rickshaw kept steady in front; and my red-whiskered friend seemed to derive great pleasure from my account of it's exact whereabouts.

'Eyes, Pansay – all Eyes, Brain, and Stomach. And the greatest of these three is Stomach. You've too much conceited Brain, too little Stomach, and thoroughly unhealthy Eyes. Get your Stomach straight and the rest follows. And all that's French for a liver pill. I'll take sole medical charge of you from this hour! for you're too interesting a phenomenon to be passed over.'

By this time we were deep in the shadow of the Blessington lower road, and the rickshaw came to a dead stop under a pine-clad, overhanging shale cliff. Instinctively I halted too, giving my reason. Heatherlegh rapped out an oath.

'Now, if you think I'm going to spend a cold night on the hillside for the sake of a Stomach-*cum*-Brain-*cum*-Eye illusion – Lord, ha' mercy! What's that?'

There was a muffled report, a blinding smother of dust just in front of us, a crack, the noise of rent boughs, and about ten yards of the cliff-side – pines, undergrowth, and all – slid down into the road below, completely blocking it up. The uprooted trees swayed and tottered for a moment like drunken giants in the gloom, and then fell prone among their fellows with a thunderous crash. Our two horses stood motionless and sweating with fear. As soon as the rattle of falling earth and stone had subsided, my companion muttered: 'Man, if we'd gone forward we should have been ten feet deep in our graves by now. "There are more things in heaven and earth"[13] . . . Come home, Pansay, and thank God. I want a peg badly.'

We retraced our way over the Church Ridge, and I arrived at Dr Heatherlegh's house shortly after midnight.

His attempts towards my cure commenced almost immediately, and for a week I never left his sight. Many a time in the course of that week did I bless the good-fortune which had thrown me in contact with Simla's best and kindest doctor. Day by day my spirits grew lighter and more equable. Day by day, too, I became more and more inclined to fall in with Heatherlegh's 'spectral illusion'[14] theory, implicating eyes, brain, and stomach. I wrote to Kitty, telling her that a slight sprain caused by a fall from my horse kept me indoors for a few days; and that I should be recovered before she had time to regret my absence.

Heatherlegh's treatment was simple to a degree. It consisted of liver pills, cold-water baths, and strong exercise, taken in the dusk or at early dawn – for, as he sagely observed: 'A man with a sprained ankle doesn't walk a dozen miles a day, and your young woman might be wondering if she saw you.'

At the end of the week, after much examination of pupil and pulse, and strict injunctions as to diet and pedestrianism, Heatherlegh dismissed me as brusquely as he had taken charge of me. Here is his parting benediction: 'Man, I certify to your mental cure, and that's as much as to say I've cured most of your bodily ailments. Now, get your traps out of this as soon as you can; and be off to make love to Miss Kitty.'

I was endeavouring to express my thanks for his kindness. He cut me short.

'Don't think I did this because I like you. I gather that you've behaved like a blackguard all through. But, all the same, you're a phenomenon, and as queer a phenomenon as you are a blackguard. No!' – checking me a second time – 'not a rupee, please. Go out and see if you can find the eyes-brain-and-stomach business again. I'll give you a lakh for each time you see it.'

Half an hour later I was in the Mannerings' drawing-room with Kitty – drunk with the intoxication of present happiness and the foreknowledge that I should never more be troubled with Its hideous presence. Strong in the sense of my newfound security, I proposed a ride at once; and, by preference, a canter round Jakko.

Never had I felt so well, so overladen with vitality and mere animal spirits, as I did on the afternoon of the 30th of April. Kitty was delighted at the change in my appearance, and complimented me on it in her delightfully frank and outspoken manner. We left the Mannerings' house together, laughing and talking, and cantered along the Chota Simla road as of old.

I was in haste to reach the Sanjowlie Reservoir and there to make my assurance doubly sure. The horses did their best, but seemed all too slow to my impatient mind. Kitty was astonished at my boisterousness. 'Why, Jack!' she cried at last, 'you are behaving like a child. What are you doing?'

We were just below the Convent, and from sheer wantonness I was making my Waler plunge and curvet across the road as I tickled it with the loop of my riding-whip.

'Doing?' I answered; 'nothing, dear. That's just it. If you'd been doing nothing for a week except lie up, you'd be as riotous as I.

> 'Singing and murmuring in your feastful mirth,
>   Joying to feel yourself alive;
> Lord over Nature, Lord of the visible Earth,
>   Lord of the senses five.'[15]

My quotation was hardly out of my lips before we had rounded the corner above the Convent, and a few yards on could see across to Sanjowlie. In the centre of the level road stood the black and white liveries, the yellow-panelled rickshaw, and Mrs Keith-Wessington. I pulled up, looked, rubbed my eyes, and, I believe, must have said something. The next thing I knew was that I was lying face downward on the road, with Kitty kneeling above me in tears.

'Has it gone, child!' I gasped. Kitty only wept more bitterly.

'Has what gone, Jack dear? what does it all mean? There must be some hideous mistake somewhere, Jack. A hideous mistake.' Her last words brought me to my feet – mad – raving for the time being.

'Yes, there *is* a mistake somewhere,' I repeated, 'a hideous mistake. Come and look at It.'

I have an indistinct idea that I dragged Kitty by the wrist

along the road up to where It stood, and implored her for pity's sake to speak to It; to tell It that we were betrothed; that neither Death nor Hell could break the tie between us: and Kitty only knows how much more to the same effect. Now and again I appealed passionately to the Terror in the rickshaw to bear witness to all I had said, and to release me from a torture that was killing me. As I talked I suppose I must have told Kitty of my old relations with Mrs Wessington, for I saw her listen intently with white face and blazing eyes.

'Thank you, Mr Pansay,' she said, 'that's *quite* enough. *Syce ghora láo.*'[16]

The syces, impassive as Orientals always are, had come up with the recaptured horses; and as Kitty sprang into her saddle I caught hold of her bridle, entreating her to hear me out and forgive. My answer was the cut of her riding-whip across my face from mouth to eye, and a word or two of farewell that even now I cannot write down. So I judged, and judged rightly, that Kitty knew all; and I staggered back to the side of the rickshaw. My face was cut and bleeding, and the blow of the riding-whip had raised a livid blue wheal on it. I had no self-respect. Just then, Heatherlegh, who must have been following Kitty and me at a distance, cantered up.

'Doctor,' I said, pointing to my face, 'here's Miss Mannering's signature to my order of dismissal and – I'll thank you for that lakh as soon as convenient.'

Heatherlegh's face, even in my abject misery, moved me to laughter.

'I'll stake my professional reputation –' he began.

'Don't be a fool,' I whispered. 'I've lost my life's happiness and you'd better take me home.'

As I spoke the rickshaw was gone. Then I lost all knowledge of what was passing. The crest of Jakko seemed to heave and roll like the crest of a cloud and fall in upon me.

Seven days later (on the 7th of May, that is to say) I was aware that I was lying in Heatherlegh's room as weak as a little child. Heatherlegh was watching me intently from behind the papers on his writing-table. His first words were not encouraging; but I was too far spent to be much moved by them.

'Here's Miss Kitty has sent back your letters. You corresponded a good deal, you young people. Here's a packet that looks like a ring, and a cheerful sort of a note from Mannering Papa, which, I've taken the liberty of reading and burning. The old gentleman's not pleased with you.'

'And Kitty?' I asked dully.

'Rather more drawn than her father from what she says. By the same token you must have been letting out any number of queer reminiscences just before I met you. 'Says that a man who would have behaved to a woman as you did to Mrs Wessington ought to kill himself out of sheer pity for his kind. She's a hot-headed little virago, your mash. 'Will have it too that you were suffering from D.T. when that row on the Jakko road turned up. 'Says she'll die before she ever speaks to you again.'

I groaned and turned over on the other side.

'Now you've got your choice, my friend. This engagement has to be broken off; and the Mannerings don't want to be too hard on you. Was it broken through D.T. or epileptic fits? Sorry I can't offer you a better exchange unless you'd prefer hereditary insanity. Say the word and I'll tell 'em it's fits. All Simla knows about that scene on the Ladies' Mile. Come! I'll give you five minutes to think over it.'

During those five minutes I believe that I explored thoroughly the lowest circles of the Inferno which it is permitted man to tread on earth. And at the same time I myself was watching myself faltering through the dark labyrinths of doubt, misery, and utter despair. I wondered, as Heatherlegh in his chair might have wondered, which dreadful alternative I should adopt. Presently I heard myself answering in a voice that I hardly recognized –

'They're confoundedly particular about morality in these parts. Give 'em fits, Heatherlegh, and my love. Now let me sleep a bit longer.'

Then my two selves joined, and it was only I (half-crazed, devil-driven I) that tossed in my bed tracing step by step the history of the past month.

'But I am in Simla,' I kept repeating to myself. 'I, Jack

Pansay, am in Simla, and there are no ghosts here. It's unreasonable of that woman to pretend there are. Why couldn't Agnes have left me alone? I never did her any harm. It might just as well have been me as well as Agnes. Only I'd never have come back on purpose to kill *her*. Why can't I be left alone – left alone and happy?'

It was the high noon when I first awoke; and the sun was low in the sky before I slept – slept as the tortured criminal sleeps on his rack, too worn to feel further pain.

Next day I could not leave my bed. Heatherlegh told me in the morning that he had received an answer from Mr Mannering, and that, thanks to his (Heatherlegh's) friendly offices, the story of my affliction had travelled through the length and breadth of Simla, where I was on all sides much pitied.

'And that's rather more than you deserve,' he concluded pleasantly, 'though the Lord knows you've been going through a pretty severe mill. Never mind; we'll cure you yet, you perverse phenomenon.'

I declined firmly to be cured. 'You've been much too good to me already, old man,' said I; 'but I don't think I need trouble you further.'

In my heart I knew that nothing Heatherlegh could do would lighten the burden that had been laid upon me.

With that knowledge came also a sense of hopeless, impotent rebellion against the unreasonableness of it all. There were scores of men no better than I whose punishments had at least been reserved for another world; and I felt that it was bitterly, cruelly unfair that I alone should have been singled out for so hideous a fate. This mood would in time give place to another where it seemed that the rickshaw and I were the only realities in a world of shadows; that Kitty was a ghost; that Mannering, Heatherlegh, and all the other men and women I knew were all ghosts; and the great grey hills themselves but vain shadows devised to torture me. From mood to mood I tossed backwards and forwards for seven weary days; my body growing daily stronger and stronger, until the bedroom looking-glass told me that I had returned to everyday life, and was as other men once more. Curiously enough my face showed no signs of the struggle I had gone through. It was pale indeed, but as expressionless and commonplace as ever. I had expected some permanent alteration – visible evidence of the disease that was eating me away. I found nothing.

On the 15th of May I left Heatherlegh's house at eleven o'clock in the morning; and the instinct of the bachelor drove me to the Club. There I found that every man knew my story as told by Heatherlegh, and was, in clumsy fashion, abnormally kind and attentive. Nevertheless I recognized that for the rest of my natural life I should be among but not of my fellows; and I envied very bitterly indeed the laughing coolies on the Mall below. I lunched at the Club, and at four o'clock wandered aimlessly down the Mall in the vague hope of meeting Kitty. Close to the Band-stand the black and white liveries joined me; and I heard Mrs Wessington's old appeal at my side. I had been expecting this ever since I came out, and was only surprised at her delay. The phantom rickshaw and I went side by side along the Chota Simla road in silence. Close to the bazar, Kitty and a man on horseback overtook and passed us. For any sign she gave I might have been a dog in the road. She did not even pay me the compliment of quickening her pace, though the rainy afternoon had served for an excuse.

So Kitty and her companion, and I and my ghostly Light-o'-Love, crept round Jakko in couples. The road was streaming with water; the pines dripped like roof-pipes on the rocks below, and the air was full of fine driving rain. Two or three times I found myself saying to myself almost aloud: 'I'm Jack Pansay on leave at Simla – *at Simla*! Everyday, ordinary Simla. I mustn't forget that – I mustn't forget that.' Then I would try to recollect some of the gossip I had heard at the Club: the prices of So-and-So's horses – anything, in fact, that related to the workaday Anglo-Indian world I knew so well. I even repeated the multiplication-table rapidly to myself, to make quite sure that I was not taking leave of my senses. It gave me much comfort, and must have prevented my hearing Mrs Wessington for a time.

Once more I wearily climbed the Convent slope and entered the level road. Here Kitty and the man started off at a canter, and I was left alone with Mrs Wessington. 'Agnes,' said I, 'will you put back your hood and tell me what it all means?' The hood dropped noiselessly, and I was face to face with my dead and buried mistress. She was wearing the dress in which I had last seen her alive; carried the same tiny handkerchief in her right hand, and the same card-case in her left. (A woman eight months dead with a card-case!) I had to pin myself down to the multiplication-table, and to set both hands on the stone parapet of the road, to assure myself that that at least was real.

'Agnes,' I repeated, 'for pity's sake tell me what it all means.' Mrs Wessington leaned forward, with that odd, quick turn of the head I used to know so well, and spoke.

If my story had not already so madly overleaped the bounds of all human belief I should apologize to you now. As I know that no one – no, not even Kitty, for whom it is written as some sort of justification of my conduct – will believe me, I will go on. Mrs Wessington spoke, and I walked with her from the Sanjowlic road to the turning below the Commander-in-Chief's house as I might walk by the side of any living woman's rickshaw, deep in conversation. The second and most tormenting of my moods of sickness had suddenly laid hold upon me, and, like the Prince in Tennyson's poem,[17] 'I seemed to move amid a world of ghosts.' There had been a garden-party at the Commander-in-Chief's, and we two joined the crowd of homeward-bound folk. As I saw them it seemed that *they* were the shadows – impalpable fantastic shadows – that divided for Mrs Wessington's rickshaw to pass through. What we said during the course of that weird interview I cannot – indeed, I dare not – tell. Heatherlegh's comment would have been a short laugh and a remark that I had been 'mashing a brain-eye-and-stomach chimera'. It was a ghastly and yet in some indefinable way a marvellously dear experience. Could it be possible, I wondered, that I was in this life to woo a second time the woman I had killed by my own neglect and cruelty?

I met Kitty on the homeward road – a shadow among shadows.

If I were to describe all the incidents of the next fortnight in their order, my story would never come to an end, and your patience would be exhausted. Morning after morning and evening after evening the ghostly rickshaw and I used to wander through Simla together. Wherever I went there the four black and white liveries followed me and bore me company to and from my hotel. At the Theatre I found them amid the crowd of yelling *jhampanies*; outside the Club verandah, after a long evening of whist; at the Birthday Ball, waiting patiently for my reappearance; and in broad daylight when I went calling. Save that it cast no shadow, the rickshaw was in every respect as real to look upon as one of wood and iron. More than once, indeed, I have had to check myself from warning some hard-riding friend against cantering over it. More than once I have walked down the Mall deep in conversaion with Mrs Wessington, to the unspeakable amazement of the passers-by.

Before I had been out and about a week I learned that the 'fit' theory had been discarded in favour of insanity. However, I made no change in my mode of life. I called, rode, and dined out as freely as ever. I had a passion for the society of my kind which I had never felt before; I hungered to be among the realities of life; and at the same time I felt vaguely unhappy when I had been separated too long from my ghostly companion. It would be almost impossible to describe my varying moods from the 15th of May up to today.

The presence of the rickshaw filled me by turns with horror, blind fear, a dim sort of pleasure, and utter despair. I dared not leave Simla; and I knew that my stay there was killing me. I knew, moreover, that it was my destiny to die slowly and a little every day. My only anxiety was to get the penance over as quietly as might be. Alternatively I hungered for a sight of Kitty, and watched her outrageous flirtations with my successor – to speak more accurately, my successors – with amused interest. She was as much out of my life as I was out of hers. By day I wandered with Mrs Wessington almost content. By night I implored Heaven to let me return to the world as I used to know it. Above all these varying moods lay the sensation of dull, numbing wonder that the seen and the Unseen should mingle so strangely on this earth to hound one poor soul to the grave.

August 27. – Heatherlegh has been indefatigable in his attendance on me; and only yesterday told me that I ought to send in an application for sick leave. An application to escape the company of a phantom! A request that the Government would graciously permit me to get rid of five ghosts and an airy rickshaw by going to England! Heatherlegh's proposition moved me to almost hysterical laughter. I told him that I should await the end quietly at Simla; and I am sure that the end is not far off. Believe me that I dread its advent more than any word can say; and I torture myself nightly with a thousand speculations as to the manner of my death.

Shall I die in my bed decently as an English gentleman should die; or, in one last walk on the Mall, will my soul be wrenched from me to take its place for ever and ever by the side of that ghastly phantasm? Shall I return to my old lost allegiance in the next world, or shall I meet Agnes loathing her and bound to her side through all eternity? Shall we two hover over the scene of our lives till the end of Time? As the day of my death draws nearer, the intense horror that all living flesh feels toward escaped spirits from beyond the grave grows more and more powerful. It is an awful thing to go down quick among the dead with scarcely one-half of your life completed. It is a thousand times more awful to wait as I do in your midst, for I know not what unimaginable terror. Pity me, at least on the score of my 'delusion', for I know you will never believe what I have written here. Yet as surely as ever a man was done to death by the Powers of Darkness I am that man.

In justice, too, pity her. For as surely as ever woman was killed by man, I killed Mrs Wessington. And the last portion of my punishment is even now upon me.

{ My Own True Ghost Story[1] }

As I came through the Desert thus it was –
As I came through the Desert.[2]
The City of Dreadful Night

This story deals entirely with ghosts. There are, in India, ghosts
who take the form of fat, cold, pobby[3] corpses, and hide in trees
near the roadside till a traveller passes. Then they drop upon
his neck and remain. There are also terrible ghosts of women
who have died in childbed. These wander along the pathways at
dusk, or hide in the crops near a village, and call seductively.
But to answer their call is death in this world and the next.
Their feet are turned backwards that all sober men may recognize them. There are ghosts of little children who have been
thrown into wells. These haunt well-curbs and the fringes of
jungles, and wail under the stars, or catch women by the wrist
and beg to be taken up and carried. These and the corpse-
ghosts, however, are only vernacular articles and do not attack
Sahibs. No native ghost has yet been authentically reported to
have frightened an Englishman; but many English ghosts have
scared the life out of both white and black.

Nearly every other Station owns a ghost. There are said to be
two at Simla, not counting the woman who blows the bellows at
Syree dâk-bungalow on the Old Road; Mussoorie has a house
haunted by a very lively Thing; a White Lady is supposed to do
night-watchman round a house in Lahore; Dalhousie says that
one of her houses 'repeats' on autumn evenings all the incidents
of a horrible horse-and-precipice accident; Murree has a merry
ghost, and, now that she has been swept by cholera, will have
room for a sorrowful one; there are Officers' Quarters in Mian
Mir whose doors open without reason, and whose furniture is

guaranteed to creak, not with the heat of June, but with the weight of Invisibles who come to lounge in the chairs; Peshawar possesses houses that none will willingly rent; and there is something – not fever – wrong with a big bungalow in Allahabad. The older Provinces[4] simply bristle with haunted houses, and march phantom armies along their main thoroughfares.

Some of the dâk bungalows on the Grand Trunk Road have handy little cemeteries in their compound – witnesses to the 'changes and chances of this mortal life'[5] in the days when men drove from Calcutta to the North-West. These bungalows are objectionable places to put up in. They are generally very old, always dirty, while the *khansamah*[6] is as ancient as the bungalow. He either chatters senilely, or falls into the long trances of age. In both moods he is useless. If you get angry with him, he refers to some Sahib dead and buried these thirty years, and says that when he was in that Sahib's service not a *khansamah* in the Province could touch him. Then he jabbers and mows and trembles and fidgets among the dishes, and you repent of your irritation.

Not long ago it was my business to live in dâk-bungalows. I never inhabited the same house for three nights running, and grew to be learned in the breed. I lived in Government-built ones with brick walls and rail ceilings, an inventory of the furniture posted in every room, and an excited cobra on the threshold to give welcome. I lived in 'converted' ones – old houses officiating as dâk-bungalows – where nothing was in its proper place and there was not even a fowl for dinner. I lived in second-hand palaces where the wind blew through open-work marble tracery just as uncomfortably as through a broken pane. I lived in dâk-bungalows where the last entry in the visitor's book was fifteen months old, and where they slashed off the curry-kid's head with a sword. It was my good luck to meet all sorts of men, from sober travelling missionaries and deserters flying from British Regiments, to drunken loafers who threw whisky bottles at all who passed; and my still greater good fortune just to escape a maternity case. Seeing that a fair proportion of the tragedy of our lives in India acted itself in dâk-bungalows, I wondered that I had met no ghosts. A ghost that would voluntarily hang about a dâk-bungalow would be mad, of course; but so many men have died mad in dâk-bungalows that there must be a fair percentage of lunatic ghosts.

In due time I found my ghost, or ghosts rather, for there were two of them.[7]

We will call the bungalow Katmal dâk-bungalow; but *that* was the smallest part of the horror. A man with a sensitive hide has no right to sleep in dâk-bungalows. He should marry. Katmal dâk-bungalow was old and rotten and unrepaired. The floor was of worn brick, the walls were filthy, and the windows were nearly black with grime. It stood on a bypath largely used by native Sub-Deputy Assistants of all kinds, from Finance to Forests; but real Sahibs were rare.[8] The *khansamah*, who was bent nearly double with old age, said so.

When I arrived, there was a fitful, undecided rain on the face of the land, accompanied by a restless wind, and every gust made a noise like a rattling of dry bones in the stiff toddy-palms outside. The *khansamah* completely lost his head on my arrival. He had served a Sahib once. Did I know that Sahib? He gave me the name of a well-known man who has been buried for more than a quarter of a century, and showed me an ancient daguerreotype of that man in his prehistoric youth. I had seen a steel engraving of him at the head of a double volume of Memoirs[9] a month before, and I felt ancient beyond telling.

The day shut in and the *khansamah* went to get me food. He did not go through the pretence of calling it '*khana*', – man's victuals. He said '*ratub*', and that means, among other things, 'grub' – dog's rations. There was no insult in his choice of the term. He had forgotten the other word, I suppose.

While he was cutting up the dead bodies of animals, I settled myself down, after exploring the dâk-bungalow. There were three rooms besides my own, which was a corner kennel, each giving into the other through dingy white doors fastened with long iron bars. The bungalow was a very solid one, but the partition-walls of the rooms were almost jerry-built in their flimsiness. Every step or bang of a trunk echoed from my room down the other three, and every footfall came back tremulously from the far walls. For this reason I shut the door. There were no lamps —only candles in long glass shades. An oil wick was set in the bathroom.

For bleak, unadulterated misery that dâk-bungalow was the worst of the many that I had ever set foot in. There was no fireplace, and the windows would not open; so a brazier of charcoal would have been useless. The rain and the wind splashed and gurgled and moaned round the house, and the toddy-palms[10] rattled and roared. Half-a-dozen jackals went through the compound singing, and a hyena stood afar off and mocked them. A hyena would convince a Sadducee[11] of the Resurrection of the Dead – the worst sort of Dead. Then came the *ratub* – a curious meal, half native and half English in composition – with the old *khansamah* babbling behind my chair about dead-and-gone English people, and the wind-blown candles playing shadow-bo-peep with the bed and the mosquito-curtains. It was just the sort of dinner and evening to make a man think of every single one of his past sins, and of all the others that he intended to commit if he lived.

Sleep, for several hundred reasons, was not easy. The lamp in the bathroom threw the most absurd shadows into the room, and the wind was beginning to talk nonsense.

Just when the reasons were drowsy with bloodsucking I heard the regular – 'Let-us-take-and-heave-him-over' grunt of the doolie-bearers in the compound. First one doolie came in, then a second, and then a third. I heard the doolies dumped on the ground and the shutter in front of my door shook.

'That's someone trying to come in,' I said. But no one spoke, and I persuaded myself that it was the gusty wind. The shutter of the room next to mine was attacked, flung back, and the inner door opened. 'That's some Sub-Deputy Assistant,' I said, 'and he has brought his friends with him. Now they'll talk and spit and smoke for an hour.'

But there were no voices and no footsteps. No one was putting his luggage into the next room. The door shut, and I thanked Providence that I was to be left in peace. But I was curious to know where the doolies had gone. I got out of bed and looked into the darkness. There was never a sign of a doolie. Just as I was getting into bed again, I heard, in the next room, the sound that no man in his senses can possibly mistake – the whir of a billiard ball down the length of the slate when the striker is stringing for break. No other sound is like it. A minute afterwards there was another whir, and I got into bed. I was not frightened – indeed I was not. I was very curious to know what had become of the doolies. I jumped into bed for that reason.

Next minute I heard the double click of a cannon, and my hair sat up. It is a mistake to say that hair stands up. The skin of the head tightens, and you can feel a faint, prickly bristling all over the scalp. That is the hair sitting up.

There was a whir and a click, and both sounds could only have been made by one thing – a billiard ball. I argued the matter out at great length with myself; and the more I argued the less probable it seemed that one bed, one table and two chairs – all the furniture of the room next to mine – could so exactly duplicate the sounds of a game of billiards. After another cannon, a three-cushion one to judge by the whir, I argued no more. I had found my ghost, and would have given worlds to have escaped from that dâk-bungalow. I listened, and with each listen the game grew clearer. There was whir on whir and click on click. Sometimes there was a double click and a whir and another click. Beyond any sort of doubt, people were playing billiards in the next room. And the next room was not big enough to hold a billiard table!

Between the pauses of the wind I heard the game go forward – stroke after stroke. I tried to believe that I could not hear voices; but that attempt was a failure.

Do you know what fear is? Not ordinary fear of insult, injury, or death, but abject, quivering dread of something that you cannot see – fear that dries the inside of the mouth and half of the throat – fear that makes you sweat on the palms of the hands, and gulp in order to keep the uvula at work? This is a fine Fear – a great cowardice, and must be felt to be appreciated. The very improbability of billiards in a dâk-bungalow proved the reality of the thing. No man – drunk or sober – could imagine a game at billiards, or invent the spitting crack of a 'screw cannon'.

A severe course of dâk-bungalows has this disadvantage – it breeds infinite credulity. If a man said to a confirmed dâk-bungalow-haunter: 'There is a corpse in the next room, and there's a mad girl in the next one, and the woman and man on that camel have just eloped from a place sixty miles away,' the hearer would not disbelieve, because he would know that nothing is too wild, grotesque, or horrible to happen in a dâk-bungalow.

This credulity, unfortunately, extends to ghosts. A rational person fresh from his own house would have turned on his side and slept. I did not. So surely as I was given up for a dry carcase by the scores of things in the bed, because the bulk of my blood was in my heart, so surely did I hear every stroke of a long game at billiards played in the echoing room behind the iron-barred door. My dominant fear was that the players might want a marker. It was an absurd fear; because creatures who could play in the dark would be above such superfluities. I only know that that was my terror; and it was real.

After a long, long while the game stopped, and the door banged. I slept because I was dead tired. Otherwise I should have preferred to have kept awake. Not for everything in Asia would I have dropped the door-bar and peered into the dark of the next room.

When the morning came I considered that I had done well and wisely, and inquired for the means of departure.

'By the way, *khansamah*,' I said, 'what were those three doolies doing in my compound in the night?'

'There were no doolies,' said the *khansamah*.

I went into the next room, and the daylight streamed through the open door. I was immensely brave. I would, at that hour, have played Black Pool with the owner of the big Black Pool down below.

'Has this place always been a dâk-bungalow?' I asked.

'No,' said the *khansamah*. 'Ten or twenty years ago, I have forgotten how long, it was a billiard room.'

'A what!'

'A billiard room for the Sahibs who built the Railway. I was *khansamah* then in the big house where all the Railway-Sahibs lived, and I used to come across with brandy-*shrab*.[12] These three rooms were all one, and they held a big table on which the Sahibs played every evening. But the Sahibs are all dead now, and the Railway runs, you say, nearly to Kabul.'

'Do you remember anything about the Sahibs?'

'It is long ago, but I remember that one Sahib, a fat man, and always angry, was playing here one night, and he said to me: "Mangal Khan, brandy-*pani do*,"[13] and I filled the glass, and he bent over the table to strike, and his head fell lower and lower till it hit the table, and his spectacles came off, and when we – the Sahibs and I myself – ran to lift him he was dead. I helped to carry him out. Aha, he was a strong Sahib! But he is dead, and I, old Mangal Kahn, am still living, by your favour.'

That was more than enough! I had my ghost – a first-hand, authenticated article. I would write to the Society for Psychical Research[14] – I would paralyse the Empire with the news! But I would, first of all, put eighty miles of assessed crop-land between myself and that dâk-bungalow before nightfall. The Society might send their regular agent to investigate later on.

I went into my own room and prepared to pack, after noting down the facts of the case. As I smoked I heard the game begin again – with a miss in balk this time, for the whir was a short one.

The door was open, and I could see into the room. *Click – click!* That was a cannon, I entered the room without fear, for there was sunlight within and a fresh breeze without. The unseen game was going on at a tremendous rate. And well it might, when a restless little rat was running to and fro inside the dingy ceiling-cloth, and a piece of loose window-sash was making fifty breaks off the window-bolt as it shook in the breeze!

Impossible to mistake the sound of billiard balls! Impossible to mistake the whir of a ball over the slate! But I was to be excused. Even when I shut my enlightened eyes the sound was marvellously like that of a fast game.

Entered angrily the faithful partner of my sorrows, Kadir Baksh.[15]

'This bungalow is very bad and low-caste! No wonder the Presence was disturbed and is speckled. Three sets of doolie-bearers came to the bungalow late last night when I was sleeping outside, and said that it was their custom to rest in the rooms set apart for the English people! What honour has the *khansamah?* They tried to enter, but I told them to go. No wonder, if these *Oorias*[16] have been here, that the Presence is sorely spotted. It is shame, and the work of a dirty man!'

Kadir Baksh did not say that he had taken from each gang two annas for rent in advance, and then, beyond my earshot, had beaten them with the big green umbrella whose use I could never before divine. But Kadir Baksh has no notions of morality.

There was an interview with the *khansamah*, but as he promptly lost his head, wrath gave place to pity, and pity led to a long conversation, in the course of which he put the fat Engineer-Sahib's tragic death in three separate stations – two of them fifty miles away. The third shift was to Calcutta, and there the Sahib died while driving a dog-cart.

I did not go away as soon as I intended. I stayed for the night, while the wind and the rat and the sash and the window-bolt played a ding-dong 'hundred and fifty up'. Then the wind ran out and the billiards stopped, and I felt that I had ruined my one genuine ghost story.

Had I only ceased investigating at the proper time I could have made *anything* out of it.

That was the bitterest thought of all.

⁅ The Strange Ride of Morrowbie Jukes[1] ⁆

Alive or dead – there is no other way.
Native Proverb

There is no invention about this tale.[2] Jukes by accident stumbled upon a village that is well known to exist, though he is the only Englishman who has been there. A somewhat similar institution used to flourish on the outskirts of Calcutta, and there is a story that if you go into the heart of Bikanir, which is in the heart of the Great Indian Desert, you shall come across, not a village, but a town where the Dead who did not die, but may not live, have established their headquarters. And, since it is perfectly true that in the same Desert is a wonderful city where all the rich money-lenders[3] retreat after they have made their fortunes (fortunes so vast that the owners cannot trust even the strong hand of the Government to protect them, but take refuge in the waterless sands), and drive sumptuous C-spring barouches, and buy beautiful girls, and decorate their palaces with gold and ivory and Minton tiles and mother-o'-pearl, I do not see why Jukes's tale should not be true. He is a Civil Engineer, with a head for plans and distances and things of that kind, and he certainly would not take the trouble to invent imaginary traps. He could earn more by doing his legitimate work. He never varies the tale in the telling, and grows very hot and indignant when he thinks of the disrespectful treatment he received. He wrote this quite straightforwardly at first, but he has touched it up in places and introduced Moral Reflections: thus:

In the beginning[4] it all arose from a slight attack of fever. My work necessitated my being in camp for some months between

Pakpattan and Mubarakpur – a desolate sandy stretch of country as every one who has the misfortune to go there may know. My coolies were neither more nor less exasperating than other gangs, and my work demanded sufficient attention to keep me from moping, had I been inclined to so unmanly a weakness.

On the 23rd December 1884[5] I felt a little feverish. There was a full moon at the time, and, in consequence, every dog near my tent was baying it. The brutes assembled in twos or threes and drove me frantic. A few days previously I had shot one loud-mouthed singer and suspended his carcase *in terrorem* about fifty yards from my tent-door, but his friends fell upon, fought for, and ultimately devoured the body; and, as it seemed to me, sang their hymns of thanksgiving afterwards with renewed energy.

The light-headedness which accompanies fever acts differently on different men. My irritation gave way, after a short time, to a fixed determination to slaughter one huge black and white beast who had been foremost in song and first in flight throughout the evening. Thanks to a shaking hand and a giddy head I had already missed him twice with both barrels of my shot-gun, when it struck me that my best plan would be to ride him down in the open and finish him off with a hog-spear.[6] This, of course, was merely the semi-delirious notion of a fever-patient; but I remember that it struck me at the time as being eminently practical and feasible.

I therefore ordered my groom to saddle Pornic and bring him round quietly to the rear of my tent. When the pony was ready, I stood at his head prepared to mount and dash out as soon as the dog should again lift up his voice. Pornic, by the way, had not been out of his pickets[7] for a couple of days; the night air was crisp and chilly; and I was armed with a specially long and sharp pair of persuaders[8] with which I had been rousing a sluggish cob that afternoon. You will easily believe, then, that when he was let go he went quickly. In one moment, for the brute bolted as straight as a die, the tent was left far behind, and we were flying over the smooth sandy soil at racing speed. In another we had passed the wretched dog, and I had almost forgotten why it was that I had taken horse and hog-spear.

The delirium of fever and the excitement of the rapid motion through the air must have taken away the remnant of my senses. I have a faint recollection of standing upright in my stirrups, and of brandishing my hog-spear at the great white moon that looked down so calmly on my mad gallop; and of shouting challenges to the camelthorn bushes as they whizzed past. Once or twice, I believe, I swayed forward on Pornic's neck, and literally hung on by my spurs – as the marks next morning showed.

The wretched beast went forward like a thing possessed, over what seemed to be a limitless expanse of moonlit sand. Next, I remember, the ground rose suddenly in front of us, and as we topped the ascent I saw the waters of the Sutlej[9] shining like a silver bar below. Then Pornic blundered heavily on his nose, and we rolled together down some unseen slope.

I must have lost consciousness, for when I recovered I was lying on my stomach in a heap of soft white sand, and the dawn was beginning to break dimly over the edge of the slope down which I had fallen. As the light grew stronger I saw I was at the bottom of a horseshoe-shaped crater of sand, opening on one side directly on the shoals of the Sutlej. My fever had altogether left me, and, with the exception of a slight dizziness in the head, I felt no bad effects from the fall overnight.

Pornic, who was standing a few yards away, was naturally a good deal exhausted, but had not hurt himself in the least. His saddle, a favourite polo one, was much knocked about, and had been twisted under his belly. It took me some time to put him to rights, and in the meantime I had ample opportunities of observing the spot into which I had so foolishly dropped.

At the risk of being considered tedious, I must describe it at length; inasmuch as an accurate mental picture of its peculiarities will be of material assistance in enabling the reader to understand what follows.

Imagine then, as I have said before, a horseshoe-shaped crater of sand with steeply-graded sand walls about thirty-five feet high. (The slope, I fancy, must have been about 65°.) This crater enclosed a level piece of ground about fifty yards long by thirty at its broadest part, with a rude well in the centre. Round the bottom of the crater, about three feet from the level of the ground proper, ran a series of eighty-three semicircular, ovoid, square, and multilateral holes, all about three feet at the mouth. Each hole on inspection showed that it was carefully shored internally with drift-wood and bamboos, and even the mouth a wooden drip-board projected, like the peak of a jockey's cap, for two feet. No sign of life was visible in these tunnels, but a most sickening stench pervaded the entire amphitheatre – a stench fouler than any which my wanderings in Indian villages have introduced me to.

Having remounted Pornic, who was as anxious as I to get back to camp, I rode round the base of the horseshoe to find some place whence an exit would be practicable. The inhabitants, whoever they might be, had not thought fit to put in an appearance, so I was left to my own devices. My first attempt to 'rush' Pornic up the steep sand-banks showed me that I had fallen into a trap exactly on the same model as that which the ant-lion[10] sets for its prey. At each step the shifting sand poured down from above in tons, and rattled on the drip-boards of the holes like small shot. A couple of ineffectual charges sent us both rolling down to the bottom, half choked with the torrents of sand; and I was constrained to turn my attention to the river-bank.

Here everything seemed easy enough. The sand-hills ran down to the river edge, it is true, but there were plenty of shoals and shallows across which I could gallop Pornic, and find my way back to *terra firma* by turning sharply to the right or the left. As I led Pornic over the sands I was startled by the faint pop of a rifle across the river; and at the same moment a bullet dropped with a sharp '*whit*' close to Pornic's head.

There was no mistaking the nature of the missile – a regulation Martini–Henry[11] 'picket'. About five hundred yards away a country-boat was anchored in mid-stream; and a jet of smoke drifting away from its bows in the still morning air showed me whence the delicate attention had come. Was ever a respectable gentleman in such an *impasse?* The treacherous sand-slope allowed no escape from a spot which I had visited most involuntarily, and a promenade on the river frontage was the signal for a bombardment from some insane native in a boat. I'm afraid that I lost my temper very much indeed.

Another bullet reminded me that I had better save my breath to cool my porridge; and I retreated hastily up the sands and back to the horseshoe, where I saw that the noise of the rifle had drawn sixty-five human beings from the badger-holes which I had up till that point supposed to be untenanted. I found myself in the midst of a crowd of spectators – about forty men, twenty women, and one child who could not have been more than five years old. They were all scantily clothed in that salmon-coloured cloth which one associates with Hindu mendicants, and, at first sight, gave me the impression of a band of loathsome *fakirs*. The filth and repulsiveness of the assembly were beyond all description, and I shuddered to think what their life in the badger-holes must be.

Even in these days, when local self-government[12] has destroyed the greater part of a native's respect for a Sahib, I have been accustomed to a certain amount of civility from my inferiors, and on approaching the crowd naturally expected that there would be some recognition of my presence. As a matter of fact there was, but it was by no means what I had looked for.

The ragged crew actually laughed at me – such laughter I hope I may never hear again. They cackled, yelled, whistled, and howled as I walked into their midst; some of them literally throwing themselves down on the ground in convulsions of unholy mirth. In a moment I had let go Pornic's head, and, irritated beyond expression at the morning's adventure, commenced cuffing those nearest to me with all the force I could. The wretches dropped under my blows like ninepins, and the laughter gave place to wails for mercy; while those yet untouched clasped me round the knees imploring me in all sorts of uncouth tongues to spare them.

In the tumult, and just when I was feeling very much ashamed of myself for having thus easily given way to my temper, a thin high voice murmured in English from behind my shoulder: 'Sahib! Sahib! Do you not know me? Sahib, it is Gunga Dass, the telegraph-master.'

I spun round quickly and faced the speaker.

Gunga Dass (I have, of course, no hesitation in mentioning the man's real name) I had known four years before as a Deccanee Brahmin[13] lent by the Punjab Government to one of the Khalsia States. He was in charge of a branch telegraph-office there, and when I had last met him was a jovial, full-stomached, portly Government servant with a marvellous capacity for making bad puns in English – a peculiarity which made me remember him long after I had forgotten his services to me in his official capacity. It is seldom that a Hindu makes English puns.

Now, however, the man was changed beyond all recognition. Caste-mark, stomach, slate-coloured continuations,[14] and unctuous speech were all gone. I looked at the withered skeleton, turbanless and almost naked, with long matted hair and deep-set codfish-eyes. But for a crescent-shaped scar on the left cheek – the result of an accident for which I was responsible – I should never have known him. But it was indubitably Gunga Dass, and – for this I was thankful – an English-speaking native who might at least tell me the meaning of all that I had gone through that day.

The crowd retreated to some distance as I turned towards the miserable figure, and ordered him to show me some method of escaping from the crater. He held a freshly-plucked crow in his hand, and in reply to my question climbed slowly to a platform of sand which ran in front of the holes, and commenced lighting a fire there in silence. Dried bents, sand-poppies, and driftwood burn quickly; and I derived much consolation from the fact that he lit them with an ordinary sulphur match. When they were in a bright glow and the crow was neatly spitted in front thereof, Gunga Dass began without a word of preamble:

'There are only two kinds of men, Sar – the alive and the dead. When you are dead you are dead, but when you are alive you live.' (Here the crow demanded his attention for an instant

as it twirled before the fire in danger of being burnt to a cinder.)
'If you die at home and do not die when you come to the ghât to
be burnt[15] you come here.'

The nature of the reeking village was made plain now, and all
that I had known or read of the grotesque and the horrible
paled before the fact just communicated by the ex-Brahmin.
Sixteen years ago, when I first landed in Bombay, I had been
told by a wandering Armenian of the existence, somewhere in
India, of a place to which such Hindus as had the misfortune to
recover from trance or catalepsy were conveyed and kept, and I
recollect laughing heartily at what I was then pleased to consider
a traveller's tale.[16] Sitting at the bottom of the sand-trap, the
memory of Watson's Hotel, with its swinging punkahs, white-
robed servants, and the sallow-faced Armenian, rose up in my
mind as vividly as a photograph, and I burst into a loud fit of
laughter. The contrast was too absurd!

Gunga Dass, as he bent over the unclean bird, watched me
curiously. Hindus seldom laugh, and his surroundings were not
such as to move him that way. He removed the crow solemnly
from the wooden spit and as solemnly devoured it. Then he
continued his story, which I give in his own words:

'In epidemics of the cholera you are carried to be burnt almost
before you are dead. When you come to the riverside the cold
air, perhaps, makes you alive, and then, if you are only little
alive, mud is put on your nose and mouth and you die con-
clusively. If you are rather more alive, more mud is put; but if
you are too lively you let you go and take you away. I was too
lively, and made protestation with anger against the indignities
that they endeavoured to press upon me. In those days I was
Brahmin and proud man. Now I am dead man and eat' – here
he eyed the well-gnawed breast-bone with the first sign of
emotion that I had seen in him since we met – 'crows, and –
other things. They took me from my sheets when they saw that I
was too lively and gave me medicines for one week, and I
survived successfully. Then they sent me by rail from my place
to Okara Station, with a man to take care of me; and at Okara
Station we met two other men, and they conducted we three on

camels, in the night, from Okara Station to this place, and they propelled me from the top to the bottom, and the other two succeeded, and I have been here ever since two and a half years. Once I was Brahmin and proud man, and now I eat crows.'

'There is no way of getting out?'

'None of what kind at all. When I first came I made experiments frequently, and all the others also, but we have always succumbed to the sand which is precipitated upon our heads.'

'But surely,' I broke in at this point, 'the river-front is open, and it is worth while dodging the bullets; while at night –'

I had already matured a rough plan of escape which a natural instinct of selfishness forbade me sharing with Gunga Dass. He, however, divined my unspoken thought almost as soon as it was formed; and, to my intense astonishment, gave vent to a long low chuckle of derision – the laughter, be it understood, of a superior or at least of an equal.

'You will not' – he had dropped the Sir after his first sentence – 'make any escape that way. But you can try. I have tried. Once only.'

The sensation of nameless terror which I had in vain attempted to strive against overmastered me completely. My long fast – it was now close upon ten o'clock, and I had eaten nothing since tiffin on the previous day – combined with the violent agitation of the ride had exhausted me, and I verily believe that, for a few minutes, I acted as one mad. I hurled myself against the sand-slope. I ran round the base of the crater, blaspheming and praying by turns. I crawled out among the sedges of the river-front, only to be driven back each time in an agony of nervous dread by the rifle-bullets which cut up the sand round me – for I dared not face the death of a mad dog among that hideous crowd – and so fell, spent and raving, at the curb of the well. No one had taken the slightest notice of an exhibition which makes me blush hotly even when I think of it now.

Two or three men trod on my panting body as they drew water, but they were evidently used to this sort of thing, and had no time to waste upon me. Gunga Dass, indeed, when he had banked the embers of his fire with sand, was at some pains to throw half a cupful of fetid water over my head, an attention for which I could have fallen on my knees and thanked him, but he was laughing all the while in the same mirthless, wheezy key that greeted me on my first attempt to force the shoals. And so, in a half-fainting state, I lay till noon. Then, being only a man after all, I felt hungry, and said as much to Gunga Dass, whom I had begun to regard as my natural protector. Following the impulse of the outer world when dealing with natives, I put my hand into my pocket and drew out four annas.[17] The absurdity of the gift struck me at once, and I was about to replace the money.

Gunga Dass, however, cried: 'Give me the money, all you have, or I will get help, and we will kill you!'

A Briton's first impulse, I believe, is to guard the contents of his pockets; but a moment's thought showed me the folly of differing with the one man who had it in his power to make me comfortable; and with whose help it was possible that I might eventually escape from the crater. I gave him all the money in my possession, Rs. 9–8–5 – nine rupees, eight annas, and five pie[18] – for I always keep small change as *bakshish* when I am in camp. Gunga Dass clutched the coins, and hid them at once in his ragged loin-cloth, looking round to assure himself that no one had observed us.

'*Now* I will give you something to eat,' said he.

What pleasure my money could have given him I am unable to say; but inasmuch as it did please him I was not sorry that I had parted with it so readily, for I had no doubt that he would have had me killed if I had refused. One does not protest against the doings of a den of wild beasts; and my companions were lower than any beasts. While I ate what Gunga Dass had provided, a coarse *chapatti*[19] and a cupful of the foul well-water, the people showed not the faintest sign of curiosity – that curiosity which is so rampant, as a rule, in an Indian village.

I could even fancy that they despised me. At all events they treated me with the most chilling indifference, and Gunga Dass was nearly as bad. I plied him with questions about the terrible village, and received extremely unsatisfactory answers. So far as I could gather, it had been in existence from time immemorial – whence I concluded that it was at least a century old – and during that time no one had ever been known to escape from it. (I had to control myself here with both hands, lest the blind terror should lay hold of me a second time and drive me raving round the crater.) Gunga Dass took a malicious pleasure in emphasizing this point and in watching me wince. Nothing that I could do would induce him to tell me who the mysterious 'They' were.

'It is so ordered,' he would reply, 'and I do not yet know anyone who has disobeyed the orders.'

'Only wait till my servants find that I am missing,' I retorted, 'and I promise you that this place shall be cleared off the face of the earth, and I'll give you a lesson in civility, too, my friend.'

'Your servants would be torn in pieces before they came near this place; and, besides, you are dead, my dear friend. It is not your fault, of course, but none the less you are dead *and* buried.'

At irregular intervals supplies of food, I was told, were dropped down from the land side into the amphitheatre, and the inhabitants fought for them like wild beasts. When a man felt his death coming on he retreated to his lair and died there. The body was sometimes dragged out of the hole and thrown on to the sand, or allowed to rot where it lay.

The phrase 'thrown on to the sand' caught my attention, and I asked Gunga Dass whether this sort of thing was not likely to breed a pestilence.

'That,' said he, with another of his wheezy chuckles, 'you may see for yourself subsequently. You will have much time to make observations.'

Whereat, to his great delight, I winced once more and hastily continued the conversation: 'And how do you live here from day to day? What do you do?' The question elicited exactly the same answer as before – coupled with the information that 'this place is like your European heaven;[20] there is neither marrying nor giving in marriage.'

Gunga Dass had been educated at a Mission School, and, as he himself admitted, had he only changed his religion 'like a wise man', might have avoided the living grave which was now his portion. But as long as I was with him I fancy he was happy.

Here was a Sahib, a representative of the dominant race, helpless as a child and completely at the mercy of his native neighbours. In a deliberate lazy way he set himself to torture me as a schoolboy would devote a rapturous half-hour to watching the agonies of an impaled beetle, or as a ferret in a blind burrow might glue himself comfortably to the neck of a rabbit. The burden of his conversation was that there was no escape 'of no kind whatever', and that I should stay here till I died and was 'thrown on to the sand'. If it were possible to forejudge the conversation of the Damned on the advent of a new soul in their abode, I should say that they would speak as Gunga Dass did to me throughout that long afternoon. I was powerless to protest or answer; all my energies being devoted to a struggle against the inexplicable terror that threatened to overwhelm me again and again. I can compare the feeling to nothing except the struggles of a man against the overpowering nausea of the Channel passage – only my agony was of the spirit and infinitely more terrible.

As the day wore on, the inhabitants began to appear in full strength to catch the rays of the afternoon sun, which were now sloping in at the mouth of the crater. They assembled by little knots, and talked among themselves without even throwing a glance in my direction. About four o'clock, so far as I could judge, Gunga Dass rose and dived into his lair for a moment, emerging with a live crow in his hands. The wretched bird was in a most draggled and deplorable condition, but seemed to be in no way afraid of its master. Advancing cautiously to the river-front, Gunga Dass stepped from tussock to tussock until he had reached a smooth patch of sand directly in the line of the boat's fire. The occupants of the boat took no notice. Here he stopped, and, with a couple of dexterous turns of the wrist, pegged the bird on its back with outstretched wings. As was only natural, the crow began to shriek at once and beat the air with its claws. In a few seconds the clamour had attracted the attention of a bevy of wild crows on a shoal a few hundred yards away, where they were discussing something that looked like a corpse. Half-a-dozen crows flew over at once to see what was going on, and also, as it proved, to attack the pinioned bird. Gunga Dass, who had lain down on a tussock, motioned to me to be quiet, though I fancy this was a needless precaution. In a moment, and before I could see how it happened, a wild crow, which had grappled with the shrieking and helpless bird, was entangled in the latter's claws, swiftly disengaged by Gunga Dass, and pegged down beside its companion in adversity. Curiosity, it seemed, overpowered the rest of the flock, and almost before Gunga Dass and I had time to withdraw to the tussock, two more captives were struggling in the upturned claws of the decoys. So the chase[21] – if I can give it so dignified a name – continued until Gunga Dass had captured seven crows. Five of them he throttled at once, reserving two for further operations another day. I was a good deal impressed by this, to me, novel method of securing food, and complimented Gunga Dass on his skill.

'It is nothing to do,' said he. 'Tomorrow you must do it for me. You are stronger than I am.'

This calm assumption of superiority upset me not a little, and I answered peremptorily: 'Indeed, you old ruffian? What do you think I have given you money for?'

'Very well,' was the unmoved reply. 'Perhaps not tomorrow, nor the day after, nor subsequently; but in the end, and for many years, you will catch crows and eat crows, and you will thank your European God that you have crows to catch and eat.'

I could have cheerfully strangled him for this, but judged it best under the circumstances to smother my resentment. An hour later I was eating one of the crows; and, as Gunga Dass had said, thanking my God that I had a crow to eat. Never as long as I live shall I forget that evening meal. The whole population were squatting on the hard sand platform opposite their dens, huddled over tiny fires of refuse and dried rushes. Death, having once laid his hand upon these men and forborne to strike, seemed to stand aloof from them now; for most of our company were old men, bent and worn and twisted with years, and women aged to all appearance as the Fates themselves. They sat together in knots and talked – God only knows what they found to discuss – in low equable tones, curiously in contrast to the strident babble with which natives are accustomed to make day hideous. Now and then an access of that sudden fury which had possessed me in the morning would lay hold on a man or woman; and with yells and imprecations the sufferer would attack the steep slope until, baffled and bleeding, he fell back on the platform incapable of moving a limb. The others would never even raise their eyes when this happened, as men too well aware of the futility of their fellows' attempts and wearied with their useless repetition. I saw four such outbursts in the course of that evening.

Gunga Dass took an eminently business-like view of my situation, and while we were dining – I can afford to laugh at the recollection now, but it was painful enough at the time – propounded the terms on which he would consent to 'do' for me. My nine rupees eight annas, he argued, at the rate of three annas a day, would provide me with food for fifty-one days, or about seven weeks; that is to say, he would be willing to cater for me for that length of time. At the end of it I was to look after myself. For a further consideration – *videlicet* [22] my boots – he would be willing to allow me to occupy the den next to his own, and would supply me with as much dried grass for bedding as he could spare.

'Very well, Gunga Dass,' I replied; 'to the first terms I cheerfully agree, but, as there is nothing on earth to prevent my killing you as you sit here and taking everything that you have' (I thought of the two invaluable crows at the time), 'I flatly refuse to give you my boots and shall take whichever den I please.'

The stroke was a bold one, and I was glad when I saw that it had succeeded. Gunga Dass changed his tone immediately, and disavowed all intention of asking for my boots. At the time it did not strike me as at all strange that I, a Civil Engineer, a man of thirteen years' standing in the Service, and, I trust, an average Englishman, should thus calmly threaten murder and violence against the man who had, for a consideration it is true, taken me under his wing. I had left the world, it seemed, for centuries. I was as certain then as I am now of my own existence, that in the accursed settlement there was no law save that of the strongest;[23] that the living dead men had thrown behind them every canon of the world which had cast them out; and that I had to depend for my own life on my strength and vigilance alone. The crew of the ill-fated *Mignonette*[24] are the only men who would understand my frame of mind. 'At present,' I argued to myself, 'I am strong and a match for six of these wretches. It is imperatively necessary that I should, for my own sake, keep both health and strength until the hour of my release comes – if it ever does.'

Fortified with these resolutions, I ate and drank as much as I could, and made Gunga Dass understand that I intended to be his master, and that the least sign of insubordination on his part would be visited with the only punishment I had it in my power to inflict – sudden and violent death. Shortly after this I went to bed. That is to say, Gunga Dass gave me a double armful of dried bents which I thrust down the mouth of the lair to the right of his, and followed myself, feet foremost; the hole running about nine feet into the sand with a slight downward inclination, and being neatly shored with timbers. From my den, which faced the river-front, I was able to watch the waters of the Sutlej flowing past under the light of a young moon and compose myself to sleep as best I might.

The horrors of that night I shall never forget. My den was nearly as narrow as a coffin, and the sides had been worn smooth and greasy by the contact of innumerable naked bodies, added to which it smelt abominably. Sleep was altogether out of the question to one in my excited frame of mind. As the night wore on, it seemed that the entire amphitheatre was filled with legions of unclean devils that, trooping up from the shoals below, mocked the unfortunates in their lairs.

Personally I am not of an imaginative temperament – very few Engineers are – but on that occasion I was as completely prostrated with nervous terror as any woman. After half an hour or so, however, I was able once more to calmly review my chances of escape. Any exit by the steep sand walls was, of course, impracticable. I had been thoroughly convinced of this some time before. It was possible, just possible, that I might, in the uncertain moonlight, safely run the gauntlet of the rifle shots. The place was so full of terror for me that I was prepared to undergo any risk in leaving it. Imagine my delight, then, when after creeping stealthily to the river-front I found that the infernal boat was not there. My freedom lay before me in the next few steps!

By walking out to the first shallow pool that lay at the foot of the projecting left horn of the horseshoe, I could wade across, turn the flank of the crater, and make my way inland. Without a moment's hesitation I marched briskly past the tussocks where Gunga Dass had snared the crows, and out in the direction of the smooth white sand beyond. My first step from the tufts of dried grass showed me how utterly futile was any hope of escape; for, as I put my foot down, I felt an indescribable drawing, sucking motion of the sand below. Another moment and my leg was swallowed up nearly to the knee. In the moonlight the whole surface of the sand seemed to be shaken with devilish delight at my disappointment. I struggled clear, sweating with terror and exertion, back to the tussocks behind me and fell on my face.

My only means of escape from the semicircle was protected by a quicksand!

How long I lay I have not the faintest idea; but I was roused at last by the malevolent chuckle of Gunga Dass at my ear. 'I would advise you, Protector of the Poor' (the ruffian was speaking English) 'to return to your house. It is unhealthy to lie down here. Moreover, when the boat returns you will most certainly be rifled at.' He stood over me in the dim light of the dawn,[25] chuckling and laughing to himself. Suppressing my first impulse to catch the man by the neck and throw him on to the quicksand, I rose sullenly and followed him to the platform below the burrows.

Suddenly, and futilely as I thought while I spoke, I asked: 'Gunga Dass, what is the good of the boat if I can't get out *anyhow*?' I recollect that even in my deepest trouble I had been speculating vaguely on the waste of ammunition in guarding an already well-protected foreshore.

Gunga Dass laughed again and made answer: 'They have the boat only in daytime. It is for the reason that *there is a way*. I hope we shall have the pleasure of your company for much longer time. It is a pleasant spot when you have been here some years and eaten roast crow long enough.'

I staggered, numbed and helpless, towards the fetid burrow allotted to me, and fell asleep. An hour or so later I was awakened by a piercing scream – the shrill, high-pitched scream of a horse in pain. Those who have once heard that will never forget the sound. I found some little difficulty in scrambling out of the burrow. When I was in the open, I saw Pornic, my poor old Pornic, lying dead on the sandy soil. How they had killed him I cannot guess. Gunga Dass explained that horse was better than crow, and 'greatest good of greatest number[26] is political maxim. We are now Republic, Mister Jukes, and you are entitled to a fair share of the beast. If you like, we will pass a vote of thanks. Shall I propose?'

Yes, we were a Republic indeed! A Republic of wild beasts penned at the bottom of a pit, to eat and fight and sleep till we died. I attempted no protest of any kind, but sat down and stared at the hideous sight in front of me. In less time almost than it takes me to write this, Pornic's body was divided, in some unclean way or other; the men and woman had dragged the fragments on to the platform and were preparing their morning meal. Gunga Dass cooked mine. The almost irresistible impulse to fly at the sand walls until I was wearied laid hold of me afresh, and I had to struggle against it with all my might. Gunga Dass was offensively jocular till I told him that if he addressed another remark of any kind whatever to me I should strangle him where he sat. This silenced him till the silence became insupportable, and I bade him say something.

'You will live here till you die like the other Feringhi,' he said coolly, watching me over the fragment of gristle that he was gnawing.

'What other Sahib, you swine? Speak at once, and don't stop to tell me a lie.'

'He is over there,' answered Gunga Dass, pointing to a burrow-mouth about four doors to the left of my own. 'You can see for yourself. He died in the burrow as you will die, and I will die, and as all these men and women and the one child will also die.'

'For pity's sake tell me all you know about him. Who was he? When did he come, and when did he die?'

This appeal was a weak step on my part. Gunga Dass only leered and replied: 'I will not – unless you give me something first.'

Then I recollected where I was, and struck the man between the eyes, partially stunning him. He stepped down from the platform at once, and, cringing and fawning and weeping and attempting to embrace my feet, led me round to the burrow which he had indicated.

'I know nothing whatever about the gentleman. Your God be my witness that I do not. He was as anxious to escape as you were, and he was shot from the boat, though we all did all things to prevent him from attempting. He was shot here.' Gunga Dass laid his hand on his lean stomach and bowed to the earth.

'Well, and what then? Go on!'

'And then – and then, Your Honour, we carried him into his house and gave him water, and put wet cloths on the wound, and he laid down in his house and gave up the ghost.'

'In how long? In how long?'

'About half an hour after he received his wound. I call Vishnu[27] to witness,' yelled the wretched man, 'that I did everything for him. Everything which was possible, that I did!'

He threw himself down on the ground and clasped my ankles. But I had my doubts about Gunga Dass's benevolence, and kicked him off as he lay protesting.

'I believe you robbed him of everything he had. But I can find out in a minute or two. How long was the Sahib here?'

'Nearly a year and a half. I think he must have gone mad. But hear me swear, Protector of the Poor! Won't Your Honour hear me swear that I never touched an article that belonged to him? What is Your Worship going to do?'

I had taken Gunga Dass by the waist and had hauled him on to the platform opposite the deserted burrow. As I did so I thought of my wretched fellow-prisoner's unspeakable misery among all these horrors for eighteen months, and the final agony of dying like a rat in a hole, with a bullet-wound in the stomach. Gunga Dass fancied I was going to kill him and howled pitifully. The rest of the population, in the plethora that follows a full flesh meal, watched us without stirring.

'Go inside, Gunga Dass,' said I, 'and fetch it out.'

I was feeling sick and faint with horror now. Gunga Dass nearly rolled off the platform and howled aloud.

'But I am Brahmin, Sahib – a high-caste Brahmin. By your soul by your father's soul, do not make me do this thing!'

'Brahmin or no Brahmin, by my soul and my father's soul, in you go!' I said, and, seizing him by the shoulders, I crammed his head into the mouth of the burrow, kicked the rest of him in, and, sitting down, covered my face with my hands.

At the end of a few minutes I heard a rustle and a creak; then Gunga Dass in a sobbing, choking whisper speaking to himself; then a soft thud – and I uncovered my eyes.

The dry sand had turned the corpse entrusted to its keeping into a yellow-brown mummy. I told Gunga Dass to stand off while I examined it. The body – clad in an olive-green hunting-suit much stained and worn, with leather pads on the shoulders – was that of a man between thirty and forty, above middle height, with light sandy hair, long moustache, and a rough unkempt beard. The left canine of the upper jaw was missing, and a portion of the lobe of the right ear was gone. On the second finger of the left hand was a ring – a shield-shaped bloodstone set in gold, with a monogram that might have been either 'B.K.' or 'B.L.' On the third finger of the right hand was a silver ring in the shape of a coiled cobra, much worn and tarnished. Gunga Dass deposited a handful of trifles he had picked out of the burrow at my feet, and, covering the face of the body with my handkerchief, I turned to examine these. I give the full list in the hope that it may lead to the identification of the unfortunate man:

1. Bowl of a briarwood pipe, serrated at the edge; much worn and blackened; bound with string at the screw.

2. Two patent-lever keys; wards of both broken.

3. Tortoise-shell-handled penknife, silver or nickel, name-plate marked with monogram 'B.K.'

4. Envelope, postmark undecipherable, bearing a Victorian stamp, addressed to 'Miss Mon—' (rest illegible) '—ham' '—nt'.

5. Imitation crocodile-skin notebook with pencil. First forty-five pages blank; four and a half illegible; fifteen others filled with private memoranda relating chiefly to three persons – a Mrs L. Singleton, abbreviated several times to 'Lot Single', 'Mrs S. May', and 'Garmison', referred to in places as 'Jerry' or 'Jack'.

6. Handle of small-sized hunting-knife. Blade snapped short. Buck's horn, diamond-cut, with swivel and ring on the butt; fragment of cotton cord attached.

It must not be supposed that I inventoried all these things on the spot as fully as I have here written them down. The notebook first attracted my attention, and I put it in my pocket with a view to studying it later on. The rest of the articles I conveyed to my burrow for safety's sake, and there, being a methodical man, I inventoried them. I then returned to the corpse and ordered Gunga Dass to help me to carry it out to the riverfront. While we were engaged in this, the exploded shell of an old brown cartridge dropped out of one of the pockets and rolled at my feet. Gunga Dass had not seen it; and I fell to thinking that a man does not carry exploded cartridge-cases, especially 'browns', which will not bear loading twice, about with him when shooting. In other words, that cartridge-case had been fired inside the crater. Consequently there must be a gun somewhere. I was on the verge of asking Gunga Dass, but checked myself, knowing that he would lie. We laid the body down on the edge of the quicksand by the tussocks. It was my intention to push it out and let it be swallowed up – the only possible mode of burial that I could think of. I ordered Gunga Dass to go away.

Then I gingerly put the corpse out on the quicksand. In doing so – it was lying face downward – I tore the frail and rotten khaki shooting-coat open, disclosing a hideous cavity in the back. I have already told you that the dry sand had, as it were, mummified the body. A moment's glance showed that the gaping hole had been caused by a gunshot wound; the gun must have been fired with the muzzle almost touching the back. The shooting-coat, being intact, had been drawn over the body after death, which must have been instantaneous. The secret of the poor wretch's death was plain to me in a flash. Some one of the crater, presumably Gunga Dass, must have shot him with his own gun – the gun that fitted the brown cartridges. He had never attempted to escape in the face of the rifle-fire from the boat.

I pushed the corpse out hastily, and saw it sink from sight literally in a few seconds. I shuddered as I watched. In a dazed, half-conscious way I turned to peruse the notebook. A stained and discoloured slip of paper had been inserted between the binding and the back, and dropped out as I opened the pages. This is what it contained: '*Four out from crow-clump; three left; nine out; two right; three back; two left; fourteen out; two left; seven out; one left; nine back; two right; six back; four right; seven back.*' The paper had been burnt and charred at the edges. What it meant I could not understand. I sat down on the dried bents turning it over and over between my fingers, until I was aware of Gunga Dass standing immediately behind me with glowing eyes and outstretched hands.

'Have you got it?' he panted. 'Will you not let me look at it also? I swear that I will return it.'

'Got what? Return what?' I asked.

'That which you have in your hands. It will help us both.' He stretched out his long bird-like talons, trembling with eagerness.

'I could never find it,' he continued. 'He had secreted it about his person. Therefore I shot him, but nevertheless I was unable to obtain it.'

Gunga Dass had quite forgotten his little fiction about the rifle-bullet. I heard him calmly. Morality is blunted by consorting with the Dead who are alive.

'What on earth are you raving about? What is it you want me to give you?'

'The piece of paper in the notebook. It will help us both. Oh, you fool! You fool! Can you not see what it will do for us? We shall escape!'

His voice rose almost to a scream, and he danced with excitement before me. I own I was moved at the chance of getting away.

'Do you mean to say that this slip of paper will help us? What does it mean?'

'Read it aloud! Read it aloud! I beg and I pray to you to read it aloud.'

I did so. Gunga Dass listened delightedly, and drew an irregular line in the sand with his fingers.

'See now! It was the length of his gun-barrels without the stock. I have those barrels. Four gun-barrels out from the place where I caught crows. Straight out; do you mind me? Then three left. Ah! Now well I remember how that man worked it out night after night. Then nine out, and so on. Out is always straight before you across the quicksand to the north. He told me so before I killed him.'

'But if you knew all this why didn't you get out before?'

'I did *not* know it. He told me that he was working it out a year and a half ago, and how he was working it out night after night when the boat had gone away, and he could get out near the quicksand safely. Then he said that we would get away together. But I was afraid that he would leave me behind one night when he had worked it all out, and so I shot him. Besides, it is not advisable that the men who once get in here should escape. Only I, and *I* am a Brahmin.'

The hope of escape had brought Gunga Dass's caste back to

him. He stood up, walked about, and gesticulated violently. Eventually I managed to make him talk soberly, and he told me how this Englishman had spent six months night after night in exploring, inch by inch, the passage across the quicksand; how he had declared it to be simplicity itself up to within about twenty yards of the river bank after turning the flank of the left horn of the horseshoe. This much he had evidently not completed when Gunga Dass shot him with his own gun.

In my frenzy of delight at the possibilities of escape I recollect shaking hands wildly with Gunga Dass, after we had decided that we were to make an attempt to get away that very night. It was weary work waiting throughout the afternoon.

About ten o'clock, as far as I could judge, when the moon had just risen above the lip of the crater, Gunga Dass made a move for his burrow to bring out the gun-barrels whereby to measure our path. All the other wretched inhabitants had retired to their lairs long ago. The guardian boat drifted down-stream some hours before, and we were utterly alone by the crow-clump. Gunga Dass, while carrying the gun-barrels, let slip the piece of paper which was to be our guide. I stooped down hastily to recover it, and, as I did so, I was aware that the creature was aiming a violent blow at the back of my head with the gun-barrels. It was too late to turn round. I must have received the blow somewhere on the nape of my neck, for I fell senseless at the edge of the quicksand.

When I recovered consciousness the moon was going down, and I was sensible of intolerable pain in the back of my head. Gunga Dass had disappeared and my mouth was full of blood. I lay down again and prayed that I might die without more ado. Then the unreasoning fury which I have before mentioned laid hold upon me, and I staggered inland towards the walls of the crater. It seemed that some one was calling to me in a whisper – 'Sahib! Sahib! Sahib!' exactly as my bearer used to call me in the mornings. I fancied that I was delirious until a handful of sand fell at my feet. Then I looked up and saw a head peering down into the amphitheatre – the head of Dunnoo, my dog-boy, who attended to my collies. As soon as he had attracted my attention, he held up his hand and showed a rope. I motioned, staggering to and fro the while, that he should throw it down. It was a couple of leather punkah-ropes knotted together, with a loop at one end. I slipped the loop over my head and under my arms; heard Dunnoo urge something foward; was conscious that I was being dragged, face downward, up the steep sand-slope, and the next instant found myself choked and half-fainting on the sand-hills overlooking the crater. Dunnoo, with his face ashy grey in the moonlight, implored me not to stay, but to get back to my tent at once.

It seems that he had tracked Pornic's footprints fourteen miles across the sands to the crater; had returned and told my servants, who flatly refused to meddle with anyone, white or black, once fallen into the hideous Village of the Dead; where-upon Dunnoo had taken one of my ponies and a couple of punkah ropes, returned to the crater, and hauled me out as I have described.[28]

⟨ The Man who would be King [1] ⟩

Brother to a Prince and fellow to a beggar if he be found worthy. [2]

The Law, [3] as quoted, lays down a fair conduct of life, and one
not easy to follow. I have been fellow to a beggar again and
again under circumstances which prevented either of us finding
out whether the other was worthy. I have still to be brother to a
Prince, though I once came near to kinship with what might
have been a veritable King, and was promised the reversion of a
Kingdom – army, law-courts, revenue, and policy all complete.
But, today, I greatly fear that my King is dead, and if I want a
crown I must go hunt it for myself.

The beginning of everything was in a railway train upon the
road to Mhow from Ajmir. [4] There had been a Deficit in the
Budget, which necessitated travelling, not Second-class, which
is only half as dear as First-class, but by Intermediate, which is
very awful indeed. There are no cushions in the Intermediate
class, and the population are either Intermediate, which is
Eurasian, or native, which for a long night journey is nasty, or
Loafer, [5] which is amusing though intoxicated. Intermediates
do not buy from refreshment-rooms. They carry their food in
bundles and pots, and buy sweets from the native sweetmeat-
sellers, and drink the road-side water. That is why in the hot
weather Intermediates are taken out of the carriages dead, and
in all weathers are most properly looked down upon.

My particular Intermediate happened to be empty till I
reached Nasirabad, when a big black-browed gentleman in
shirt-sleeves entered, and, following the custom of Intermediates,
passed the time of day. He was a wanderer and a vagabond like
myself, but with an educated taste for whisky. He told tales of

things he had seen and done, of out-of-the-way corners of the Empire into which he had penetrated, and of adventures in which he risked his life for a few days' food.

'If India was filled with men like you and me, not knowing more than the crows where they'd get their next day's rations, it isn't seventy millions of revenue the land would be paying – it's seven hundred millions,' said he; and as I looked at his mouth and chin I was disposed to agree with him.

We talked politics – the politics of Loaferdom,[6] that sees things from the underside where the lath and plaster is not smoothed off – and we talked postal arrangements because my friend wanted to send a telegram back from the next station to Ajmir, the turning-off place from the Bombay to the Mhow line as you travel westward. My friend had no money beyond eight annas, which he wanted for dinner, and I had no money at all, owing to the hitch in the Budget before mentioned. Further, I was going into a wilderness where, though I should resume touch with the Treasury, there were no telegraph offices. I was, therefore, unable to help him in any way.

'We might threaten a Station-master, and make him send a wire on tick,' said my friend, 'but that'd mean inquiries for you and for me, and *I*'ve got my hands full these days. Did you say you are travelling back along this line within any days?'

'Within ten,' I said.

'Can't you make it eight?' said he. 'Mine is rather urgent business.'

'I can send your telegram within ten days if that will serve you,' I said.

'I couldn't trust the wire to fetch him now I think of it. It's this way. He leaves Delhi on the 23rd for Bombay. That means he'll be running through Ajmir about the night of the 23rd.'

'But I'm going into the Indian Desert,' I explained.

'Well *and* good,' said he. 'You'll be changing at Marwar Junction to get into Jodhpore territory – you must do that – and he'll be coming through Marwar Junction in the early morning of the 24th by the Bombay Mail. Can you be at Marwar

Junction on that time? 'Twon't be inconveniencing you because I know that there's precious few pickings to be got out of these Central India States – even though you pretend to be correspondent of the *Backwoodsman*.'

'Have you ever tried that trick?' I asked.

'Again and again, but the Residents find you out, and then you get escorted to the Border before you've time to get your knife into them. But about my friend here. I *must* give him a word o' mouth to tell him what's come to me or else he won't know where to go. I would take it more than kind of you if you was to come out of Central India in time to catch him at Marwar Junction, and say to him: "He has gone South for the week." He'll know what that means. He's a big man with a red beard, and a great swell he is. You'll find him sleeping like a gentleman with all his luggage round him in a Second-class compartment. But don't you be afraid. Slip down the window, and say: "He has gone South for the week," and he'll tumble. It's only cutting your time of stay in those parts by two days. I ask you as a stranger – going to the West,'[7] he said with emphasis.

'Where have *you* come from?' said I.

'From the East,' said he, 'and I am hoping that you will give him the message on the Square – for the sake of my Mother as well as your own.'

Englishmen are not usually softened by appeals to the memory of their mothers, but for certain reasons, which will be fully apparent, I saw fit to agree.

'It's more than a little matter,' said he, 'and that's why I asked you to do it – and now I know that I can depend on you doing it. A Second-class carriage at Marwar Junction, and a red-haired man asleep in it. You'll be sure to remember. I get out at the next station, and I must hold on there till he comes or sends me what I want.'

'I'll give the message if I catch him,' I said, 'and for the sake of your Mother as well as mine I'll give you a word of advice. Don't try to run the Central India States just now as the correspondent of the *Backwoodsman*. There's a real one knocking about here, and it might lead to trouble.'

211

'Thank you,' said he simply, 'and when will the swine be gone? I can't starve because he's ruining my work. I wanted to get hold of the Degumber Rajah down here about his father's widow, and give him a jump.'

'What did he do to his father's widow, then?'

'Filled her up with red pepper and slippered her to death as she hung from a beam. I found that out myself, and I'm the only man that would dare going into the State to get hush-money for it. They'll try to poison me, same as they did in Chortumna when I went on the loot there. But you'll give the man at Marwar Junction my message?'

He got out at a little roadside station, and I reflected. I had heard, more than once, of men personating correspondents of newspapers and bleeding small Native States with threats of exposure, but I had never met any of the caste before. They led a hard life, and generally die with great suddenness. The Native States have a wholesome horror of English newspapers [8] which may throw light on their peculiar methods of government, and do their best to choke correspondents with champagne, or drive them out of their mind with four-in-hand barouches. They do not understand that nobody cares a straw for the internal administration of Native States so long as oppression and crime are kept within decent limits, and the ruler is not drugged, drunk, or diseased from one end of the year to the other. They are the dark places of the earth, full of unimaginable cruelty, touching the Railway and the Telegraph on one side, and, on the other, the days of Harun-al-Raschid. [9] When I left the train I did business with divers Kings, and in eight days passed through many changes of life. Sometimes I wore dress-clothes and consorted with Princes and Politicals, [10] drinking from crystal and eating from silver. Sometimes I lay out upon the ground and devoured what I could get, from a plate made of leaves, and drank the running water, and slept under the same rug as my servant. It was all in the day's work.

Then I headed for the Great Indian Desert upon the proper date, as I had promised, and the night Mail set me down at Marwar Junction, where a funny, little, happy-go-lucky,

native-managed railway runs to Jodhpore. The Bombay Mail
from Delhi makes a short halt at Marwar. She arrived as I got
in, and I had just time to hurry to her platform and go down the
carriages. There was only one Second-class on the train. I slipped the window and looked down upon a flaming red beard,
half covered by a railway rug. That was my man, fast asleep,
and I dug him gently in the ribs. He woke with a grunt, and I
saw his face in the light of the lamps. It was a great and shining
face.

'Tickets again?' said he.

'No,' said I. 'I am to tell you that he is gone South for the
week. He has gone South for the week!'

The train had begun to move out. The red man rubbed his
eyes. 'He has gone South for the week,' he repeated. 'Now
that's just like his impidence. Did he say that I was to give you
anything? 'Cause I won't.'

'He didn't,' I said, and dropped away, and watched the red
lights die out in the dark. It was horribly cold because the wind
was blowing off the sands. I climbed into my own train – not an
Intermediate Carriage this time – and went to sleep.

If the man with the beard had given me a rupee I should
have kept it as a memento of a rather curious affair. But the
consciousness of having done my duty was my only reward.

Later on I reflected that two gentlemen like my friends could
not do any good if they forgathered and personated correspondents of newspapers, and might, if they black-mailed one
of the little rat-trap states of Central India or Southern Rajputana, get themselves into serious difficulties. I therefore took
some trouble to describe them as accurately as I could remember
to people who would be interested in deporting them; and
succeeded, so I was later informed, in having them headed back
from the Degumber borders.

Then I became respectable, and returned to an Office where
there were no Kings and no incidents outside the daily manufacture of a newspaper. A newspaper office seems to attract every
conceivable sort of person, to the prejudice of discipline.
Zenana-mission ladies [11] arrive, and beg that the Editor will

instantly abandon all his duties to describe a Christian prize-giving in a back-slum of a perfectly inaccessible village; Colonels who have been overpassed for command sit down and sketch the outline of a series of ten, twelve, or twenty-four leading articles on Seniority *versus* Selection; Missionaries wish to know why they have not been permitted to escape from their regular vehicles of abuse and swear at a brother-missionary under special patronage of the editorial We; stranded theatrical companies troop up to explain that they cannot pay for their advertisements, but on their return from New Zealand or Tahiti will do so with interest; inventors of patent punkah-pulling machines, carriage couplings, and unbreakable swords and axle-trees, call with specifications in their pockets and hours at their disposal; tea-companies enter and elaborate their prospectuses with the office pens; secretaries of ball-committees clamour to have the glories of their last dance more fully described; strange ladies rustle in and say, 'I want a hundred lady's cards printed *at once*, please,' which is manifestly part of an Editor's duty; and every dissolute ruffian that ever tramped the Grand Trunk Road makes it his business to ask for employment as a proof-reader. And, all the time, the telephone-bell is ringing madly, and Kings are being killed on the Continent, and Empires are saying, 'You're another,' and Mister Gladstone[12] is calling down brimstone upon the British Dominions, and the little black copy-boys are whining, '*kaa-pi chay-ha-yeh*'[13] (copy wanted) like tired bees, and most of the paper is as blank as Modred's shield.[14]

But that is the amusing part of the year. There are six other months when none ever comes to call, and the thermometer walks inch by inch up to the top of the glass, and the office is darkened to just above reading-light, and the press-machines are red-hot of touch, and nobody writes anything but accounts of amusements in the Hill-stations or obituary notices. Then the telephone becomes a tinkling terror, because it tells you of the sudden deaths of men and women that you knew intimately, and the prickly-heat covers you with a garment, and you sit down and write: 'A slight increase of sickness is reported from

the Khuda Janta Khan [15] District. The outbreak is purely spor-
adic in its nature, and, thanks to the energetic efforts of the
District authorities, is now almost at an end. It is, however,
with deep regret we record the death, etc.'

Then the sickness really breaks out, and the less recording
and reporting the better for the peace of the subscribers. But
the Empires and the Kings continue to divert themselves as
selfishly as before, and the Foreman thinks that a daily paper
really ought to come out once in twenty-four hours, and all the
people at the Hill-stations in the middle of their amusements
say: 'Good gracious! Why can't the paper be sparkling? I'm
sure there's plenty going on up here.'

That is the dark half of the moon, and, as the advertisements
say, 'must be experienced to be appreciated'.

It was in that season, and a remarkably evil season, that the
paper began running the last issue of the week on Saturday
night, which is to say Sunday morning, after the custom of a
London paper. This was a great convenience, for immediately
after the paper was put to bed, the dawn would lower the
thermometer from 96° to almost 84° for half an hour, and in
that chill – you have no idea how cold is 84° on the grass until
you begin to pray for it – a very tired man could get off to sleep
ere the heat roused him.

One Saturday night it was my pleasant duty to put the paper
to bed alone. A King or courtier or a courtesan or a Community
was going to die or get a new Constitution, or do something that
was important on the other side of the world, and the paper was
to be held open till the latest possible minute in order to catch
the telegram.

It was a pitchy black night, as stifling as a June night can be,
and the *loo*, the red-hot wind from the westward, was booming
among the tinder-dry trees and pretending that the rain was on
its heels. Now and again a spot of almost boiling water would
fall on the dust with the flop of a frog, but all our weary world
knew that was only pretence. It was a shade cooler in the press-
room than the office, so I sat there, while the type ticked and
clicked, and the night-jars hooted at the windows, and the all

but naked compositors wiped the sweat from their foreheads, and called for water. The thing that was keeping us back, whatever it was, would not come off, though the *loo* dropped and the last type was set, and the whole round earth stood still in the choking heat, with its finger on its lip, to wait the event. I drowsed, and wondered whether the telegraph was a blessing, and whether this dying man, or struggling people, might be aware of the inconvenience the delay was causing. There was no special reason beyond the heat and worry to make tension, but, as the clock-hands crept up to three o'clock, and the machines spun their fly-wheels two or three times to see that all was in order before I said the word that would set them off, I could have shrieked aloud.

Then the roar and rattle of the wheels shivered the quiet into little bits. I rose to go away, but two men in white clothes stood in front of me. The first one said: 'It's him!' The second said: 'So it is!' And they both laughed almost as loudly as the machinery roared, and mopped their foreheads. 'We seed there was a light burning across the road, and we were sleeping in that ditch there for coolness, and I said to my friend here, The office is open. Let's come along and speak to him as turned us back from the Degumber State,' said the smaller of the two. He was the man I had met in the Mhow train, and his fellow was the red-bearded man of Marwar Junction. There was no mistaking the eyebrows of the one or the beard of the other.

I was not pleased, because I wished to go to sleep, not to squabble with loafers. 'What do you want?' I asked.

'Half an hour's talk with you, cool and comfortable, in the office,' said the red-bearded man. 'We'd *like* some drink – the Contrack doesn't begin yet, Peachey, so you needn't look – but what we really want is advice. We don't want money. We ask you as a favour, because we found out you did us a bad turn about Degumber State.'

I led from the press-room to the stifling office with the maps on the walls, and the red-haired man rubbed his hands. 'That's something like,' said he. 'This was the proper shop to come to. Now, Sir, let me introduce to you Brother [16] Peachey Carnehan, that's him, and Brother Daniel Dravot, that is *me*, and the less said about our professions the better, for we have been most things in our time. Soldier, sailor, compositor, photographer, proof-reader, street-preacher, and correspondents of the *Backwoodsman* when we thought the paper wanted one. Carnehan is sober, and so am I. Look at us first, and see that's sure. It will save you cutting into my talk. We'll take one of your cigars apiece, and you shall see us light up.'

I watched the test. The men were absolutely sober, so I gave them each a tepid whisky and soda.

'Well *and* good,' said Carnehan of the eyebrows, wiping the froth from his moustache. 'Let me talk now, Dan. We have been all over India, mostly on foot. We have been boiler-fitters, engine-drivers, petty contractors, and all that, and we have decided that India isn't big enough for such as us.'

They certainly were too big for the office. Dravot's beard seemed to fill half the room and Carnehan's shoulders the other half, as they sat on the big table. Carnehan continued: 'The country isn't half worked out because they that governs it won't let you touch it. They spend all their blessed time in governing it, and you can't lift a spade, nor chip a rock, nor look for oil, nor anything like that, without all the Government saying, "Leave it alone, and let us govern." Therefore, such *as* it is, we will let it alone, and go away to some other place where a man isn't crowded and can come to his own. We are not little men, and there is nothing that we are afraid of except Drink, and we have signed a Contrack on that. *Therefore*, we are going away to be Kings.'

'Kings in our own right,' muttered Dravot.

'Yes, of course,' I said. 'You've been tramping in the sun, and it's a very warm night, and hadn't you better sleep over the notion? Come tomorrow.'

'Neither drunk nor sunstruck,' said Dravot. 'We have slept over the notion half a year, and require to see Books and Atlases, and we have decided that there is only one place now in the world that two strong men can Sar-a-*whack*. They call it Kafiristan.[17] By my reckoning it's the top right-hand corner of

Afghanistan, not more than three hundred miles from Peshawar. They have two-and-thirty heathen idols there, and we'll be the thirty-third and fourth. It's a mountaineous country, and the women of those parts are very beautiful.'

'But that is provided against in the Contrack,' said Carnehan. 'Neither Woman nor Liqu-or, Daniel.'

'And that's all we know, except that no one has gone there, and they fight, and in any place where they fight a man who knows how to drill men can always be a King. We shall go to those parts and say to any King we find – "D'you want to vanquish your foes?" and we will show him how to drill men; for that we know better than anything else. Then we will subvert that King and seize his Throne and establish a Dy-nasty.'

'You'll be cut to pieces before you're fifty miles across the Border,' I said. 'You have to travel through Afghanistan to get to that country. It's one mass of mountains and peaks and glaciers, and no Englishman has been through it. The people are utter brutes, and even if you reached them you couldn't do anything.'

'That's more like,' said Carnehan. 'If you could think us a little more mad we would be more pleased. We have come to you to know about this country, to read a book about it, and to be shown maps. We want you to tell us that we are fools and to show us your books.' He turned to the bookcases.

'Are you at all in earnest?' I said.

'A little,' said Dravot sweetly. 'As big a map as you have got, even if it's all blank where Kafiristan is, and any books you've got. We can read, though we aren't very educated.'

I uncased the big thirty-two-miles-to-the-inch map of India, and two smaller Frontier maps, hauled down volume I N F–K A N of the *Encyclopaedia Britannica*, and the men consulted them.

'See here!' said Dravot, his thumb on the map. 'Up to Jagdallak, Peachey and me know the road. We was there with Roberts' Army.[18] We'll have to turn off to the right at Jagdallak through Laghmann territory. Then we get among the hills – fourteen thousand feet – fifteen thousand – it will be cold work there, but it don't look very far on the map.'

I handed him Wood on the *Sources of the Oxus*. Carnehan was deep in the *Encyclopaedia*.

'They're a mixed lot,' said Dravot reflectively; 'and it won't help us to know the names of their tribes. The more tribes the more they'll fight, and the better for us. From Jagdallak to Ashang H'mm!'

'But all the information about the country is as sketchy and inaccurate as can be,' I protested. 'No one knows anything about it really. Here's the file of the *United Services' Institute*. Read what Bellew says.'

'Blow Bellew!' said Carnehan. 'Dan, they're a stinkin' lot of heathens, but this book here says they think they're related to us English.'[19]

I smoked while the men poured over Raverty,[20] Wood, the maps, and the *Encyclopaedia*.

'There is no use your waiting,' said Dravot politely. 'It's about four o'clock now. We'll go before six o'clock if you want to sleep, and we won't steal any of the papers. Don't you sit up. We're two harmless lunatics, and if you come tomorrow evening down to the Serai[21] we'll say good-bye to you.'

'You *are* two fools,' I answered. 'You'll be turned back at the Frontier or cut up the minute you set foot in Afghanistan. Do you want any money or a recommendation down-country? I can help you to the chance of work next week.'

'Next week we shall be hard at work ourselves, thank you,' said Dravot. 'It isn't so easy being a King as it looks. When we've got our Kingdom in going order we'll let you know, and you can come up and help us to govern it.'

'Would two lunatics make a contrack like that?' said Carnehan, with subdued pride, showing me a greasy half-sheet of notepaper on which was written the following. I copied it, then and there, as a curiosity —

This Contract between me and you persuing witnesseth in the name of God — Amen and so forth.

  (One)   That me and you will settle this matter together; i.e. to be Kings of Kafiristan.

(*Two*) *That you and me will not, while this matter is being settled, look at any Liquor, nor any Woman black, white, or brown, so as to get mixed up with one or the other harmful.*

(*Three*) *That we conduct ourselves with Dignity and Discretion, and if one of us gets into trouble the other will stay by him.*

> *Signed by you and me this day,*
> *Peachey Taliaferro Carnehan*
> *Daniel Dravot*
> *Both Gentlemen at Large*

'There was no need for the last article,' said Carnehan, blushing modestly; 'but it looks regular. Now you know the sort of men that loafers are – we *are* loafers, Dan, until we get out of India – and *do* you think that we would sign a Contrack like that unless we was in earnest? We have kept away from the two things that make life worth having.'

'You won't enjoy your lives much longer if you are going to try this idiotic adventure. Don't set the office on fire,' I said, 'and go away before nine o'clock.'

I left them still poring over the maps and making notes on the back of the 'Contrack'. 'Be sure to come down to the Serai tomorrow,' were their parting words.

The Kumharsen Serai is the great four-square sink of humanity where the strings of camels and horses from the North load and unload. All the nationalities of Central Asia may be found there, and most of the folk of India proper. Balkh and Bokhara there meet Bengal and Bombay, and try to draw eye-teeth.[22] You can buy ponies, turquoises, Persian pussy-cats, saddle-bags, fat-tailed sheep and musk in the Kumharsen Serai, and get many strange things for nothing. In the afternoon I went down to see whether my friends intended to keep their word or were lying there drunk.

A priest[23] attired in fragments of ribbons and rags stalked up to me, gravely twisting a child's paper whirligig. Behind him was his servant bending under the load of a crate of mud toys. The two were loading up two camels, and the inhabitants of the Serai watched them with shrieks of laughter.

'The priest is mad,' said a horse-dealer to me. 'He is going up to Kabul to sell toys to the Amir. He will either be raised to honour or have his head cut off. He came in here this morning and has been behaving madly ever since.'

'The witless are under the protection of God,' stammered a flat-cheeked Usbeg in broken Hindi. 'They foretell future events.'

'Would they could have foretold that my caravan would have been cut up by the Shinwaris almost within shadow of the Pass!' grunted the Eusufzai agent of a Rajputana trading-house whose goods had been diverted into the hands of other robbers just across the Border, and whose misfortunes were the laughing-stock of the bazar. 'Ohé, priest, whence come you and whither do you go?'

'From Roum [24] have I come,' shouted the priest, waving his whirligig; 'from Roum, blown by the breath of a hundred devils across the sea! O thieves, robbers, liars, the blessing of Pir Khan [25] on pigs, dogs, and perjurers! Who will take the Protected of God to the North to sell charms that are never still to the Amir? The camels shall not gall, the sons shall not fall sick, and the wives shall remain faithful while they are away, of the men who give me place in their caravan. Who will assist me to slipper the King of the Roos [26] with a golden slipper with a silver heel? The protection of Pir Khan be upon his labours!' He spread out the skirts of his gaberdine and pirouetted between the lines of tethered horses.

'There starts a caravan from Peshawar to Kabul in twenty days, *Huzrut*,' [27] said the Eusufzai trader. 'My camels go therewith. Do thou also go and bring us good luck.'

'I will go even now!' shouted the priest. 'I will depart upon my winged camels, and be at Peshawar in a day! Ho! Hazar [28] Mir Khan,' he yelled to his servant, 'drive out the camels, but let me first mount my own.'

He leaped on the back of his beast as it knelt, and, turning round to me, cried: 'Come thou also, Sahib, a little along the road, and I will sell thee a charm – an amulet that shall make thee King of Kafiristan.'

Then the light broke upon me, and I followed the two camels out of the Serai till we reached open road and the priest halted.

'What d'you think o' that?' said he in English. 'Carnehan can't talk their patter, so I've made him my servant. He makes a handsome servant. 'Tisn't for nothing that I've been knocking about the country for fourteen years. Didn't I do that talk neat? We'll hitch on to a caravan at Peshawar till we get to Jagdallak, and then we'll see if we can get donkeys for our camels, and strike into Kafiristan. Whirligigs for the Amir, O Lor! Put your hand under the camel-bags and tell me what you feel.'

I felt the butt of a Martini,[29] and another and another.

'Twenty of 'em,' said Dravot placidly. 'Twenty of 'em and ammunition to correspond, under the whirligigs and the mud dolls.'

'Heaven help you if you are caught with those things!' I said. 'A Martini is worth her weight in silver among the Pathans.'

'Fifteen hundred rupees of capital – every rupee we could beg, borrow, or steal – are invested on these two camels,' said Dravot. 'We won't get caught. We're going through the Khaiber with a regular caravan. Who'd touch a poor mad priest?'

'Have you got everything you want?' I asked, overcome with astonishment.

'Not yet, but we shall soon. Give us a memento of your kindness, *Brother*. You did me a service, yesterday, and that time in Marwar. Half my Kingdom shall you have,[30] as the saying is.' I slipped a small charm compass from my watch-chain and handed it up to the priest.

'Good-bye,' said Dravot, giving me hand cautiously. 'It's the last time we'll shake hands with an Englishman these many days. Shake hands with him, Carnehan,' he cried, as the second camel passed me.

Carnehan leaned down and shook hands. Then the camels passed away along the dusty road, and I was left alone to wonder. My eye could detect no failure in the disguises. The scene in the Serai proved that they were complete to the native mind. There was just the chance, therefore, that Carnehan and Dravot would be able to wander through Afghanistan without detection. But, beyond, they would find death – certain and awful death.

Ten days later a native correspondent giving me the news of

the day from Peshawar, wound up his letter with: 'There has been much laughter here on account of a certain mad priest who is going in his estimation to sell petty gauds and insignificant trinkets which he ascribes as great charms to H.H. the Amir of Bokhara. He passed through Peshawar and associated himself to the Second Summer caravan that goes to Kabul. The merchants are pleased because through superstition they imagine that such mad fellows bring good fortune.'

The two, then, were beyond the Border. I would have prayed for them, but, that night, a real King died in Europe, and demanded an obituary notice.

The wheel of the world swings through the same phases again and again. Summer passed and winter thereafter, and came and passed again. The daily paper continued and I with it, and upon the third summer there fell a hot night, a night-issue, and a strained waiting for something to be telegraphed from the other side of the world, exactly as had happened before. A few great men had died in the past two years, the machines worked with more clatter, and some of the trees in the office garden were a few feet taller. But that was all the difference.

I passed over to the press-room, and went through just such a scene as I have already described. The nervous tension was stronger than it had been two years before, and I felt the heat more acutely. At three o'clock I cried, 'Print off,' and turned to go, when there crept to my chair what was left of a man. He was bent into a circle, his head was sunk between his shoulders, and he moved his feet one over the other like a bear. I could hardly see whether he walked or crawled – this rag-wrapped, whining cripple who addressed me by name, crying that he was come back. 'Can you give me a drink?' he whimpered. 'For the Lord's sake give me a drink!'

I went back to the office, the man following with groans of pain, and I turned up the lamp.

'Don't you know me?' he gasped, dropping into a chair, and he turned his drawn face, surmounted by a shock of grey hair, to the light.

I looked at him intently. Once before had I seen eyebrows that met over the nose in an inch-broad black band, but for the life of me I could not tell where.

'I don't know you,' I said, handing him the whisky. 'What can I do for you?'

He took a gulp of the spirit raw, and shivered in spite of the suffocating heat.

'I've come back,' he repeated; 'and I was the King of Kafiristan — me and Dravot — crowned Kings we was! In this office we settled it — you setting there and giving us the books. I am Peachey —Peachey Taliaferro Carnehan, and you've been setting here ever since — O Lord!'

I was more than a little astonished, and expresssed my feelings accordingly.

'It's true,' said Carnehan, with a dry cackle, nursing his feet, which were wrapped in rags. 'True as gospel. Kings we were, with crowns upon our heads — me and Dravot — poor Dan — oh, poor, poor Dan, that would never take advice, not though I begged of him!'

'Take the whisky,' I said, 'and take your own time. Tell me all you can recollect of everything from beginning to end. You got across the Border on your camels, Dravot dressed as a mad priest and you his servant. Do you remember that?'

'I ain't mad — yet, but I shall be that way soon. Of course I remember. Keep looking at me, or maybe my words will go all to pieces. Keep looking at me in my eyes and don't say anything.'

I leaned forward and looked into his face as steadily as I could. He dropped one hand upon the table and I grasped it by the wrist. It was twisted like a bird's claw, and upon the back was a ragged red diamond-shaped scar.

'No, don't look there. Look at *me*,' said Carnehan. 'That comes afterwards, but for the Lord's sake don't distrack me. We left with that caravan, me and Dravot playing all sorts of antics to amuse the people we were with. Dravot used to make us laugh in the evenings when all the people was cooking their dinners — cooking their dinners, and . . . what did they do then?

They lit little fires with sparks that went into Dravot's beard, and we all laughed – fit to die. Little red fires they was, going into Dravot's big red beard – so funny.' His eyes left mine and he smiled foolishly.

'You went as far as Jagdallak with that caravan,' I said at a venture, 'after you had lit those fires. To Jagdallak, where you turned off to try to get into Kafiristan.'

'No, we didn't neither. What are you talking about? We turned off before Jagdallak, because we heard the roads was good. But they wasn't good enough for our two camels – mine and Dravot's. When we left the caravan, Dravot took off all his clothes and mine too, and said we would be heathen, because the Kafirs didn't allow Mohammedans to talk to them. So we dressed betwixt and between, and such a sight as Daniel Dravot I never saw yet nor expect to see again. He burned half his beard, and slung a sheep-skin over his shoulder, and shaved his head into patterns. He shaved mine, too, and made me wear outrageous things to look like a heathen. That was in a most mountaineous country, and our camels couldn't go along any more because of the mountains. They were tall and black, and coming home I saw them fight like wild goats – there are lots of goats in Kafiristan. And these mountains, they never keep still, no more than the goats. Always fighting they are, and don't let you sleep at night.'

'Take some more whisky,' I said very slowly. 'What did you and Daniel Dravot do when the camels could go no farther because of the rough roads that led into Kafiristan?'

'What did which do? There was a party called Peachey Taliaferro Carnehan that was with Dravot. Shall I tell you about him? He died out there in the cold. Slap from the bridge fell old Peachey, turning and twisting in the air like a penny whirligig that you can sell to the Amir – No; they was two for three-ha'pence, those whirligigs, or I am much mistaken and woful sore . . . And then these camels were no use, and Peachey said to Dravot – "For the Lord's sake let's get out of this before our heads are chopped off," and with that they killed the camels all among the mountains, not having anything in particular to eat, but first they took off the boxes with the guns and the ammunition, till two men came along driving four mules. Dravot up and dances in front of them, singing – "Sell me four mules." Says the first man – "If you are rich enough to buy, you are rich enough to rob"; but before ever he could put his hand to his knife, Dravot breaks his neck over his knee, and the other party runs away. So Carnehan loaded the mules with the rifles that was taken off the camels, and together we starts forward into those bitter cold mountaineous parts, and never a road broader than the back of your hand.'

He paused for a moment, while I asked him if he could remember the nature of the country through which he had journeyed.

'I am telling you as straight as I can, but my head isn't as good as it might be. They drove nails through it to make me hear better how Dravot died. The country was mountaineous and the mules were most contrary, and the inhabitants was dispersed and solitary. They went up and up, and down and down, and that other party, Carnehan, was imploring of Dravot not to sing and whistle so loud, for fear of bringing down the tremenjus avalanches. But Dravot says that if a King couldn't sing it wasn't worth being King, and whacked the mules over the rump, and never took no heed for ten cold days. We came to a big level valley all among the mountains, and the mules were near dead, so we killed them, not having anything in special for them or us to eat. We sat upon the boxes, and played odd and even [31] with the cartridges that was jolted out.

'Then ten men with bows and arrows ran down that valley, chasing twenty men with bows and arrows, and the row was tremenjus. They was fair men – fairer than you or me – with yellow hair and remarkable well built. Says Dravot, unpacking the guns – "This is the beginning of the business. We'll fight for the ten men," and with that he fires two rifles at the twenty men, and drops one of them at two hundred yards from the rock where he was sitting. The other men began to run, but Carnehan and Dravot sits on the boxes picking them off at all ranges, up and down the valley. Then we goes up to the ten

men that had run across the snow too, and they fires a footy
little arrow at us. Dravot he shoots above their heads and they
all falls down flat. Then he walks over them and kicks them, and
then he lifts them up and shakes hands all round to make them
friendly like. He calls them and gives them the boxes to carry,
and waves his hand for all the world as though hc was King
already. They takes the boxes and him across the valley and up
the hill into a pine wood on the top, where there was half-a-
dozen big stone idols. Dravot he goes to the biggest – a fellow
they call Imbra – and lays a rifle and a cartridge at his feet,
rubbing his nose respectful with his own nose, patting him on
the head, and saluting in front of it. He turns round to the men
and nods his head, and says – "That's all right. I'm in the know
too, and all these old jim-jams are my friends." Then he opens
his mouth and points down it, and when the first man brings
him food, he says – "No"; and when the second man brings
him food he says – "No"; but when one of the old priests and
the boss of the village brings him food, he says – "Yes," very
haughty, and eats it slow. That was how we came to our first
village, without any trouble, just as though we had tumbled
from the skies. But we tumbled from one of those damned
rope-bridges, you see, and – you couldn't expect a man to laugh
much after that?'

'Take some more whisky and go on,' I said. 'That was the
first village you came into. How did you get to be King?'

'I wasn't King,' said Carnehan. 'Dravot he was the King,
and a handsome man he looked with the gold crown on his head
and all. Him and the other party stayed in that village, and
every morning Dravot sat by the side of old Imbra, and the
people came and worshipped. That was Dravot's order. Then a
lot of men came into the valley, and Carnehan and Dravot picks
them off with the rifles before they knew where they was, and
runs down into the valley and up again the other side and finds
another village, same as the first one, and the people all falls
down flat on their faces, and Dravot says – "Now what is the
trouble between you two villages?" and the people points to a
woman, as fair as you or me, that was carried off, and Dravot

takes her back to the first village and counts up the dead – eight there was. For each dead man Dravot pours a little milk on the ground and waves his arms like a whirligig, and "That's all right," says he. Then he and Carnehan takes the big boss of each village by the arm and walks them down into the valley, and shows them how to scratch a line with a spear right down the valley, and gives each a sod of turf from both sides of the line. Then all the people comes down and shouts like the devil and all, and Dravot says –"Go and dig the land, and be fruitful and multiply,"³² which they did, though they didn't understand. Then we asks the names of things in their lingo – bread and water and fire and idols and such, and Dravot leads the priest of each village up to the idol, and says he must sit there and judge the people, and if anything goes wrong he is to be shot.

'Next week they was all turning up the land in the valley as quiet as bees and much prettier, and the priests heard all the complaints and told Dravot in dumb show what it was about. "That's just the beginning," says Dravot. "They think we're Gods." He and Carnehan picks out twenty good men and shows them how to click off a rifle, and form fours, and advance in line, and they was very pleased to do so, and clever to see the hang of it. Then he takes out his pipe and his baccy-pouch and leaves one at one village, and one at the other, and off we two goes to see what was to be done in the next valley. That was all rock, and there was a little village there, and Carnehan says – "Send 'em to the old valley to plant," and takes 'em there, and gives 'em some land that wasn't took before. They were a poor lot, and we blooded 'em³³ with a kid before letting 'em into the new Kingdom. That was to impress the people, and then they settled down quiet, and Carnehan went back to Dravot who had got into another valley, all snow and ice and most mountaineous. There was no people there and the Army got afraid, so Dravot shoots one of them, and goes on till he finds some people in a village, and the Army explains that unless the people wants to be killed they had better not shoot their little matchlocks; for they had matchlocks. We makes friends with the priest, and I

stays there alone with two of the Army, teaching the men how to
drill, and a thundering big Chief comes across the snow with
kettle-drums and horns twanging, because he heard there was a
new God kicking about. Carnehan sights for the brown [34] of the
men half a mile across the snow and wings one of them. Then
he sends a message to the Chief that, unless he wished to be
killed, he must come and shake hands with me and leave his
arms behind. The Chief comes alone first, and Carnehan shakes
hands with him and whirls his arms about, same as Dravot
used, and very much surprised that Chief was, and strokes my
eyebrows. Then Carnehan goes alone to the Chief, and asks
him in dumb show if he had an enemy he hated. "I have," says
the Chief. So Carnehan weeds out the pick of his men, and sets
the two of the Army to show them drill, and at the end of two
weeks the men can manoeuvre about as well as Volunteers. [35]
So he marches with the Chief to a great big plain on the top of a
mountain, and the Chief's men rushes into a village and takes
it; we three Martinis firing into the brown of the enemy. So
we took that village too, and I gives the Chief a rag from my
coat and says, "Occupy till I come"; which was scriptural. [36] By
way of a reminder, when me and the Army was eighteen hundred yards away, I drops a bullet near him standing on the
snow, and all the people falls flat on their faces. Then I sends a
letter to Dravot wherever he be by land or by sea.'

At the risk of throwing the creature out of train I interrupted
– 'How could you write a letter up yonder?'

'The letter? – Oh! – The letter! Keep looking at me between
the eyes, please. It was a string-talk letter, that we'd learned the
way of it from a blind beggar in the Punjab.'

I remember that there had once come to the office a blind
man with a knotted twig and a piece of string which he wound
round the twig according to some cipher of his own. He could,
after the lapse of days or hours, repeat the sentence which he
had reeled up. He had reduced the alphabet to eleven primitive
sounds, and tried to teach me his method, but I could not understand.

'I sent that letter to Dravot,' said Carnehan; 'and told him to come back because this Kingdom was growing too big for me to handle, and then I struck for the first valley, to see how the priests were working. They called the village we took along with the Chief, Bashkai, and the first village we took, Er-Heb. The priests at Er-Heb was doing all right, but they had a lot of pending cases about land to show me, and some men from another village had been firing arrows at night. I went out and looked for that village, and fired four rounds at it from a thousand yards. That used all the cartridges I cared to spend, and I waited for Dravot, who had been away two or three months, and I kept my people quiet.

'One morning I heard the devil's own noise of drums and horns, and Dan Dravot marches down the hill with his Army and a tail of hundreds of men, and, which was the most amazing, a great gold crown on his head. "My Gord, Carnehan," says Daniel, "this is a tremenjus business, and we've got the whole country as far as it's worth having. I am the son of Alexander by Queen Semiramis,[37] and you're my younger brother and a God too! It's the biggest thing we've ever seen. I've been marching and fighting for six weeks with the Army, and every footy little village for fifty miles has come in rejoiceful; and more than that, I've got the key of the whole show, as you'll see, and I've got a crown for you! I told 'em to make two of 'em at a place called Shu, where the gold lies in the rock like suet in mutton. Gold I've seen, and turquoise I've kicked out of the cliffs, and there's garnets in the sands of the river, and here's a chunk of amber that a man brought me. Call up all the priests and, here, take your crown."

'One of the men opens a black hair bag, and I slips the crown on. It was too small and too heavy, but I wore it for the glory. Hammered gold it was – five pound weight, like a hoop of a barrel.

'"Peachey," says Dravot, "we don't want to fight no more. The Craft's[38] the trick, so help me!" and he brings forward that same Chief that I left at Bashkai – Billy Fish we called him afterwards, because he was so like Billy Fish that drove the big tank-engine at Mach on the Bolan in the old days. "Shake hands with him," says Dravot, and I shook hands and nearly dropped, for Billy Fish gave me the Grip. I said nothing, but tried him with the Fellow Craft Grip. He answers all right, and I tried the Master's Grip, but that was a slip. "A Fellow Craft he is!" I says to Dan. "Does he know the word?" – "He does," says Dan, "and all the priests know. It's a miracle! The Chiefs and the priests can work a Fellow Craft Lodge in a way that's very like ours, and they've cut the marks on the rocks, but they don't know the Third Degree, and they've come to find out. It's Gord's Truth. I've known these long years that the Afghans knew up to the Fellow Craft Degree, but this is a miracle. A God and a Grand-Master of the Craft am I, and a Lodge in the Third Degree I will open, and we'll raise the head priests and the Chiefs of the villages."

'"It's against all the law," I says, "holding a Lodge without warrant from any one; and you know we never held office in any Lodge."

'"It's a master-stroke o' policy," says Dravot. "It means running the country as easy as a four-wheeled bogie[39] on a down grade. We can't stop to inquire now, or they'll turn against us. I've forty Chiefs at my heel, and passed and raised according to their merit they shall be. Billet these men on the villages, and see that we run up a Lodge of some kind. The temple of Imbra will do for the Lodge-room. The women must make aprons as you show them. I'll hold a levee of Chiefs tonight and Lodge tomorrow."

'I was fair run off my legs, but I wasn't such a fool as not to see what a pull this Craft business gave us. I showed the priests' families how to make aprons of the degrees, but for Dravot's apron the blue border and marks was made of turquoise lumps on white hide, not cloth. We took a great square stone in the temple for the Master's chair, and little stones for the officers' chairs, and painted the black pavement with white squares, and did what we could to make things regular.

'At the levee which was held that night on the hillside with big bonfires, Dravot gives out that him and me were Gods and sons of Alexander, and Past Grand-Masters in the Craft, and was come to make Kafiristan a country where every man should eat in peace and drink in quiet, and specially obey us. Then the Chiefs come round to shake hands, and they were so hairy and white and fair it was just shaking hands with old friends. We gave them names according as they was like men we had known in India – Billy Fish, Holly Dilworth, Pikky Kergan, that was Bazar-master [40] when I was at Mhow, and so on, and so on.

'*The* most amazing miracles was at Lodge next night. One of the old priests was watching us continuous, and I felt uneasy, for I knew we'd have to fudge the Ritual, and I didn't know what the men knew. The old priest was a stranger come in from beyond the village of Bashkai. The minute Dravot puts on the Master's apron that the girls had made for him, the priest fetches a whoop and a howl, and tries to overturn the stone that Dravot was sitting on. "It's all up now," I says. "That comes of meddling with the Craft without warrant!" Dravot never winked an eye, not when ten priests took and tilted over the Grand-Master's chair – which was to say the stone of Imbra. The priests begins rubbing the bottom end of it to clear away the black dirt, and presently he shows all the other priests the Master's Mark, same as was on Dravot's apron, cut into the stone. Not even the priests of the temple of Imbra knew it was there. The old chap falls flat on his face at Dravot's feet and kisses.'em. "Luck again," says Dravot, across the Lodge to me; "they say it's the Missing Mark that no one could understand the why of. We're more than safe now." Then he bangs the butt of his gun for a gavel and says: "By virtue of the authority vested in me by my own right hand and the help of Peachey, I declare myself Grand-Master of all Freemasonry in Kafiristan in this the Mother Lodge o' the country, and King of Kafiristan equally with Peachey!" [41] At that he puts on his crown and I puts on mine – I was doing Senior Warden – and we opens the Lodge in most ample form. It was a amazing miracle! The priests moved in Lodge through the first two degrees almost without telling, as if the memory was coming back to them. After that, Peachey and Dravot raised [42] such as was worthy – high priests and Chiefs of far-off villages. Billy Fish was the first, and I can tell you we scared the soul out of him. It was not in any way according to Ritual, but it served our turn. We didn't raise more than ten of the biggest men, because we didn't want to make the Degree common. And they was clamouring to be raised.

'"In another six months," says Dravot, "we'll hold another Communication, and see how you are working." Then he asks them about their villages, and learns that they was fighting one against the other, and were sick and tired of it. And when they wasn't doing that they was fighting with the Mohammedans. "You can fight those when they come into our country," says Dravot. "Tell off every tenth man of your tribes for a Frontier guard, and send two hundred at a time to this valley to be drilled. Nobody is going to be shot or speared any more so long as he does well, and I know that you won't cheat me, because you're white people – sons of Alexander – and not like common, black Mohammedans. You are *my* people, and by God," says he, running off into English at the end – "I'll make a damned fine Nation of you, or I'll die in the making!"

'I can't tell all we did for the next six months, because Dravot did a lot I couldn't see the hang of, and he learned their lingo in a way I never could. My work was to help the people plough, and now and again go out with some of the Army and see what the other villages were doing, and make 'em throw rope-bridges across the ravines which cut up the country horrid. Dravot was very kind to me, but when he walked up and down in the pine wood pulling that bloody red beard of his with both fists I knew he was thinking plans I could not advise about, and I just waited for orders.

'But Dravot never showed me disrespect before the people. They were afraid of me and the Army, but they loved Dan. He was the best of friends with the priests and the Chiefs; but anyone could come across the hills with a complaint, and Dravot would hear him out fair, and call four priests together and say what was to be done. He used to call in Billy Fish from Bashkai, and Pikky Kergan from Shu, and an old Chief we called Kafu-zelum [43] – it was like enough to his real name – and hold councils

233

with 'em when there was any fighting to be done in small villages. That was his Council of War, and the four priests of Bashkai, Shu, Khawak, and Madora was his Privy Council. Between the lot of 'em they sent me, with forty men and twenty rifles and sixty men carrying turquoises, into the Ghorband country to buy those hand-made Martini rifles, that come out of the Amir's workshops at Kabul, from one of the Amir's Herati regiments that would have sold the very teeth out of their mouths for turquoises.

'I stayed in Ghorband a month, and gave the Governor there the pick of my baskets for hush-money, and bribed the Colonel of the regiment some more, and, between the two and the tribespeople, we got more than a hundred hand-made Martinis, a hundred good Kohat Jezails[44] that'll throw to six hundred yards, and forty man-loads of very bad ammunition for the rifles. I came back with what I had, and distributed 'em among the men that the Chiefs sent in to me to drill. Dravot was too busy to attend to those things, but the old Army that we first made helped me, and we turned out five hundred men that could drill, and two hundred that knew how to hold arms pretty straight. Even those cork-screwed, hand-made guns was a miracle to them. Dravot talked big about powder-shops and factories, walking up and down in the pine wood when the winter was coming on.

'"I won't make a Nation," says he. "I'll make an Empire! These men aren't niggers;[45] they're English! Look at their eyes – look at their mouths. Look at the way they stand up. They sit on chairs in their own houses. They're the Lost Tribes, or something like it, and they've grown to be English. I'll take a census in the spring if the priests don't get frightened. There must be a fair two million of 'em in these hills. The villages are full o' little children. Two million people – two hundred and fifty thousand fighting men – and all English! They only want the rifles and a little drilling. Two hundred and fifty thousand men, ready to cut in on Russia's right flank when she tries for India! Peachey, man," he says, chewing his beard in great hunks, "we shall be Emperors – Emperors of the Earth! Rajah Brooke will be a suckling to us. I'll treat with the Viceroy on equal terms. I'll ask him to send me twelve picked English – twelve that I know of – to help us govern a bit. There's Mackray, Sergeant-pensioner at Segowli – many's the good dinner he's given me, and his wife a pair of trousers. There's Donkin, the Warder of Tounghoo Jail; there's hundreds that I could lay my hand on if I was in India. The Viceroy shall do it for me. I'll send a man through in the spring for those men, and I'll write for a dispensation from the Grand Lodge for what I've done as Grand-Master. That – and all the Sniders [46] that'll be thrown out when the native troops in India take up the Martini. They'll be worn smooth, but they'll do for fighting in these hills. Twelve English, a hundred thousand Sniders run through the Amir's country in driblets – I'd be content with twenty thousand in one year – and we'd be an Empire. When everything was ship-shape, I'd hand over the crown – this crown I'm wearing now – to Queen Victoria on my knees, and she'd say: 'Rise up, Sir Daniel Dravot.' Oh, it's big! It's big, I tell you! But there's so much to be done in every place – Bashkai, Khawak, Shu, and everywhere else."

"'What is it?' I says. "There are no more men coming in to be drilled this autumn. Look at those fat, black clouds. They're bringing the snow."

"'It isn't that,' says Daniel, putting his hand very hard on my shoulder; "and I don't wish to say anything that's against you, for no other living man would have followed me and made me what I am as you have done. You're a first-class Commander-in-Chief, and the people know you; but – it's a big country, and somehow you can't help me, Peachey, in the way I want to be helped."

"'Go to your blasted priests, then!" I said, and I was sorry when I made that remark, but it did hurt me sore to find Daniel talking so superior when I'd drilled all the men, and done all he told me.

"'Don't let's quarrel, Peachey,' says Daniel without cursing. "You're a King too, and the half of this Kingdom is yours; but can't you see, Peachey, we want cleverer men than us now –

three or four of 'em, that we can scatter about for our Deputies. It's a hugeous great State, and I can't always tell the right thing to do, and I haven't time for all I want to do, and here's the winter coming on and all." He put half his beard into his mouth, all red like the gold of his crown.

"'I'm sorry, Daniel," says I. "I've done all I could. I've drilled the men and shown the people how to stack their oats better; and I've brought in those tinware rifles from Ghorband – but I know what you're driving at. I take it Kings always feel oppressed that way."

"'There's another thing too," says Dravot, walking up and down. "The winter's coming and these people won't be giving much trouble, and if they do we can't move about. I want a wife."

"'For Gord's sake leave the women alone!" I says. "We've both got all the work we can, though I *am* a fool. Remember the Contrack, and keep clear o' women."

"'The Contrack only lasted till such time as we was Kings; and Kings we have been these months past," says Dravot, weighing his crown in his hand. "You go get a wife too, Peachey – a nice, strappin', plump girl that'll keep you warm in the winter. They're prettier than English girls, and we can take the pick of 'em. Boil 'em once or twice in hot water and they'll come out like chicken and ham."

"'Don't tempt me!" I says. "I will not have any dealings with a woman not till we are a dam' side more settled than we are now. I've been doing the work o' two men, and you've been doing the work o' three. Let's lie off a bit, and see if we can get some better tobacco from Afghan country and run in some good liquor; but no women."

"'Who's talking o' *women?*" says Dravot. "I said *wife* – a Queen to breed a King's son for the King. A Queen out of the strongest tribe, that'll make them your blood-brothers, and that'll lie by your side and tell you all the people thinks about you and their own affairs. That's what I want."

"'Do you remember that Bengali woman I kept at Mogul Serai when I was a plate-layer?" says I. "A fat lot o' good she was to me. She taught me the lingo and one or two other things; but what happened? She ran away with the Station-master's servant and half my month's pay. Then she turned up at Dadur Junction in tow of a half-caste, and had the impidence to say I was her husband — all among the drivers in the running-shed too!"

'"We've done with that," says Dravot; "these women are whiter than you or me, and a Queen I will have for the winter months."

'"For the last time o' asking, Dan, do *not*," I says. "It'll only bring us harm. The Bible says that Kings ain't to waste their strength on women,[47] 'specially when they've got a new raw Kingdom to work over."

'"For the last time of answering[48] I will," said Dravot, and he went away through the pine-trees looking like a big red devil, the sun being on his crown and beard and all.

'But getting a wife was not as easy as Dan thought. He put it before the Council, and there was no answer till Billy Fish said that he'd better ask the girls. Dravot damned them all round. "What's wrong with me?" he shouts, standing by the idol Imbra. "Am I a dog or am I not enough of a man for your wenches? Haven't I put the shadow of my hand over this country? Who stopped the last Afghan raid?" It was me really, but Dravot was too angry to remember. "Who bought your guns? Who repaired the bridges? Who's the Grand-Master of the sign cut in the stone?" says he, and he thumped his hand on the block that he used to sit on in Lodge, and at Council, which opened like Lodge always. Billy Fish said nothing and no more did the others. "Keep your hair on, Dan," said I; "and ask the girls. That's how it's done at Home, and these people are quite English."

'"The marriage of the King is a matter of State," says Dan, in a white-hot rage, for he could feel, I hope, that he was going against his better mind. He walked out of the Council-room, and the others sat still, looking at the ground.

'"Billy Fish," says I to the Chief of Bashkai, "what's the difficulty here? A straight answer to a true friend."

'"You know," says Billy Fish. "How should a man tell you who knows everything? How can daughters of men[49] marry Gods or Devils? It's not proper."

'I remembered something like that in the Bible; but if, after seeing us as long as they had, they still believed we were Gods, it wasn't for me to undeceive them.

'"A God can do anything," says I. "If the King is fond of a girl he'll not let her die." – "She'll have to," said Billy Fish. "There are all sorts of Gods and Devils in these mountains, and now and again a girl marries one of them and isn't seen any more. Besides, you two know the Mark cut in the stone. Only the Gods know that. We thought you were men till you showed the sign of the Master."

'I wished then that we had explained about the loss of the genuine secrets of a Master-Mason at the first go-off; but I said nothing. All that night there was a blowing of horns in a little dark temple half-way down the hill, and I heard a girl crying fit to die. One of the priests told us that she was being prepared to marry the King.

'"I'll have no nonsense of that kind," says Dan. "I don't want to interfere with your customs, but I'll take my own wife." – "The girl's a little bit afraid," says the priest. "She thinks she's going to die, and they are a-heartening of her up down in the temple."

'"Hearten her very tender, then," says Dravot, "or I'll hearten you with the butt of a gun so you'll never want to be heartened again." He licked his lips, did Dan, and stayed up walking about more than half the night, thinking of the wife that he was going to get in the morning. I wasn't any means comfortable, for I knew that dealings with a woman in foreign parts, though you was a crowned King twenty times over, could not but be risky. I got up very early in the morning while Dravot was asleep, and I saw the priests talking together in whispers, and the Chiefs talking together too, and they looked at me out of the corners of their eyes.

'"What is up, Fish?" I say to the Bashkai man, who was wrapped up in his furs and looking splendid to behold.

'"I can't rightly say," says he; "but if you can make the King drop all this nonsense about marriage, you'll be doing him and me and yourself a great service."

'"That I do believe," says I. "But sure, you know, Billy, as well as me, having fought against and for us, that the King and me are nothing more than two of the finest men that God Almighty ever made. Nothing more, I do assure you."

'"That may be," says Billy Fish, "and yet I should be sorry if it was." He sinks his head upon his great fur cloak for a minute and thinks. "King," says he, "be you man or God or Devil, I'll stick by you today. I have twenty of my men with me, and they will follow me. We'll go to Bashkai until the storm blows over."

'A little snow had fallen in the night, and everything was white except the greasy fat clouds that blew down and down from the north. Dravot came out with his crown on his head, swinging his arms and stamping his feet, and looking more pleased than Punch.

'"For the last time, drop it, Dan," says I in a whisper, "Billy Fish here says that there will be a row."

'"A row among my people!" says Dravot. "Not much. Peachey, you're a fool not to get a wife too. Where's the girl?" says he with a voice as loud as the braying of a jackass. "Call up all the Chiefs and priests, and let the Emperor see if his wife suits him."

'There was no need to call anyone. They were all there leaning on their guns and spears round the clearing in the centre of the pine wood. A lot of priests went down to the little temple to bring up the girl, and the horns blew fit to wake the dead. Billy Fish saunters round and gets as close to Daniel as he could, and behind him stood his twenty men with matchlocks. Not a man of them under six feet. I was next to Dravot, and behind me was twenty men of the regular Army. Up comes the girl, and a strapping wench she was, covered with silver and turquoises, but white as death, and looking back every minute at the priests.

'"She'll do," said Dan, looking her over. "What's to be

afraid of, lass? Come and kiss me." He puts his arm round her. She shuts her eyes, gives a bit of a squeak, and down goes her face in the side of Dan's flaming red beard.

'"The slut's bitten me!" says he, clapping his hand to his neck, and, sure enough, his hand was red with blood. Billy Fish and two of his matchlock-men catches hold of Dan by the shoulders and drags him into the Bashkai lot, while the priests howls in their lingo —"Neither God nor Devil but a man!" I was all taken aback, for a priest cut at me in front, and the Army behind began firing into the Bashkai men.

'"God A'mighty!" says Dan. "What is the meaning o' this?"

'"Come back! Come away!" says Billy Fish. "Ruin and Mutiny is the matter. We'll break for Bashkai if we can."

'I tried to give some sort of orders to my men — the men o' the Regular Army — but it was no use, so I fired into the brown of 'em with an English Martini and drilled three beggars in a line. The valley was full of shouting, howling creatures, and every soul was shrieking, "Not a God or a Devil but only a man!" The Bashkai troops stuck to Billy Fish for all they were worth, but their matchlocks wasn't half as good as the Kabul breech-loaders, and four of them dropped. Dan was bellowing like a bull, for he was very wrathy; and Billy Fish had a hard job to prevent him running out at the crowd.

'"We can't stand," says Billy Fish. "Make a run for it down the valley! The whole place is against us." The matchlock-men ran, and we went down the valley in spite of Dravot. He was swearing horribly and crying out he was King. The priests rolled great stones on us, and the regular Army fired hard, and there wasn't more than six men, not counting Dan, Billy Fish, and Me, that came down to the bottom of the valley alive.

'Then they stopped firing and the horns in the temple blew again. "Come away — for God's sake come away!" says Billy Fish. "They'll send runners out to all the villages before ever we get to Bashkai. I can protect you there, but I can't do anything now."

'My own notion is that Dan began to go mad in his head from that hour. He stared up and down like a stuck pig. Then he was all for walking back alone and killing the priests with his bare hands; which he could have done. "An Emperor am I," says Daniel, "and next year I shall be a Knight of the Queen."

'"All right, Dan," says I; "but come along now while there's time."

'"It's your fault," says he, "for not looking after your Army better. There was mutiny in the midst, and you didn't know – you damned engine-driving, plate-laying, missionary's-pass-hunting hound!" He sat upon a rock and called me every foul name he could lay tongue to. I was too heart-sick to care, though it was all his foolishness that brought the smash.

'"I'm sorry, Dan," says I, "but there's no accounting for natives. This business is our Fifty-Seven.[50] Maybe we'll make something out of it yet, when we've got to Bashkai."

'"Let's get to Bashkai, then," says Dan, "and, by God, when I come back here again I'll sweep the valley so there isn't a bug in a blanket left!"

'We walked all that day, and all that night Dan was stumping up and down on the snow, chewing his beard and muttering to himself.

'"There's no hope o' getting clear," said Billy Fish. "The priests will have sent runners to the villages to say that you are only men. Why didn't you stick on as Gods till things was more settled? I'm a dead man," says Billy Fish, and he throws himself down on the snow and begins to pray to his Gods.

'Next morning we was in a cruel bad country –all up and down, no level ground at all, and no food either. The six Bashkai men looked at Billy Fish hungry-way as if they wanted to ask something, but they said never a word. At noon we came to the top of a flat mountain all covered with snow, and when we climbed up into it, behold, there was an Army in position waiting in the middle!

'"The runners have been very quick," says Billy Fish, with a little bit of a laugh. "They are waiting for us."

'Three or four men began to fire from the enemy's side, and a chance shot took Daniel in the calf of the leg. That brought him to his senses. He looks across the snow at the Army, and sees the rifles that we had brought into the country.

'"We're done for," says he. "They are Englishmen, these people – and it's my blasted nonsense that has brought you to this. Get back, Billy Fish, and take your men away; you've done what you could, and now cut for it. Carnehan," says he, "shake hands with me and go along with Billy. Maybe they won't kill you. I'll go and meet 'em alone. It's me that did it. Me, the King!"

'"Go!" says I. "Go to Hell, Dan! I'm with you here. Billy Fish, you clear out, and we two will meet those folk."

'"I'm a Chief," says Billy Fish, quite quiet. "I stay with you. My men can go."

'The Bashkai fellows didn't wait for a second word, but ran off, and Dan and Me and Billy Fish walked across to where the drums were drumming and the horns were horning. It was cold – awful cold. I've got that cold in the back of my head now. There's a lump of it there.'

The punkah-coolies had gone to sleep. Two kerosene lamps were blazing in the office, and the perspiration poured down my face and splashed on the blotter as I leaned forward. Carnehan was shivering, and I feared that his mind might go. I wiped my face, took a fresh grip of the piteously mangled hands, and said: 'What happened after that?'

The momentary shift of my eyes had broken the clear current.

'What was you pleased to say?' whined Carnehan. 'They took them without any sound. Not a little whisper all along the snow, not though the King knocked down the first man that set hand on him – not though old Peachey fired his last cartridge into the brown of 'em. Not a single solitary sound did those swines make. They just closed up tight, and I tell you their furs stunk. There was a man called Billy Fish, a good friend of us all, and they cut his throat, Sir, then and there, like a pig; and the King kicks up the bloody snow and says: "We've had a dashed fine run for our money. What's coming next?" But Peachey, Peachey Taliaferro, I tell you, Sir, in confidence as betwixt two friends, he lost his head, Sir. No, he didn't neither. The King lost his head, so he did, all along o' one of those cunning rope-bridges. Kindly let me have the paper-cutter, Sir. It tilted this way. They marched him a mile across that snow to a rope-bridge over a ravine with a river at the bottom. You may have seen such. They prodded him behind like an ox. "Damn your eyes!" says the King. "D'you suppose I can't die like a gentleman?" He turns to Peachey – Peachey that was crying like a child. "I've brought you to this, Peachey," says he. "Brought you out of your happy life to be killed in Kafiristan, where you was late Commander-in-Chief of the Emperor's forces. Say you forgive me, Peachey." – "I do," says Peachey. "Fully and freely do I forgive you, Dan." – "Shake hands, Peachey," says he. "I'm going now." Out he goes, looking neither right nor left, and when he was plumb in the middle of those dizzy looking ropes – "Cut, you beggars," he shouts; and they cut, and old Dan fell, turning round and round and round, twenty thousand miles, for he took half an hour to fall till he struck the water, and I could see his body caught on a rock with the gold crown close beside.

'But do you know what they did to Peachey between two pine-trees? They crucified him, Sir, as Peachey's hand will show. They used wooden pegs for his hands and his feet; and he didn't die. He hung there and screamed, and they took him down next day, and said it was a miracle that he wasn't dead. They took him down – poor old Peachey that hadn't done them any harm – that hadn't done them any –'

He rocked to and fro and wept bitterly, wiping his eyes with the back of his scarred hands and moaning like a child for some ten minutes.

'They was cruel enough to feed him up in the temple, because they said he was more of a God than old Daniel that was a man. Then they turned him out on the snow, and told him to go home, and Peachey came home in about a year, begging along the roads quite safe; for Daniel Dravot he walked before and said: "Come along Peachey. It's a big thing we're doing." The mountains they danced at night, and the mountains they tried to fall on Peachy's head, but Dan he held up his hand, and Peachey came along bent double. He never let go of Dan's hand, and he never let go of Dan's head. They gave it to him as a present in the temple, to remind him not to come again, and though the crown was pure gold, and Peachey was starving, never would Peachey sell the same. You knew Dravot, Sir! You knew Right Worshipful Brother Dravot! Look at him now!'

He fumbled in the mass of rags round his bent waist; brought out a black horsehair bag embroidered with silver thread, and shook therefrom on to my table – the dried withered head of Daniel Dravot! The morning sun that had long been paling the lamps struck the red beard and blind sunken eyes; struck, too, a heavy circlet of gold studded with raw turquoises, that Carnehan placed tenderly on the battered temples.

'You be'old now,' said Carnehan, 'the Emperor in his 'abit as he lived[51] – the King of Kafiristan with his crown upon his head. Poor old Daniel that was a monarch once!'

I shuddered, for, in spite of defacements manifold, I recognized the head of the man of Marwar Junction. Carnehan rose to go. I attempted to stop him. He was not fit to walk abroad. 'Let me take away the whisky, and give me a little money,' he gasped. 'I was a King once. I'll go to the Deputy Commissioner and ask to set in the Poorhouse till I get my health. No, thank you, I can't wait till you get a carriage for me. I've urgent private affairs – in the south – at Marwar.'

He shambled out of the office and departed in the direction of the Deputy Commissioner's house. That day at noon I had occasion to go down the blinding hot Mall, and I saw a crooked man crawling along the white dust of the roadside, his hat in his hand, quavering dolorously after the fashion of street-singers at Home. There was not a soul in sight, and he was out of all possible earshot of the houses. And he sang through his nose, turning his head from right to left:

'The Son of Man goes forth to war,
    A golden crown to gain;
His blood-red banner streams afar –
    Who follows in his train?'[52]

I waited to hear no more, but put the poor wretch into my carriage and drove him off to the nearest missionary for eventual transfer to the Asylum. He repeated the hymn twice while he was with me whom he did not in the least recognize, and I left him singing it to the missionary.

Two days later I inquired after his welfare of the Superintendent of the Asylum.

'He was admitted suffering from sunstroke. He died early yesterday morning,' said the Superintendent. 'Is it true that he was half an hour bare-headed in the sun at mid-day?'

'Yes,' said I, 'but do you happen to know if he had anything upon him by any chance when he died?'

'Not to my knowledge,' said the Superintendent.

And there the matter rests.

WEE WILLIE WINKIE
AND OTHER STORIES[1]

¶ Wee Willie Winkie [1] §

An officer and a gentleman.

His full name was Percival William Williams, but he picked up the other name in a nursery-book,[2] and that was the end of the christened titles. His mother's *ayah* called him Willie-*Baba*, but as he never paid the faintest attention to anything that the *ayah* said, her wisdom did not help matters.

His father was the Colonel of the 195th, and as soon as Wee Willie Winkie was old enough to understand what Military Discipline meant, Colonel Williams put him under it. There was no other way of managing the child. When he was good for a week, he drew good-conduct pay; and when he was bad, he was deprived of his good-conduct stripe. Generally he was bad, for India offers many chances of going wrong to little six-year-olds.

Children resent familiarity from strangers, and Wee Willie Winkie was a very particular child. Once he accepted an acquaintance, he was graciously pleased to thaw. He accepted Brandis, a subaltern of the 195th, on sight. Brandis was having tea at the Colonel's, and Wee Willie Winkie entered strong in the possession of a good-conduct badge won for not chasing the hens round the compound. He regarded Brandis with gravity for at least ten minutes, and then delivered himself of his opinion.

'I like you,' said he slowly, getting off his chair and coming over to Brandis. 'I like you. I shall call you Coppy, because of your hair. Do you *mind* being called Coppy? It is because of ve hair, you know.'

Here was one of the most embarrassing of Wee Willie Winkie's peculiarities. He would look at a stranger for some time, and then, without warning or explanation, would give him a name. And the name stuck. No regimental penalties could break Wee Willie Winkie off this habit. He lost his good-conduct badge for christening the Commissioner's wife 'Pobs'; but nothing that the Colonel could do made the Station forego the nickname, and Mrs Collen remained 'Pobs' till the end of her stay. So Brandis was christened 'Coppy', and rose, therefore, in the estimation of the regiment.

If Wee Willie Winkie took an interest in any one, the fortunate man was envied alike by the mess and the rank and file. And in their envy lay no suspicion of self-interest. 'The Colonel's son' was idolized on his own merits entirely. Yet Wee Willie Winkie was not lovely. His face was permanently freckled, as his legs were permanently scratched, and in spite of his mother's almost tearful remonstrances he had insisted upon having his long yellow locks cut short in the military fashion. 'I want my hair like Sergeant Tummil's,' said Wee Willie Winkie, and, his father abetting, the sacrifice was accomplished.

Three weeks after the bestowal of his youthful affections on Lieutenant Brandis – henceforward to be called 'Coppy' for the sake of brevity – Wee Willie Winkie was destined to behold strange things and far beyond his comprehension.

Coppy returned his liking with interest. Coppy had let him wear for five rapturous minutes his own big sword – just as tall as Wee Willie Winkie. Coppy had promised him a terrier puppy; and Coppy had permitted him to witness the miraculous operation of shaving. Nay, more – Coppy had said that even he, Wee Willie Winkie, would rise in time to the ownership of a box of shiny knives, a silver soap-box, and a silver-handled 'sputter-brush', as Wee Willie Winkie called it. Decidedly, there was no one except his father, who could give or take away good-conduct badges at pleasure, half so wise, strong, and valiant as Coppy with the Afghan and Egyptian medals on his breast. Why, then, should Coppy be guilty of the unmanly weakness of kissing – vehemently kissing – a 'big girl', Miss Allardyce to wit? In the course of a morning ride Wee Willie Winkie had seen Coppy so doing, and, like the gentleman he was, had promptly wheeled round and cantered back to his groom, lest the groom should also see.

Under ordinary circumstances he would have spoken to his father, but he felt instinctively that this was a matter on which Coppy ought first to be consulted.

'Coppy,' shouted Wee Willie Winkie, reining up outside that subaltern's bungalow early one morning – 'I want to see you, Coppy!'

'Come in, young 'un,' returned Coppy, who was at early breakfast in the midst of his dogs. 'What mischief have you been getting into now?'

Wee Willie Winkie had done nothing notoriously bad for three days, and so stood on a pinnacle of virtue.

'*I've* been doing nothing bad,' said he, curling himself into a long chair with a studious affectation of the Colonel's languor after a hot parade. He buried his freckled nose in a tea-cup and, with eyes staring roundly over the rim, asked: 'I say, Coppy, is it pwoper to kiss big girls?'

'By Jove! You're beginning early. Who do you want to kiss?'

'No one. My muvver's always kissing me if I don't stop her. If it isn't pwoper, how was you kissing Major Allardyce's big girl last morning, by ve canal?'

Coppy's brow wrinkled. He and Miss Allardyce had with great craft managed to keep their engagement secret for a fortnight. There were urgent and imperative reasons why Major Allardyce should not know how matters stood for at least another month, and this small marplot[3] had discovered a great deal too much.

'I saw you,' said Wee Willie Winkie calmly. 'But ve *sais* didn't see. I said, "*Hut jao!*"'[4]

'Oh, you had that much sense, you young Rip,' groaned poor Coppy, half amused and half angry. 'And how many people may you have told about it?'

'Only me myself. You didn't tell when I twied to wide ve buffalo ven my pony was lame; and I fought you wouldn't like.'

'Winkie,' said Coppy enthusiastically, shaking the small hand, 'you're the best of good fellows. Look here, you can't understand all these things. One of these days – hang it, how can I make you see it! – I'm going to marry Miss Allardyce, and then she'll be Mrs Coppy, as you say. If your young mind is so scandalized at the idea of kissing big girls, go and tell your father.'

'What will happen?' said Wee Willie Winkie, who firmly believed that his father was omnipotent.

'I shall get into trouble,' said Coppy, playing his trump card with an appealing look at the holder of the ace.

'Ven I won't,' said Wee Willie Winkie briefly. 'But my faver says it's un-man-ly to be always kissing, and I didn't fink *you'd* do vat, Coppy.'

'I'm not always kissing, old chap. It's only now and then, and when you're bigger you'll do it too. Your father meant it's not good for little boys.'

'Ah!' said Wee Willie Winkie, now fully enlightened. 'It's like ve sputter-brush?'

'Exactly,' said Coppy gravely.

'But I don't fink I'll ever want to kiss big girls, nor no one, 'cept my muvver. And I *must* vat, you know.'

There was a long pause, broken by Wee Willie Winkie.

'Are you fond of vis big girl, Coppy?'

'Awfully!' said Coppy.

'Fonder van you are of Bell or ve Butcha[5] – or me?'

'It's in a different way,' said Coppy. 'You see, one of these days Miss Allardyce will belong to me, but you'll grow up and command the Regiment and – all sorts of things. It's quite different, you see.'

'Very well,' said Wee Willie Winkie, rising. 'If you're fond of ve big girl I won't tell any one. I must go now.'

Coppy rose and escorted his small guest to the door, adding – 'You're the best of little fellows, Winkie. I tell you what. In thirty days from now you can tell if you like – tell anyone you like.'

Thus the secret of the Brandis-Allardyce engagement was dependent on a little child's word. Coppy, who knew Wee Willie Winkie's idea of truth, was at ease, for he felt that he would not break promises. Wee Willie Winkie betrayed a special and unusual interest in Miss Allardyce, and, slowly revolving round that embarrassed young lady, was used to regard her gravely with unwinking eye. He was trying to discover why Coppy should have kissed her. She was not half so nice as his own mother. On the other hand, she was Coppy's property, and would in time belong to him. Therefore it behoved him to treat her with as much respect as Coppy's big sword or shiny pistol.

The idea that he shared a great secret in common with Coppy kept Wee Willie Winkie unusually virtuous for three weeks. Then the Old Adam[6] broke out, and he made what he called a 'camp-fire' at the bottom of the garden. How could he have foreseen that the flying sparks would have lighted the Colonel's little hay-rick and consumed a week's store for the horses? Sudden and swift was the punishment − deprivation of the good-conduct badge and, most sorrowful of all, two days' confinement to barracks − the house and verandah − coupled with the withdrawal of the light of his father's countenance.

He took the sentence like the man he strove to be, drew himself up with a quivering under-lip, saluted, and, once clear of the room, ran to weep bitterly in his nursery − called by him 'my quarters'. Coppy came in the afternoon and attempted to console the culprit.

'I'm under awwest,' said Wee Willie Winkie mournfully, 'and I didn't ought to speak to you.'

Very early the next morning he climbed on to the roof of the house − that was not forbidden − and beheld Miss Allardyce going for a ride.

'Where are you going?' cried Wee Willie Winkie.

'Across the river,' she answered, and trotted forward.

Now the cantonment in which the 195th lay was bounded on the north by a river − dry in the winter. From his earliest years, Wee Willie Winkie had been forbidden to go across the river, and had noted that even Coppy − the almost almighty Coppy − had never set foot beyond it. Wee Willie Winkie had once been read to, out of a big blue book, the history of the Princess and the Goblins[7] − a most wonderful tale of a land where the

Goblins were always warring with the children of men until they were defeated by one Curdie. Ever since that date it seemed to him that the bare black and purple hills across the river were inhabited by Goblins, and, in truth, every one had said that there lived the Bad Men. Even in his own house the lower halves of the windows were covered with green paper on account of the Bad Men who might, if allowed clear view, fire into peaceful drawing-rooms and comfortable bedrooms. Certainly, beyond the river, which was the end of all the Earth, lived the Bad Men. And here was Major Allardyce's big girl, Coppy's property, preparing to venture into their borders! What would Coppy say if anything happened to her? If the Goblins ran off with her as they did with Curdie's Princess? She must at all hazards be turned back.

The house was still. Wee Willie Winkie reflected for a moment on the very terrible wrath of his father; and then – broke his arrest! It was a crime unspeakable. The low sun threw his shadow, very large and very black, on the trim garden-paths, as he went down to the stables and ordered his pony. It seemed to him in the hush of the dawn that all the big world had been bidden to stand still and look at Wee Willie Winkie guilty of mutiny. The drowsy *sais* gave him his mount, and, since the one great sin made all others insignificant, Wee Willie Winkie said that he was going to ride over to Coppy Sahib, and went out at a foot-pace, stepping on the soft mould of the flower-borders.

The devastating track of the pony's feet was the last misdeed that cut him off from all sympathy of Humanity. He turned into the road, leaned forward, and rode as fast as the pony could put foot to the ground in the direction of the river.

But the liveliest of twelve-two[8] ponies can do little against the long canter of a Waler. Miss Allardyce was far ahead, had passed through the crops, beyond the Police-posts, when all the guards were asleep, and her mount was scattering the pebbles of the river-bed as Wee Willie Winkie left the cantonment and British India behind him. Bowed forward and still flogging, Wee Willie Winkie shot into Afghan territory, and could just see Miss Allardyce, a black speck, flickering across the stony plain. The reason of her wandering was simple enough. Coppy, in a tone of too-hastily-assumed authority, had told her overnight that she must not ride out by the river. And she had gone to prove her own spirit and teach Coppy a lesson.

Almost at the foot of the inhospitable hills, Wee Willie Winkie saw the Waler blunder and come down heavily. Miss Allardyce struggled clear, but her ankle had been severely twisted, and she could not stand. Having fully shown her spirit, she wept, and was surprised by the apparition of a white, wide-eyed child in khaki, on a nearly spent pony.

'Are you badly, badly hurted?' shouted Wee Willie Winkie, as soon as he was within range. 'You didn't ought to be here.'

'I don't know,' said Miss Allardyce ruefully, ignoring the reproof. 'Good gracious, child, what are *you* doing here?'

'You said you was going acwoss ve wiver,' panted Wee Willie Winkie, throwing himself off his pony. 'And nobody – not even Coppy – must go acwoss ve wiver, and I came after you ever so hard, but you wouldn't stop, and now you've hurted yourself, and Coppy will be angwy wiv me, and – I've bwoken my awwest! I've bwoken my awwest!'

The future Colonel of the 195th sat down and sobbed. In spite of the pain in her ankle the girl was moved.

'Have you ridden all the way from cantonments, little man? What for?'

'You belonged to Coppy. Coppy told me so!' wailed Wee Willie Winkie disconsolately. 'I saw him kissing you, and he said he was fonder of you van Bell or ve Butcha or me. And so I came. You must get up and come back. You didn't ought to be here. Vis is a bad place, and I've bwoken my awwest.'

'I can't move, Winkie,' said Miss Allardyce, with a groan. 'I've hurt my foot. What shall I do?'

She showed a readiness to weep anew, which steadied Wee Willie Winkie, who had been brought up to believe that tears were the depth of unmanliness. Still, when one is as great a sinner as Wee Willie Winkie, even a man may be permitted to break down.

'Winkie,' said Miss Allardyce, 'when you've rested a little, ride back and tell them to send out something to carry me back in. It hurts fearfully.'

The child sat still for a little time and Miss Allardyce closed her eyes; the pain was nearly making her faint. She was roused by Wee Willie Winkie tying up the reins on his pony's neck and setting it free with a vicious cut of his whip that made it whicker. The little animal headed towards the cantonments.

'Oh, Winkie, what are you doing?'

'Hush!' said Wee Willie Winkie. 'Vere's a man coming – one of ve Bad Men. I must stay wiv you. My faver says a man must *always* look after a girl. Jack will go home, and ven vey'll come and look for us. Vat's why I let him go.'

Not one man but two or three had appeared from behind the rocks of the hills, and the heart of Wee Willie Winkie sank within him, for just in this manner were the Goblins wont to steal out and vex Curdie's soul. Thus had they played in Curdie's garden – he had seen the picture – and thus had they frightened the Princess's nurse.[9] He heard them talking to each other, and recognized with joy the bastard Pushto that he had picked up from one of his father's grooms lately dismissed. People who spoke that tongue could not be the Bad Men. They were only natives after all.[10]

They came up to the boulders on which Miss Allardyce's horse had blundered.

Then rose from the rock Wee Willie Winkie, child of the Dominant Race, aged six and three-quarters, and said briefly and emphatically '*Jao!*' The pony had crossed the river-bed.

The men laughed, and laughter from natives was the one thing Wee Willie Winkie could not tolerate. He asked them what they wanted and why they did not depart. Other men with most evil faces and crooked-stocked guns crept out of the shadows of the hills, till, soon, Wee Willie Winkie was face to face with an audience some twenty strong. Miss Allardyce screamed.

'Who are you?' said one of the men.

'I am the Colonel Sahib's son, and my order is that you go at once. You black men are frightening the Miss Sahib. One of you must run into cantonments and take the news that the Miss Sahib has hurt herself, and that the Colonel's son is here with her.'

'Put our feet into the trap?' was the laughing reply. 'Hear this boy's speech!'

'Say that I sent you – I, the Colonel's son. They will give you money.'

'What is the use of this talk? Take up the child and the girl, and we can at least ask for the ransom. Ours are the villages on the heights,' said a voice in the background.

These *were* the Bad Men – worse than Goblins – and it needed all Wee Willie Winkie's training to prevent him from bursting into tears. But he felt that to cry before a native, excepting only his mother's *ayah*, would be an infamy greater than any mutiny. Moreover, he, as future Colonel of the 195th, had that grim regiment at his back.

'Are you going to carry us away?' said Wee Willie Winkie, very blanched and uncomfortable.

'Yes, my little *Sahib Bahadur*,'[11] said the tallest of the men, 'and eat you afterwards.'

'That is child's talk,' said Wee Willie Winkie. 'Men do not eat men.'

A yell of laughter interrupted him, but he went on firmly – 'And if you do carry us away, I tell you that all my regiment will come up in a day and kill you all without leaving one. Who will take my message to the Colonel Sahib?'

Speech in any vernacular – and Wee Willie Winkie had a colloquial acquaintance with three – was easy to the boy who could not yet manage his 'r's' and 'th's' aright.

Another man joined the conference, crying: 'O foolish men! What this babe says is true. He is the heart's heart of those white troops. For the sake of peace let them go both, for if he be taken, the regiment will break loose and gut the valley. *Our* villages are in the valley, and we shall not escape. That regiment are devils. They broke Khoda Yar's breastbone with kicks when he tried to take the rifles; and if we touch this child they will fire and rape and plunder for a month, till nothing remains. Better to send a man back to take the message and get a reward. I say that this child is their God, and that they will spare none of us, nor our women, if we harm him.'

It was Din Mahommed, the dismissed groom of the Colonel, who made the diversion, and an angry and heated discussion followed. Wee Willie Winkie, standing over Miss Allardyce, waited the upshot. Surely his 'wegiment', his own 'wegiment', would not desert him if they knew of his extremity.

The riderless pony brought the news to the 195th, though there had been consternation in the Colonel's household for an hour before. The little beast came in through the parade-ground in front of the main barracks, where the men were settling down to play Spoil-five till the afternoon. Devlin, the Colour-Sergeant of E Company, glanced at the empty saddle and tumbled through the barrack-rooms, kicking up each Room Corporal as he passed. 'Up, ye beggars! There's something happened to the Colonel's son,' he shouted.

'He couldn't fall off! S'elp me, 'e *couldn't* fall off,' blubbered a drummer-boy. 'Go an' hunt acrost the river. He's over there if he's anywhere, an' maybe those Pathans have got 'im. For the love o'Gawd don't look for 'im in the nullahs!¹² Let's go over the river.'

'There's sense in Mott yet,' said Devlin. 'E Company, double out to the river – sharp!'

So E Company, in its shirt-sleeves mainly, doubled for the dear life, and in the rear toiled the perspiring Sergeant, adjuring it to double yet faster. The cantonment was alive with the men of the 195th hunting for Wee Willie Winkie, and the Colonel finally overtook E Company, far too exhausted to swear, struggling in the pebbles of the river-bed.

Up the hill under which Wee Willie Winkie's Bad Men were discussing the wisdom of carrying off the child and the girl, a look-out fired two shots.

'What have I said?' shouted Din Mahommed. 'There is the warning! The *pulton*¹³ are out already and are coming across the plain! Get away! Let us not be seen with the boy.'

The men waited for an instant, and then, as another shot was fired, withdrew into the hills, silently as they had appeared.

'The wegiment is coming,' said Wee Willie Winkie confidently to Miss Allardyce, 'and it's all wight. Don't cwy!'

He needed the advice himself, for ten minutes later, when his father came up, he was weeping bitterly with his head in Miss Allardyce's lap.

And the men of the 195th carried him home with shouts and rejoicings; and Coppy, who had ridden a horse into a lather, met him, and, to his intense disgust, kissed him openly in the presence of the men.

But there was balm for his dignity. His father assured him that not only would the breaking of arrest be condoned, but that the good-conduct badge would be restored as soon as his mother could sew it on his blouse-sleeve. Miss Allardyce had told the Colonel a story that made him proud of his son.

'She belonged to you, Coppy,' said Wee Willie Winkie, indicating Miss Allardyce with a grimy forefinger. 'I *knew* she didn't ought to go acwoss ve wiver, and I knew ve wegiment would come to me if I sent Jack home.'

'You're a hero, Winkie,' said Coppy – 'a *pukka* hero!'

'I don't know what vat means,' said Wee Willie Winkie, 'but you mustn't call me Winkie any no more. I'm Percival Will'am Will'ams.'

And in this manner did Wee Willie Winkie enter into his manhood.

✝ Baa Baa, Black Sheep[1] ⚓

Baa Baa, Black Sheep,
Have you any wool?
Yes, Sir, yes, Sir, three bags full.
One for the Master, one for the Dame –
None for the Little Boy that cries down the lane.

Nursery Rhyme

The First Bag

When I was in my father's house, I was in a better place[2]

They were putting Punch[3] to bed – the *ayah* and the *hamal* and Meeta, the big *Surti*[4] boy, with the red and gold turban. Judy, already tucked inside her mosquito-curtains, was nearly asleep. Punch had been allowed to stay up for dinner. Many privileges had been accorded to Punch within the last ten days, and a greater kindness from the people of his world had encompassed his ways and works, which were mostly obstreperous. He sat on the edge of his bed and swung his bare legs defiantly.

'Punch-*baba* going to bye-lo?' said the *ayah* suggestively.

'No,' said Punch. 'Punch-*baba* wants the story about the Ranee that was turned into a tiger. Meeta must tell it, and the *hamal* shall hide behind the door and make tiger-noises at the proper time.'

'But Judy-*baba* will wake up,' said the *ayah*.

'Judy-*baba* is waked,' piped a small voice from the mosquito-curtains. 'There was a Ranee that lived at Delhi. Go on, Meeta,' and she fell fast asleep again while Meeta began the story.

Never had Punch secured the telling of that tale with so little opposition. He reflected for a long time. The *Hamal* made the tiger-noises in twenty different keys.

'"Top!' said Punch authoritatively. 'Why doesn't Papa come in and say he is going to give me *put-put?*'

'Punch-*baba* is going away,' said the *ayah*. 'In another week there will be no Punch-*baba* to pull my hair any more.' She sighed softly, for the boy of the household was very dear to her heart.

'Up the Ghauts[5] in a train?' said Punch, standing on his bed. 'All the way to Nassick where the Ranee-Tiger lives?'

'Not to Nassick this year, little Sahib,' said Meeta, lifting him on his shoulder. 'Down to the sea where the cocoa-nuts are thrown, and across the sea in a big ship. Will you take Meeta with you to *Belait?*'[6]

'You shall all come,' said Punch, from the height of Meeta's strong arms. 'Meeta and the *ayah* and the *hamal* and Bhini-in-the-Garden, and the salaam-Captain-Sahib-snake-man.'

There was no mockery in Meeta's voice when he replied – 'Great is the Sahib's favour,' and laid the little man down in the bed, while the *ayah*, sitting in the moonlight at the doorway, lulled him to sleep with an interminable canticle such as they sing in the Roman Catholic Church at Parel.[7] Punch curled himself into a ball and slept.

Next morning Judy shouted that there was a rat in the nursery, and thus he forget to tell her the wonderful news. It did not much matter, for Judy was only three and she would not have understood. But Punch was five; and he knew that going to England would be much nicer than a trip to Nassick.

Papa and Mamma sold the brougham and the piano, and stripped the house, and curtailed the allowance of crockery for the daily meals, and took long counsel together over a bundle of letters bearing the Rocklington postmark.

'The worst of it is that one can't be certain of anything,' said Papa, pulling his moustache. 'The letters in themselves are excellent, and the terms are moderate enough.'

'The worst of it is that the children will grow up away from me,' thought Mamma; but she did not say it aloud.

'We are only one case among hundreds,' said Papa bitterly. 'You shall go Home again in five years, dear.'

'Punch will be ten then – and Judy eight. Oh, how long and long and long and long the time will be! And we have to leave them among strangers.'

'Punch is a cheery little chap. He's sure to make friends wherever he goes.'

'And who could help loving my Ju?'

They were standing over the cots in the nursery late at night, and I think that Mamma was crying softly. After Papa had gone away, she knelt down by the side of Judy's cot. The *ayah* saw her and put up a prayer that the *memsahib* might never find the love of her children taken away from her and given to a stranger.

Mamma's own prayer was a slightly illogical one. Summarized it ran: 'Let strangers love my children and be as good to them as I should be, but let *me* preserve their love and their confidence for ever and ever. Amen.' Punch scratched himself in his sleep, and Judy moaned a little.

Next day they all went down to the sea, and there was a scene at the Apollo Bunder[8] when Punch discovered that Meeta could not come too, and Judy learned that the *ayah* must be left behind. But Punch found a thousand fascinating things in the rope, block, and steam-pipe line on the big P. and O. Steamer long before Meeta and the *ayah* had dried their tears.

'Come back, Punch-*baba*,' said the *ayah*.

'Come back,' said Meeta, 'and be a *Burra Sahib*' (a big man).

'Yes,' said Punch, lifted up in his father's arms to wave good-bye. 'Yes, I will come back, and I will be a *Burra Sahib Bahadur*!' (a very big man indeed).

At the end of the first day Punch demanded to be set down in England, which he was certain must be close at hand. Next day there was a merry breeze, and Punch was very sick. 'When I come back to Bombay,' said Punch on his recovery, 'I will come by the road – in a broom-*gharri*.[9] This is a very naughty ship.'

The Swedish boatswain consoled him, and he modified his opinions as the voyage went on. There was so much to see and to handle and ask questions about that Punch nearly forgot the *ayah* and Meeta and the *hamal*, and with difficulty remembered a few words of the Hindustani once his second-speech.[10]

But Judy was much worse. The day before the steamer reached Southampton, Mamma asked her if she would not like to see the *ayah* again. Judy's blue eyes turned to the stretch of sea that swallowed all her tiny past, and she said: '*Ayah!* What *ayah?*'

Mamma cried over her and Punch marvelled. It was then that he heard for the first time Mamma's passionate appeal to him never to let Judy forget Mamma. Seeing that Judy was young, ridiculously young, and that Mamma, every evening for four weeks past, had come into the cabin to sing her and Punch to sleep with a mysterious rune that he called 'Sonny, my soul,'[11] Punch could not understand what Mamma meant. But he strove to do his duty; for, the moment Mamma left the cabin, he said to Judy: 'Ju, you bemember Mamma?'

''Torse I do,' said Judy.

'Then *always* bemember Mamma, 'r else I won't give you the paper ducks that the red-haired Captain Sahib cut out for me.'

So Judy promised always to 'bemember Mamma'.

Many and many a time was Mamma's command laid upon Punch, and Papa would say the same thing with an insistence that awed the child.

'You must make haste and learn to write, Punch,' said Papa, 'and then you'll be able to write letters to us in Bombay.'

'I'll come into your room,' said Punch, and Papa choked.

Papa and Mamma were always choking in those days. If Punch took Judy to task for not 'bemembering', they choked. If Punch sprawled on the sofa in the Southampton lodging-house and sketched his future in purple and gold, they choked; and so they did if Judy put up her mouth for a kiss.

Through many days all four were vagabonds on the face of the earth – Punch with no one to give orders to, Judy too young for anything, and Papa and Mamma grave, distracted, and choking.

'Where,' demanded Punch, wearied of a loathsome contrivance on four wheels with a mound of luggage atop – '*where* is our broom-*gharri?* This thing talks so much that *I* can't talk.

Where is our *own* broom-*gharri*? When I was at Bandstand before we comed away, I asked Inverarity Sahib why he was sitting in it, and he said it was his own. And I said, "I will *give* it you" – I like Inverarity Sahib – and I said, "Can you put your legs through the pully-wag loops by the windows?" And Inverarity Sahib said No, and laughed. *I* can put my legs through the pully-wag loops. I can put my legs through *these* pully-wag loops. Look! Oh, Mamma's crying again! I didn't know I wasn't not to do *so*.'

Punch drew his legs out of the loops of the four-wheeler: the door opened and he slid to the earth, in a cascade of parcels, at the door of an austere little villa whose gates bore the legend 'Downe Lodge'. Punch gathered himself together and eyed the house with disfavour. It stood on a sandy road, and a cold wind tickled his knickerbockered legs.

'Let us go away,' said Punch. 'This is not a pretty place.'

But Mamma and Papa and Judy had left the cab, and all the luggage was being taken into the house. At the doorstep stood a woman in black, and she smiled largely, with dry chapped lips. Behind her was a man, big, bony, grey, and lame as to one leg – behind him a boy of twelve, black-haired and oily in appearance. Punch surveyed the trio, and advanced without fear, as he had been accustomed to do in Bombay when callers came and he happened to be playing in the verandah.

'How do you do?' said he. 'I am Punch.' But they were all looking at the luggage – all except the grey man, who shook hands with Punch, and said he was 'a smart little fellow'. There was much running about and banging of boxes, and Punch curled himself up on the sofa in the dining-room and considered things.

'I don't like these people,' said Punch. 'But never mind. We'll go away soon. We have always went away soon from everywhere. I wish we was gone back to Bombay *soon*.'

The wish bore no fruit. For six days Mamma wept at intervals, and showed the woman in black all Punch's clothes – a liberty which Punch resented. 'But p'raps she's a new white *ayah*,' he thought. 'I'm to call her Antirosa, but she doesn't call *me* Sahib. She says just Punch,' he confided to Judy. 'What is Antirosa?'[12]

Judy didn't know. Neither she nor Punch had heard anything of an animal called an aunt. Their world had been Papa and Mamma, who knew everything, permitted everything, and loved everybody – even Punch when he used to go into the garden at Bombay and fill his nails with mould after the weekly nail-cutting, because, as he explained between two strokes of the slipper to his sorely-tried Father, his fingers 'felt so new at the ends'.

In an undefined way Punch judged it advisable to keep both parents between himself and the woman in black and the boy in black hair. He did not approve of them. He liked the grey man, who had expressed a wish to be called 'Uncleharri'. They nodded at each other when they met, and the grey man showed him a little ship with rigging that took up and down.

'She is a model of the *Brisk* – the little *Brisk* that was sore exposed that day at Navarino.'[13] The grey man hummed the last words and fell into a reverie. 'I'll tell you about Navarino, Punch, when we go for walks together; and you mustn't touch the ship, because she's the *Brisk*.'

Long before that walk, the first of many, was taken, they roused Punch and Judy in the chill dawn of a February morning to say Good-bye; and of all people in the wide earth to Papa and Mamma – both crying this time. Punch was very sleepy and Judy was cross.

'Don't forget us,' pleaded Mamma. 'Oh, my little son, don't forget us, and see that Judy remembers too.'

'I've told Judy to bemember,' said Punch, wriggling, for his father's beard tickled his neck, 'I've told Judy – ten – forty – 'leven thousand times. But Ju's so young – quite a baby – isn't she?'

'Yes,' said Papa, 'quite a baby, and you must be good to Judy, and make haste to learn to write and – and – and –'

Punch was back in his bed again. Judy was fast asleep, and there was the rattle of a cab below. Papa and Mamma had gone away. Not to Nassick; that was across the sea. To some place much nearer, of course, and equally of course they would return. They came back after dinner-parties, and Papa had come back after he had been to a place called 'The Snows', and Mamma with him, to Punch and Judy at Mrs Inverarity's house in Marine Lines. Assuredly they would come back again. So Punch fell asleep till the true morning, when the black-haired boy met him with the information that Papa and Mamma had gone to Bombay, and that he and Judy were to stay at Downe Lodge 'for ever'. Antirosa, tearfully appealed to for a contradiction, said that Harry had spoken the truth, and that it behoved Punch to fold up his clothes neatly on going to bed. Punch went out and wept bitterly with Judy, into whose fair head he had driven some ideas of the meaning of separation.

When a matured man discovers that he has been deserted by Providence, deprived of his God, and cast without help, comfort, or sympathy, upon a world which is new and strange to him, his despair, which may find expression in evil-living, the writing of his experiences, or the more satisfactory diversion of suicide, is generally supposed to be impressive. A child, under exactly similar circumstances as far as its knowledge goes, cannot very well curse God and die. It howls till its nose is red, its eyes are sore, and its head aches. Punch and Judy, through no fault of their own, had lost all their world. They sat in the hall and cried; the black-haired boy looking on from afar.

The model of the ship availed nothing, though the grey man assured Punch that he might pull the rigging up and down as much as he pleased; and Judy was promised free entry into the kitchen. They wanted Papa and Mamma gone to Bombay beyond the seas, and their grief while it lasted was without remedy.

When the tears ceased the house was very still. Antirosa had decided that it was better to let the children 'have their cry out', and the boy had gone to school. Punch raised his head from the floor and sniffed mournfully. Judy was nearly asleep. Three short years had not taught her how to bear sorrow with full knowledge. There was a distant, dull boom in the air – a repeated heavy thud. Punch knew that sound in Bombay in the Monsoon.

It was the sea – the sea that must be traversed before any one could get to Bombay.

'Quick, Ju!' he cried, 'we're close to the sea. I can hear it! Listen! That's where they've went. P'haps we can catch them if we was in time. They didn't mean to go without us. They've only forgot.'

'Iss,' said Judy. 'They've only forgotted. Less go to the sea.'

The hall-door was open and so was the garden-gate.

'It's very, very big, this place,' he said, looking cautiously down the road, 'and we will get lost; but *I* will find a man and order him to take me back to my house – like I did in Bombay.'

He took Judy by the hand, and the two ran hatless in the direction of the sound of the sea. Downe Villa was almost the last of a range of newly-built houses running out, through a field of brick-mounds, to a heath where gypsies occasionally camped and where the Garrison Artillery of Rocklington practised. There were few people to be seen, and the children might have been taken for those of the soldiery who ranged far. Half an hour the wearied little legs tramped across heath, potato-patch, and sand-dune.

'I'se so tired,' said Judy, 'and Mamma will be angry.'

'Mamma's *never* angry. I suppose she is waiting at the sea now while Papa gets tickets. We'll find them and go along with them. Ju, you mustn't sit down. Only a little more and we'll come to the sea. Ju, if you sit down I'll *thmack* you!' said Punch.

They climbed another dune, and came upon the great gray sea at low tide. Hundreds of crabs were scuttling about the beach, but there was no trace of Papa and Mamma, not even of a ship upon the waters – nothing but sand and mud for miles and miles.

And 'Uncleharri' found them by chance – very muddy and very forlorn – Punch dissolved in tears, but trying to divert Judy with an 'ickle trab', and Judy wailing to the pitiless horizon for 'Mamma, Mamma!' – and again 'Mamma!'

Wee Willie Winkie

The Second Bag

Ah, well-a-day, for we are souls bereaved!
Of all the creatures under Heaven's wide scope
We are most hopeless, who had once most hope,
And most beliefless, who had most believed.[14]

The City of Dreadful Night

All this time not a word about Black Sheep. He came later, and Harry the black-haired boy was mainly responsible for his coming.

Judy – who could help loving little Judy? – passed, by special permit, into the kitchen and thence straight to Aunty Rosa's heart. Harry was Aunty Rosa's one child, and Punch was the extra boy about the house. There was no special place for him or his little affairs, and he was forbidden to sprawl on sofas and explain his ideas about the manufacture of this world and his hopes for his future. Sprawling was lazy and wore out sofas, and little boys were not expected to talk. They were talked to, and the talking to was intended for the benefit of their morals. As the unquestioned despot of the house at Bombay, Punch could not quite understand how he came to be of no account in this his new life.

Harry might reach across the table and take what he wanted; Judy might point and get what she wanted. Punch was forbidden to do either. The grey man was his great hope and stand-by for many months after Mamma and Papa left, and he had forgotten to tell Judy to 'bemember Mamma'.

This lapse was excusable, because in the interval he had been introduced by Aunty Rosa to two very impressive things – an abstraction called God,[15] the intimate friend and ally of Aunty Rosa, generally believed to live behind the kitchen-range because it was hot there – and a dirty brown book filled with unintelligible dots and marks. Punch was always anxious to oblige everybody. He therefore welded the story of the Creation on to what he could recollect of his Indian fairy tales,[16] and scandalized Aunty Rosa by repeating the result to Judy. It was a sin, a grievous sin, and Punch was talked to for a quarter of an

268

hour. He could not understand where the iniquity came in, but was careful not to repeat the offence, because Aunty Rosa told him that God had heard every word he had said and was very angry. If this were true why didn't God come and say so, thought Punch, and dismissed the matter from his mind. Afterwards he learned to know the Lord as the only thing in the world more awful than Aunty Rosa – as a Creature that stood in the background and counted the strokes of the cane.

But the reading was, just then, a much more serious matter than any creed. Aunty Rosa sat him upon a table and told him that A B meant ab.

'Why?' said Punch. 'A is a and B is bee. *Why* does A B mean ab?'

'Because I tell you it does,' said Aunty Rosa, 'and you've got to say it.'

Punch said it accordingly, and for a month, hugely against his will, stumbled through the brown book, not in the least comprehending what it meant. But Uncle Harry, who walked much and generally alone, was wont to come into the nursery and suggest to Aunty Rosa that Punch should walk with him. He seldom spoke, but he showed Punch all Rocklington, from the mud-banks and the sand of the back-bay to the great harbours where ships lay at anchor, and the dockyards where the hammers were never still, and the marine-store shops, and the shiny brass counters in the Offices where Uncle Harry went once every three months with a slip of blue paper and received sovereigns in exchange; for he held a wound-pension. Punch heard, too, from his lips the story of the battle of Navarino, where the sailors of the Fleet, for three days afterwards, were deaf as posts and could only sign to each other. 'That was because of the noise of the guns,' said Uncle Harry, 'and I have got the wadding of a bullet somewhere inside me now.'

Punch regarded him with curiosity. He had not the least idea what wadding was, and his notion of a bullet was a dockyard cannon-ball bigger than his own head. How could Uncle Harry keep a cannon-ball inside him? He was ashamed to ask, for fear Uncle Harry might be angry.

Punch had never known what anger – real anger – meant until one terrible day when Harry had taken his paint-box to paint a boat with, and Punch had protested. Then Uncle Harry had appeared on the scene and, muttering something about 'strangers' children', had with a stick smitten the black-haired boy across the shoulders till he wept and yelled, and Aunty Rosa came in and abused Uncle Harry for cruelty to his own flesh and blood, and Punch shuddered to the tips of his shoes. 'It wasn't my fault,' he explained to the boy, but both Harry and Aunty Rosa said that it was, and that Punch had told tales, and for a week there were no more walks with Uncle Harry.

But that week brought a great joy to Punch.

He had repeated till he was thrice weary the statement that 'the Cat lay on the Mat and the Rat came in'.

'Now I can truly read,'[17] said Punch, 'and now I will never read anything in the world.'

He put the brown book in the cupboard where his school-books lived and accidentally tumbled out a venerable volume, without covers, labelled *Sharpe's Magazine*.[18] There was the most portentous picture of a griffin on the first page, with verses below. The griffin carried off one sheep a day from a German village, till a man came with a 'falchion' and split the griffin open. Goodness only knew what a falchion was, but there was the Griffin, and his history was an improvement upon the eternal Cat.

'This,' said Punch, 'means things, and now I will know all about everything in all the world.' He read till the light failed, not understanding a tithe of the meaning, but tantalized by glimpses of new worlds hereafter to be revealed.

'What is a "falchion"? What is a "e-wee lamb"? What is a "base *us*surper"? What is a "verdant me-ad"?' he demanded with flushed cheeks, at bedtime, of the astonished Aunty Rosa.

'Say your prayers and go to sleep,' she replied, and that was all the help Punch then or afterwards found at her hands in the new and delightful exercise of reading.

'Aunty Rosa only knows about God and things like that,' argued Punch. 'Uncle Harry will tell me.'

The next walk proved that Uncle Harry could not help either; but he allowed Punch to talk, and even sat down on a bench to hear about the Griffin. Other walks brought other stories as Punch ranged farther afield, for the house held large store of old books that no one ever opened – from *Frank Fairlegh*[19] in serial numbers, and the earlier poems of Tennyson, contributed anonymously to *Sharpe's Magazine*, to '62 Exhibition Catalogues, gay with colours and delightfully incomprehensible, and odd leaves of *Gulliver's Travels*.

As soon as Punch could string a few pot-hooks together he wrote to Bombay, demanding by return of post 'all the books in all the world'. Papa could not comply with this modest indent, but sent *Grimm's Fairy Tales* and a Hans Andersen.[20] That was enough. If he were only left alone Punch could pass, at any hour he chose, into a land of his own, beyond reach of Aunty Rosa and her God, Harry and his teasements, and Judy's claims to be played with.

'Don't disturve me, I'm reading. Go and play in the kitchen,' grunted Punch. 'Aunty Rosa lets *you* go there.' Judy was cutting her second teeth and was fretful. She appealed to Aunty Rosa, who descended on Punch.

'I was reading,' he explained, 'reading a book I *want* to read.'

'You're only doing that to show off,' said Aunty Rosa. 'But we'll see. Play with Judy now, and don't open a book for a week.'[21]

Judy did not pass a very enjoyable playtime with Punch, who was consumed with indignation. There was a pettiness at the bottom of the prohibition which puzzled him.

'It's what I like to do,' he said, 'and she's found out that and stopped me. Don't cry, Ju – it wasn't your fault – *please* don't cry, or she'll say I made you.'

Ju loyally mopped up her tears, and the two played in their nursery, a room in the basement and half underground, to which they were regularly sent after the mid-day dinner while Aunty Rosa slept. She drank wine – that is to say, something from a bottle in the cellaret – for her stomach's sake, but if she did not fall asleep she would sometimes come into the nursery to see that the children were really playing. Now bricks, wooden hoops, ninepins, and chinaware cannot amuse for ever, especially when all Fairyland is to be won by the mere opening of a book, and, as often as not, Punch would be discovered reading to Judy or telling her interminable tales. That was an offence in the eyes of the law, and Judy would be whisked off by Aunty Rosa, while Punch was left to play alone, 'and be sure that I hear you doing it'.

It was not a cheering employ, for he had to make a playful noise. At last, with infinite craft, he devised an arrangement whereby the table could be supported as to three legs on toy bricks, leaving the fourth clear to bring down on the floor. He could work the table with one hand and hold a book with the other. This he did till an evil day when Aunty Rosa pounced upon him unawares and told him that he was 'acting a lie'.

'If you're old enough to do that,' she said – her temper was always worst after dinner – 'you're old enough to be beaten.'

'But – I'm – I'm not a animal!' said Punch aghast. He remembered Uncle Harry and the stick, and turned white. Aunty Rosa had hidden a light cane behind her, and Punch was beaten then and there over the shoulders. It was a revelation to him. The room-door was shut, and he was left to weep himself into repentance and work out his own gospel of life.

Aunty Rosa, he argued, had the power to beat him with many stripes. It was unjust and cruel, and Mamma and Papa would never have allowed it. Unless perhaps, as Aunty Rosa seemed to imply, they had sent secret orders. In which case he was abandoned indeed. It would be discreet in the future to propitiate Aunty Rosa, but, then, again, even in matters in which he was innocent, he had been accused of wishing to 'show off'. He had 'shown off' before visitors when he had attacked a strange gentleman – Harry's uncle, not his own – with requests for information about the Griffin and the falchion, and the precise nature of the Tilbury[22] in which Frank Fairlegh rode – all points of paramount interest which he was bursting to understand. Clearly it would not do to pretend to care for Aunty Rosa.

At this point Harry entered and stood afar off, eyeing Punch, a dishevelled heap in the corner of the room, with disgust.

'You're a liar – a young liar,' said Harry, with great unction, 'and you're to have tea down here because you're not fit to speak to us. And you're not to speak to Judy again till Mother gives you leave. You'll corrupt her. You're only fit to associate with the servant. Mother says so.'

Having reduced Punch to a second agony of tears, Harry departed upstairs with the news that Punch was still rebellious.

Uncle Harry sat uneasily in the dining-room. 'Damn it all, Rosa,' said he at last, 'can't you leave the child alone? He's a good enough little chap when I meet him.'

'He puts on his best manners with you, Henry,' said Aunty Rosa, 'but I'm afraid, I'm very much afraid, that he is the Black Sheep of the family.'

Harry heard and stored up the name for future use. Judy cried till she was bidden to stop, her brother not being worth tears; and the evening concluded with the return of Punch to the upper regions and a private sitting at which all the blinding horrors of Hell were revealed to Punch with such store of imagery as Aunty Rosa's narrow mind possessed.

Most grievous of all was Judy's round-eyed reproach, and Punch went to bed in the depths of the Valley of Humiliation.[23] He shared his room with Harry and knew the torture in store. For an hour and a half he had to answer that young gentleman's questions as to his motives for telling a lie, and a grievous lie, the precise quantity of punishment inflicted by Aunty Rosa, and had also to profess his deep gratitude for such religious instruction as Harry thought fit to impart.

From that day began the downfall of Punch, now Black Sheep.

'Untrustworthy in one thing, untrustworthy in all,' said Aunty Rosa, and Harry felt that Black Sheep was delivered into his hands. He would wake him up in the night to ask him why he was such a liar.

'I don't know,' Punch would reply.

'Then don't you think you ought to get up and pray to God for a new heart?'

'Y-yess.'

'Get out and pray, then!' And Punch would get out of bed with raging hate in his heart against all the world, seen and unseen. He was always tumbling into trouble. Harry had a knack of cross-examining him as to his day's doings, which seldom failed to lead him, sleepy and savage, into half-a-dozen contradictions – all duly reported to Aunty Rosa next morning.

'But it *wasn't* a lie,'[24] Punch would begin, charging into a laboured explanation that landed him more hopelessly in the mire. 'I said that I didn't say my prayers *twice* over in the day, and *that* was on Tuesday. *Once* I did. I *know* I did, but Harry said I didn't,' and so forth, till the tension brought tears, and he was dismissed from the table in disgrace.

'You usen't to be as bad as this,' said Judy, awe-stricken at the catalogue of Black Sheep's crimes. 'Why are you so bad now?'

'I don't know,' Black Sheep would reply. 'I'm not, if I only wasn't bothered upside down. I knew what I *did*, and I want to say so; but Harry always makes it out different somehow, and Aunty Rosa doesn't believe a word I say. Oh, Ju! don't *you* say I'm bad too.'

'Aunty Rosa says you are,' said Judy. 'She told the Vicar so when he came yesterday.'

'Why does she tell all the people outside the house about me? It isn't fair,' said Black Sheep. 'When I was in Bombay, and was bad – *doing* bad, not made-up bad like this – Mamma told Papa, and Papa told me he knew, and that was all. *Outside* people didn't know too – even Meeta didn't know.'

'I don't remember,' said Judy wistfully. 'I was all little then. Mamma was just as fond of you as she was of me, wasn't she?'

''Course she was. So was Papa. So was everybody.'

'Aunty Rosa likes me more than she does you. She says that you are a Trial and a Black Sheep, and I'm not to speak to you more than I can help.'

'Always? Not outside of the times when you mustn't speak to me at all?'

Judy nodded her head mournfully. Black Sheep turned away in despair, but Judy's arms were round his neck.

'Never mind, Punch,' she whispered. 'I *will* speak to you just the same as ever and ever. You're my own own brother though you are – though Aunty Rosa says you're bad, and Harry says you are a little coward. He says that if I pulled your hair hard, you'd cry.'

'Pull, then,' said Punch.

Judy pulled gingerly.

'Pull harder – as hard as you can! There! I don't mind how much you pull it *now*. If you'll speak to me same as ever I'll let you pull it as much as you like – pull it out if you like. But I know if Harry came and stood by and made you do it I'd cry.'

So the two children sealed the compact with a kiss, and Black Sheep's heart was cheered within him, and by extreme caution and careful avoidance of Harry he acquired virtue, and was allowed to read undisturbed for a week. Uncle Harry took him for walks, and consoled him with rough tenderness, never calling him Black Sheep. 'It's good for you, I suppose, Punch,' he used to say. 'Let us sit down. I'm getting tired.' His steps led him now not to the beach, but to the Cemetery of Rocklington, amid the potato-fields. For hours the grey man would sit on a tombstone, while Black Sheep would read epitaphs, and then with a sigh would stump home again.

'I shall lie there soon,' said he to Black Sheep, one winter evening, when his face showed white as a worn silver coin under the light of the lych-gate. 'You needn't tell Aunty Rosa.'

A month later he turned sharp round, ere half a morning walk was completed, and stumped back to the house. 'Put me to bed, Rosa,' he muttered. 'I've walked my last. The wadding has found me out.'

They put him to bed, and for a fortnight the shadow of his sickness lay upon the house, and Black Sheep went to and fro unobserved. Papa had sent him some new books, and he was told to keep quiet. He retired into his own world, and was perfectly happy. Even at night his felicity was unbroken. He could lie in bed and string himself tales of travel and adventure while Harry was downstairs.

'Uncle Harry's going to die,' said Judy, who now lived almost entirely with Aunty Rosa.

'I'm very sorry,' said Black Sheep soberly. 'He told me that a long time ago.'

Aunty Rosa heard the conversation. 'Will nothing check your wicked tongue?' she said angrily. There were blue circles round her eyes.

Black Sheep retreated to the nursery and read *Cometh up as a Flower*[25] with deep and uncomprehending interest. He had been forbidden to open it on account of its 'sinfulness', but the bonds of the Universe were crumbling, and Aunty Rosa was in great grief.

'I'm glad,' said Black Sheep. 'She's unhappy now. It wasn't a lie, though. *I* knew. He told me not to tell.'

That night Black Sheep woke with a start. Harry was not in his room, and there was a sound of sobbing on the next floor. Then the voice of Uncle Harry, singing the song of the Battle of Navarino,[26] came through the darkness:

> 'Our vanship was the Asia –
> The Albion and Genoa!'

'He's getting well,' thought Black Sheep, who knew the song through all its seventeen verses. But the blood froze at his little heart as he thought. The voice leapt an octave, and rang shrill as a boatswain's pipe:

> 'And next came on the lovely Rose,
> The Philomel, her fire-ship, closed,
> And the little Brisk was sore exposed
> That day at Navarino.'

'That day at Navarino, Uncle Harry!' shouted Black Sheep, half wild with excitement and fear of he knew not what.

A door opened, and Aunty Rosa screamed up the staircase: 'Hush! For God's sake hush, you little devil. Uncle Harry is *dead*!'

Baa Baa, Black Sheep
The Third Bag

Journeys end in lovers' meeting,
Every wise man's son doth know.[27]

'I wonder what will happen to me now,' thought Black Sheep,
when semi-pagan rites peculiar to the burial of the Dead in
middle-class houses had been accomplished, and Aunty Rosa,
awful in black crape, had returned to this life. 'I don't think
I've done anything bad that she knows of. I suppose I will soon.
She will be very cross after Uncle Harry's dying, and Harry will
be cross too. I'll keep in the nursery.'

Unfortunately for Punch's plans, it was decided that he
should be sent to a day-school which Harry attended. This
meant a morning walk with Harry, and perhaps an evening one;
but the prospect of freedom in the interval was refreshing.
'Harry'll tell everything I do, but I won't do anything,' said
Black Sheep. Fortified with this virtuous resolution, he went to
school only to find that Harry's version of his character had
preceded him, and that life was a burden in consequence. He
took stock of his associates. Some of them were unclean, some
of them talked in dialect, many dropped their h's, and there
were two Jews and a negro, or someone quite as dark, in the
assembly. 'That's a *hubshi*,'[28] said Black Sheep to himself.
'Even Meeta used to laugh at a *hubshi*. I don't think this is a
proper place.' He was indignant for at least an hour, till he
reflected that any expostulation on his part would be by Aunty
Rosa construed into 'showing off', and that Harry would tell
the boys.

'How do you like school?' said Aunty Rosa at the end of the
day.

'I think it is a very nice place,' said Punch quietly.

'I suppose you warned the boys of Black Sheep's character?'
said Aunty Rosa to Harry.

'Oh yes,' said the censor of Black Sheep's morals. 'They
know all about him.'

'If I was with my father,' said Black Sheep, stung to the
quick, 'I shouldn't *speak* to those boys. He wouldn't let me.

277

They live in shops. I saw them go into shops – where their fathers live and sell things.'

'You're too good for that school, are you?' said Aunty Rosa, with a bitter smile. 'You ought to be grateful, Black Sheep, that those boys speak to you at all. It isn't every school that takes little liars.'

Harry did not fail to make much capital out of Black Sheep's ill-considered remark; with the result that several boys, including the *hubshi*, demonstrated to Black Sheep the eternal equality of the human race by smacking his head, and his consolation from Aunty Rosa was that it 'served him right for being vain'. He learned, however, to keep his opinions to himself, and by propitiating Harry in carrying books and the like to get a little peace. His existence was not too joyful. From nine till twelve he was at school, and from two to four, except on Saturdays. In the evenings he was sent down into the nursery to prepare his lessons for the next day, and every night came the dreaded cross-questionings at Harry's hand. Of Judy he saw but little. She was deeply religious – at six years of age Religion is easy to come by – and sorely divided between her natural love for Black Sheep and her love for Aunty Rosa, who could do no wrong.

The lean woman returned that love with interest, and Judy, when she dared, took advantage of this for the remission of Black Sheep's penalties. Failures in lessons at school were punished at home by a week without reading other than school-books, and Harry brought the news of such a failure with glee. Further, Black Sheep was then bound to repeat his lessons at bedtime to Harry, who generally succeeded in making him break down, and consoled him by gloomiest forebodings for the morrow. Harry was at once spy, practical joker, inquisitor, and Aunty Rosa's deputy executioner. He filled his many posts to admiration. From his actions, now that Uncle Harry was dead, there was no appeal. Black Sheep had not been permitted to keep any self-respect at school: at home he was, of course, utterly discredited, and grateful for any pity that the servant girls – they changed frequently at Downe Lodge because they, too, were liars – might show. 'You're just fit to row in the same

boat with Black Sheep,' was a sentiment that each new Jane or
Eliza might expect to hear, before a month was over, from
Aunty Rosa's lips; and Black Sheep was used to ask new girls
whether they had yet been compared to him. Harry was 'Master
Harry' in their mouths; Judy was officially 'Miss Judy'; but
Black Sheep was never anything more than Black Sheep *tout
court*.[29]

As time went on and the memory of Papa and Mamma
became wholly overlaid by the unpleasant task of writing them
letters, under Aunty Rosa's eye, each Sunday, Black Sheep
forgot what manner of life he had led in the beginning of things.
Even Judy's appeals to 'try and remember about Bombay' failed
to quicken him.

'I can't remember,' he said. 'I know I used to give orders and
Mamma kissed me.'

'Aunty Rosa will kiss you if you are good,' pleaded Judy.

'Ugh! I don't want to be kissed by Aunty Rosa. She'd say I
was doing it to get something more to eat.'

The weeks lengthened into months, and the holidays came;
but just before the holidays Black Sheep fell into deadly sin.

Among the many boys whom Harry had incited to 'punch Black
Sheep's head because he daren't hit back', was one more aggravat-
ing than the rest, who, in an unlucky moment, fell upon Black
Sheep when Harry was not near. The blows stung, and Black
Sheep struck back at random with all the power at his command.
The boy dropped and whimpered. Black Sheep was astounded at
his own act, but, feeling the unresisting body under him, shook it
with both hands in blind fury and then began to throttle his
enemy; meaning honestly to slay him. There was a scuffle, and
Black Sheep was torn off the body by Harry and some colleagues,
and cuffed home tingling but exultant. Aunty Rosa was out:
pending her arrival, Harry set himself to lecture Black Sheep on
the sin of murder – which he described as the offence of Cain.

'Why didn't you fight him fair? What did you hit him when
he was down for, you little cur?'

Black Sheep looked up at Harry's throat and then at a knife
on the dinner-table.

'I don't understand,' he said wearily. 'You always set him on me and told me I was a coward when I blubbed. Will you leave me alone until Aunty Rosa comes in? She'll beat me if you tell her I ought to be beaten; so it's all right.'

'It's all wrong,' said Harry magisterially. 'You nearly killed him, and I shouldn't wonder if he dies.'

'Will he die?' said Black Sheep.

'I daresay,' said Harry, 'and then you'll be hanged, and go to Hell.'

'All right,' said Black Sheep, picking up the table-knife. 'Then I'll kill *you* now. You say things and do things and – and *I* don't know how things happen, and you never leave me alone – and I don't care *what* happens!'

He ran at the boy with the knife, and Harry fled upstairs to his room, promising Black Sheep the finest thrashing in the world when Aunty Rosa returned. Black Sheep sat at the bottom of the stairs, the table-knife in his hand, and wept for that he had not killed Harry. The servant-girl came up from the kitchen, took the knife away, and consoled him. But Black Sheep was beyond consolation. He would be badly beaten by Aunty Rosa; then there would be another beating at Harry's hands; then Judy would not be allowed to speak to him; then the tale would be told at school, and then –

There was no one to help and no one to care, and the best way out of the business was by death. A knife would hurt, but Aunty Rosa had told him, a year ago, that if he sucked paint he would die. He went into the nursery, unearthed the now disused Noah's Ark, and sucked the paint off as many animals as remained. It tasted abominable, but he had licked Noah's Dove clean by the time Aunty Rosa and Judy returned. He went upstairs and greeted them with: 'Please, Aunty Rosa, I believe I've nearly killed a boy at school, and I've tried to kill Harry, and when you've done all about God and Hell, will you beat me and get it over?'

The tale of the assault as told by Harry could only be explained on the ground of possession by the Devil. Wherefore Black Sheep was not only most excellently beaten, once by

Aunty Rosa and once, when thoroughly cowed down, by Harry, but he was further prayed for at family prayers, together with Jane who had stolen a cold rissole from the pantry, and snuffled audibly as her sin was brought before the Throne of Grace. Black Sheep was sore and stiff but triumphant. He would die that very night and be rid of them all. No, he would ask for no forgiveness from Harry, and at bed-time would stand no questioning at Harry's hands, even though addressed as 'Young Cain'.

'I've been beaten,' said he, 'and I've done other things. I don't care what I do. If you speak to me tonight, Harry, I'll get out and try to kill you. Now you can kill me if you like.'

Harry took his bed into the spare room, and Black Sheep lay down to die.

It may be that the makers of Noah's Arks know that their animals are likely to find their way into young mouths, and paint them accordingly. Certain it is that the common, weary next morning broke through the windows and found Black Sheep quite well and a good deal ashamed of himself, but richer by the knowledge that he could, in extremity, secure himself against Harry for the future.

When he descended to breakfast on the first day of the holidays, he was greeted with the news that Harry, Aunty Rosa, and Judy were going away to Brighton, while Black Sheep was to stay in the house with the servant. His latest outbreak suited Aunty Rosa's plans admirably. It gave her good excuse for leaving the extra boy behind. Papa in Bombay, who really seemed to know a young sinner's wants to the hour, sent, that week, a package of new books. And with these, and the society of Jane on board-wages, Black Sheep was left alone for a month.

The books lasted for ten days. They were eaten too quickly in long gulps of twelve hours at a time. Then came days of doing absolutely nothing, of dreaming dreams and marching imaginary armies up and downstairs, of counting the number of banisters, and of measuring the length and breadth of every room in handspans – fifty down the side, thirty across, and fifty back again. Jane made many friends, and, after receiving Black Sheep's assurance that he would not tell of her absences, went out daily for long hours. Black Sheep would follow the rays of the sinking sun from the kitchen to the dining-room and thence upward to his own bedroom until all was grey dark, and he ran down to the kitchen fire and read by its light. He was happy in that he was left alone and could read as much as he pleased. But, later, he grew afraid of the shadows of window-curtains and the flapping of doors and the creaking of shutters. He went out into the garden, and the rustling of the laurel-bushes frightened him.

He was glad when they all returned – Aunty Rosa, Harry, and Judy – full of news, and Judy laden with gifts. Who could help loving loyal little Judy? In return for all her merry babblement, Black Sheep confided to her that the distance from the hall-door to the top of the first landing was exactly one hundred and eighty-four handspans. He had found it out himself.

Then the old life recommenced; but with a difference, and a new sin. To his other iniquities Black Sheep had now added a phenomenal clumsiness – was as unfit to trust in action as he was in word. He himself could not account for spilling everything he touched, upsetting glasses as he put his hand out, and bumping his head against doors that were manifestly shut. There was a grey haze upon all his world, and it narrowed month by month, until at last it left Black Sheep almost alone with the flapping curtains that were so like ghosts, and the nameless terrors [30] of broad daylight that were only coats on pegs after all.

Holidays came and holidays went, and Black Sheep was taken to see many people whose faces were all exactly alike; was beaten when occasion demanded, and tortured by Harry on all possible occasions; but defended by Judy through good and evil report, though she hereby drew upon herself the wrath of Aunty Rosa.

The weeks were interminable, and Papa and Mamma were clean forgotten. Harry had left school and was a clerk in a Banking-Office. Freed from his presence, Black Sheep resolved that he should no longer be deprived of his allowance of pleasure-reading. Consequently when he failed at school he reported that all was well, and conceived a large contempt for Aunty Rosa as he saw how easy it was to deceive her. [31] 'She says I'm a little liar when I don't tell lies, and now I do, she doesn't know,' thought Black Sheep. Aunty Rosa had credited him in the past with petty cunning and stratagem that had never entered into his head. By the light of the sordid knowledge that she had revealed to him he paid her back full tale. In a household where the most innocent of his motives, his natural yearning for a little affection, had been interpreted into a desire for more bread and jam, or to ingratiate himself with strangers and so put Harry into the background, his work was easy. Aunty Rosa could penetrate certain kinds of hypocrisy, but not all. He set his child's wits against hers and was no more beaten. It grew monthly more and more of a trouble to read the schoolbooks, and even the pages of the open-print story-books danced and were dim. So Black Sheep brooded in the shadows that fell about him and cut him off from the world, inventing horrible punishments for 'dear Harry', or plotting another line of the tangled web of deception that he wrapped round Aunty Rosa.

Then the crash came and the cobwebs were broken. It was impossible to foresee everything. Aunty Rosa made personal inquiries as to Black Sheep's progress and received information that startled her. Step by step, with a delight as keen as when she convicted an underfed housemaid of the theft of cold meats, she followed the trail of Black Sheep's delinquencies. For weeks and weeks, in order to escape banishment from the book-shelves, he had made a fool of Aunty Rosa, of Harry, of God, of all the world! Horrible, most horrible, and evidence of an utterly depraved mind.

Black Sheep counted the cost. 'It will only be one big beating and then she'll put a card with "Liar" on my back,[32] same as she did before. Harry will whack me and pray for me, and she will pray for me at prayers and tell me I'm a Child of the Devil and give me hymns to learn. But I've done all my reading and she never knew. She'll say she knew all along. She's an old liar too,' said he.

For three days Black Sheep was shut in his own bedroom — to prepare his heart. 'That means two beatings. One at school and one here. *That* one will hurt most.' And it fell even as he thought. He was thrashed at school before the Jews and the *hubshi* for the heinous crime of carrying home false reports of progress. He was thrashed at home by Aunty Rosa on the same count, and then the placard was produced. Aunty Rosa stitched it between his shoulders and bade him go for a walk with it upon him.

'If you make me do that,' said Black Sheep very quietly, 'I shall burn this house down, and perhaps I'll kill you. I don't know whether I *can* kill you – you're so bony – but I'll try.'

No punishment followed this blasphemy, though Black Sheep held himself ready to work his way to Aunty Rosa's withered throat, and grip there till he was beaten off. Perhaps Aunty Rosa was afraid, for Black Sheep, having reached the Nadir of Sin, bore himself with a new recklessness.

In the midst of all the trouble there came a visitor from over the seas to Downe Lodge, who knew Papa and Mamma, and was commissioned to see Punch and Judy. Black Sheep was sent to the drawing-room and charged into a solid tea-table laden with china.

'Gently, gently, little man,' said the visitor, turning Black Sheep's face to the light slowly. 'What's that big bird on the palings?'

'What bird?' asked Black Sheep.

The visitor looked deep down into Black Sheep's eyes for half a minute, and then said suddenly: 'Good God, the little chap's nearly blind!' [33]

It was a most business-like visitor. He gave orders, on his own responsibility, that Black Sheep was not to go to school or open a book until Mamma came home. 'She'll be here in three weeks, as you know of course,' said he, 'and I'm Inverarity Sahib. I ushered you into this wicked world, young man, and a nice use you seem to have made of your time. You must do nothing whatever. Can you do that?'

'Yes,' said Punch in a dazed way. He had not [34] known that Mamma was coming. There was a chance, then, of another beating. Thank Heaven, Papa wasn't coming too. Aunty Rosa had said of late that he ought to be beaten by a man.

For the next three weeks Black Sheep was strictly allowed to do nothing. He spent his time in the old nursery looking at the broken toys, for all of which account must be rendered to Mamma. Aunty Rosa hit him over the hands if even a wooden boat were broken. But that sin was of small importance compared to the other revelations, so darkly hinted at by Aunty Rosa. 'When your Mother comes, and hears what I have to tell her, she may appreciate you properly,' she said grimly, and mounted guard over Judy lest that small maiden should attempt to comfort her brother, to the peril of her soul.

And Mamma came – in a four-wheeler – fluttered with tender excitement. Such a Mamma! She was young, frivolously young, and beautiful, with delicately-flushed cheeks, eyes that shone like stars, and a voice that needed no appeal of outstretched arms to draw little ones to her heart. Judy ran straight to her, but Black Sheep hesitated. Could this wonder be 'showing off'? She would not put out her arms when she knew of his crimes. Meantime was it possible that by fondling she wanted to get anything out of Black Sheep? Only all his love and all his confidence; but that Black Sheep did not know. Aunty Rosa withdrew and left Mamma, kneeling between her children, half laughing, half crying, in the very hall where Punch and Judy had wept five years before.

'Well, chicks, do you remember me?'

'No,' said Judy frankly, 'but I said, "God bless Papa and Mamma" ev'vy night.'

'A little,' said Black Sheep. 'Remember I wrote to you every week, anyhow. That isn't to show off, but 'cause of what comes afterwards.'

'What comes after? What should come after, my darling boy?' And she drew him to her again. He came awkwardly, with many angles. 'Not used to petting,' said the quick Mother-soul. 'The girl is.'

'She's too little to hurt anyone,' thought Black Sheep, 'and if I said I'd kill her, she'd be afraid. I wonder what Aunty Rosa will tell.'

There was a constrained late dinner, at the end of which

Mamma picked up Judy and put her to bed with endearments manifold. Faithless little Judy had shown her defection from Aunty Rosa already. And that lady resented it bitterly. Black Sheep rose to leave the room.

'Come and say good-night,' said Aunty Rosa, offering a withered cheek.

'Huh!' said Black Sheep. 'I never kiss you, and I'm not going to show off. Tell that woman what I've done, and see what she says.'

Black Sheep climbed into bed feeling that he had lost Heaven after a glimpse through the gates. In half an hour 'that woman' was bending over him. Black Sheep flung up his right arm.[35] It wasn't fair to come and hit him in the dark. Even Aunty Rosa never tried that. But no blow followed.

'Are you showing off? I won't tell you anything more than Aunty Rosa has, and *she* doesn't know everything,' said Black Sheep as clearly as he could for the arms round his neck.

'Oh, my son – my little, little son! It was my fault – *my* fault, darling – and yet how could we help it? Fogive me, Punch.' The voice died out in a broken whisper, and two hot tears fell on Black Sheep's forehead.

'Has she been making you cry too?' he asked. 'You should see Jane cry. But you're nice, and Jane is a Born Liar – Aunty Rosa says so.'

'Hush, Punch, hush! My boy, don't talk like that. Try to love me a little bit – a little bit. You don't know how I want it. Punch-*baba*, come back to me! I am your Mother – your own Mother – and never mind the rest. I know – yes, I know, dear. It doesn't matter now. Punch, won't you care for me a little?'

It is astonishing how much petting a big boy of ten can endure when he is quite sure that there is no one to laugh at him. Black Sheep had never been made much of before, and here was this beautiful woman treating him – Black Sheep, the Child of the Devil and the inheritor of undying flame – as though he were a small God.

'I care for you a great deal, Mother dear,' he whispered at

last, 'and I'm glad you've come back; but are you sure Aunty Rosa told you everything?'

'Everything. What *does* it matter? But —' the voice broke with a sob that was also laughter — 'Punch, my poor, dear, half-blind darling, don't you think it was a little foolish of you?'

'*No*. It saved a lickin'.'

Mamma shuddered and slipped away in the darkness to write a long letter to Papa. Here is an extract:

... Judy is a dear, plump little prig who adores the woman, and wears with as much gravity as her religious opinions – only eight, Jack! – a venerable horse-hair atrocity which she calls her Bustle! I have just burnt it, and the child is asleep in my bed as I write. She will come to me at once. Punch I cannot quite understand. He is well nourished, but seems to have been worried into a system of small deceptions which the woman magnifies into deadly sins. Don't you recollect our own upbringing, dear, when the Fear of the Lord [36] was so often the beginning of falsehood? I shall win Punch to me before long. I am taking the children away [37] into the country to get them to know me, and, on the whole, I am content, or shall be when you come home, dear boy, and then, thank God, we shall be all under one roof again at last!

Three months later, Punch, no longer Black Sheep, has discovered that he is the veritable owner of a real, live, lovely Mamma, who is also a sister, comforter, and friend, and that he must protect her till the Father comes home. Deception does not suit the part of a protector, and, when one can do anything without question, where is the use of deception?

'Mother would be awfully cross if you walked through that ditch,' says Judy, continuing a conversation.

'Mother's never angry,' says Punch. 'She'd just say, "You're a little *pagal*"; [38] and that's not nice, but I'll show.'

Punch walks through the ditch and mires himself to the knees. 'Mother, dear,' he shouts, 'I'm just as dirty as I can pos-*sib*-ly be!'

'Then change your clothes as quickly as you pos-*sib*-ly can!' Mother's clear voice rings out from the house. 'And don't be a little *pagal*!'

'There! 'Told you so,' says Punch. 'It's all different now, and we are just as much Mother's as if she had never gone.'

Not altogether, O Punch, for when young lips have drunk deep of the bitter waters of Hate, Suspicion, and Despair, all the Love in the world will not wholly take away that knowledge; though it may turn darkened eyes for a while to the light, and teach Faith where no Faith was.

⟨ His Majesty the King [1] ⟩

Where the word of a King is, there is power: And who may say unto him –
What doest thou? [2]

'Yeth! And Chimo to sleep at ve foot of ve bed, and ve pink
pikky-book, and ve bwead – 'cause I will be hungwy in ve night
– and vat's all, Miss Biddums. And now give me one kiss and I'll
go to sleep – So! Kite quiet. Ow! Ve pink pikky-book has
slidded under ve pillow and ve bwead is cwumbling! Miss Biddums! Miss *Bid*-dums! I'm *so* uncomfy! Come and tuck me
up, Miss Biddums.'

His Majesty the King was going to bed; and poor, patient
Miss Biddums, who had advertised herself humbly as a 'young
person, European, accustomed to the care of little children',
was forced to wait upon his royal caprices. The going to bed
was always a lengthy process, because His Majesty had a convenient knack of forgetting which of his many friends, from the
mehter's [3] son to the Commissioner's daughter, he had prayed
for, and, lest the Deity should take offence, was used to toil
through his little prayers, in all reverence, five times in one
evening. His Majesty the King believed in the efficacy of prayer
as devoutly as he believed in Chimo the patient spaniel, or Miss
Biddums, who could reach him down his gun – 'with cursuffun
caps [4] – *reel* ones' – from the upper shelves of the big nursery cupboard.

At the door of the nursery his authority stopped. Beyond lay
the empire of his father and mother – two very terrible people
who had no time to waste upon His Majesty the King. His
voice was lowered when he passed the frontier of his own dominions, his actions were fettered, and his soul was filled with
awe because of the grim man who lived among a wilderness of

pigeon-holes and the most fascinating pieces of red tape, and the wonderful woman who was always getting into or stepping out of the big carriage.

To the one belonged the mysteries of the '*duftar*-room',[5] to the other the great, reflected wilderness of the 'Memsahib's room', where the shiny, scented dresses hung on pegs, miles and miles up in the air, and the just-seen plateau of the toilet-table revealed an acreage of speckly combs, broidered 'hanafitch-bags', and 'white-headed' brushes.

There was no room for His Majesty the King either in official reserve or worldly gorgeousness. He had discovered that, ages and ages ago – before even Chimo came to the house, or Miss Biddums had ceased grizzling over a packet of greasy letters which appeared to be her chief treasure on earth. His Majesty the King, therefore, wisely confined himself to his own territories, where only Miss Biddums, and she feebly, disputed his sway.

From Miss Biddums he had picked up his simple theology and welded it to the legends of gods and devils that he had learned in the servants' quarters.

To Miss Biddums he confided with equal trust his tattered garments and his more serious griefs. She would make everything whole. She knew exactly how the Earth had been born, and had reassured the trembling soul of His Majesty the King that terrible time in July when it rained continuously for seven days and seven nights, and – there was no Ark ready and all the ravens had flown away! She was the most powerful person with whom he was brought into contact – always excepting the two remote and silent people beyond the nursery door.

How was His Majesty the King to know that, six years ago, in the summer of his birth, Mrs Austell, turning over her husband's papers, had come upon the intemperate letter of a foolish woman who had been carried away by the silent man's strength and personal beauty? How could he tell what evil the overlooked slip of notepaper had wrought in the mind of a desperately jealous wife? How could he, despite his wisdom, guess that his mother had chosen to make of it excuse for a bar and a division between herself and her husband, that strengthened and grew harder to break with each year; that she, having unearthed this skeleton in the cupboard, had trained it into a household God which should be about their path and about their bed, and poison all their ways?

These things were beyond the province of His Majesty the King. He only knew that his father was daily absorbed in some mysterious work for a thing called the *Sirkar*,[6] and that his mother was the victim alternately of the *Nautch* and the *Bur rakhana*.[7] To these entertainments she was escorted by a Captain-Man for whom His Majesty the King had no regard.

'He *doesn't* laugh,' he argued with Miss Biddums, who would fain have taught him charity. 'He only makes faces wiv his mouf, and when he wants to o-muse me I am *not* o-mused.' And His Majesty the King shook his head as one who knew the deceitfulness of this world.

Morning and evening it was his duty to salute his father and mother — the former with a grave shake of the hand, and the latter with an equally grave kiss. Once, indeed, he had put his arms round his mother's neck, in the fashion he used towards Miss Biddums. The openwork of his sleeve-edge caught in an earring, and the last stage of His Majesty's little overture was a suppressed scream and summary dismissal to the nursery.

'It is w'ong,' thought His Majesty the King, 'to hug Memsahibs wiv fings in veir ears. I will amember.' He never repeated the experiment.

Miss Biddums, it must be confessed, spoilt him as much as his nature admitted, in some sort of recompense for what she called 'the hard ways of his Papa and Mamma'. She, like her charge, knew nothing of the trouble between man and wife — the savage contempt for a woman's stupidity on the one side, or the dull, rankling anger on the other. Miss Biddums had looked after many little children in her time, and served in many establishments. Being a discreet woman, she observed little and said less, and, when her pupils went over the sea to the Great Unknown, which she, with touching confidence in her hearers, called 'Home', packed up her slender belongings and sought for employment afresh, lavishing all her love on each successive batch of ingrates. Only His Majesty the King had repaid her affection with interest; and in his uncomprehending ears she had told the tale of nearly all her hopes, her aspirations, the hopes that were dead, and the dazzling glories of her ancestral home in '*Cal*cutta, close to Wellington Square'.

Everything above the average was in the eyes of His Majesty the King 'Calcutta good'. When Miss Biddums had crossed his royal will, he reversed the epithet to vex that estimable lady, and all things evil were, until the tears of repentance swept away spite, 'Calcutta bad'.

Now and again Miss Biddums begged for him the rare pleasure of a day in the society of the Commissioner's child – the wilful four-year-old Patsie, who, to the intense amazement of His Majesty the King, was idolized by her parents. On thinking the question out at length, by roads unknown to those who have left childhood behind, he came to the conclusion that Patsie was petted because she wore a big blue sash and yellow hair.

This precious discovery he kept to himself. The yellow hair was absolutely beyond his power, his own tousled wig being potato-brown; but something might be done towards the blue sash. He tied a large knot in his mosquito-curtains in order to remember to consult Patsie on their next meeting. She was the only child he had ever spoken to, and almost the only one that he had ever seen. The little memory and the very large and ragged knot held good.

'Patsie, lend me your blue wiband,' said His Majesty the King.

'You'll bewy it,' said Patsie doubtfully, mindful of certain atrocities committed on her doll.

'No, I won't – twoofanhonour.[8] It's for me to wear.'

'Pooh!' said Patsie. 'Boys don't wear sa-ashes. Zey's only for dirls.'

'I didn't know.' The face of His Majesty the King fell.

'Who wants ribands? Are you playing horses, chickabiddies?' said the Commissioner's wife, stepping into the verandah.

'Toby wanted my sash,' explained Patsie.

'I don't now,' said His Majesty the King hastily, feeling that with one of these terrible 'grown-ups' his poor little secret would be shamelessly wrenched from him, and perhaps – most burning desecration of all – laughed at.

'I'll give you a cracker-cap,' said the Commissioner's wife. 'Come along with me, Toby, and we'll choose it.'

The cracker-cap was a stiff, three-pointed vermilion-and-tinsel splendour. His Majesty the King fitted it on his royal brow. The Commissioner's wife had a face that children instinctively trusted, and her action, as she adjusted the toppling middle spike, was tender.

'Will it do as well?' stammered His Majesty the King.

'As what, little one?'

'As ve wiban?'

'Oh, quite. Go and look at yourself in the glass.'

The words were spoken in all sincerity, and to help forward any absurd 'dressing-up' amusement that the children might take into their minds. But the young savage has a keen sense of the ludicrous. His Majesty the King swung the great cheval-glass down, and saw his head crowned with the staring horror of a fool's cap – a thing which his father would rend to pieces if it ever came into his office. He plucked it off, and burst into tears.

'Toby,' said the Commissioner's wife gravely, 'you shouldn't give way to temper. I am very sorry to see it. It's wrong.'

His Majesty the King sobbed inconsolably, and the heart of Patsie's mother was touched. She drew the child on to her knee. Clearly it was not temper alone.

'What is it, Toby? Won't you tell me? Aren't you well?'

The torrent of sobs and speech met, and fought for a time, with chokings and gulpings and gasps. Then, in a sudden rush, His Majesty the King was delivered of a few inarticulate sounds, followed by the words – 'Go a – way you – dirty – little debbil!'

'Toby! What do you mean?'

'It's what he'd say. I *know* it is! He said vat when vere was only a little, little eggy mess, on my t-t-unic; and he'd say it again, and laugh, if I went in wif vat on my head.'

'Who would say that?'

'M-m-my Papa! And I fought if I had ve blue wiban, he'd let me play in ve waste-paper basket under ve table.'

'*What* blue riband, childie?'

'Ve same vat Patsie had – ve big blue wiban w-w-wound my t-t-tummy!'

'What is it, Toby? There's something on your mind. Tell me all about it, and perhaps I can help.'

'Isn't anyfing,' sniffed His Majesty, mindful of his manhood, and raising his head from the motherly bosom upon which it was resting. 'I only fought vat you – you petted Patsie 'cause she had ve blue wiban, and – and if I'd had ve blue wiban too, m-my Papa w-would pet me.'

The secret was out, and His Majesty the King sobbed bitterly in spite of the arms around him and the murmur of comfort on his heated little forehead.

Enter Patsie tumultuously, embarrassed by several lengths of the Commissioner's pet *mahseer*-rod.[9] 'Tum along, Toby! Zere's a *chu-chu* lizard[10] in ze *chick*,[11] and I've told Chimo to watch him till we tum. If we poke him wiz zis his tail will go *wiggle-wiggle* and fall off. Tum along! I can't weach.'

'I'm comin',' said His Majesty the King, climbing down from the Commissioner's wife's knee after a hasty kiss.

Two minutes later, the *chu-chu* lizard's tail was wriggling on the matting of the verandah, and the children were gravely poking it with splinters from the *chick*, to urge its exhausted vitality into 'just one wiggle more, 'cause it doesn't hurt *chu-chu*'.

The Commissioner's wife stood in the doorway and watched – 'Poor little mite! A blue sash – and my own precious Patsie! I wonder if the best of us, or we who love them best, ever understood what goes on in their topsy-turvy little heads.'

She went indoors to devise a tea for His Majesty the King.

'Their souls aren't in their tummies at that age in this climate,' said the Commissioner's wife, 'but they are not far off. I wonder if I could make Mrs Austell understand. Poor little fellow!'

With simple craft, the Commissioner's wife called on Mrs

Austell and spoke long and lovingly about children; inquiring specially for His Majesty the King.

'He's with his governess,' said Mrs Austell, and the tone showed that she was not interested.

The Commissioner's wife, unskilled in the art of war, continued her questionings. 'I don't know,' said Mrs Austell. 'These things are left to Miss Biddums, and, of course, she does not ill-treat the child.'

The Commissioner's wife left hastily. The last sentence jarred upon her nerves. 'Doesn't *ill-treat* the child! As if that were all! I wonder what Tom would say if I only "didn't ill-treat" Patsie!'

Thenceforward, His Majesty the King was an honoured guest at the Commissioner's house, and the chosen friend of Patsie, with whom he blundered into as many scrapes as the compound and the servants' quarters afforded. Patsie's Mamma was always ready to give counsel, help, and sympathy, and, if need were and callers few, to enter into their games with an *abandon* that would have shocked the sleek-haired subalterns who squirmed painfully in their chairs when they came to call on her whom they profanely nicknamed 'Mother Bunch'.[12]

Yet, in spite of Patsie and Patsie's Mamma, and the love that these two lavished upon him, His Majesty the King fell grievously from grace, and committed no less a sin than that of theft – unknown, it is true, but burdensome.

There came a man to the door one day, when His Majesty was playing in the hall and the bearer had gone to dinner, with a packet for His Majesty's Mamma. And he put it upon the hall-table, and said that there was no answer, and departed.

Presently, the pattern of the dado ceased to interest His Majesty, while the packet, a white, neatly-wrapped one of fascinating shape, interested him very much indeed. His Mamma was out, so was Miss Biddums, and there was pink string round the packet. He greatly desired pink string. It would help him in many of his little businesses – the haulage across the floor of his small cane-chair, the torturing of Chimo, who could never understand harness – and so forth. If he took the string it would be his own, and nobody would be any the wiser. He certainly could not pluck up sufficient courage to ask Mamma for it. Wherefore, mounting upon a chair, he carefully untied the string and, behold, the stiff white paper spread out in four directions, and revealed a beautiful little leather box with gold lines upon it! He tried to replace the string, but that was a failure. So he opened the box to get full satisfaction for his iniquity, and saw a most beautiful Star that shone and winked, and was altogether lovely and desirable.

'Vat,' said His Majesty meditatively, 'is a 'parkle cwown, like what I will wear when I go to heaven. I will wear it on my head – Miss Biddums says so. I would like to wear it *now*. I would like to play wiv it. I will take it away and play wiv it, very careful, until Mamma asks for it. I fink it was brought for me to play wiv – same as my cart.'

His Majesty the King was arguing against his conscience, and he knew it, for he thought immediately after: 'Never mind, I will keep it to play wiv until Mamma says where is it, and then I will say – "I tookt it and I am sorry." I will not hurt it because it is a 'parkle cwown. But Miss Biddums will tell me to put it back. I will not show it to Miss Biddums.'

If Mamma had come in at that moment all would have gone well. She did not, and His Majesty the King stuffed paper, case, and jewel into the breast of his blouse and marched to the nursery.

'When Mamma asks I will tell,' was the salve that he laid upon his conscience. But Mamma never asked, and for three whole days His Majesty the King gloated over his treasure. It was of no earthly use to him, but it was splendid, and, for aught he knew, something dropped from the heavens themselves. Still Mamma made no inquiries, and it seemed to him, in his furtive peeps, as though the shiny stones grew dim. What was the use of a 'parkle cwown if it made a little boy feel all bad in his inside? He had the pink string as well as the other treasure, but greatly he wished that he had not gone beyond the string. It was his first experience of iniquity, and it pained him after the flush of possession and secret delight in the ''parkle cwown' had died away.

Each day that he delayed rendered confession to the people beyond the nursery doors more impossible. Now and again he determined to put himself in the path of the beautifully-attired lady as she was going out, and explain that he and no one else was the possessor of a ''parkle cwown', most beautiful and quite uninquired for. But she passed hurriedly to her carriage, and the opportunity was gone before His Majesty the King could draw the deep breath which clinches noble resolve. The dread secret cut him off from Miss Biddums, Patsie, and the Commissioner's wife, and – doubly hard fate – when he brooded over it Patsie said, and told her mother, that he was cross.

The days were very long to His Majesty the King, and the nights longer still. Miss Biddums had informed him, more than once, what was the ultimate destiny of 'fieves', and when he passed the interminable mud flanks of the Central Jail, he shook in his little strapped shoes.

But release came after an afternoon spent in playing boats by the edge of the tank at the bottom of the garden. His Majesty the King went to tea, and, for the first time in his memory, the meal revolted him. His nose was very cold, and his cheeks were burning hot. There was a weight about his feet, and he pressed his head several times to make sure that it was not swelling as he sat.

'I feel vevy funny,' said His Majesty the King, rubbing his nose. 'Vere's a buzz-buzz in my head.'

He went to bed quietly. Miss Biddums was out and the bearer undressed him.

The sin of the ''parkle cwown' was forgotten in the acuteness of the discomfort to which he roused after a leaden sleep of some hours. He was thirsty, and the bearer had forgotten to leave the drinking-water. 'Miss Biddums! Miss Biddums! I'm so kirsty!'

No answer. Miss Biddums had leave to attend the wedding of a Calcutta schoolmate. His Majesty the King had forgotten that.

'I want a dwink of water,' he cried, but his voice was dried up in his throat. 'I want a drink! Vere is ve glass?'

He sat up in bed and looked round. There was a murmur of voices from the other side of the nursery door. It was better to face the terrible unknown than to choke in the dark. He slipped out of bed, but his feet were strangely wilful, and he reeled once or twice. Then he pushed the door open and staggered – a puffed and purple-faced little figure – into the brilliant light of the dining-room full of pretty ladies.

'I'm vevy hot! I'm vevy uncomfitivle,' moaned His Majesty the King, clinging to the portière, 'and vere's no water in ve glass, and I'm *so* kirsty. Give me a dwink of water.'

An apparition in black and white – His Majesty the King could hardly see distinctly – lifted him up to the level of the table, and felt his wrists and forehead. The water came, and he drank deeply, his teeth chattering against the edge of the tumbler. Then everyone seemed to go away – everyone except the huge man in black and white, who carried him back to his bed; the mother and father following. And the sin of the ''parkle cwown' rushed back and took possession of the terrified soul.

'I'm a fief!' he gasped. 'I want to tell Miss Biddums vat I'm a fief. Vere is Miss Biddums?'

Miss Biddums had come and was bending over him. 'I'm a fief,' he whispered. 'A fief – like ve men in ve pwison. But I'll tell now. I tookt – I tookt ve 'parkle cwown when ve man that came left it in ve hall. I bwoke ve paper and ve little bwown box, and it looked shiny, and I tookt it to play wif, and I was afwaid. It's in ve dooly-box at ve bottom. No one *never* asked for it, but I was afwaid. Oh, go an' get ve dooly-box!'

Miss Biddums obediently stooped to the lowest shelf of the *almirah*¹³ and unearthed the big paper box in which His Majesty the King kept his dearest possessions. Under the tin soldiers, and a layer of mud pellets for a pellet-bow, winked and blazed a diamond star, wrapped roughly in a half-sheet of notepaper whereon were a few words.

Somebody was crying at the head of the bed, and a man's hand touched the forehead of His Majesty the King, who grasped the packet and spread it on the bed.

'Vat is ve 'parkle cwown,' he said, and wept bitterly; for now that he had made restitution he would fain have kept the shining splendour with him.

'It concerns you too,' said a voice at the head of the bed. 'Read the note. This is not the time to keep back anything.'

The note was curt, very much to the point, and signed by a single initial. *'If you wear this tomorrow night I shall know what to expect.'* The date was three weeks old.

A whisper followed, and the deeper voice returned: 'And you drifted as far apart as *that*! I think it makes us quite now, doesn't it? Oh, can't we drop this folly once and for all? Is it worth it, darling?'

'Kiss me too,' said His Majesty the King dreamily. 'You isn't *vevy* angwy, is you?'

The fever burned itself out, and His Majesty the King slept.

When he waked, it was in a new world – peopled by his father and mother as well as Miss Biddums; and there was much love in that world and no morsel of fear, and more petting than was good for several little boys. His Majesty the King was too young to moralize on the uncertainty of things human, or he would have been impressed with the singular advantages of crime – ay, black sin. Behold, he had stolen the ''parkle cwown', and his reward was Love, and the right to play in the waste-paper basket under the table 'for always'.

He trotted over to spend an afternoon with Patsie, and the Commissioner's wife would have kissed him. 'No, not vere,' said His Majesty the King, with superb insolence, fencing one corner of his mouth with his hand. 'Vat's my Mamma's place – vere *she* kisses me.'

'Oh!' said the Commissioner's wife briefly. Then to herself: 'Well, I suppose I ought to be glad for his sake. Children are selfish little grubs and – I've got my Patsie.'

⟨ The Drums of the Fore and Aft [1] ⟩

In the Army List they still stand as 'The Fore and Fit Princess Hohenzollern-Sigmaringen-Auspach's Merthyr-Tydfilshire Own Royal Loyal Light Infantry, Regimental District 329A', but the Army through all its barracks and canteens knows them now as the 'Fore and Aft'. They may in time do something that shall make their new title honourable, but at present they are bitterly ashamed, and the man who calls them 'Fore and Aft' does so at the risk of the head which is on his shoulders.

Two words breathed into the stables of a certain Cavalry Regiment will bring the men out into the streets with belts and mops and bad language; but a whisper of 'Fore and Aft' will bring out this regiment with rifles.

Their own excuse is that they came again and did their best to finish the job in style. But for a time all their world knows that they were openly beaten, whipped, dumb-cowed, shaking, and afraid. The men know it; their officers know it; the Horse Guards [2] know it, and when the next war comes the enemy will know it also. There are two or three regiments of the Line that have a black mark against their names which they will then wipe out; and it will be excessively inconvenient for the troops upon whom they do their wiping.

The courage of the British soldier is officially supposed to be above proof, and, as a general rule, it is so. The exceptions are decently shovelled out of sight, only to be referred to in the freshest of unguarded talk, that occasionally swamps a Mess-table at midnight. Then one hears strange and horrible stories of men not following their officers, of orders being given by those who had no right to give them, and of disgrace that, but for the standing luck of the British Army, might have ended in brilliant disaster. These are unpleasant stories to listen to, and the Messes tell them under their breath, sitting by the big wood

300

fires, and the young officer bows his head and thinks to himself, please God, his men shall never behave unhandily.

The British soldier is not altogether to be blamed for occasional lapses; but this verdict he should not know. A moderately intelligent General will waste six months in mastering the craft of the particular war that he may be waging; a Colonel may utterly misunderstand the capacity of his regiment for three months after it has taken the field; and even a Company Commander may err and be deceived as to the temper and temperament of his own handful: wherefore the soldier, and the soldier of today more particularly, should not be blamed for falling back. He should be shot or hanged afterwards – to encourage the others; but he should not be vilified in newspapers, for that is want of tact and waste of space.

He has, let us say, been in the service of the Empress for, perhaps, four years. He will leave in another two years. He has no inherited morals, and four years are not sufficient to drive toughness into his fibre, or to teach him how holy a thing is his Regiment. He wants to drink, he wants to enjoy himself – in India he wants to save money – and he does not in the least like getting hurt. He has received just sufficient education to make him understand half the purport of the orders he receives, and to speculate on the nature of clean, incised, and shattering wounds. Thus, if he is told to deploy under fire preparatory to an attack, he knows that he runs a very great risk of being killed while he is deploying, and suspects that he is being thrown away to gain ten minutes' time. He may either deploy with desperate swiftness, or he may shuffle, or bunch, or break, according to the discipline under which he has lain for four years.

Armed with imperfect knowledge, cursed with the rudiments of an imagination, hampered by the intense selfishness of the lower classes, and unsupported by any regimental associations, this young man is suddenly introduced to an enemy who in eastern lands is always ugly, generally tall and hairy, and frequently noisy. If he looks to the right and the left and sees old soldiers – men of twelve years' service, who, he knows, know what they are about – taking a charge, rush, or demonstration without embarrassment, he is consoled and applies his shoulder to the butt of his rifle with a stout heart. His peace is the greater if he hears a senior, who has taught him his soldiering and broken his head on occasion, whispering: 'They'll shout and carry on like this for five minutes. Then they'll rush in, and then we've got 'em by the short hairs!'

But, on the other hand, if he sees only men of his own term of service turning white and playing with their triggers, and saying: 'What the Hell's up now?' while the Company Commanders are sweating into their sword-hilts and shouting: 'Front-rank, fix bayonets. Steady there – steady! Sight for three hundred [3] – no, for five! Lie down, all! Steady! Front-rank kneel!' and so forth, he becomes unhappy; and grows acutely miserable when he hears a comrade turn over with the rattle of fire-irons falling into the fender, and the grunt of a pole-axed ox. If he can be moved about a little and allowed to watch the effect of his own fire on the enemy he feels merrier, and may be then worked up to the blind passion of fighting, which is, contrary to general belief, controlled by a chilly Devil and shakes men like ague. If he is not moved about, and begins to feel cold at the pit of the stomach, and in that crisis is badly mauled, and hears orders that were never given, he will break, and he will break badly; and of all things under the light of the Sun there is nothing more terrible than a broken British regiment. When the worst comes to the worst and the panic is really epidemic, the men must be e'en let go, and the Company Commanders had better escape to the enemy and stay there for safety's sake. If they can be made to come again they are not pleasant men to meet; because they will not break twice.

About thirty years from this date, when we have succeeded in half-educating everything that wears trousers, our Army will be a beautifully unreliable machine. It will know too much and it will do too little. Later still, when all men are the mental level of the officer of today it will sweep the earth. Speaking roughly, you must employ either blackguards or gentlemen, or, best of all, blackguards commanded by gentlemen, to do butcher's work with efficiency and despatch. The ideal soldier should, of course, think for himself – the *Pocket-book* [4] says so. Unfortunately, to attain this virtue he has to pass through the phase of thinking of himself, and that is misdirected genius. A blackguard may be slow to think for himself, but he is genuinely anxious to kill, and a little punishment teaches him how to guard his own skin and perforate another's. A powerfully prayerful Highland Regiment, officered by rank Presbyterians, is, perhaps, one degree more terrible in action than a hard-bitten thousand of irresponsible Irish ruffians led by most improper young unbelievers. But these things prove the rule – which is that the midway men are not to be trusted alone. They have ideas about the value of life and an upbringing that has not taught them to go on and take the chances. They are carefully unprovided with a backing of comrades who have been shot over, and until that backing is re-introduced, as a great many Regimental Commanders intend it shall be, they are more liable to disgrace themselves than the size of the Empire or the dignity of the Army allows. Their officers are as good as good can be, because their training begins early, and God has arranged that a clean-run youth of the British middle classes shall, in the matter of backbone, brains, and bowels, surpass all other youths. For this reason a child of eighteen will stand up, doing nothing, with a tin sword in his hand and joy in his heart until he is dropped. If he dies, he dies like a gentleman. If he lives, he writes Home that he has been 'potted', 'sniped', 'chipped', or 'cut over', and sits down to besiege Government for a wound-gratuity until the next little war breaks out, when he perjures himself before a Medical Board, blarneys his Colonel, burns incense round his Adjutant, and is allowed to go to the Front once more.

Which homily brings me directly to a brace of the most finished little fiends that ever banged drum or tootled fife in the Band of a British Regiment. They ended their sinful career by open and flagrant mutiny and were shot for it. Their names were Jakin and Lew – Piggy Lew – and they were bold, bad drummer-boys, both of them frequently birched by the Drum-Major of the Fore and Aft.

Jakin was a stunted child of fourteen, and Lew was about the same age. When not looked after, they smoked and drank. They swore habitually after the manner of the Barrack-room, which is cold-swearing and comes from between clinched teeth; and they fought religiously once a week. Jakin had sprung from some London gutter and may or may not have passed through Dr Barnardo's [5] hands ere he arrived at the dignity of drummer-boy. Lew could remember nothing except the regiment and the delight of listening to the Band from his earliest years. He hid somewhere in his grimy little soul a genuine love for music, and was most mistakenly furnished with the head of a cherub: insomuch that beautiful ladies who watched the Regiment in church were wont to speak of him as a 'darling'. They never heard his vitriolic comments on their manners and morals, as he walked back to barracks with the Band and matured fresh causes of offence against Jakin.

The other drummer-boys hated both lads on account of their illogical conduct. Jakin might be pounding Lew, or Lew might be rubbing Jakin's head in the dirt, but any attempt at aggression on the part of an outsider was met by the combined forces of Lew and Jakin; and the consequences were painful. The boys were the Ishmaels [6] of the corps, but wealthy Ishmaels, for they sold battles in alternate weeks for the sport of the barracks when they were not pitted against other boys; and thus amassed money.

On this particular day there was dissension in the camp. They had just been convicted afresh of smoking, which is bad for little boys who use plug-tobacco, and Lew's contention was that Jakin had 'stunk so 'orrid bad from keepin' the pipe in pocket', that he and he alone was responsible for the birching they were both tingling under.

'I tell you I 'id the pipe back o' barracks,' said Jakin pacifically.

'You're a bloomin' liar,' said Lew without heat.

'You're a bloomin' little barstard,' said Jakin, strong in the knowledge that his own ancestry was unknown.

Now there is one word in the extended vocabulary of

barrack-room abuse that cannot pass without comment. You may call a man a thief and risk nothing. You may even call him a coward, without finding more than a boot whiz past your ear, but you must not call a man a bastard unless you are prepared to prove it on his front teeth.

'You might ha' kep' that till I wasn't so sore,' said Lew sorrowfully, dodging round Jakin's guard.

'I'll make you sorer,' said Jakin genially, and got home on Lew's alabaster forehead. All would have gone well and this story, as the books say, would never have been written, had not his evil fate prompted the Bazar-Sergeant's son, a long, employ-less man of five-and-twenty, to put in an appearance after the first round. He was eternally in need of money, and knew that the boys had silver.

'Fighting again,' said he. 'I'll report you to my father, and he'll report you to the Colour-Sergeant.'

'What's that to you?' said Jakin with an unpleasant dilation of the nostrils.

'Oh! nothing to *me*. You'll get in to trouble, and you've been up too often to afford that.'

'What the Hell do you know about what we've done?' asked Lew the Seraph. '*You* aren't in the Army, you lousy, cadging civilian.'

He closed in on the man's left flank.

'Jes' 'cause you find two gentlemen settlin' their diff'rences with their fistes you stick in your ugly nose where you aren't wanted. Run 'ome to your 'arf-caste slut of a Ma – or we'll give you what-for,' said Jakin.

The man attempted reprisals by knocking the boys' heads together. The scheme would have succeeded had not Jakin punched him vehemently in the stomach, or had Lew refrained from kicking his shins. They fought together, bleeding and breathless, for half an hour, and, after heavy punishment, tri-umphantly pulled down their opponent as terriers pull down a jackal.

'Now,' gasped Jakin, 'I'll give you what-for.' He proceeded to pound the man's features while Lew stamped on the outlying portions of his anatomy. Chivalry is not a strong point in the composition of the average drummer-boy. He fights, as do his betters, to make his mark.

Ghastly was the ruin that escaped, and awful was the wrath of the Bazar-Sergeant. Awful, too, was the scene in Orderly-room when the two reprobates appeared to answer the charge of half-murdering a 'civilian'. The Bazar-Sergeant thirsted for a criminal action, and his son lied. The boys stood to attention while the black clouds of evidence accumulated.

'You little devils are more trouble than the rest of the Regiment put together,' said the Colonel angrily. 'One might as well admonish thistledown, and I can't well put you in cells or under stoppages. You must be birched again.'

'Beg y' pardon, Sir. Can't we say nothin' in our own defence, Sir?' shrilled Jakin.

'Hey! What? Are you going to argue with *me?*' said the Colonel.

'No, Sir,' said Lew. 'But if a man come to you, Sir, and said he was going to report you, Sir, for 'aving a bit of a turn-up with a friend, Sir, an' wanted to get money out o' you, Sir –'

The Orderly-room exploded in a roar of laughter. 'Well?' said the Colonel.

'That was what that measly *jarnwar* [7] there did, Sir, and 'e'd 'a' *done* it, Sir, if we 'adn't prevented 'im. We didn't 'it' 'im much, Sir. 'E 'adn't no manner o' right to interfere with us, Sir. I don't mind being' birched by the Drum-Major, Sir, nor yet reported by *any* Corp'ral, but I'm – but I don't think it's fair, Sir, for a civilian to come an' talk over a man in the Army.'

A second shout of laughter shook the Orderly-room, but the Colonel was grave.

'What sort of characters have these boys?' he asked of the Regimental Sergeant-Major.

'Accordin' to the Bandmaster, Sir,' returned that revered official – the only soul in the regiment whom the boys feared – 'they do everything *but* lie, Sir.'

'Is it like we'd go for that man for fun, Sir?' said Lew, pointing to the plaintiff.

'Oh, admonished – admonished!' said the Colonel testily, and when the boys had gone he read the Bazar-Sergeant's son a lecture on the sin of unprofitable meddling, and gave orders that the Bandmaster should keep the Drums in better discipline.

'If either of you comes to practice again with so much as a scratch on your two ugly little faces,' thundered the Bandmaster, 'I'll tell the Drum-Major to take the skin off your backs. Understand that, you young devils.'

Then he repented of his speech for just the length of time that Lew, looking like a Seraph in red worsted embellishments, took the place of one of the trumpets – in hospital – and rendered the echo of a battle-piece. Lew certainly was a musician, and had often in his more exalted moments expressed a yearning to master every instrument of the Band.

'There's nothing to prevent your becoming a Bandmaster, Lew,' said the Bandmaster, who had composed waltzes of his own, and worked day and night in the interests of the Band.

'What did he say?' demanded Jakin after practice.

''Said I might be a bloomin' Bandmaster, an' be asked in to 'ave a glass o' sherry-wine on Mess-nights.' [8]

'Ho! 'Said you might be a bloomin' non-combatant, did 'e! That's just about wot 'e would say. When I've put in my boy's service – it's a bloomin' shame that doesn't count for pension – I'll take on as a privit. Then I'll be a Lance in a year – knowin' what I know about the ins an' outs o' things. In three years I'll be a bloomin' Sergeant. I won't marry then, not I! I'll 'old on and learn the orf'cers' ways an' apply for exchange into a reg'-ment that doesn't know all about me. Then I'll be a bloomin' orf'cer. Then I'll ask you to 'ave a glass o' sherry-wine, *Mister* Lew, an' you'll bloomin' well 'ave to stay in the hanty-room [9] while the Mess-Sergeant brings it to your dirty 'ands.'

''S'pose I'm going to a be a Bandmaster? Not I, quite. I'll be a orf'cer too. There's nothin' like taking to a thing an' stickin' to it, the Schoolmaster says. The reg'ment don't go 'ome for another seven years. I'll be a Lance then or near to.'

Thus the boys discussed their futures, and conducted themselves piously for a week. That is to say, Lew started a flirtation with the Colour-Sergeant's daughter, aged thirteen – 'not', as he explained to Jakin, 'with any intention o' matrimony, but by way o' keeping' my 'and in'. And the black-haired Cris Delighan enjoyed that flirtation more than previous ones, and the other drummer-boys raged furiously together,[10] and Jakin preached sermons on the dangers of 'bein' tangled along o' petticoats'.

But neither love nor virtue would have held Lew long in the paths of propriety had not the rumour gone abroad that the Regiment was to be sent on active service, to take part in a war which, for the sake of brevity, we will call 'The War of the Lost Tribes'.[11]

The barracks had the rumour almost before the Mess-room, and of all the nine hundred men in barracks not ten had seen a shot fired in anger. The Colonel had, twenty years ago, assisted at a Frontier expedition; one of the Majors had seen service at the Cape; a confirmed deserter in E Company had helped to clear streets in Ireland; but that was all. The Regiment had been put by for many years. The overwhelming mass of its rank and file had from three to four years' service; the non-commissioned officers were under thirty years old; and men and sergeants alike had forgotten to speak of the stories written in brief upon the Colours[12] – the New Colours that had been formally blessed by an Archbishop in England ere the Regiment came away.

They wanted to go to the Front – they were enthusiastically anxious to go – but they had no knowledge of what war meant, and there was none to tell them. They were an educated regiment, the percentage of school-certificates in their ranks was high, and most of the men could do more than read and write. They had been recruited in loyal observance of the territorial idea;[13] but they themselves had no notion of that idea. They were made up of drafts from an over-populated manufacturing district. The system had put flesh and muscle upon their small bones, but it could not put heart into the sons of those who for generations had done overmuch work for over-scanty pay, had sweated in drying-rooms, stooped over looms, coughed among white-lead, and shivered on lime-barges. The men had found food and rest in the Army, and now they were going to fight 'niggers' – people who ran away if you shook a stick at them. Wherefore they cheered lustily when the rumour ran, and the shrewd, clerkly non-commissioned officers speculated on the chances of batta [14] and of saving their pay. At Headquarters men said: 'The Fore and Fit have never been under fire within the last generation. Let us, therefore, break them in easily by setting them to guard lines of communication ' And this would have been done but for the fact that British Regiments were wanted – badly wanted – at the Front, and there were doubtful Native Regiments that could fill the minor duties. 'Brigade 'em with two strong Regiments,' said Headquarters. 'They may be knocked about a bit, but they'll learn their business before they come through. Nothing like a night-alarm and a little cutting-up of stragglers to make a Regiment smart in the field. Wait till they've had half-a-dozen sentries' throats cut.'

The Colonel wrote with delight that the temper of his men was excellent, that the Regiment was all that could be wished, and as sound as a bell. The Majors smiled with a sober joy, and the subalterns waltzed in pairs down the Mess-room after dinner, and nearly shot themselves at revolver-practice. But there was consternation in the hearts of Jakin and Lew. What was to be done with the Drums? Would the Band go to the Front? How many of the Drums would accompany the Regiment?

They took counsel together, sitting in a tree and smoking.

'It's more than a bloomin' toss-up they'll leave us be'ind at the Depot with the women. You'll like that,' said Jakin sarcastically.

''Cause o' Cris, y' mean? Wot's a woman, or a 'ole bloomin' depot o' women, 'longside o' the chanst of field-service? You know I'm as keen on goin' as you,' said Lew.

''Wish I was a bloomin' bugler,' said Jakin sadly. 'They'll take Tom Kidd along, that I can plaster a wall with, an' like as not they won't take us.'

'Then let's go an' make Tom Kidd so bloomin' sick 'e can't

bugle no more. You 'old is' 'ands an' I'll kick him,' said Lew, wriggling on the branch.

'That ain't no good neither. We ain't the sort o' characters to presoom on our rep'tations – they're bad. If they leave the Band at the Depot we don't go, and no error *there*. If they take the Band we may get cast for medical unfitness. Are you medical fit, Piggy?' said Jakin, digging Lew in the ribs with force.

'Yus,' said Lew with an oath. 'The Doctor says your 'eart's weak through smokin' on an empty stummick. Throw a chest an' I'll try yer.'

Jakin thew out his chest, which Lew smote with all his might. Jakin turned very pale, gasped, crowed, screwed up his eyes, and said – 'That's all right.'

'You'll do,' said Lew. 'I've 'eard o' men dying when you 'it 'em fair on the breastbone.'

'Don't bring us no nearer goin', though,' said Jakin. 'Do you know where we're ordered?'

'Gawd knows, an' 'E won't split on a pal. Somewheres up to the Front to kill Paythans [15] – hairy big beggars that turn you inside out if they get 'old o' you. They say their women are good-looking, too.'

'Any loot?' asked the abandoned Jakin.

'Not a bloomin' anna, they say, unless you dig up the ground an' see what the niggers 'ave 'id. They're a poor lot.' Jakin stood upright on the branch and gazed across the plain.

'Lew,' said he, 'there's the Colonel coming. 'Colonel's a good old beggar. Let's go an' talk to 'im.'

Lew nearly fell out of the tree at the audacity of the suggestion. Like Jakin he feared not God, neither regarded he Man, but there are limits even to the audacity of drummer-boy, and to speak to a Colonel was –

But Jakin had slid down the trunk and doubled in the direction of the Colonel. That officer was walking wrapped in thought and visions of a C.B. – yes, even a K.C.B., [16] for had he not at command one of the best Regiments of the Line – the Fore and Fit? And he was aware of two small boys charging down upon him. Once before it had been solemnly reported to

him that 'the Drums were in a state of mutiny', Jakin and Lew
being the ringleaders. This looked like an organized conspiracy.

The boys halted at twenty yards, walked to the regulation
four paces, and saluted together, each as well-set-up as a ramrod
and little taller.

The Colonel was in a genial mood; the boys appeared very
forlorn and unprotected on the desolate plain, and one of them
was handsome.

'Well!' said the Colonel, recognizing them. 'Are you going to
pull me down in the open? I'm sure I never interfere with you,
even though' – he sniffed suspiciously – 'you have been smoking.'

It was time to strike while the iron was hot. Their hearts beat
tumultuously.

'Beg y' pardon, Sir,' began Jakin. 'The Reg'ment's ordered
on active service, Sir?'

'So I believe,' said the Colonel courteously.

'Is the Band goin', Sir?' said both together. Then, without
pause, 'We're goin', Sir, ain't we?'

'You!' said the Colonel, stepping back the more fully to take
in the two small figures. 'You! You'd die in the first march.'

'No, we wouldn't, Sir. We can march with the Reg'ment
anywheres – p'rade an' anywhere else,' said Jakin.

'If Tom Kidd goes 'e'll shut up like a clasp-knife,' said Lew.
'Tom 'as very-close veins [17] in both 'is legs, Sir.'

'Very how much?'

'Very-close veins, Sir. That's why they swells after long
p'rade, Sir. If 'e can go, we can go, Sir.'

Again the Colonel looked at them long and intently.

'Yes, the Band is going,' he said as gravely as though he had
been addressing a brother officer. 'Have you any parents, either
of you two?'

'No, Sir,' rejoicingly from Lew and Jakin. 'We're both or-
phans, Sir. There's no one to be considered of on our account,
Sir.'

'You poor little sprats, and you want to go up to the Front
with the Regiment, do you? Why?'

'I've wore the Queen's Uniform for two years,' said Jakin. 'It's very 'ard, Sir, that a man don't get no recompense for doin' of 'is dooty, Sir.'

'An' – an' if I don't go, Sir,' interrupted Lew, 'the Bandmaster 'e says 'e'll catch an' make a bloo – a blessed musician o' me, Sir. Before I've seen any service, Sir.'

The Colonel made no answer for a long time. Then he said quietly: 'If you're passed by the Doctor I daresay you can go. I shouldn't smoke if I were you.'

The boys saluted and disappeared. The Colonel walked home and told the story to his wife, who nearly cried over it. The Colonel was well pleased. If that was the temper of the children, what would not the men do?

Jakin and Lew entered the boys' barrack-room with great stateliness, and refused to hold any conversation with their comrades for at least ten minutes. Then, bursting with pride, Jakin drawled: 'I've bin intervooin' the Colonel. Good old beggar is the Colonel. Says I to 'im, "Colonel," says I, "let me go to the Front, along o' the Reg'ment." – "To the Front you shall go," says 'e, "an' I only wish there was more like you among the dirty little devils that bang the bloomin' drums." Kidd, if you throw your 'courtrements at me for tellin' you the truth to your own advantage, your legs'll swell.'

None the less there was a Battle-Royal in the barrack-room, for the boys were consumed with envy and hate, and neither Jakin nor Lew behaved in conciliatory wise.

'I'm goin' out to say adoo to my girl,' said Lew, to cap the climax. 'Don't none o' you touch my kit because it's wanted for active service; me bein' specially invited to go by the Colonel.'

He strolled forth and whistled in the clump of trees at the back of the Married Quarters till Cris came to him, and, the preliminary kisses being given and taken, Lew began to explain the situation.

'I'm goin' to the Front with the Reg'ment,' he said valiantly.

'Piggy, you're a little liar,' said Cris, but her heart misgave her, for Lew was not in the habit of lying.

'Liar yourself, Cris,' said Lew, slipping an arm round her.

'I'm going'. When the Reg'ment marches out you'll see me with 'em, all galliant and gay. Give us another kiss, Cris, on the strength of it.'

'If you'd on'y a-stayed at the Depot – where you *ought* to ha' bin – you could get as many of 'em as – as you dam please,' whimpered Cris, putting up her mouth.

'It's 'ard, Cris. I grant you it's 'ard. But what's a man to do? If I'd a-stayed at the Depot, you wouldn't think anything of me.'

'Like as not, but I'd 'ave you with me, Piggy. An' all the thinkin' in the world isn't like kissin'.'

'An' all the kissin' in the world isn't like 'avin' a medal to wear on the front o' your coat.'

'*You* won't get no medal.'

'Oh yus, I shall though. Me an' Jakin are the only acting-drummers that'll be took along. All the rest is full men, an' we'll get our medals with them.'

'They might ha' taken anybody but you, Piggy. You'll get killed – you're so venturesome. Stay with me, Piggy darlin', down at the Depot, an' I'll love you true, for ever.'

'Ain't you goin' to do that *now*, Cris? You said you was.'

'O' course I am, but th' other's more comfortable. Wait till you've growed a bit, Piggy. You aren't no taller than me now.'

'I've bin in the Army for two years an' I'm not goin' to get out of a chanst o' seein' service, an' don't you try to make me do so. I'll come back, Cris, an' when I take on as a man I'll marry you – marry you when I'm a Lance.'

'Promise, Piggy?'

Lew reflected on the future as arranged by Jakin a short time previously, but Cris's mouth was very near to his own.

'I promise, s'elp me Gawd!' said he.

Cris slid an arm round his neck.

'I won't 'old you back no more, Piggy. Go away an' get your medal, an' I'll make you a new button-bag as nice as I know how,' she whispered.

'Put some o' your 'air into it, Cris, an' I'll keep it in my pocket so long's I'm alive.'

Then Cris wept anew, and the interview ended. Public feeling among the drummer-boys rose to fever pitch and the lives of Jakin and Lew became unenviable. Not only had they been permitted to enlist two years before the regulation boy's age – fourteen – but, by virtue, it seemed, of their extreme youth, they were allowed to go to the Front – which thing had not happened to acting-drummers within the knowledge of boy. The Band which was to accompany the Regiment had been cut down to the regulation twenty men, the surplus returning to the ranks. Jakin and Lew were attached to the Band as supernumeraries, though they would much have preferred being Company buglers.

''Don't matter much,' said Jakin, after the medical inspection. 'Be thankful that we're 'lowed to go at all. The Doctor 'e said that if we could stand what we took from the Bazar-Sergeant's son we'd stand pretty nigh anything.'

'Which we will,' said Lew, looking tenderly at the ragged and ill-made housewife [18] that Cris had given him, with a lock of her hair worked into a sprawling 'L' upon the cover.

'It was the best I could,' she sobbed. 'I wouldn't let mother nor the Sergeants' tailor 'elp me. Keep it always, Piggy, an' remember I love you true.'

They marched to the railway station, nine hundred and sixty strong, and every soul in cantonments turned out to see them go. The drummers gnashed their teeth at Jakin and Lew marching with the Band, the married women wept upon the platform, and the Regiment cheered its noble self black in the face.

'A nice level lot,' said the Colonel to the Second-in-Command as they watched the first four companies entraining.

'Fit to do anything,' said the Second-in-Command enthusiastically. 'But it seems to me they're a thought too young and tender for the work in hand. It's bitter cold up at the Front now.'

'They're sound enough,' said the Colonel. 'We must take our chance of sick casualties.'

So they went northward, ever northward, past droves and droves of camels, armies of camp followers, and legions of laden mules, the throng thickening day by day, till with a shriek the train pulled up at a hopelessly-congested junction where six lines of temporary track accommodated six forty-waggon trains; where whistles blew, Babus[19] sweated, and Commissariat officers swore from dawn till far into the night amid the wind-driven chaff of the fodder-bales and the lowing of a thousand steers.

'Hurry up – you're badly wanted at the Front,' was the message that greeted the Fore and Aft, and the occupants of the Red Cross carriages told the same tale.

''Tisn't so much the bloomin' fightin',' gasped a headbound trooper of Hussars to a knot of admiring Fore and Afts. ''Tisn't so much the bloomin' fightin', though there's enough o' that. It's the bloomin' food an' the bloomin' climate. Frost all night 'cept when it hails, and biling sun all day, and the water stinks fit to knock you down. I got my 'ead chipped like a egg; I've got pneumonia too, an' my guts is all out o' order. 'Tain't no bloomin' picnic in those parts, I can tell you.'

'Wot are the niggers like?' demanded a private.

'There's some prisoners in that train yonder. Go an' look at 'em. They're the aristocracy o' the country. The common folk are a dashed sight uglier. If you want to know what they fight with, reach under my seat an' pull out the long knife that's there.'

They dragged out and beheld for the first time the grim, bone-handled, triangular Afghan knife. It was almost as long as Lew.

'That's the thing to jint ye,' said the trooper feebly. 'It can take off a man's arm at the shoulder as easy as slicing butter. I halved the beggar that used that 'un, but there's more of his likes up above. They don't understand thrustin', but they're devils to slice.'

The men strolled across the tracks to inspect the Afghan prisoners. They were unlike any 'niggers' that the Fore and Aft had ever met – these huge, black-haired, scowling sons of the Beni-Israel.[20] As the men stared the Afghans spat freely and muttered one to another with lowered eyes.

315

'My eyes! Wot awful swine!' said Jakin, who was in the rear of the procession. 'Say, old man, how you got *puckrowed*,[21] eh? *Kiswasti* you wasn't hanged for your ugly face, hey?'

The tallest of the company turned, his leg-irons clanking at the movement, and stared at the boy. 'See!' he cried to his fellows in Pushto. 'They send children against us. What a people, and what fools!'

'*Hya!*' said Jakin, nodding his head cheerily. 'You go down-country. *Khana* get, *peenikapanee* get – live like a bloomin' Raja *ke marfik*. That's a better *bandobust* than baynit get it in your innards. Good-bye, ole man. Take care o' your beautiful figure-'ed, an' try to look *kushy*.'[22]

The men laughed and fell in for their first march, when they began to realize that a soldier's life was not all beer and skittles. They were much impressed with the size and bestial ferocity of the niggers whom they had now learned to call 'Paythans', and more with the exceeding discomfort of their own surroundings. Twenty old soldiers in the corps would have taught them how to make themselves moderately snug at night, but they had no old soldiers, and, as the troops on the line of march said, 'they lived like pigs'. They learned the heart-breaking cussedness of camp-kitchens and camels and the depravity of an E.P. tent[23] and a wither-wrung mule. They studied animalculae in water, and developed a few cases of dysentery in their study.

At the end of their third march they were disagreeably surprised by the arrival in their camp of a hammered iron slug which, fired from a steady rest at seven hundred yards, flicked out the brains of a private seated by the fire. This robbed them of their peace for a night, and was the beginning of a long-range fire carefully calculated to that end. In the daytime they saw nothing except an unpleasant puff of smoke from a crag above the line of march. At night there were distant spurts of flame and occasional casualities, which set the whole camp blazing into the gloom and, occasionally, into opposite tents. Then they swore vehemently, and vowed that this was magnificent but not war.[24]

Indeed it was not. The Regiment could not halt for reprisals against the sharpshooters of the countryside. Its duty was to go forward and make connection with the Scotch and Gurkha troops with which it was brigaded. The Afghans knew this, and knew too, after their first tentative shots, that they were dealing with a raw regiment. Thereafter they devoted themselves to the task of keeping the Fore and Aft on the strain. Not for anything would they have taken equal liberties with a seasoned corps – with the wicked little Gurkhas, whose delight it was to lie out in the open on a dark night and stalk their stalkers – with the terrible, big men dressed in women's clothes, who could be heard praying to their God in the night-watches, and whose peace of mind no amount of 'sniping' could shake – or with those vile Sikhs, who marched so ostentatiously unprepared, and who dealt out such grim reward to those who tried to profit by that unpreparedness. This white regiment was different – quite different. It slept like a hog, and, like a hog, charged in every direction when it was roused. Its sentries walked with a footfall that could be heard for a quarter of a mile; would fire at anything that moved – even a driven donkey – and when they had once fired, could be scientifically 'rushed' and laid out a horror and an offence against the morning sun. Then there were camp-followers who straggled and could be cut up without fear. Their shrieks would disturb the white boys, and the loss of their services would inconvenience them sorely.

Thus, at every march, the hidden enemy became bolder and the regiment writhed and twisted under attacks it could not avenge. The crowning triumph was a sudden night-rush ending in the cutting of many tent-ropes, the collapse of the sodden canvas, and a glorious knifing of the men who struggled and kicked below. It was a great deed, neatly carried out, and it shook the already shaken nerves of the Fore and Aft. All the courage that they had been required to exercise up to this point was the 'two o'clock in the morning courage'; and, so far, they had only succeeded in shooting their comrades and losing their sleep.

Sullen, discontented, cold, savage, sick with their uniforms dulled and unclean, the Fore and Aft joined their Brigade.

'I hear you had a tough time of it coming up,' said the Brigadier. But when he saw the hospital-sheets his face fell.

'This is bad,' said he to himself. 'They're as rotten as sheep.' And aloud to the Colonel – 'I'm afraid we can't spare you just yet. We want all we have, else I should have given you ten days to recover in.'

The Colonel winced. 'On my honour, Sir,' he returned, 'there is not the least necessity to think of sparing us. My men have been rather mauled and upset without a fair return. They only want to go in somewhere where they can see what's before them.'

'Can't say I think much of the Fore and Fit,' said the Brigadier in confidence to his Brigade-Major. 'They've lost all their soldiering, and, by the trim of them, might have marched through the country from the other side. A more fagged-out set of men I never put eyes on.'

'Oh, they'll improve as the work goes on. The parade gloss has been rubbed off a little, but they'll put on field polish before long,' said the Brigade-Major. 'They've been mauled, and they quite don't understand it.'

They did not. All the hitting was on one side, and it was cruelly hard hitting with accessories that made them sick. There was also the real sickness that laid hold of a strong man and dragged him howling to the grave. Worst of all, their officers knew just as little of the country as the men themselves, and looked as if they did. The Fore and Aft were in a thoroughly unsatisfactory condition, but they believed that all would be well if they could once get a fair go-in at the enemy. Pot-shots up and down the valleys were unsatisfactory, and the bayonet never seemed to get a chance. Perhaps it was as well, for a long-limbed Afghan with a knife had a reach of eight feet, and could carry away lead that would disable three Englishmen.

The Fore and Fit would like some rifle-practice at the enemy – all seven hundred rifles blazing together. That wish showed the mood of the men.

The Gurkhas walked into their camp, and in broken, barrack-room English strove to fraternize with them; offered them pipes of tobacco and stood them treat at the canteen. But the Fore and Aft, not knowing much of the nature of the Gurkhas, treated them as they would treat any other 'niggers', and the little men in green trotted back to their firm friends the Highlanders, and with many grins confided to them: 'That dam white regiment no dam use. Sulky – ugh! Dirty – ugh! Hya, any tot for Johnny?' Whereat the Highlanders smote the Gurkhas as to the head, and told them not to vilify a British Regiment, and the Gurkhas grinned cavernously, for the Highlanders were their elder brothers and entitled to the privileges of kinship. The common soldier who touches a Gurkha is more than likely to have his head sliced open.

Three days later the Brigadier arranged a battle according to the rules of war and the peculiarity of the Afghan temperament. The enemy were massing in inconvenient strength among the hills, and the moving of many green standards[25] warned him that the tribes were 'up' in aid of the Afghan regular troops. A squadron and a half of Bengal Lancers represented the available Cavalry, and two screw-guns[26] borrowed from a column thirty miles away, the Artillery at the General's disposal.

'If they stand, as I've a very strong notion that they will, I fancy we shall see an infantry fight that will be worth watching,' said the Brigadier. 'We'll do it in style. Each regiment shall be played into action by its Band, and we'll hold the Cavalry in reserve.'

'For *all* the reserve?' somebody asked.

'For all the reserve; because we're going to crumple them up,' said the Brigadier, who was an extraordinary Brigadier, and did not believe in the value of a reserve when dealing with Asiatics. Indeed, when you come to think of it, had the British Army consistently waited for reserves in all its little affairs, the boundaries of Our Empire would have stopped at Brighton beach.

That battle was to be a glorious battle.

The three regiments debouching from three separate gorges, after duly crowning the heights above, were to converge from the centre, left, and right upon what we will call the Afghan army, then stationed towards the lower extremity of a flat-bottomed valley. Thus it will be seen that three sides of the valley practically belonged to the English, while the fourth was strictly Afghan property. In the event of defeat the Afghans had the rocky hills to fly to, where the fire from the guerrilla tribes in aid would cover their retreat. In the event of victory these same tribes would rush down and lend their weight to the rout of the British.

The screw-guns were to shell the head of each Afghan rush that was made in close formation, and the Cavalry, held in reserve in the right valley, were to gently stimulate the break-up which would follow on the combined attack. The Brigadier, sitting upon a rock overlooking the valley, would watch the battle unrolled at his feet. The Fore and Aft would debouch from the central gorge, the Gurkhas from the left, and the Highlanders from the right, for the reason that the left flank of the enemy seemed as though it required the most hammering. It was not every day that an Afghan force would take ground in the open, and the Brigadier was resolved to make the most of it.

'If we only had a few more men,' he said plaintively, 'we could surround the creatures and crumple 'em up thoroughly. As it is, I'm afraid we can only cut them up as they run. It's a great pity.'

The Fore and Aft had enjoyed unbroken peace for five days, and were beginning, in spite of dysentery, to recover their nerve. But they were not happy, for they did not know the work in hand, and had they known, would not have known how to do it. Throughout those five days in which old soldiers might have taught them the craft of the game, they discussed together their misadventures in the past – how such an one was alive at dawn and dead ere the dusk, and with what shrieks and struggles such another had given up his soul under the Afghan knife. Death was a new and horrible thing to the sons of mechanics who were used to die decently of zymotic disease;[26] and their careful conservation in barracks had done nothing to make them look upon it with less dread.

Very early in the dawn the bugles began to blow, and the

Fore and Aft, filled with a misguided enthusiasm, turned out without waiting for a cup of coffee and a biscuit; and were rewarded by being kept under arms in the cold while the other regiments leisurely prepared for the fray. All the world knows that it is ill taking the breeks off a Highlander.[28] It is much iller to try to make him stir unless he is convinced of the necessity for haste.

The Fore and Aft waited, leaning upon their rifles and listening to the protests of their empty stomachs. The Colonel did his best to remedy the default of lining as soon as it was borne in upon him that the affair would not begin at once, and so well did he succeed that the coffee was just ready when – the men moved off, their Band leading. Even then there had been a mistake in time, and the Fore and Aft came out into the valley ten minutes before the proper hour. Their Band wheeled to the right after reaching the open, and retired behind a little rocky knoll still playing while the regiment went past.

It was not a pleasant sight that opened on the uninstructed view, for the lower end of the valley appeared to be filled by an army in position – real and actual regiments attired in red coats, and – of this there was no doubt – firing Martini-Henry bullets which cut up the ground a hundred yards in front of the leading company. Over that pock-marked ground the regiment had to pass, and it opened the ball with a general and profound courtesy to the piping pickets; ducking in perfect time, as though it had been brazed on a rod. Being half-capable of thinking for itself, it fired a volley by the simple process of pitching its rifle into its shoulder and pulling the trigger. The bullets may have accounted for some of the watchers on the hillside, but they certainly did not affect the mass of enemy in front, while the noise of the rifles drowned any orders that might have been given.

'Good God!' said the Brigadier, sitting on the rock high above all. 'That regiment has spoilt the whole show. Hurry up the others, and let the screw-guns get off.'

But the screw-guns, in working round the heights, had stumbled upon a wasp's nest of a small mud fort which they incontinently shelled at eight hundred yards, to the huge discomfort of the occupants, who were unaccustomed to weapons of such devilish precision.

The Fore and Aft continued to go forward, but with shortened stride. Where were the other regiments, and why did these niggers use Martinis? They took open order instinctively, lying down and firing at random, rushing a few paces forward and lying down again, according to the regulations. Once in this formation, each man felt himself desperately alone, and edged in towards his fellow for comfort's sake.

Then the crack of his neighbour's rifle at his ear led him to fire as rapidly as he could – again for the sake of the comfort of the noise. The reward was not long delayed. Five volleys plunged the files in banked smoke impenetrable to the eye, and the bullets began to take ground twenty or thirty yards in front of the firers, as the weight of the bayonet dragged down and to the right arms wearied with holding the kick of the leaping Martini. The Company Commanders peered helplessly through the smoke, the more nervous mechanically trying to fan it away with their helmets.

'High and to the left!' bawled a Captain till he was hoarse. 'No good! Cease firing, and let it drift away a bit.'

Three and four times the bugles shrieked the order, and when it was obeyed the Fore and Aft looked that their foe should be lying before them in mown swaths of men. A light wind drove the smoke to leeward, and showed the enemy still in position and apparently unaffected. A quarter of a ton of lead had been buried a furlong in front of them, as the ragged earth attested.

That was not demoralizing to the Afghans, who have not European nerves. They were waiting for the mad riot to die down, and were firing quietly into the heart of the smoke. A private of the Fore and Aft spun up his company shrieking with agony, another was kicking the earth and gasping, and a third, ripped through the lower intestines by a jagged bullet, was calling aloud on his comrades to put him out of his pain. These were the casualties, and they were not soothing to hear or see. The smoke cleared to a dull haze.

Then the foe began to shout with a great shouting, and a mass – a black mass – detached itself from the main body, and rolled over the ground at horrid speed. It was composed of, perhaps, three hundred men, who would shout and fire and slash if the rush of their fifty comrades who were determined to die carried home. The fifty were Ghazis,[29] half-maddened with drugs and wholly mad with religious fanaticism. When they rushed the British fire ceased, and in the lull the order was given to close ranks and meet them with the bayonet.

Anyone who knew the business could have told the Fore and Aft that the only way of dealing with a Ghazi rush is by volleys at long ranges; because a man who means to die, who desires to die, who will gain heaven by dying, must, in nine cases out of ten, kill a man who has a lingering prejudice in favour of life. Where they should have closed and gone forward, the Fore and Aft opened out and skirmished, and where they should have opened out and fired, they closed and waited.

A man dragged from his blankets half awake and unfed is never in a pleasant frame of mind. Nor does his happiness increase when he watches the whites of the eyes of three hundred six-foot fiends upon whose beards the foam is lying, upon whose tongues is a roar of wrath, and in whose hands are yard-long knives.

The Fore and Aft heard the Gurkha bugles bringing that regiment forward at the double, while the neighing of the Highland pipes came from the left. They strove to stay where they were, though the bayonets wavered down the line like the oars of a ragged boat. Then they felt body to body the amazing physical strength of their foes; a shriek of pain ended the rush, and the knives fell amid scenes not to be told. The men clubbed together and smote blindly – as often as not at their own fellows. Their front crumpled like paper, and the fifty Ghazis passed on; their backers, now drunk with success, fighting as madly as they.

Then the rear-ranks were bidden to close up, and the subalterns dashed into the stew – alone. For the rear-rank had heard the clamour in front, the yells and the howls of pain, and had seen the dark stale blood that makes afraid. They were not going to stay. It was the rushing of the camps over again. Let their officers go to Hell, if they chose; they would get away from the knives.

'Come on!' shrieked the subalterns, and their men, cursing them, drew back, each closing into his neighbour and wheeling round.

Charteris and Devlin, subalterns of the last company, faced their death alone in the belief that their men would follow.

'You've killed me, you cowards,' sobbed Devlin and dropped, cut from the shoulder-strap to the centre of the chest, and a fresh detachment of his men retreating, always retreating, trampled him under foot as they made for the pass whence they had emerged.

> I kissed her in the kitchen and I kissed her in the hall.
>   Child'un, child'un, follow me!
> Oh Golly, said the cook, is he gwine to kiss us all?
>   Halla – Halla – Halla – Hallelujah! [30]

The Gurkhas were pouring through the left gorge and over the heights at the double to the invitation of their Regimental Quick-step. The black rocks were crowned with dark green spiders as the bugles gave tongue jubilantly:

> In the morning! In the morning *by* the bright light!
> When Gabriel blows his trumpet in the morning! [31]

The Gurkha rear-companies tripped and blundered over loose stones. The front-files halted for a moment to take stock of the valley and to settle stray boot-laces. Then a happy little sigh of contentment soughed down the ranks, and it was as though the land smiled, for behold there below was the enemy, and it was to meet them that the Gurkhas had doubled so hastily. There was much enemy. There would be amusement. The little men hitched their *kukris* [32] well to hand, and gaped expectantly at their officers as terriers grin ere the stone is cast for them to fetch. The Gurkhas' ground sloped downward to the valley, and they enjoyed a fair view of the proceedings. They sat upon the boulders to watch, for their officers were not going to waste their wind in assisting to repulse a Ghazi rush more than half a mile away. Let the white men look to their own front.

'Hi! yi!' said the Subadar-Major,[33] who was sweating profusely. 'Dam fools yonder, stand close-order! This is no time for close order, it is the time for volleys. Ugh!'

Horrified, amused, and indignant, the Gurkhas beheld the retirement of the Fore and Aft with a running chorus of oaths and commentaries.

'They run! The white men run! Colonel Sahib, may *we* also do a little running?' murmured Runbir Thappa, the Senior Jemadar.[34]

But the Colonel would have none of it. 'Let the beggars be cut up a little,' said he wrathfully. ''Serves 'em right. They'll be prodded into facing round in a minute.' He looked through his field-glasses, and caught the glint of an officer's sword.

'Beating 'em with the flat — damned conscripts! How the Ghazis are walking into them!' said he.

The Fore and Aft, heading back, bore with them their officers. The narrowness of the pass forced the mob into solid formation, and the rear-rank delivered some sort of a wavering volley. The Ghazis drew off, for they did not know what reserves the gorge might hide. Moreover, it was never wise to chase white men too far. They returned as wolves return to cover, satisfied with the slaughter that they had done, and only stopping to slash at the wounded on the ground. A quarter of a mile had the Fore and Aft retreated, and now, jammed in the pass, was quivering with pain, shaken and demoralized with fear, while the officers, maddened beyond control, smote the men with the hilts and the flats of their swords.

'Get back! Get back, you cowards — you women! Right about face — column of companies, form — you hounds!' shouted the Colonel, and the subalterns swore aloud. But the Regiment wanted to go — to go anywhere out of the range of those merciless knives. It swayed to and fro irresolutely with shouts and outcries, while from the right the Gurkhas dropped volley after volley of cripple-stopper Snider[35] bullets at long range into the mob of the Ghazis returning to their own troops.

The Fore and Aft Band, though protected from direct fire by the rocky knoll under which it had sat down, fled at the first rush. Jakin and Lew would have fled also, but their short legs left them fifty yards in the rear, and by the time the Band had mixed with the regiment, they were painfully aware that they would have to close in alone and unsupported.

'Get back to that rock,' gasped Jakin. 'They won't see us there.'

And they returned to the scattered instruments of the Band, their hearts nearly bursting their ribs.

'Here's a nice show for *us*,' said Jakin, throwing himself full length on the ground. 'A bloomin' fine show for British Infantry! Oh, the devils! They've gone an' left us alone here! Wot'll we do?'

Lew took possession of a cast-off water bottle, which naturally was full of canteen rum, and drank till he coughed again.

'Drink,' said he shortly. 'They'll come back in a minute or two – you see.'

Jakin drank, but there was no sign of the regiment's return. They could hear a dull clamour from the head of the valley of retreat, and saw the Ghazis slink back, quickening their pace as the Gurkhas fired at them.

'We're all that's left of the Band, an' we'll be cut up as sure as death,' said Jakin.

'I'll die game, then,' said Lew thickly, fumbling with his tiny drummer's sword. The drink was working on his brain as it was on Jakin's.

''Old on! I know something better than fightin',' said Jakin, 'stung by the splendour of a sudden thought' [36] due chiefly to rum. 'Tip our bloomin' cowards yonder the word to come back. The Paythan beggars are well away. Come on, Lew! We won't get hurt. Take the fife an' give me the drum. The Old Step for all your bloomin' guts are worth! There's a few of our men coming back now. Stand up, ye drunken little defaulter. By your right – quick march!'

He slipped the drum-sling over his shoulder, thrust the fife into Lew's hand, and the two boys marched out of the cover of the rock into the open, making a hideous hash of the first bars of the 'British Grenadiers'.[37]

As Lew had said, a few of the Fore and Aft were coming back sullenly and shamefacedly under the stimulus of blows and abuse; their red coats shone at the head of the valley, and behind them were wavering bayonets. But between this shattered line and the enemy, who with Afghan suspicion feared that the hasty retreat meant an ambush, and had not moved therefore, lay half a mile of level ground dotted only by the wounded.

The tune settled into full swing and the boys kept shoulder to shoulder, Jakin banging the drum as one possessed. The one fife made a thin and pitiful squeaking, but the tune carried far, even to the Gurkhas.

'Come on, you dogs!' muttered Jakin to himself. 'Are we to play forhever?' Lew was staring straight in front of him and marching more stiffly than ever he had done on parade.

And in bitter mockery of the distant mob, the old tune of the Old Line shrilled and rattled:

> Some talk of Alexander,
>   And some of Hercules;
> Of Hector and Lysander,
>   And such great names as these!

There was a far-off clapping of hands from the Gurkhas, and a roar from the Highlanders in the distance, but never a shot was fired by British or Afghan. The two little red dots moved forward in the open parallel to the enemy's front.

> But of all the world's great heroes
>   There's none that can compare,
> With a tow-row-row-row-row-row,
>   To the British Grenadier!

The men of the Fore and Aft were gathering thick at the entrance to the plain. The Brigadier on the heights far above was speechless with rage. Still no movement from the enemy. The day stayed to watch the children.

Jakin halted and beat the long roll of the Assembly, while the fife squealed despairingly.

'Right about face! Hold up, Lew, you're drunk,' said Jakin. They wheeled and marched back:

> Those heroes of antiquity
> Ne'er saw a cannon-ball,
> Nor knew the force o' powder,

'Here they come!' said Jakin. 'Go on, Lew':

> To scare their foes withal!

The Fore and Aft were pouring out of the valley. What officers had said to men in that time of shame and humiliation will never be known; for neither officers nor men speak of it now.

'They are coming anew!' shouted a priest[38] among the Afghans. 'Do not kill the boys! Take them alive, and they shall be of our faith.'

But the first volley had been fired, and Lew dropped on his face. Jakin stood for a minute, spun round and collapsed, as the Fore and Aft came forward, the curses of their officers in their ears, and in their hearts the shame of open shame.

Half the men had seen the drummers die, and they made no sign. They did not even shout. They doubled out straight across the plain in open order, and they did not fire.

'This,' said the Colonel of Gurkhas, softly, 'is the real attack, as it should have been delivered. Come on, my children.'

'Ulu-lu-lu-lu!' squealed the Gurkhas, and came down with a joyful clicking of *kukris* – those vicious Gurkha knives.

On the right there was no rush. The Highlanders, cannily commending their souls to God (for it matters as much to a dead man whether he has been shot in a Border scuffle[39] or at Waterloo), opened out and fired according to their custom, that is to say, without heat and without intervals, while the screw-guns, having disposed of the impertinent mud fort aforementioned, dropped shell after shell into the clusters round the flickering green standards on the heights.

'Charrging is an unfortunate necessity,' murmured the Colour-Sergeant of the right company of the Highlanders. 'It makes the men sweer so, but I am thinkin' that it will come to a charrge if these black devils stand much longer. Stewarrt, man, you're firing into the eye of the sun, and he'll not take any harm for Government ammuneetion. A foot lower and a great deal slower! What are the English doing? They're very quiet there in the centre. Running again?'

The English were not running. They were hacking and hewing and stabbing, for though one white man is seldom physically a match for an Afghan in a sheepskin or wadded coat, yet, through the pressure of many white men behind, and a certain thirst for revenge in his heart, he becomes capable of doing much with both ends of his rifle. The Fore and Aft held their fire till one bullet could drive through five or six men, and the front of the Afghan force gave on the volley. They then selected their men, and slew them with deep gasps and short hacking coughs, and groanings of leather belts against strained bodies, and realized for the first time that an Afghan attacked is far less formidable than an Afghan attacking: which fact old soldiers might have told them.

But they had no old soldiers in their ranks.

The Gurkhas' stall at the bazar was the noisiest, for the men were engaged – to a nasty noise as of beef being cut on the block – with the *kukri*, which they preferred to the bayonet; well knowing how the Afghan hates the half-moon blade.

As the Afghans wavered, the green standards on the mountain moved down to assist them in a last rally. This was unwise. The Lancers chafing in the right gorge had thrice despatched their only subaltern as galloper to report on the progress of affairs. On the third occasion he returned, with a bullet-graze on his knee, swearing strange oaths in Hindustani, and saying that all things were ready. So that Squadron swung round the right of the Highlanders with a wicked whistling of wind in the pennons of its lances, and fell upon the remnant just when, according to all the rules of war, it should have waited for the foe to show more signs of wavering.

But it was a dainty charge, deftly delivered, and it ended by the Cavalry finding itself at the head of the pass by which the Afghans intended to retreat; and down the track that the lances had made streamed two companies of the Highlanders, which was never intended by the Brigadier. The new development was successful. It detached the enemy from his base as a sponge is torn from a rock, and left him ringed about with fire in that pitiless plain. And as a sponge is chased round the bath-tub by the hand of the bather, so were the Afghans chased till they broke into little detachments much more difficult to dispose of than large masses.

'See!' quoth the Brigadier. 'Everything has come as I arranged. We've cut their base, and now we'll bucket 'em to pieces.'

A direct hammering was all that the Brigadier had dared to hope for, considering the size of the force at his disposal; but men who stand or fall by the errors of their opponents may be forgiven for turning Chance into Design. The bucketing went forward merrily. The Afghan forces were upon the run – the run of wearied wolves who snarl and bite over their shoulders. The red lances dipped by twos and threes, and, with a shriek, up rose the lance-butt, like a spar on a stormy sea, as the trooper cantering forward cleared his point. The Lancers kept between their prey and the steep hills, for all who could were trying to escape from the valley of death.[40] The Highlanders gave the fugitives two hundred yards' law,[41] and then brought them down, gasping and choking, ere they could reach the protection of the boulders above. The Gurkhas followed suit; but the Fore and Aft were killing on their own account, for they had penned a mass of men between their bayonets and a wall of rock, and the flash of the rifles was lighting the wadded coats.

'We cannot hold them, Captain Sahib!' panted a Ressaldar[42] of Lancers. 'Let us try the carbine. The lance is good, but it wastes time.'

They tried the carbine, and still the enemy melted away – fled up the hills by hundreds when there were only twenty bullets to stop them. On the heights the screw-guns ceased firing – they had run out of ammunition – and the Brigadier groaned, for the musketry fire could not sufficiently smash the retreat. Long before the last volleys were fired the doolies[43] were out in force looking for the wounded. The battle was over, and, but for want of fresh troops, the Afghans would have been wiped off the earth. As it was they counted their dead by hundreds, and nowhere were the dead thicker than in the track of the Fore and Aft.

But the Regiment did not cheer with the Highlanders, nor did they dance uncouth dances with the Gurkhas among the dead. They looked under their brows at the Colonel as they leaned upon their rifles and panted.

'Get back to camp, you. Haven't you disgraced yourself enough for one day! Go and look to the wounded. It's all you're fit for,' said the Colonel. Yet for the past hour the Fore and Aft had been doing all that mortal commander could expect. They had lost heavily because they did not know how to set about their business with proper skill, but they had borne themselves gallantly, and this was their reward.

A young and sprightly Colour-Sergeant, who had begun to imagine himself a hero, offered his water-bottle to a Highlander, whose tongue was black with thirst. 'I drink with no cowards,' answered the youngster huskily, and, turning to a Gurkha, said, 'Hya, Johnny! Drink water got it?' The Gurkha grinned and passed his bottle. The Fore and Aft said no word.

They went back to camp when the field of strife had been a little mopped up and made presentable, and the Brigadier, who saw himself a Knight in three months, was the only soul who was complimentary to them. The Colonel was heart-broken, and the officers were savage and sullen.

'Well,' said the Brigadier, 'they are young troops of course, and it was not unnatural that they should retire in disorder for a bit.'

'Oh, my only Aunt Maria!' murmured a junior Staff Officer. 'Retire in disorder! It was a bally run!'

'But they came again, as we all know,' cooed the Brigadier, the Colonel's ashy-white face before him, 'and they behaved as well as could possibly be expected. Behaved beautifully, indeed. I was watching them. It's not a matter to take to heart, Colonel. As some German General said of his men, they wanted to be shooted over a little, that was all.' To himself he said – 'Now they're blooded I can give 'em responsible work. It's as well that they got what they did. 'Teach 'em more than half-a-dozen rifle flirtations, that will – later – run alone and bite. Poor old Colonel, though.'

All that afternoon the heliograph winked and flickered on the hills, striving to tell the good news to a mountain forty miles away. And in the evening there arrived, dusty, sweating, and sore, a misguided Correspondent who had gone out to assist at a trumpery village-burning, and who had read off the message from afar, cursing his luck the while.

'Let's have the details somehow – as full as ever you can, please. It's the first time I've ever been left this campaign,' said the Correspondent to the Brigadier, and the Brigadier, nothing loath, told him how an Army of Communication had been crumpled up, destroyed, and all but annihilated by the craft, strategy, wisdom, and foresight of the Brigadier.

But some say, and among these be the Gurkhas who watched on the hillside, that that battle was won by Jakin and Lew, whose little bodies were borne up just in time to fit two gaps at the head of the big ditch-grave for the dead under the heights of Jagai.

APPENDIX

﹛ A Supplementary Chapter[1] ﹜

Shall I not one day remember thy Bower –
One day when all days are one day to me?
Thinking I stirred not and yet had the power,
Yearning – ah, God, if again it might be!
– *The Song of the Bower*[2]

This is a base betrayal of confidence, but the sin is Mrs Hauksbee's and not mine.

If you remember a certain foolish tale called 'The Education of Otis Yeere', you will not forget that Mrs Mallowe laughed at the wrong time which was a single, and at Mrs Hauksbee, which was a double, offence. An experiment had gone wrong, and it seems that Mrs Mallowe had said some quaint things about the experimentrix.

'I am not angry,' said Mrs Hauksbee, 'and I admire Polly in spite of her evil counsels to me. But I shall wait – I shall wait, like the frog footman in *Alice in Wonderland*,[3] and Providence will deliver Polly into my hands. It always does if you wait.' And she departed to vex the soul of the 'Hawley boy', who says that she is singularly '*uninstruite*[4] and childlike'. He got that first word out of a Ouida[5] novel. I do not know what it means, but am prepared to make an affidavit before the Collector[6] that it does not mean Mrs Hauksbee.

Mrs Hauksbee's ideas of waiting are very liberal. She told the 'Hawley boy' that he dared not tell Mrs Reiver that 'she was an intellectual woman with a gift for attracting men', and she offered another man two waltzes if he would repeat the same thing in the same ears. But he said: 'Timeo Danaos et dona ferentes,'[7] which means 'Mistrust all waltzes except those you get for legitimate asking.'

The 'Hawley boy' did as he was told because he believes in

Mrs Hauksbee. He was the instrument in the hand of a Higher Power, and he wore *jharun* coats, like 'the scoriac rivers that roll their sulphurous torrents down Yahek, in the realms of the Boreal Pole,'[8] that made your temples throb when seen early in the morning. I will introduce him to you some day if all goes well. He is worth knowing.

Unpleasant things have already been written about Mrs Reiver in other places.

She was a person without invention. She used to get her ideas from the men she captured, and this led to some eccentric changes of character. For a month or two she would act *à la* Madonna, and try Théo for a change if she fancied Théo's ways suited her beauty. Then she would attempt the dark and fiery Lilith,[9] and so and so on, exactly as she had absorbed the new notion. But there was always Mrs Reiver – hard, selfish, stupid Mrs Reiver – at the back of each transformation. Mrs Hauksbee christened her the Magic Lantern on account of this borrowed mutability. 'It just depends upon the slide,' said Mrs Hauksbee. 'The case is the only permanent thing in the exhibition. But that, thank Heaven, is getting old.'

There was a Fancy Ball at Government House and Mrs Reiver came attired in some sort of '98 costume, with her hair pulled up to the top of her head, showing the clear outline on the back of the neck like the Récamier[10] engravings. Mrs Hauksbee had chosen to be loud, not to say vulgar, that evening, and went as The Black Death – a curious arrangement of barred velvet, black domino and flame-coloured satin puffery coming up the neck and the wrists, with one of those shrieking keel-backed cicalas in the hair. The scream of the creature made people jump. It sounded so unearthly in the ballroom.

I heard her say to someone: 'Let me introduce you to Madame Récamier,' and I saw a man dressed as Autolycus[11] bowing to Mrs Reiver, while The Black Death looked more than usually saintly. It was a very pleasant evening, and Autolycus and Madame Récamier – I heard her ask Autolycus who Madame Récamier was, by the way – danced together ever so much. Mrs

Hauksbee was in a meditative mood, but she laughed once or twice in the back of her throat, and that meant trouble.

Autolycus was Trewinnard, the man whom Mrs Mallowe had told Mrs Hauksbee about – the Platonic Paragon, as Mrs Hauksbee called him. He was amiable, but his moustache hid his mouth, and so he did not explain himself all at once. If you stared at him, he turned his eyes away, and through the rest of the dinner kept looking at you to see whether you were looking again. He took stares as a tribute to his merits, which were generally known and recognized. When he played billiards he apologized at length between each bad stroke, and explained what would have happened if the red had been somewhere else, or the bearer had trimmed the third lamp, or the wind hadn't made the door bang. Also he wriggled in his chair more than was becoming to one of his inches. Little men may wriggle and fidget without attracting notice. It doesn't suit big-framed men. He was the Main Girder Boom of the Kutcha, Pukka, Bundobust and Benaoti Department and corresponded direct with the Three Taped Bashaw.[12] Everyone knows what *that* means. The men in his own office said that where anything was to be gained, even temporarily, he would never hesitate for a moment over handing up a subordinate to be hanged and drawn and quartered. He didn't back up his underlings, and for that reason they dreaded taking responsibility on their shoulders, and the strength of the Department was crippled.

A weak Department can, and often does, do a power of good work simply because its chief sees it through thick and thin. Mistakes may be born of this policy, but it is safer and sounder than giving orders which may be read in two ways and reserving to yourself the right of interpretation according to subsequent failure or success. Offices prefer administration to diplomacy. They are very like Empires.

Hatchett of the Almirah and Thannicutch[13] – a vicious little three-cornered Department that was always stamping on the toes of the Elect – had the fairest estimate of Trewinnard, when he said: 'I don't believe he is as good as he is.' They always quoted that verdict as an instance of the blind jealousy of the Uncovenanted,[14] but Hatchett was quite right. Trewinnard was just as good and no better than Mrs Mallowe could make him; and she had been engaged on the work for three years. Hatchett has a narrow-minded partiality for the more than naked – the anatomized Truth – but he can gauge a man.

Trewinnard had been spoilt by over-much petting, and the devil of vanity that rides nine hundred and ninety-nine men out of a thousand made him believe as he did. He had been too long one woman's property; and that belief will sometimes drive a man to throw the best things in the world behind him, from rank perversity. Perhaps he only meant to stray temporarily and then return, but in arranging for this excursion he misunderstood both Mrs Mallowe and Mrs Reiver. The one made no sign, she would have died first; and the other – well, the high-falutin mindsome lay was her craze for the time being. She had never tried it before and several men had hinted that it would eminently become her. Trewinnard was in himself pleasant, with the great merit of belonging to somebody else. He was what they call 'intellectual', and vain to the marrow. Mrs Reiver returned his lead in the first, and hopelessly out-trumped him in the second suit. Put down all that comes after this to Providence or The Black Death.

Trewinnard never realized how far he had fallen from his allegiance till Mrs Reiver referred to some official matter that he had been telling her about as 'ours'. He remembered then how that word had been sacred to Mrs Mallowe and how she had asked his permission to use it. Opium is intoxicating, and so is whisky, but more intoxicating than either to a certain build of mind is the first occasion on which a woman – especially if she has asked leave for the 'honour' – identifies herself with a man's work. The second time is not so pleasant. The answer has been given before, and the treachery comes to the top and tastes coppery in the mouth.

Trewinnard swallowed the shame – he felt dimly that he was not doing Mrs Reiver any great wrong by untruth – and told and told and continued to tell, for the snare of this form of open-heartedness is than no man, unless he be a consummate liar, knows where to stop. The office door of all others must be either open wide or shut tight with a *shaprassi*[15] to keep off callers.

Mrs Mallowe made no sign to show that she felt Trewinnard's desertion till a piece of information that could only have come from *one* quarter ran about Simla like quicksilver. She met Trewinnard at a dinner. 'Choose your *confidantes* better, Harold,' she whispered as she passed him in the drawing-room. He turned salmon-colour, and swore very hard to himself that Babu Durga Charan Laha must go – must go – must go. He almost believed in that grey-headed old oyster's guilt.

And so another of those upside down tragedies that we call a Simla Season wore through to the end – from the Birthday Ball to the 'tripping' to Naldera and Kotghar. And fools gave feasts and wise men ate them, and they were bidden to the wedding and sat down to bake, and those who had nuts had no teeth and they staked the substance for the shadow, and carried coals to Newcastle, and in the dark all cats were grey, as it was in the days of the great Curé of Meudon.[16]

Late in the year there developed itself a battle-royal between the K.P.B. and B. Department and the Almirah and Thannicutch. Three columns of this paper[17] would be needed to supply you with the outlines of the difficulty; and then you would not be grateful. Hatchett snuffed the fray from afar[18] and went into it with his teeth bared to the gums, while his Department stood behind him solid to a man. They believed in him, and their answer to the fury of men who detested him was: 'Ah! But you'll admit he's d–d right in what he says.'

'The head of Trewinnard in a Government Resolution,' said Hatchett, and he told the *daftri*[19] to put a new pad on his blotter, and smiled a bleak smile as he spread out his notes. Hatchett is a Thug[20] in his systematic way of butchering a man's reputation.

'What are you going to do?' asked Trewinnard's Department. 'Sit tight,' said Trewinnard, which was tantamount to saying 'Lord knows.' The Department groaned and said: 'Which of us poor beggars is to be Jonahed *this* time?' They knew Trewinnard's vice.

The dispute was essentially not one for the K.P.B. and B. under its then direction to fight out. It should have been compromised, or at the worst sent up to the Supreme Government with a private and confidential note directing justice into the proper paths.

Some people say that the Supreme Government is the Devil. It is more like the Deep Sea. Anything that you throw into it disappears for weeks, and comes to light hacked and furred at the edges, crusted with weeds and shells and almost unrecognizable. The bold man who would dare to give it a file of love-letters would be amply rewarded. It would overlay them with original comments and marginal notes, and work them piecemeal into D. O.[21] dockets. Few things, from a letter or a whirlpool to a sausage-machine or a hatching hen, are more interesting and peculiar than the Supreme Government.

'What shall we do?' said Trewinnard, who had fallen from grace into sin. 'Fight,' said Mrs Reiver, or words to that effect; and no one can say how far aimless desire to test her powers, and how far belief in the man she had brought to her feet prompted the judgement. Of the merits of the case she knew just as much as any *ayah*.

Then Mrs Mallowe, upon an evil word that went through Simla, put on her visiting-garb and attired herself for the sacrifice, and went to call – to call upon Mrs Reiver, knowing what the torture would be. From half-past twelve till twenty-five minutes to two she sat, her hand upon her card-case, and let Mrs Reiver stab at her, all for the sake of information. Mrs Reiver double-acted her part, but she played into Mrs Mallowe's hand by this defect. The assumptions of ownership, the little intentional slips, were overdone, and so also was the pretence of intimate knowledge. Mrs Mallowe never winced. She repeated to herself: 'And he has trusted this – this Thing. She knows nothing and she cares nothing, and she has digged this trap for him.'[22] The main feature of the case was abundantly clear. Trewinnard, whose capacities Mrs Mallowe knew to the utmost farthing, to whom public and departmental petting were as the breath of his delicately-cut nostrils – Trewinnard, with his nervous dread of dispraise, was to be pitted against the Paul de Cassagnac[23] of the Almirah and Thannicutch – the unspeakable Hatchett, who fought with the venom of a woman and the skill of a Red Indian. Unless his cause was triply just, Trewinnard was already under the guillotine, and if he had been under this 'Thing's' dominance, small hope for the justice of his case. 'Oh, why did I let him go without putting out a hand to fetch him back?' said Mrs Mallowe, as she got into her rickshaw.

Now, *Tim*, her fox-terrier, is the only person who knows what Mrs Mallowe did that afternoon, and as I found him loafing on the Mall in a very disconsolate condition and as he recognized me effusively and suggested going for a monkey-hunt – a thing he had never done before – my impression is that Mrs Mallowe stayed at home till the light fell and thought. If she did this, it is of course hopeless to account for her actions. So you must fill in the gap for yourself.

That evening it rained heavily, and horses mired their riders. But not one of all the habits was so plastered with mud as the habit of Mrs Mallowe when she pulled up under the scrub oaks and sent in her name by the astounded bearer to Trewinnard. 'Folly! downright folly!' she said as she sat in the steam of the dripping horse. 'But it's all a horrible jumble together.'

It may be as well to mention that ladies do not usually call upon bachelors at their houses. Bachelors would scream and run away. Trewinnard came into the light of the verandah with a nervous, undecided smile upon his lips, and he wished – in the bottomless bottom of his bad heart – he wished that Mrs Reiver was there to see. A minute later he was profoundly glad that he was alone, for Mrs Mallowe was standing in his office room and calling him names that reflected no credit on his intellect. 'What have you done? What have you said?' she asked. 'Be quick! Be *quick*! And have the horse led round to the back. Can you speak? What have you written? Show me!'

She had interrupted him in the middle of what he was pleased to call his reply; for Hatchett's first shell had already fallen in his camp. He stood back and offered her the seat at the *duftar* table. Her elbow left a great wet stain on the baize, for she was soaked through and through.

'Say exactly how the matter stands,' she said, and laughed a weak little laugh, which emboldened Trewinnard to say loftily: 'Pardon me, Mrs Mallowe, but I hardly recognize your –'

'Idiot! Will you show me the papers, will you speak, and *will* you be quick?'

Her most reverent admirers would hardly have recognized the soft-spoken, slow-gestured, quiet-eyed Mrs Mallowe in the indignant woman who was drumming on Trewinnard's desk. He submitted to the voice of authority, as he had submitted in the old times, and explained as quickly as might be the cause of the war between the two Departments. In conclusion he handed over the rough sheets of his reply. As she read he watched her with the expectant sickly half-smile of the unaccustomed writer who is doubtful of the success of his work. And another smile followed, but died away as he saw Mrs Mallowe read his production. All the old phrases out of which she had so carefully drilled him had returned; the unpruned fluency of diction was there, the more luxuriant for being so long cut back; the reckless riotousness of assertion that sacrificed all – even the vital truth that Hatchett would be so sure to take advantage of – for the sake of scoring a point, was there; and through and between every line ran the weak, wilful vanity of the man. Mrs Mallowe's mouth hardened.

'And you wrote this!' she said. Then to herself: '*He* wrote this!'

Trewinnard stepped forward with a gesture habitual to him when he wished to explain. Mrs Reiver had never asked for explanations. She had told him that all his ways were perfect. Therefore he loved her.

Mrs Mallowe tore up the papers one by one, saying as she did so: '*You* were going to cross swords with Hatchett. Do you know your own strength? Oh, Harold, Harold, it is *too* pitiable! I thought – I thought –' Then the great anger that had been growing in her broke out, and she cried: 'Oh, you fool! You blind, blind, *blind*, trumpery fool! Why do I help you? You miserable man! Sit down and write as I dictate. Quickly! And I had chosen *you* out of a hundred other *men*! Write!' It is a terrible thing to be found out by a mere unseeing male – Thackeray has said it. It is worse, by far to be found out by a woman, and in that hour after long years to discover her worth. For ten minutes Trewinnard's pen scratched across the paper, and Mrs Mallowe spoke. 'And that is all,' she said bitterly. 'As you value yourself – your noble, honourable, modest self – keep within that.'

But that was not all – by any means. At least as far as Trewinnard was concerned.

He rose from his chair and delivered his soul of many mad and futile thoughts – such things as a man babbles when he is deserted of the gods, has missed his hold upon the door-latch of Opportunity – and cannot see that the ways are shut. Mrs Mallowe bore with him to the end, and he stood before her – no enviable creature to look upon.

'A cur as well as a fool!' she said. 'Will you be good enough to tell them to bring my horse? I do not trust to your honour – you have none – but I believe that your sense of shame will keep you from speaking of my visit.'

So he was left in the verandah crying 'Come back' like a distracted guinea-fowl.

'He's done us in the eye,' grunted Hatchett as he perused the K.P.B. and B. reply. 'Look at the cunning of the brute in shifting the issue on to India in that carneying, blarneying way! Only wait until I can get my knife into him again. I'll stop every bolt-hole before the hunt begins.'

Oh, I believe I have forgotten to mention the success of Mrs Hauksbee's revenge. It was so brilliant and overwhelming that she had to cry in Mrs Mallowe's arms for the better part of half an hour; and Mrs Mallowe was just as bad, though she thanked Mrs Hauksbee several times in the course of the interview, and Mrs Hauksbee said that she would repent and reform, and Mrs

Mallowe said: 'Hush, dear, hush! I don't think either of us had anything to be proud of.' And Mrs Hauksbee said: 'Oh, but I didn't *mean* it, Polly, I didn't *mean* it!' And I stood with my hat in my hand trying to make two very indignant ladies understand that the bearer really *had* given me '*salaam bolta*'.[24]

That was an evil quarter minute.

⦃ Mrs Hauksbee Sits Out ⦄

Persons Chiefly Interested

His Excellency the Viceroy and Governor-General of India
Charles Hilton Hawley (lieutenant at large)
Lieutenant-Colonel J. Scriffshaw (not so much at large)
Major Decker (a persuasive Irishman)
Peroo (an Aryan butler)
Mrs Hauksbee (a lady with a will of her own)
Mrs Scriffshaw (a lady who believes she has a will of her own)
May Holt (niece of the above)
Assunta (an Aryan lady's-maid)
Aides-de-Camp, Dancers, Horses and Devils as Required

⁅ Mrs Hauksbee Sits Out [1] ⁆

An Unhistorical Extravaganza

Scene – *The imperial city of Simla, on a pine-clad mountain seven thousand feet above the level of the sea. Grey roofs of houses peering through green; white clouds going to bed in the valley below; purple clouds of sunset sitting on the peaks above. Smell of wood-smoke and pine-cones. A curtained verandah-room in* MRS HAUKSBEE'S *house, overlooking Simla, shows* MRS HAUKSBEE, *in black cachemire tea-gown opening over cream front, seated in a red-cushioned chair, her foot on a Khokand rug, Russian china tea-things on red lacquered table beneath red-shaded lamps. On a cushion at her feet,* MISS HOLT – *grey riding-habit, soft grey felt terai hat, blue and gold puggree,[2] buff gauntlets in lap, and glimpse of spurred riding-boot. They have been talking as the twilight gathers.* MRS HAUKSBEE *crosses over to piano in a natural pause of the conversation and begins to play.*

MAY. (*Without changing her position*) Yes. That's nice. Play something.

MRS H. What?

MAY. Oh! Anything. Only I don't want to hear about sighing over tombs, and saying Nevermore.[3]

MRS H. Have you ever known me do that? May, you're in one of your little tempers this afternoon.

MAY. So would a Saint be. I've told you why. Horrid old *thing!* – isn't she?

MRS H. (*Without prelude*) –

> Fair Eve [4] knelt close to the guarded gate in the hush
>   of an Eastern spring,
> She saw the flash of the Angel's sword, the gleam
>   of the Angel's wing –

345

MAY. (*Impetuously*) And now *you're* laughing at me!

MRS H. (*Shaking her head, continues the song for a verse; then crescendo*) –

> And because she was so beautiful, and because she could not see
> How fair were the pure white cyclamens crushed dying at her knee.

(That's the society of your aunt, my dear.)

> He plucked a Rose from the Eden Tree where the four great rivers met

MAY. Yes. I know you're laughing at me. Now somebody's going to die, of course. They always do.

MRS H. No. Wait and see what is going to happen. (*The puckers pass out of* MAY'S *face as she listens*) –

> And though for many a Cycle past that Rose in the dust hath lain
> With her who bore it upon her breast when she passed from grief and pain,

(*Retard*) –

> There was never a daughter of Eve but once, ere the tale of her years be done,
> Shall know the scent of the Eden Rose, but once beneath the sun!
> Though the years may bring her joy or pain, fame, sorrow, or sacrifice,
> The hour that brought her the scent of the Rose she lived it in Paradise!

(*Concludes with arpeggio chords*)

MAY. (*Shuddering*) Ah! don't. How good that is! What is it?

MRS H. Something called 'The Eden Rose'. An old song to a new setting.

MAY. Play it again!

MRS H. (I thought it would tell.) No, dear. (*Returning to her place by the tea-things*) And so that amiable aunt of yours won't let you go to the dance?

MAY. She says dancing's wicked and sinful; and it's only a Volunteer ball,[5] after all.

MRS H. Then why are you so anxious to go?

MAY. Because she says I mustn't! Isn't that sufficient reason? And because –

MRS H. Ah, it's that 'because' I want to hear about, dear.

MAY. Because I choose. Mrs Hauksbee – *dear* Mrs Hauksbee – you will help me, won't you?

MRS H. (*Slowly*) Ye-es. Because *I* choose. Well?

MAY. In the first place, you'll take me under your wing, won't you? And, in the second, you'll keep me there, won't you?

MRS H. That will depend a great deal on the Hawley Boy's[6] pleasure, won't it?

MAY. (*Flushing*) Char – Mr Hawley has nothing whatever to do with it.

MRS H. Of course not. But what will your aunt say?

MAY. She will be angry with *me*, but not with you. She is pious – oh! so pious! – and she would give anything to be put on that lady's committee for –what is it? – giving pretty dresses to half-caste girls. Lady Bieldar is the secretary, and she won't speak to Aunt on the Mall. You're Lady Bieldar's friend. Aunt daren't quarrel with you, and, besides, if I come here after dinner tonight, how are you to know that everything isn't correct?

MRS H. On your own pretty head be the talking to! I'm willing to chaperon to an unlimited extent.

MAY. Bless you! and I'll love you *always* for it!

MRS H. There, again, the Hawley Boy might have something to say. You've been a well-conducted little maiden so far, May. Whence this sudden passion for Volunteer balls? (*Turning down lamp and lowering voice as she takes the girl's hand*) Won't you tell me? I'm not very young, but I'm not a grim griffin, and I think I'd understand, dear.

MAY. (*After a pause, and swiftly*) His leave is nearly ended. He goes down to the plains to his regiment the day after tomorrow, and –

MRS H. Has he said anything?

MAY. I don't know. I don't think so. Don't laugh at me,

please! But I believe it would nearly break my heart if he didn't.

Mrs H. (*Smiling to herself*) Poor child! And how long has this been going on?

May. Ever so long! Since the beginning of the world – or the beginning of the season. I couldn't help it. I didn't want to help it. And last time we met I was just as rude as I could be – and – and he thought I meant it.

Mrs H. How strange! Seeing that he is a man, too – (*half aloud*) – and probably with experiences of his own!

May. (*Dropping* Mrs H.'s *hand*) I don't believe that, and – I won't. He couldn't!

Mrs H. No, dear. Of course he hasn't had experiences. Why should he? I was only teasing! But when do I pick you up tonight, and how?

May. Aunt's dining out somewhere – with goody-goody people. I dine alone with Uncle John – and he sleeps after dinner. I shall dress then. I simply daren't order my rickshaw. The trampling of four coolies in the verandah would wake the dead. I shall have Dandy brought round quietly, and slip away.

Mrs H. But won't riding crumple your frock horribly?

May. (*Rising*) Not in the least, if you know how. I've ridden ten miles to a dance, and come in as fresh as though I had just left my brougham. A plain head hunting-saddle – swing up carefully – throw a waterproof over the skirt and an old shawl over the body, and there you are! Nobody notices in the dark, and Dandy knows when he feels a high heel that he must behave.

Mrs H. And what are you wearing?

May. My very, very bestest – slate body, smoke-coloured tulle skirt, and the loveliest steel-worked little shoes that ever were. Mother sent them. She doesn't know Aunt's views. That, and awfully pretty yellow roses – teeny-weeny ones. And you'll wait for me here, won't you – you angel! – at half-past nine? (*Shortens habit and whirls* Mrs H. *down the verandah. Winds up with a kiss*) There!

Mrs H. (*Holding her at arm's length and looking into her eyes*) And the next one will be given to –

MAY. (*Blushing furiously*) Uncle John – when I get home.

MRS H. Hypocrite! Go along, and be happy! (*As* MAY *mounts her horse in the garden*) At half-past nine, then? And can you curl your own wig? But I shall be here to put the last touches to you.

MRS H. (*In the verandah alone, as the stars come out*) Poor child! Dear child! And Charley Hawley too! God gie us a guid conceit of oorselves![7] But I think they are made for each other! I wonder whether that Eurasian dress-reform committee is susceptible of improvements? I wonder whether – O youth, youth!

Enter PEROO, *the butler, with a note on a tray.*

MRS H. (*Reading*) 'Help! help! help! The decorations are vile – the Volunteers are fighting over them. The roses are just beginning to come in. Mrs Mallowe has a headache. I am on a step-ladder and the verge of tears! Come and restore order, if you have any regard for me! Bring things and dress; and dine with us – CONSTANCE.' How vexatious! But I must go, I suppose. I *hate* dressing in other people's rooms – and Lady Bieldar takes all the chairs. But I'll tell Assunta to wait for May. (*Passes into house, gives orders, and departs. The clock-hands in the dining-room mark half-past seven*)

Enter ASSUNTA, *the lady's-maid, to* PEROO, *squatting on the hearth-rug.*

ASSUNTA. Peroo, there is an order that I am to remain on hand till the arrival of a young lady. (*Squats at his side*)

PEROO. Hah!

ASSUNTA. I do not desire to wait so long. I wish to go to my house.

PEROO. Hah!

ASSUNTA. My house is in the bazar. There is an urgency that I should go there.

PEROO. To meet a lover?

ASSUNTA. No – black beast! To tend my children, who be honest born. Canst thou say that of thine?

PEROO. (*Without emotion*) That is a lie, and thou art a woman of notoriously immoral carriage.

ASSUNTA. For this, my husband, who is a man, shall break thy lizard's back with a bamboo.

PEROO. For that, I, who am much honoured and trusted in this house, can, by a single word, secure his dismissal, and, owing to my influence among the servants of this town, can raise the bad name against ye both. Then ye will starve for lack of employ.

ASSUNTA. (*Fawning*) That is true. Thy honour is as great as thy influence, and thou art an esteemed man. Moreover, thou art beautiful; especially as to thy moustachios.

PEROO. So other women, and of higher caste than thou, sweeper's wife, have told me.

ASSUNTA. The moustachios of a fighting-man – of a very swashbuckler! Ahi! Peroo, how many hearts hast thou broken with thy fine face and those so huge moustachios?

PEROO. (*Twirling moustache*) One or two – two or three. It is a matter of common talk in the bazars. I speak not of the matter myself. (*Hands her betel-nut and lime wrapped in the leaf. They chew in silence*)

ASSUNTA. Peroo!

PEROO. Hah!

ASSUNTA. I greatly desire to go away, and not to wait.

PEROO. Go, then!

ASSUNTA. But what wilt thou say to the mistress?

PEROO. That thou hast gone.

ASSUNTA. Nay, but thou must say that one came crying with news that my littlest babe was smitten with fever, and that I fled weeping. Else it were not wise to go.

PEROO. Be it so! But I shall need a little tobacco to solace me while I wait for the return of the mistress alone.

ASSUNTA. It shall come; and it shall be of the best. (A snake is a snake, and a bearer is a thieving ape till he dies!) I go. It was the fever of the child – the littlest babe of all – remember. (And now, if my lover finds I am late, he will beat me, judging that I have been unfaithful.) (*Exit*)

At half-past nine enter tumultuously MAY, *a heavy shawl over her shoulders, skirt of smoke-coloured tulle showing beneath.*

MAY. Mrs Hauksbee! Oh! she isn't here. And I dared not get Aunt's *ayah* to help. She would have told Uncle John – and I can't lace it myself. (PEROO *hands note.* MAY *reads*) 'So sorry. Dragged off to put the last touches to the draperies. Assunta will look after you.' Sorry! You may well be sorry, wicked woman! Draperies, indeed! You never thought of mine, and – all up the back, too. (*To* PEROO) Where's Assunta?

PEROO. (*Bowing to the earth*) By your honoured favour, there came a man but a short time ago crying that the *ayah's* baby was smitten with fever, and she fled, weeping, to tend it. Her house is a mile hence. Is there any order?

MAY. How desperately annoying! (*Looking into fire, her eyes softening*) Her baby! (*With a little shiver, passing right hand before eyes*) Poor woman! (*A pause*) But what am I to do? I can't even creep into the cloak-room as I am, and trust to some one to put me to rights; and the shawl's a horrid old plaid! Who invented dresses to lace up the back? It must have been a man! I'd like to put him into one! What *am* I to do? Perhaps the Colley-Haughton girls haven't left yet. They're sure to be dining at home. I might run up to their rooms and wait till they came. Eva wouldn't tell, I know. (*Remounts* DANDY, *and rides up the hill to house immediately above, enters glazed hall cautiously, and calls up staircase in an agonized whisper, huddling her shawl about her*) Jenny! Eva! *Eva!* Jenny! They're out too, and, of course, their *ayah's* gone!

SIR HENRY COLLEY-HAUGHTON. (*Opening door of dining-room, where he has been finishing an after-dinner cigar, and stepping into hall*) I thought I heard a – Miss Holt! I didn't know you were going with my girls. They've just left.

MAY. (*Confusedly*) I wasn't. I didn't – that is, it was partly my fault. (*With desperate earnestness*) Is Lady Haughton in?

SIR HENRY. She's with the girls. Is there anything that I can do? I'm going to the dance in a minute. Perhaps I might ride with you!

MAY. Not for worlds! Not for anything! It was a mistake. I hope the girls are quite well.

SIR HENRY. (*With bland wonder*) Perfectly, thanks. (*Moves through hall towards horse*)

MAY. (*Mounting in haste*) No! Please don't hold my stirrup!
I can manage perfectly, thanks! (*Canters out of the garden to side
road shadowed by pines. Sees beneath her the lights of Simla town
in orderly constellations, and on a bare ridge the illuminated bulk
of the Simla Town-hall, shining like a cut-paper transparency.
The main road is firefly-lighted with the moving rickshaw lamps
all climbing towards the Town-hall. The wind brings up a few bars
of a waltz. A monkey in the darkness of the wood wakes and croons
dolefully*) And no, where in the world am I to go? May, you bad
girl! This all comes of disobeying aunts and wearing dresses
that lace up the back, and – trusting Mrs Hauksbee. Everybody
is going. I must wait a little till that crowd has thinned. Perhaps
– perhaps Mrs Lefevre might help me. It's a horrid road to her
poky little house, but she's very kind, even if she is pious.
(*Thrusts* DANDY *along an almost inaccessible path; halts in the
shadow of a clump of rhododendron, and watches the lighted windows of* MRS LEFEVRE'S *small cottage*) Oh! horror! so that's
where Aunt is dining! Back, Dandy, back! Dandy, dearest, step
softly! (*Regains road, panting*) I'll never forgive Mrs Hauksbee!
– never! And there's the band beginning 'God Save the Queen',
and that means the Viceroy has come; and Charley will think
I've disappointed him on purpose, because I was so rude last
time. And I'm all but ready. Oh! it's cruel, cruel! I'll go home,
and I'll go straight to bed, and Charley may dance with any
other horrid girl he likes! (*The last of the rickshaw lights pass her
as she reaches the main road. Clatter of stones overhead and squeak
of a saddle as a big horse picks his way down a steep path above,
and a robust baritone chants*) –

> Our King went forth to Normandie
> With power of might and chivalry;
> The Lord for him wrought wondrously,
> Therefore now may England cry,
> Deo Gratias! [8]

*Swings into main road, and the young moon shows a glimpse of the
cream and silver of the Deccan Irregular Horse uniform under
rider's opened cloak.*

MAY. (*Leaning forward and taking reins short*) That's Charley! What a splendid voice! Just like a big, strong angel's! I wonder what he is so happy about? How he sits his horse! And he hasn't anything round his neck, and he'll catch his death of cold! If he sees me riding in this direction, he may stop and ask me why, and I can't explain. Fate's against me tonight. I'll canter past quickly. Bless you, Charley! (*Canters up the main road, under the shadow of the pines, as* HAWLEY *canters down.* DANDY'S *hoofs keep the tune 'There was never a daughter of Eve', etc.* ALL EARTH *wakes, and tells the* STARS. *The* OCCUPANTS *of the Little Simla Cemetery stir in their sleep*)

PINES OF THE CEMETERY (*to the* OCCUPANTS).

> Lie still, lie still! O earth to earth returning!
> Brothers beneath, what wakes you to your pain?

The OCCUPANTS (*underground*).

> Earth's call to earth – the old unstifled yearning,
> To clutch our lives again.

> By summer shrivelled and by winter frozen,
> Ye cannot thrust us wholly from the light.
> Do we not know, who were of old his chosen,
> Love rides abroad tonight?

> By all that was our own of joy or sorrow,
> By Pain fordone, Desire snatched away!
> By hopeless weight of that unsought Tomorrow,
> Which is our lot today,

> By vigil in our chambers ringing hollow,
> With Love's foot overhead to mock our dearth,
> We who have come would speak for those who follow –
> Be pitiful, O Earth!

The DEVIL OF CHANCE, *in the similitude of a grey ape, runs out on the branch of an overhanging tree, singing –*

> On a road that is pied as a panther's hide
> The shadows flicker and dance.
> And the leaves that make them, my hand shall shake them –
> The hand of the Devil of Chance.

Wee Willie Winkie

Echo from the SNOWS *on the Thibet road —*

The little blind Devil of Chance.

The DEVIL (*swinging branch furiously*) —

> Yea, chance and confusion and error
> The chain of their destiny wove;
> And the horse shall be smitten with terror,
> And the maiden made sure of her love!

DANDY *shies at the waving shadows, and cannons into* HAW-
LEY'S *horse, off shoulder to off shoulder.* HAWLEY *catches the
reins.*

The DEVIL, *above* (*letting the branch swing back*) —

> On a road that is pied as a panther's hide
> The souls of the twain shall dance!
> And the passions that shake them, my hand shall wake them —
> The hand of the Devil of Chance.

Echo —

The little blind Devil of Chance.

HAWLEY. (*Recovering himself*) Confou — er — hm! Oh, Miss
Holt! And to what am I indebted for this honour?

MAY. Dandy shied. I hope you aren't hurt.

ALL EARTH, THE FLOWERS, THE TREES, and THE
MOONLIGHT (*together to* HAWLEY). Speak now, or forever
hold your peace![9]

HAWLEY. (*Drawing reins tighter, keeping his horse's off shoulder
to* DANDY'S *side*) My fault entirely. (It comes easily now) Not
much hurt, are you (*leaning off side, and putting his arm round
her*), my May? It's awfully mean, I know, but I meant to speak
weeks ago, only you never gave a fellow the chance — specially last
time. (*Moistens his lips*) I'm not fit — I'm utterly (*in a gruff whisper*)
— I'm utterly unworthy, and — and you aren't angry, May, are you?
I thought you might have cared a little bit. *Do* you care, darl —?

MAY. (*Her head falling on his right shoulder. The arm tightens*)
Oh! don't — don't!

HAWLEY. (*Nearly tumbling off his horse*) Only one, darling. We can talk at the dance.

MAY. But I can't go to the dance!

HAWLEY. (*Taking another promptly as head is raised*) Nonsense! You *must*, dear, now. Remember I go down to my Regiment the day after tomorrow, and I shan't see you again. (*Catches glimpse of steel-grey slipper in stirrup*) Why, you're dressed for it!

MAY. Yes, but I can't go! I've - torn my dress.

HAWLEY. Run along and put on a new one; only be quick. Shall I wait here?

MAY. No! Go away! Go at once!

HAWLEY. You'll find me opposite the cloak-room.

MAY. Yes, yes! Anything! Good-night!

HAWLEY *canters up the road, and the song breaks out again fortissimo.*

MAY. (*Absently, picking up reins*) Yes, indeed. My king went forth to Normandie; and – I shall never get there. Let me think, though! Let me think! It's all over now – all over! I wonder what I ought to have said! I wonder what I did say! Hold up, Dandy; you need some one to order you about. It's nice to have some one nice to order you about. (*Flicks horse, who capers*) Oh, don't jiggit, Dandy! I feel so trembly and faint. But I sha'n't see him for ever so long ... But we understand now. (DANDY *turns down path to* MRS SCRIFFSHAW'S *house*) And I wanted to go to the dance so much before, and now I want to go worse than ever! (*Dismounts, runs into house, and weeps with her head on the drawing-room table*)

Enter SCRIFFSHAW, *grizzled Lieutenant-Colonel.*

SCRIFFSHAW. May! Bless my soul, what's all this? What's all this? (*Shawl slips*) And, bless my soul, what's all *this*?

MAY. N-nothing. Only I'm miserable and wretched.

SCRIFFSHAW. But where have you been? I thought you were in your own room.

MAY. (*With icy desperation*) I was, till you had fallen asleep.

Then I dressed myself for a dance – this dance that Aunt
has forbidden me to go to. Then I took Dandy out, and then
– (*collapsing and wriggling her shoulders*) – doesn't it show
enough?

SCRIFFSHAW. (*Critically*) It does, dear. I thought those
things – er – laced up the front.

MAY. This one doesn't. That's all. (*Weeps afresh*)

SCRIFFSHAW. Then what are you going to do? Bless my
soul, May, don't cry!

MAY. I *will* cry, and I'll sit here till Aunt comes home, and
then she'll see what I've been trying to do, and I'll tell her that
I hate her, and ask her to send me back to Calcutta!

SCRIFFSHAW. But – but if she finds you in this dress she'll
be furiously angry with *me!*

MAY. For allowing me to put it on? So much the better.
Then you'll know what it is to be scolded by Aunt.

SCRIFFSHAW. I knew that before you were born. (*Standing
by* MAY'S *bowed head*) (She's my sister's child, and I don't
think Alice has the very gentlest way with girls. I'm sure her
mother wouldn't object if we took her to twenty dances. She
can't find us amusing company – and Alice will be simply
beside herself under any circumstances. I know her tempers
after those 'refreshing evenings' at the Lefevres'.) May, dear,
don't cry like that!

MAY. I will! I will! I *will!* You – you don't know why!

SCRIFFSHAW. (*Revolving many matters*) We may just as
well be hanged for a sheep as a lamb.[10]

MAY. (*Raising head swiftly*) Uncle *John!*

SCRIFFSHAW. You see, my dear, your aunt can't be a scrap
more angry than she will be if you don't take off that frock. She
looks at the intention of things.

MAY. Yes; disobedience, of course. (And I'll only obey one
person in the wide living world.) Well?

SCRIFFSHAW. Your aunt may be back at any moment, *I*
can't face her.

MAY. Well?

SCRIFFSHAW. Let's go to the dance. I'll jump into my

uniform, and then see if I can't put those things straight. We may *just* as well be hanged for a sheep as a lamb. (And there's the chance of a rubber.) Give me five minutes, and we'll fly. (*Dives into his room, leaving* MAY *astounded*)

SCRIFFSHAW. (*From the room*) Tell them to bring round Dolly Bobs.¹¹ We can get away quicker on horseback.

MAY. But really, Uncle, hadn't you better go in a rickshaw? Aunt says –

SCRIFFSHAW. We're in open mutiny now. We'll ride. (*Emerges in full uniform*) There!

MAY. Oh, Uncle John! you look perfectly delightful – and so martial, too!

SCRIFFSHAW. I was martial once. Suppose your aunt came in? Let me see if I can lace those things of yours. That's too tight – eh?

MAY. No! Much, much tighter. You must bring the edges together. Indeed you must. And lace it *quick!* Oh! what if Aunt should come? Tie it in a knot! Any sort of knot.

SCRIFFSHAW. (*Lacing bodice after a fashion of his own devising*) Yes – yes! I see! Confound! That's all right! (*They pass into the garden and mount their horses*) Let go her head! By Jove, May, how well you ride!

MAY. (*As they race through the shadows neck and neck*) (Small blame to me. I'm riding to my love.) Go along, Dandy boy! Wasn't that Aunt's rickshaw that passed just now? She'll come to the dance and fetch us back.

SCRIFFSHAW. (*After the gallop*) Who cares?

Scene – *Main ball-room of the Simla Town-hall; dancing-floor grooved and tongued teak, vaulted roof, and gallery round the walls. Four hundred people dispersed in couples. Banners, bayonet-stars on walls; red and gold, blue and gold, chocolate, buff, rifle-green, black and other uniforms under glare of a few hundred lamps. Cloak-and supper-rooms at the sides, with alleys leading to Chinese-lanterned verandahs.* HAWLEY, *at entrance, receives* MAY *as she drops from her horse and passes towards cloak-room.*

357

HAWLEY. (*As he pretends to rearrange shawl*) Oh, my love, my love, my love!

MAY. (*Her eyes on the ground*) Let me go and get these things off. I'm trying to control my eyes, but it is written on my face. (*Dashes into cloak-room*)

NEWLY MARRIED WIFE OF CAPTAIN OF ENGINEERS TO HUSBAND. No need to ask what has happened *there*, Dick.

HUSBAND. No, bless 'em both, whoever they are!

HAWLEY. (*Under his breath*) Damn his impertinence!

MAY. *comes from cloak-room, having completely forgotten to do more than look at her face and hair in the glass.*

HAWLEY. Here's the programme, dear!

MAY. (*Returning it with pretty gesture of surrender*) Here's the programme – dear!

HAWLEY *draws line from top to bottom, initials and returns card.*

MAY. You can't! It's perfectly awful! But – I should have been angry if you hadn't. (*Taking his arm*) Is it wrong to say that?

HAWLEY. It sounds delicious. We can sit out all the squares and dance all the round dances. There are heaps of square dances at Volunteer balls. Come along!

MAY. One minute! I want to tell my chaperon something.

HAWLEY. Come along! You belong to me now.

MAY. (*Her eyes seeking* MRS HAUKSBEE, *who is seated on an easy-chair by an alcove*) But it was so awfully sudden!

HAWLEY. My dear infant! When a girl throws herself literally into a man's arms –

MAY. I didn't! Dandy shied.

HAWLEY. Don't shy to conclusions. That man is never going to let her go. Come!

MAY *catches* MRS H.'s. *Telegraphs a volume, and receives by return two. Turns to go with* HAWLEY.

MRS H. (*As she catches sight of back of* MAY'S *dress*) Oh, horror! Assunta shall die tomorrow! (*Sees* SCRIFFSHAW *fluc-*

tuating uneasily among the chaperons, and following his niece's departure with the eye of an artist)

MRS H. (*Furiously*) Colonel Scriffshaw, you – *you* did that?

SCRIFFSHAW. (*Imbecilely*) The lacing? Yes. I think it will hold.

MRS H. You monster! Go and tell her. No, don't (*Falling back in chair*) I have lived to see every proverb I believed in a lie. The maid has forgotten her attire![12] (What a handsome couple they make! Anyhow, he doesn't care, and she doesn't know.) How did *you* come here, Colonel Scriffshaw?

SCRIFFSHAW. Strictly against orders. (*Uneasily*) I'm afraid I shall have my wife looking for me.

MRS H. I fancy you will (*Sees reflection of herself in the mirrors – black-lace dinner dress, blood-red poinsettia at shoulder and girdle to secure single brace of black lace. Silver shoes, silver-handled black fan*) (You're looking pretty tonight, dear. I wish your husband were here.) (*Aloud, to drift of expectant men*) No, no, no! For the hundredth time, Mrs Hauksbee is not dancing this evening. (Her hands are full, or she is in error. Now, the chances are that I sha'n't see May again till it is time to go, and I may see Mrs Scriffshaw at any moment.) Colonel, *will* you take me to the supper-room? The hall's chilly without perpetual soups. (*Goes out on* COLONEL'S *arm. Passing the cloak-room, sees portion of* MRS SCRIFFSHAW'S *figure*.) (Before me the Deluge![13]) If I were you, Colonel Scriffshaw, I'd go to the whist-room, and – stay there. (S. *follows the line of her eye, and blanches as he flies*) She *has* come – to – take them home, and she is quite capable of it. What shall I do? (*Looks across the supper-tables. Sees* MAJOR DECKER, *a big black-haired Irishman, and attacks him among the meringues.*) Major Decker! Dear Major Decker! If ever I was a friend of yours, help me now!

MAJOR D. I will indeed. What is it?

MRS H. (*Walking him back deftly in the direction of the cloak-room door.*) I want you to be very kind to a very dear friend of mine – a Mrs Scriffshaw. She doesn't come to dances much, and, being very sensitive, she feels neglected if no one asks her to dance. She really waltzes divinely, though you might not think it. There she is, walking out of the cloak-room now, in the high dress. *Please* come and be introduced. (*Under her eyelashes*) You're an Irishman, Major, and you've got a way with you. (*Planting herself in front of* MRS S.) Mrs Scriffshaw, may I wah-wah-wah Decker? – wah-wah-wah Decker? – Mrs Scuffles. (*Flies hastily*) Saved for a moment! And now, if I can enlist the Viceroy on my side, I may do something.

MAJOR D. (*To* MRS. S.) The pleasure of a dance with you, Mrs Scruffun?

MRS SCRIFFSHAW. (*Backing, and filling in the doorway*) Sirr!

MAJOR D. (*Smiling persuasively*) You've forgotten me, I see! I had the pleasure o' meeting you – (there's missionary in every line o' that head) – at – at – the last Presbyterian Conference.

MRS S. (*Strict Wesleyan Methodist*) I was never there.

MAJOR D. (*Retiring* en échelon *towards two easy-chairs*) Were ye not, now? That's queer. Let's sit down here and talk over it, and perhaps we will strike a chord of mutual reminiscence. (*Sits down exhaustedly*) And if it was not at the Conference, where was it?

MRS S. (*Icily, looking for her husband*) I apprehend that our paths in the world are widely different.

MAJOR D. (My faith! they are!) Not in the least in the world. (MRS S. *shudders*) Are you sitting in a draught? Shall we try a turn at the waltz now?

MRS S. (*Rising to the expression of her abhorrence*) My husband is Colonel Scriffshaw. I should be much obliged if you would find him for me.

MAJOR D. (*Throwing up his chin*) Scriffshaw, begad! I saw him just now at the other end of the room. (I'll get a dance out of the old woman, or I'll die for it.) We'll just waltz up there an' inquire. (*Hurls* MRS S. *into the waltz. Revolves ponderously*) (Mrs Hauksbee has perjured herself – but not on my behalf. She's ruining my instep.) No, he's not at this end. (*Circling slowly*) We'll just go back to our chairs again. If he won't dance with so magnificent a dancer as his wife, he doesn't deserve to be here, or anywhere else. (That's my own sound knee-cap she's kicking now.) (*Halts at point of departure*) And now we'll watch for him here.

MRS S. (*Panting*) Abominable! Infamous!

MAJOR D. Oh, no! He's not so bad as that! Prob'bly playin' whist in the kyard-rooms. Will I look for him? (*Departs, leaving* MRS S. *purple in the face among the chaperons, and passes* MRS H. *in close conversation with a partner*)

MAJOR D. (*To* MRS H., *not noticing her partner*) She's kicked me to pieces. She can dance no more than a Windsor chair, an' now she's sent me to look for her husband. You owe me something for this . . . (The Viceroy, by Jove!)

MRS H. (*Turning to her partner and concluding story*) A base betrayal of confidence, of course; but the woman's absolutely without tact, and capable of making a scene at a minute's notice, besides doing her best to wreck the happiness of two lives, after her treatment at Major Decker's hands. But on the Dress Reform Committee, and under proper supervision, she would be most valuable.

HIS EXCELLENCY THE VICEROY AND GOVERNOR-GENERAL OF INDIA. (*Diplomatic uniform, stars, etc.*) But surely the work of keeping order among the waltzers is entrusted to abler hands. I cannot, cannot fight! I – I only direct armies.

MRS H. No. But your Excellency has not quite grasped the situation. (*Explains it with desperate speed, one eye on* MRS S. *panting on her chair*) So you see! Husband fled to the whist-room for refuge; girl with her lover, who goes down the day after tomorrow; and *she* is loose. She will be neither to hold nor to bind after the Major's onslaught, save by you. And on a committee – she really would –

HIS EXCELLENCY. I see. I am penetrated with an interest in Eurasian dress reform. I never felt so alive to the importance of committees before. (*Screwing up his eyes to see across the room*) But pardon me – my sight is not so good as it has been – which of that line of Mothers in Israel[14] do I attack! The wearied one who is protesting with a fan against this scene of riot and dissipation?

MRS H. Can you doubt for a moment? I'm afraid your task is a heavy one, but the happiness of two —

HIS EXCELLENCY. (*Wearily*) Hundred and fifty million souls? Ah, yes! And yet they say a Viceroy is overpaid. Let us advance. It will not talk to me about its husband's unrecognized merits, will it? You have no idea how inevitably the conversation drifts in that direction when I am left alone with a lady. They tell me of Poor Tom, or Dear Dick, or Persecuted Paul, before I have time to explain that these things are really regulated by my Secretaries. On my honour, I sometimes think that the ladies of India are polyandrous![15]

MRS H. Would it be so difficult to credit that they love their husbands?

HIS EXCELLENCY. That also is possible. One of your many claims to my regard is that you have never mentioned your husband.

MRS H. (*Sweetly*) No; and as long as he is where he is, I have not the least intention of doing so.

HIS EXCELLENCY. (*As they approach the row of eminently self-conscious chaperons*) And, by the way, where is he?

MRS H. *lays her fan lightly over her heart, bows her head, and moves on.*

HIS EXCELLENCY. (*As the chaperons become more self-conscious, drifting to vacant chair at* MRS S.'s *side*) That also is possible. I do not recall having seen him elsewhere, at any rate. (*Watching* MRS S.) How very like twenty thousand people that I could remember if I had time! (*Glides into vacant chair.* MRS S. *colours to the temples; chaperons exchange glances. In a voice of strained honey*) May I be pardoned for attacking you so brusquely on matters of public importance, Mrs Scriffshaw? But my times are not my own, and I have heard so much about the good work you carry on so successfully. (When she has quite recovered I may learn what that work was.)

MRS S., *in tones meant for the benefit of all the chaperons, discourses volubly, with little gasps, of her charitable mission work.*

HIS EXCELLENCY. How interesting! Of course, quite natural! What we want most on our dress reform committee is a firm hand and enormous local knowledge. Men are *so* tactless. You have been too proud, Mrs Scriffshaw, to offer us your help in that direction. So, you see, I come to ask it as a favour. (*Gives* MRS S. *to understand that the Eurasian dress reform committee cannot live another hour without her help and comfort*)

FIRST AIDE. (*By doorway within eye-reach of* HIS EXCELLENCY) What in the world is His Excellency tackling now?

SECOND AIDE. (*In attitude of fascination*) Looks as if it had been a woman once. Anyhow, it isn't amusing him. I know that smile when he is in acute torment.

MRS H. (*Coming up behind him*) 'Now the Serpent was more subtle than any beast of the field!'[16]

SECOND AIDE. (*Turning*) Ah! Your programme full, of course, Mrs Hauksbee?

MRS H. I'm not dancing, and you should have asked me before. You Aides have no manners.

FIRST AIDE. You must excuse him. Hugh's a blighted being. He's watching somebody dance with somebody else, and somebody's wanting to dance with him.

MRS H. (*Keenly, under her eyebrows*) You're too young for that rubbish.

SECOND AIDE. It's his imagination. *He's* all right, but Government House duty is killing me. My heart's in the plains[17] with a dear little, fat little, lively little nine-foot tiger. I want to sit out over that kill instead of watching over His Excellency.

MRS H. Don't they let the Aides out to play, then?

SECOND AIDE. Not me. I've got to do most of Duggy's work while he runs after –

MRS H. Never mind! A discontented Aide is a perpetual beast. One of you boys will take me to a chair, and then leave me. No, I don't want the delights of your conversation.

SECOND AIDE. (*As first goes off*) When Mrs Hauksbee is attired in holy simplicity it generally means – larks!

HIS EXCELLENCY. (*To* MRS SCRIFFSHAW) ... And so we all wanted to see more of you. I felt I was taking no liberty when I dashed into affairs of State at so short a notice. It was with the greatest difficulty I could find you. Indeed, I hardly believed my eyes when I saw you waltzing so divinely just now. (She will first protest, and next perjure herself.)

MRS S. (*Weakly*) But I assure you –

HIS EXCELLENCY. My eyes are not so old that they cannot recognize a good dancer when they see one.

MRS S. (*With a simper*) But only once in a way, Your Excellency.

HIS EXCELLENCY. (*Of course*) That is too seldom – much too seldom. You should set our younger folk an example. These slow swirling waltzes are tiring. I prefer – as I see you do – swifter measures.

MAJOR D. (*Entering main door in strict charge of* SCRIFF-SHAW, *who fears the judgment*) Yes! she sent me to look for you, after giving me *the* dance of the evening. I'll never forget it!

SCRIFFSHAW. (*His jaw dropping*) My – wife – danced – with – *you!* I mean – anybody!

MAJOR D. Anybody! Aren't I somebody enough? (*Looking across room*) Faith! you're right though! There she is in a corner, flirting with the Viceroy! I was not good enough for her. Well, it's no use to interrupt 'em.

SCRIFFSHAW. Certainly not! We'll – we'll get a drink and go back to the whist-rooms. (Alice must be mad! At any rate, I'm safe, I suppose.)

HIS EXCELLENCY *rises and fades away from* MRS SCRIFF-SHAW'S *side after a long and particular pressure of the hand.* MRS S. *throws herself back in her chair with the air of one surfeited with similar attentions, and the chaperons begin to talk.*

HIS EXCELLENCY. (*Leaning over* MRS H.'s *chair with an absolutely expressionless countenance*) She is a truly estimable lady – one that I shall count it an honour to number among my friends. No! she will not move from her place, because I have expressed a hope that, a little later on in the dance, we may renew our very interesting conversation. And now, if I could only get my boys together, I think I would go home. Have you seen any Aide who looked as though a Viceroy belonged to him?

MRS H. The feet of the young men are at the door without.[18] You leave early.

HIS EXCELLENCY. Have I not done enough?

MRS H. (*Half rising from her chair*) Too much, alas! Too much! Look!

HIS EXCELLENCY. (*Regarding* MRS SCRIFFSHAW, *who has risen and is moving towards a side door*) How interesting! By every law known to me she should have waited in that chair – such a comfortable chair – for my too tardy return. But now she is loose! How has this happened?

MRS H. (*Half to herself, shutting and opening fan*) She is looking for May! I know it! Oh! why wasn't she isolated? One of those women has taken revenge on Mrs Scriffshaw's new glory – *you* – by telling her that May has been sitting out too much with Mr Hawley.

HIS EXCELLENCY. Blame me! Always blame a Viceroy! (MRS H. *moves away*) What are you meditating?

MRS H. Following – watching – administering – anything! I fly! I know where they are!

HIS EXCELLENCY. The plot thickens! May I come to administer?

MRS H. (*Over her shoulder*) If you can!

MRS H. *flies down a darkened corridor speckled with occasional Chinese lanterns, and establishes herself behind a pillar as* MRS S. *sweeps by to the darkest end, where* MAY *and* HAWLEY *are sitting very close together.* HIS EXCELLENCY *follows* MRS S.

MRS S. (*To both the invisibles*) Well!

HIS EXCELLENCY. (*To* MRS H. *in a whisper*) Now I should be afraid. I should run away.

MRS S. (*In a high-pitched voice of the matron*) May, go to the cloak-room at once, and wait till I come. I wonder you expect any one to speak to you after this! (MAY *hurries down corridor very considerably agitated.*)

HIS EXCELLENCY. (*As* MAY *passes, slightly raising his voice, and with all the deference due to half a dozen Duchesses*) May an old man be permitted to offer you his arm, my dear? (*To* MRS H.) I entreat – I *command* you to delay the catastrophe till I return!

MRS H. (*Plunging into the darkness, and halting before a dead wall*) Oh! I thought there was a way round! (*Pretends to discover the two*) Mrs Scriffshaw and Mr Hawley! (*With exaggerated emphasis*) Mrs Scriffshaw – Oh! *Mrs* Scriffshaw! – how truly shocking! What will that dear, good husband of yours say? (*Smothered chuckle from* HAWLEY, *who otherwise preserves silence. Snorts of indignation from* MRS S.)

MRS H. (*Hidden by pillar of observation*) Now, in any other woman that would have been possibly weak – certainly vulgar. But I think it has answered the purpose.

HIS EXCELLENCY. (*Returning, and taking up his post at her side*) Poor little girl! She was shaking all over. What an enormous amount of facile emotion exists in the young! What is about to –

MRS S. (*In a rattling whisper to* HAWLEY) Take me to some quieter place.

HAWLEY On my word, you seem to be accustomed to *very* quiet places. I'm sorry I don't know any more secluded nook; but if you have anything to say –

MRS S. Say, indeed! I wish you to understand that I consider your conduct abominable, sir!

HAWLEY. (*In level, expressionless voice*) Yes? Explain yourself.

MRS S. In the first place, you meet my niece at an entertainment of which I utterly disapprove –

HAWLEY. To the extent of dancing with Major Decker, the most notorious loose fish in the whole room? Yes.

MRS S. (*Hotly*) That was not my fault. It was entirely against my inclination.

HAWLEY. It takes two to make a waltz. Presumably, you are capable of expressing your wishes – are you not?

MRS S. I did. It was – only – and I couldn't –

HAWLEY. (*Relentlessly*) Well, it's a most serious business. I've been talking it over with May.

MRS S. May!

HAWLEY. Yes May; and she has assured me that you do not do – er – this sort of thing often. She *assured* me of that.

MRS S. But by what right –

HAWLEY. You see, May has promised to marry me, and one can't be too careful about one's connections.

HIS EXCELLENCY. (*To* MRS H.) That young man will go far! This is invention indeed.

MRS H. He seems to have marched some paces already. (Blessed be the chance that led me to the Major! I can always say that I meant it.)

MRS S. May has promised . . . this is worse than ever! And *I* was not consulted!

HAWLEY. If I had known the precise hour, you know, I might possibly have chosen to take you into my confidence.

MRS S. May should have told *me*.

HAWLEY. You mustn't worry May about it. Is that perfectly clear to you?

HIS EXCELLENCY. (*To* MRS H.) What a singularly flat, hopeless tone he has chosen to talk in – as if he were speaking to a coolie from a distance.

MRS H. Yes. It's the one note that will rasp through her overstrained nerves.

HIS EXCELLENCY. You know him well?

MRS H. I trained him.

HIS EXCELLENCY. Then *she* collapses.

MRS H. If she does not, all my little faith in man is gone for ever.

MRS S. (*To* HAWLEY) This is perfectly monstrous! It's conduct utterly unworthy of a *man*, much less a gentleman. What do *I* know of you, or your connections, or your means?

HAWLEY. Nothing. How could you?

MRS S. How could I? . . . Because – because I insist on knowing!

HAWLEY. Then am I to understand that you are anxious to marry me? Suppose we talk to the Colonel about that?

HIS EXCELLENCY. (*To* MRS H.) Very far, indeed, will that young man go.

MRS S. (*Almost weeping with anger*) Will you let me pass? I – I want to go away. I've no language at my command that could convey to you –

HAWLEY. Then surely it would be better to wait here till the inspiration comes?

MRS S. But this is insolence!

HAWLEY. You must remember that you drove May, who, by the way, is a woman, out of this place like a hen. That was insolence, Mrs Scriffshaw – to her.

MRS S. To her? She's my husband's sister's child.

HAWLEY. And she is going to do me the honour of carrying my name. I am accountable to your husband's sister in Calcutta. Sit down, please!

HIS EXCELLENCY. She will positively assault him in a minute. I can hear her preparing for a spring.

MRS H. He will be able to deal with that too, if it happens. (I trained him. Bear witness, heaven and earth, I trained him, that his tongue should guard his head with my sex.)

MRS S. (*Feebly*) What shall I do? What *can* I do? (*Through her teeth*) I hate you!

HIS EXCELLENCY. (*Critically*) Weak. The end approaches.

MRS S. *You*'re not the sort of man I should have chosen for anybody's husband.

HAWLEY. I can't say your choice seems particularly select – Major Decker, for instance. And believe me, you are not required to choose husbands for anybody.

MRS SCRIFFSHAW *looses all the double-thonged lightnings of her tongue, condemns* HAWLEY *as no gentleman, an impostor, possibly a bigamist, a defaulter and every other unpleasant character she has ever read of; announces her unalterable intention of refusing to recognize the engagement, and of harrying* MAY *tooth and talon; and renews her request to be allowed to pass. No answer.*

HIS EXCELLENCY. What a merciful escape! She might have attacked me on the chairs in this fashion. What will he do now?

MRS H. I have faith – illimitable faith.

368

MRS S. (*At the end of her resources*) Well, what have you to say?

HAWLEY. (*In a placid and most insinuating drawl*) Aunt Alice – give – me – a – kiss.

HIS EXCELLENCY. Beautiful! Oh! thrice beautiful! And my Secretaries never told me there were men like this in the Empire.

MRS S. (*Bewilderedly, beginning to sob*) Why – why *should* I?

HAWLEY. Because you will make – you really will – a delightful aunt-in-law, and it will save such a lot of trouble when May and I are married, and you have to accept me as a relation.

MRS S. (*Weeping gently*) But – but you're taking the management of affairs into your own hands.

HAWLEY. Quite so. They are my own affairs. And do you think that my aunt is competent to manage other people's affairs when she doesn't know whether she means to dance or sit out, and when she chooses the very worst –

MRS S. (*Appealingly*) Oh, don't – don't! Please, don't! (*Bursts into tears*)

HIS EXCELLENCY. (*To* MRS H.) Unnecessarily brutal, surely? She's crying.

MRS H. No! It's nothing. We all cry – even the worst of us.

HAWLEY. Well?

MRS S. (*Snuffling, with a rustle*) There!

HAWLEY. No, no, no! I said give it to me! (*It is given*)

HIS EXCELLENCY. (*Carried away*) And I? What am I doing here, pretending to govern India, while that man languishes in a lieutenant's uniform?

MRS H. (*Speaking very swiftly and distinctly*) It rests with Your Excellency to raise him to honour. He should go down the day after tomorrow. A month at Simla, now, would mean Paradise to him, and one of your Aides is dying for a little tiger-shooting.

HIS EXCELLENCY. But would such an Archangel of Insolence condescend to run errands for me?

MRS H. You can but try.

HIS EXCELLENCY. I shall be afraid of him; but we'll see if we can get the Commander-in-Chief to lend him to me.

HAWLEY. (*To* MRS S.) There, there, there! It's nothing to make a fuss about, is it? Come along, Aunt Alice, and I'll tuck you into your rickshaw, and you shall go home quite comfy, and the Colonel and I will bring May home later. I go down to my regiment the day after tomorrow, worse luck! So you won't have me long to trouble you. But we quite understand each other, don't we? (*Emerges from the darkness, very tenderly escorting the very much shaken* MRS SCRIFF-SHAW)

HIS EXCELLENCY. (*To* MRS H. *as the captive passes*) I feel as if I ought to salute that young man; but I must go to the ball-room. Send him to me as soon as you can. (*Drifts in direction of music.* HAWLEY *returns to* MRS H.)

HAWLEY. (*Mopping his forehead*) Phew! I have had easier duties.

MRS H. How could you? How dared you? I builded better than I knew. It was cruel, but it was superb.

HAWLEY. Who taught me? Where's May?

MRS H. In the cloak-room – being put to rights – I fervently trust.

HAWLEY. (*Guiltily*) They wear their fringes so low on their foreheads that one can't –

MRS H. (*Laughing*) Oh, you goose! That wasn't it. His Excellency wants to speak to you! (HAWLEY *turns to ball-room as* MRS H. *flings herself down in a chair*)

MRS H. (*Alone*) For two seasons, at intervals, I formed the infant mind. Heavens, how raw he was in the beginning! And never one throughout his schooling did he disappoint you, dear. Never once, by word or look or sign, did he have the unspeakable audacity to fall in love with you. No, he chose his maiden, then he stopped his confidences, and conducted his own wooing, and in open fight slew his aunt-in-law. But he never, being a whole-some, dear, delightful boy, fell in love with you, Mrs Hauksbee; and I wonder whether you liked it or whether you didn't. Which? . . . You certainly never gave him a chance . . . but that was the very reason why ... (*Half aloud*) Mrs Hauksbee, you are an idiot!

Enters main ball-room just in time to see HIS EXCELLENCY *conferring with* HAWLEY, AIDES *in background.*

HIS EXCELLENCY. Have you any very pressing employment in the plains, Mr Hawley?

HAWLEY. Regimental duty. Native Cavalry, sir.

HIS EXCELLENCY. And, of course, you are anxious to return at once?

HAWLEY. Not in the least, sir.

HIS EXCELLENCY. Do you think you could relieve one of my boys here for a month?

HAWLEY. Most certainly, sir.

SECOND AIDE. (*Behind* VICEROY'S *shoulders, shouting in dumb show*) My tiger! My tiger! My tigerling!

HIS EXCELLENCY. (*Lowering his voice and regarding* HAWLEY *between his eyes*) But could we trust you — ahem! — not to insist on ordering kisses at inopportune moments from — people?

HAWLEY. (*Dropping eyes*) Not when I'm on duty, sir.

HIS EXCELLENCY. (*Turning*) Then I'll speak to the Commander-in-Chief about it.

MRS H. (*As she sees gratified expression of the* VICEROY'S *and* HAWLEY'S *lowered eyes*) I am sometimes sorry that I am a woman, but I'm very glad that I'm not a man, and — I shouldn't care to be an angel. (MRS SCRIFFSHAW *and* MAY *pass — the latter properly laced, the former regarding the lacing*) So that's settled at last. (*To* MRS S.) Your husband, Mrs Scriffshaw? Yes, I know. But don't be too hard on him. Perhaps he never did it, after all.

MRS S. (*With a grunt of infinite contempt*) Mrs Hauksbee, that man has tried to lace *me*!

MRS H. (Then he's bolder than I thought. She will avenge all her outrages on the Colonel.) May, come and talk to me a moment, dear.

FIRST AIDE. (*To* HAWLEY, *as the* VICEROY *drifts away*)

Knighted on the field of battle, by Jove! What the deuce have you been doing to His Excellency?

SECOND AIDE. I'll bet on it that Mrs Hauksbee is at the bottom of this, somehow. I told her what I wanted, and —

HAWLEY. Never look a gift tiger in the mouth. It's apt to bite. (*Departs in search of* MAY)

HIS EXCELLENCY. (*To* MRS H. *as he passes her sitting out with* MAY) No, I am not so afraid of your young friend. Have I done well?

MRS H. Exceedingly. (*In a whisper, including* MAY) She is a pretty girl, isn't she?

HIS EXCELLENCY. (*Regarding mournfully, his chin on his breast*) O youth, youth, youth! *Si la jeunesse savait — si la vieillesse pouvait.*[19]

MRS H. (*Incautiously*) Yes, but in this case we have seen that youth did know quite as much as was good for it, and — (*Stops*)

HIS EXCELLENCY. And age had power, and used it. Sufficient reward, perhaps; but I hardly expected the reminder from *you*.

MRS H. No. I won't try to excuse it. Perhaps the slip is as well, for it reminds me that I am but mortal, and in watching *you* controlling the destinies of the universe I thought I was as the gods![20]

HIS EXCELLENCY. Thank you! I go to be taken away. But it has been an interesting evening.

SCRIFFSHAW. (*Very much disturbed after the* VICEROY *has passed on, to* MRS H.) Now, what in the world was wrong with my lacing? My wife didn't appear angry about my bringing May here. I'm informed she danced several dances herself. But she — she gave it me awfully in the supper-room for my — ahem! — lady's-maid's work. Fearfully she gave it me! What was wrong? It held, didn't it?

MAY. (*From her chair*) It was beautiful, Uncle John. It was the best thing in the world you could have done. Never mind. I forgive you. (*To* HAWLEY, *behind her*) No, Charley. No more dances for just a little while. Ask Mrs Hauksbee now.

Mrs Hauksbee Sits Out

Alarums and Excursions.[21] *The ball-room is rent in twain as the* VICEROY, AIDES, *etc., file out between Lines of Volunteers and Uniforms.*

BAND IN THE GALLERY—

God save our gracious Queen,
Heaven bless our noble Queen,
> God save the Queen!
Send her victorious,
Happy and glorious,
Long to reign over us,
> God save the Queen!

HAWLEY. (*Behind* MRS H's *chair*) Amen, your Imperial Majesty!

MRS H. (*Looking up, head thrown back on left shoulder*) Thank you! Yes, you can have the next if you want it. Mrs Hauksbee isn't sitting out any more.

⁅ The Last of the Stories ¹ ⁆

Wherefore I perceive that there is nothing better than that a man should rejoice in his own works; for that is his portion.² *Ecc.* iii, 22

'Kench³ with a long hand, lazy one,' I said to the punkah coolie. 'But I am tired,' said the coolie. 'Then go to Jehannum⁴ and get another man to pull,' I replied, which was rude and, when you come to think of it, unnecessary.

'Happy thought – go to Jehannum!' said a voice at my elbow. I turned and saw, seated on the edge of my bed, a large and luminous Devil. 'I'm not afraid,' I said. 'You're an illusion bred by too much tobacco and not enough sleep. If I look at you steadily for a minute you will disappear. You are an *ignis fatuus*.'⁵

'Fatuous yourself!' answered the Devil blandly. 'Do you mean to say you don't know *me*?' He shrivelled up to the size of a blob of sediment on the end of a pen, and I recognized my old friend the Devil of Discontent, who lived in the bottom of the inkpot, but emerges half a day after each story has been printed with a host of useless suggestions for its betterment.

'Oh, it's you, is it?' I said. 'You're not due till next week. Get back to your inkpot.'

'Hush!' said the Devil 'I have an idea.'

'Too late, as usual. I know your ways.'

'No. It's a perfectly practicable one. Your swearing at the coolie suggested it. Did you ever hear of a man called Dante – charmin' fellow, friend o' mine?'

'"Dante once prepared to paint a picture,"'⁶ I quoted.

'Yes. I inspired that notion – but never mind. Are you willing to play Dante to my Virgil? I can't guarantee a nine-circle Inferno, any more than *you* can turn out a cantoed epic, but

374

there's absolutely no risk and – it will run to three columns at
least.'

'But what sort of Hell do you own?' I said. 'I fancied your
operations were mostly above ground. You have no jurisdiction
over the dead.'

'Sainted Leopardi!' [7] rapped the Devil, resuming natural size.
'Is *that* all you know? I'm proprietor of one of the largest Hells
in existence – the Limbo of Lost Endeavor, where the souls of
all the Characters go.'

'Characters? What Characters?'

'All the characters that are drawn in books, painted in novels,
sketched in magazine articles, thumb-nailed in *feuilletons* or in
any way created by anybody and everybody who has had the
fortune or misfortune to put his or her writings into print.'

'That sounds like a quotation from a prospectus. What do
you herd Characters for? Aren't there enough souls in the Universe?'

'Who possess souls and who do not? For aught you can
prove, man may be soulless and the creatures he writes about
immortal. Anyhow, about a hundred years after printing became
an established nuisance, the loose Characters used to blow about
interplanetary space in legions which interfered with traffic. So
they were collected, and their charge became mine by right.
Would you care to see them? *Your own are there.*'

'That decides me. But *is* it hotter than Northern India?'

'On my Devildom, no. Put your arms round my neck and sit
tight. I'm going to dive!'

He plunged from the bed headfirst into the floor. There was
a smell of jail-*durrie* [8] and damp earth; and then fell the black
darkness of night.

We stood before a door in a topless wall, from the further side
of which came faintly the roar of infernal fires.

'But you said there was no danger!' I cried in an extremity of
terror.

'No more there is,' said the Devil. 'That's only the Furnace
of First Edition. Will you go on? No other human being has set

375

foot here in the flesh. Let me bring the door to your notice. Pretty design, isn't it? A joke of the Master's.'

I shuddered, for the door was nothing more than a coffin, the backboard knocked out, set on end in the thickness of the wall. As I hesitated, the silence of space was cut by a sharp, shrill whistle, like that of a live shell, which rapidly grew louder and louder. 'Get away from that door,' said the Devil of Discontent quickly. 'Here's a soul coming to its place.' I took refuge under the broad vans of the Devil's wings. The whistle rose to an ear-splitting shriek and a naked soul flashed past me.

'Always the same,' said the Devil quietly. 'These little writers are *so* anxious to reach their reward. H'm, I don't think he likes *his'n*, though.' A yell of despair reached my ears and I shuddered afresh. 'Who was he?' I asked. 'Hack-writer for a pornographic firm in Belgium, exporting to London, you'll understand presently – and now we'll go in,' said the Devil. 'I must apologize for that creature's rudeness. He should have stopped at the distance-signal for line-clear. You can hear the souls whistling there now.'

'Are they the souls of men?' I whispered.

'Yes – writer-men. That's why they are so shrill and querulous. Welcome to the Limbo of Lost Endeavour!'

They passed into a domed hall, more vast than visions could embrace, crowded to its limit by men, women and children. Round the eye of the dome ran, a flickering fire, that terrible quotation from Job: 'Oh, that mine enemy had written a book!'[9]

'Neat, isn't it?' said the Devil, following my glance. 'Another joke of the Master's. Man of *Us*,[10] y' know. In the old days we used to put the Characters into a disused circle of Dante's Inferno, but they grew overcrowded. So Balzac and Théophile Gautier were commissioned to write up this building. It took them three years to complete, and is one of the finest under earth. Don't attempt to describe it unless you are *quite* sure you are equal to Balzac and Gautier in collaboration. Look at the crowds and tell me what you think of them.'

I looked long and earnestly, and saw that many of the multitude were cripples. They walked on their heels or their toes, or with a list to the right or left. A few of them possessed odd eyes and parti-coloured hair; more threw themselves into absurd and impossible attitudes; and every fourth woman seemed to be weeping.

'Who are these?' I said.

'Mainly the population of three-volume novels that never reach the six-shilling stage.[11] See that beautiful girl with one grey eye and one brown, and the black and yellow hair? Let her be an awful warning to you how you correct your proofs. She was created by a careless writer a month ago, and he changed all colours in the second volume. So she came here as you see her. There will be trouble when she meets her author. He can't alter her now, and she says she'll accept no apology.'

'But when will she meet her author?'

'Not in *my* department. Do you notice a general air of expectancy among all the Characters? They are waiting for their authors. Look! That explains the system better than I can.'

A lovely maiden, at whose feet I would willingly have fallen and worshipped, detached herself from the crowd and hastened to the door through which I had just come. There was a prolonged whistle without, a soul dashed through the coffin and fell upon her neck. The girl with the parti-coloured hair eyed the couple enviously as they departed arm in arm to the other side of the hall.

'That man,' said the Devil, 'wrote one magazine story, of twenty-four pages, ten years ago when he was desperately in love with a flesh and blood woman. He put all his heart into the work, and created the girl you have just seen. The flesh and blood woman married someone else and died – it's a way they have – but the man has this girl for his very own, and she will everlastingly grow sweeter.'

'Then the Characters are independent?'

'Slightly! Have you never known one of your Characters – even yours – get beyond control as soon as they are made?'

'That's true. Where are those two happy creatures going?'

'To the Levels. You've heard of authors finding their levels? We keep all the Levels here. As each writer enters, he picks up his Characters, or they pick *him* up, as the case may be, and to the Levels he goes.'

'I should like to see –'

'So you shall, when you come through that door a second time – whistling. I can't take you there now.'

'Do you keep only the Characters of living scribblers in this hall?'

'We should be crowded out if we didn't draft them off some-how. Step this way and I'll take you to the Master. One moment, though. There's John Ridd with Lorna Doone, and there are Mr Maliphant and the Bormalacks – clannish folk, those Besant Characters [12] – don't let the twins talk to you about Literature and Art. Come along. What's here?'

The white face of Mr John Oakhurst,[13] gambler, broke through the press. 'I wish to explain,' said he in a level voice, 'that had I been consulted I should never have blown out my brains with the Duchess and all that Poker Flat lot. I wish to add that the only woman I ever loved was the wife of Brown of Calaveras.' He pressed his hand behind him suggestively. 'All right, Mr Oakhurst,' I said hastily; 'I believe you.' '*Kin* you set it right?' he asked, dropping into the Doric [14] of the Gulches. I caught a trigger's cloth-muffled click. 'Just heavens!' I groaned. 'Must I be shot for the sake of another man's Characters?' Oakhurst levelled his revolver at my head, but the weapon was struck up by the hand of Yuba Bill. 'You durned fool!' said the stage-driver. 'Hevn't I told you no one but a blamed idiot shoots at sight *now*? Let the galoot go. You kin see by his eyes he's no party to your matrimonial arrangements.' Oakhurst re-tired with an irreproachable bow, but in my haste to escape I fell over Caliban,[15] his head in a melon and his tame orc under his arm. He spat like a wildcat.

'Manners none, customs beastly,' said the Devil. 'We'll take the Bishop with us. They all respect the Bishop.' And the great Bishop Blougram joined us, calm and smiling, with the news, for my private ear, that Mr Gigadibs despised him no longer.[16]

We were arrested by a knot of semi-nude Bacchantes kissing

a clergyman. The Bishop's eyes twinkled, and I turned to the Devil for explanation.

'That's Robert Elsmere[17] – what's left of him,' said the Devil. 'Those are French *feuilleton* women and scourings of the Opéra Comique. He has been lecturing 'em, and they don't like it.' 'He lectured *me!*' said the Bishop with a bland smile. 'He has been a nuisance ever since he came here. By the Holy Law of Proportion, he had the audacity to talk to the Master! Called him a "pot-bellied barbarian"! That is why he is walking so stiffly now,' said the Devil. 'Listen! Marie Pigeonnier is swearing deathless love to him. On my word, we ought to segregate the French characters entirely. By the way, your regiment came in very handy for Zola's importations.'[18]

'My regiment?' I said. 'How do you mean?'

'You wrote something about the Tyneside Tail-Twisters, just enough to give the outline of the regiment, and of course it came down here – one thousand and eighty strong. I told it off in hollow squares to pen up the Rougon-Macquart series. There they are.' I looked and saw the Tyneside Tail-Twisters ringing an inferno of struggling, shouting, blaspheming men and women in the costumes of the Second Empire. Now and again the shadowy ranks brought down their butts on the toes of the crowd inside the square, and shrieks of pain followed. 'You should have indicated your men more clearly; they are hardly up to their work,' said the Devil. 'If the Zola tribe increase, I'm afraid I shall have to use up your two companies of the Black Tyrone and two of the Old Regiment.'[19]

'I am proud –' I began.

'Go slow,' said the Devil. 'You won't be half so proud in a little while, and I don't think much of your regiments, anyway. But they are good enough to fight the French. Can you hear Coupeau[20] raving in the left angle of the square? He used to run about the hall seeing pink snakes, till the children's story-book Characters protested. Come along!'

Never since Caxton pulled his first proof and made for the world a new a most terrible God of Labour had mortal man such an experience as mine when I followed the Devil of Discontent through the shifting crowds below the motto of the Dome. A few – a very few – of the faces were of old friends, but there were thousands whom I did not recognize. Men in every conceivable attire and of every possible nationality, deformed by intention, or the impotence of creation that could not create – blind, unclean, heroic, mad, sinking under the weight of remorse or with eyes made splendid by the light of love and fixed endeavour; women fashioned in ignorance and mourning the errors of their creator, life and thought at variance with body and soul; perfect women such as walk rarely upon this earth, and horrors that were women only because they had not sufficient self-control to be fiends; little children, fair as the morning, who put their hands into mine and made most innocent confidences; loathsome, lank-haired infant-saints, curious as to the welfare of my soul, and delightfully mischievous boys, generalled by the irrepressible Tom Sawyer, who played among murderers, harlots, professional beauties, nuns, Italian bandits and politicians of state.

The ordered peace of Arthur's Court was broken up by the incursions of Mr John Wellington Wells, and Dagonet, the jester, found that his antics drew no attention so long as the 'dealer in magic and spells', taking Tristram's harp, sang patter-songs to the Round Table; while a Zulu Impi, headed by Allan Quatermain, wheeled and shouted in sham fight for the pleasure of Little Lord Fauntleroy.[21] Every century and every type was jumbled in the confusion of one colossal fancy-ball where all the characters were living their parts.

'Aye, look long,' said the Devil. 'You will never be able to describe it, and the next time you come you won't have the chance. Look long, and look at' – Good's passing with a maiden of the Zu-Vendi[22] must have suggested the idea – 'look at their legs.' I looked, and for the second time noticed the lameness that seemed to be almost universal in the Limbo of Lost Endeavour. Brave men and stalwart to all appearance had one leg shorter than the other; some paced a few inches above the floor, never touching it, and others found the greatest difficulty in preserving their feet at all. The stiffness and laboured gait of these thousands was pitiful to witness. I was sorry for them. I told the Devil as much.

· 'H'm,' said he reflectively, 'that's the world's work. Rather cockeye, ain't it? They do everything but stand on their feet. *You* could improve them, I suppose?' There was an unpleasant sneer in his tone, and I hastened to change the subject.

'I'm tired of walking,' I said. 'I want to see some of my own characters, and go on to the Master, whoever he may be, afterwards.'

'Reflect,' said the Devil. 'Are you certain – do you know how many they be?'

'No – but I want to see them. That's what I came for.'

'Very well. Don't abuse me if you don't like the view. There are one-and-fifty of your make up²³ to date, and – it's rather an appalling thing to be confronted with fifty-one children. However, here's a special favourite of yours. Go and shake hands with her!'

A limp-jointed, staring-eyed doll was hirpling towards me with a strained smile of recognition. I felt that I knew her only too well – if indeed she were she. 'Keep her off, Devil!' I cried, stepping back. 'I never made *that*!' ' "She began to weep and she began to cry, Lord ha' mercy on me, this is none of I!" ²⁴ You're very rude to – Mrs Hauksbee, and she wants to speak to you,' said the Devil. My face must have betrayed my dismay, for the Devil went on soothingly: 'That's as she *is*, remember. I *knew* you wouldn't like it. Now what will you give if I make her as she ought to be? No, I don't want your soul, thanks. I have it already, and many others of better quality. Will you, when you write your story, own that I am the best and greatest of all the Devils?' The doll was creeping nearer. 'Yes,' I said hurriedly. 'Anything you like. Only I can't stand her in that state.'

'You'll *have* to when you come next again. Look! No connection with Jekyll and Hyde!' The Devil pointed a lean and inky finger towards the doll, and lo! radiant, bewitching, with a smile of dainty malice, her high heels clicking on the floor like castanets, advanced Mrs Hauksbee²⁵ as I had imagined her in the beginning.

'Ah!' she said. 'You are here so soon? Not dead yet? That will come. Meantime, a thousand congratulations. And now, what do you think of me?' She put her hands on her hips, revealed a glimpse of the smallest foot in Simla and hummed: '"Just look at that . . . just look at this! And then you'll see I'm not amiss."'

'She'll use exactly the same words when you meet her next time,' said the Devil warningly. 'You dowered her with any amount of vanity, if you left out – Excuse me a minute! I'll fetch up the rest of your menagerie.' But I was looking at Mrs Hauksbee.

'Well?' she said. '*Am* I what you expected?' I forgot the Devil and all his works,[26] forgot that this was not the woman I had made, and could only murmur rapturously: 'By Jove! You *are* a beauty.' Then, incautiously: 'And you stand on your feet.' 'Good heavens!' said Mrs Hauksbee. 'Would you, at my time of life, have me stand on my head?' She folded her arms and looked me up and down. I was grinning imbecilely – the woman was so alive. 'Talk,' I said absently; 'I want to hear you talk.' 'I am not used to being spoken to like a coolie,' she replied. 'Never mind,' I said, 'that may be for outsiders, but I made you and I've a right –'

'You have a right? You made me? My dear sir, if I didn't know that we should bore each other so inextinguishably here-after I should read you an hour's lecture this instant. You made me! I suppose you will have the audacity to pretend that you understand me – that you *ever* understood me. Oh, man, man – foolish man! If you only knew!'

'Is that the person who thinks he understands us, Loo?' drawled a voice at her elbow. The Devil had returned with a cloud of witnesses, and it was Mrs Mallowe who was speaking.

'I've touched 'em all up,' said the Devil in an aside. 'You couldn't stand 'em raw. But don't run away with the notion that they are your work. I show you what they ought to be. You must find out for yourself how to make 'em so.'

'Am I allowed to remodel the batch – up above?' I asked anxiously.

'*Litera scripta manet.*[27] That's in the Delectus and Eternity.' He turned round to the semi-circle of Characters: 'Ladies and gentlemen, who are all a great deal better than you should be by virtue of *my* power, let me introduce you to your maker. If you have anything to say to him, you can say it.'

'What insolence!' said Mrs Hauksbee between her teeth. 'This isn't a Peterhoff [28] drawing-room. I haven't the slightest intention of being leveed by this person. Polly, come here and we'll watch the animals go by.' She and Mrs Mallowe stood at my side. I turned crimson with shame, for it is an awful thing to see one's Characters in the solid.

'Wal,' said Gilead P. Beck [29] as he passed, 'I would not be you at this *pre*-cise moment of time, not for all the ile in the univarsal airth. *No*, sirr! I thought my dinner-party was soul-shatterin', but it's mush – mush and milk – to your circus. Let the good work go on!'

I turned to the company and saw that they were men and women, standing upon their feet as folks should stand. Again I forgot the Devil, who stood apart and sneered. From the distant door of entry I could hear the whistle of arriving souls, from the semi-darkness at the end of the hall came the thunderous roar of the Furnace of First Edition, and everywhere the restless crowds of Characters muttered and rustled like windblown autumn leaves. But I looked upon my own people and was perfectly content as man could be.

'I have seen you study a new dress with just such an ex-pression of idiotic beatitude,' whispered Mrs Mallowe to Mrs Hauksbee. 'Hush!' said the latter. 'He thinks he understands.' Then to me: 'Please trot them out. Eternity is long enough in all conscience, but that is no reason for wasting it. *Pro*-ceed, or shall I call them up? Mrs Vansuythen, Mr Boult, Mrs Boult, Captain Kurrel and the Major!' The European population in Kashima in the Dosehri hills, the actors in the Wayside Comedy, moved towards me; and I saw with delight that they were human. 'So you wrote about us?' said Mrs Boult. 'About my confession to my husband and my hatred of that Vansuythen woman? Did you think that you understood? Are *all* men such fools?' 'That woman is bad form,' said Mrs Hauksbee, 'but she speaks the truth. I wonder what these soldiers have to say.'

Gunner Barnabas and Private Shacklock[30] stopped, saluted, and hoped I would take no offence if they gave it as their opinion that I had not 'got them down quite right'. I gasped.

A spurred Hussar succeeded, his wife on his arm. It was Captain Gadsby and Minnie, and close behind them swaggered Jack Mafflin, the Brigadier-General[31] in his arms. 'Had the cheek to try to describe our life, had you?' said Gadsby carelessly. 'Ha-hmm! S'pose he understood, Minnie?' Mrs Gadsby raised her face to her husband and murmured: 'I'm *sure* he didn't, Pip,' while Poor Dear Mamma, still in her riding-habit hissed: 'I'm sure he didn't understand *me*.' And these also went their way.

One after another they filed by – Trewinnard, the pet of his Department; Otis Yeere, lean and lanthorn-jawed; Crook O'Neil and Bobby Wick arm in arm; Janki Meah, the blind miner in the Jimahari coal fields; Afzul Khan, the policeman; the murderous Pathan horse-dealer, Durga Dass; the bunnia, Boh Da Thone; the dacoit, Dana Da, weaver of false magic; the Leander of the Barhwi ford; Peg Barney drunk as a coot; Mrs Delville, the dowd; Dinah Shadd, large, red-cheeked and resolute; Simmons, Slane and Losson; Georgie Porgie and his Burmese helpmate; a shadow in a high collar, who was all that I had ever indicated of the Hawley Boy – the nameless men and women who had trod the Hill of Illusion and lived in the Tents of Kedar, and last, His Majesty the King.[32]

Each one in passing told me the same tale, and the burden thereof was: 'You did not understand.' My heart turned sick within me. 'Where's Wee Willie Winkie?' I shouted. 'Little children don't lie.'

A clatter of pony's feet followed, and the child appeared, habited as on the day he rode into Afghan territory to warn Coppy's love against the 'bad men'. 'I've been playing,' he sobbed, 'playing on ve Levels wiv Jackanapes and Lollo,[33] an' *he* says I'm only just borrowed. I'm *isn't* borrowed. I'm Willie Wi-*inkie*! Vere's Coppy?'

'"Out of the mouths of babes and sucklings,"'[34] whispered the Devil, who had drawn nearer. 'You know the rest of the proverb. Don't look as if you were going to be shot in the morning! Here are the last of your gang.'

I turned despairingly to the Three Musketeers,[35] dearest of all my children to me – to Privates Mulvaney, Ortheris and Learoyd. Surely the Three would not turn against me as the others had done! I shook hands with Mulvaney. 'Terence, how goes? Are *you* going to make fun of me, too?' ''Tis not for me to make fun av you, sorr,' said the Irishman, 'knowin' as I *du* know, fwat good frends we've been for the matter av three years.'

'Fower,' said Ortheris, ''twas in the Helanthami barricks, H block, we was become acquaint, an' 'ere's thankin' you kindly for all the beer we've drunk twix' that and now.'

'Four ut is, then,' said Mulvaney. 'He an' Dinah Shadd are your friends, but –' He stood uneasily.

'But what?' I said.

'Savin' your presence, sorr, an' it's more than onwillin' I am to be hurtin' you; you did not ondersthand. On my sowl an' honour, sorr, you did not ondersthand. Come along, you two.'

But Ortheris stayed for a moment to whisper: 'It's Gawd's own trewth, but there's this 'ere to think. 'Tain't the bloomin' belt that's wrong, as Peg Barney sez, when he's up for bein' dirty on p'rade. 'Tain't the bloomin' belt, sir; it's the bloomin' pipeclay.' Ere I could seek an explanation he had joined his companions.

'For a private soldier, a singularly shrewd man,' said Mrs Hauksbee, and she repeated Ortheris's words. The last drop filled my cup, and I am ashamed to say that I bade her be quiet in a wholly unjustifiable tone. I was rewarded by what would have been a notable lecture on propriety, had I not said to the Devil: 'Change that woman to a d – d doll again! Change 'em all back as they were – as they are. I'm sick of them.'

'Poor wretch!' said the Devil of Discontent very quietly. 'They are changed.'

The reproof died on Mrs Hauksbee's lips, and she moved away marionette-fashion, Mrs Mallowe trailing after her. I hastened after the remainder of the Characters, and they were changed indeed – even as the Devil had said, who kept at my side.

They limped and stuttered and staggered and mouthed and. staggered round me, till I could endure no more.

'So I am the master of this idiotic puppet-show, am I?' I said bitterly, watching Mulvaney trying to come to attention by spasms.

'*In saecula saeculorum*,'[36] said the Devil, bowing his head; 'and you needn't kick, my dear fellow, because they will concern no one but yourself by the time you whistle up to the door. Stop reviling me and uncover. Here's the Master!'

Uncover! I would have dropped on my knees, had not the Devil prevented me, at sight of the portly form of Maître François Rabelais, some time Curé of Meudon. He wore a smoke-stained apron of the colours of Gargantua. I made a sign which was duly returned. 'An Entered Apprentice in difficulties with his rough ashlar, Worshipful Sir,[37] explained the Devil. I was too angry to speak.

Said the Master, rubbing his chin: 'Are those things yours?' 'Even so, Worshipful Sir,' I muttered, praying inwardly that the characters would at least keep quiet while the Master was near. He touched one or two thoughtfully, put his hand upon my shoulder and started: 'By the Great Balls of Notre Dame,[38] you are in the flesh – the warm flesh! – the flesh I quitted so long –ah, so long! And you fret and behave unseemly because of these shadows! Listen now! I, even I, would give my Three, Panurge, Gargantua and Pantagruel, for one little hour of the life that is in you. And *I* am the Master!'

. But the words gave me no comfort. I could hear Mrs Mallowe's joints cracking – or it might have been merely her stays.

'Worshipful Sir, he will not believe that,' said the Devil. 'Who live by shadows lust for shadows. Tell him something more to his need.'

The Master grunted contemptuously: 'And he is flesh and blood! Know this, then. The First Law is to make them stand upon their feet, and the Second is to make them stand upon their feet, and the Third is to make them stand upon their feet.

But, for all that, Trajan is a fisher of frogs.'[39] He passed on, and I could hear him say to himself: 'One hour – one minute – of life in the flesh, and I would sell the Great Perhaps thrice over!'

'Well,' said the Devil, 'you've made the Master angry, seen about all there is to be seen, except the Furnace of First Edition, and, as the Master is in charge of that, I should avoid it. Now you'd better go. You know what you ought to do?'

'I don't need all Hell –'

'Pardon me. Better men than you have called this Paradise.'

'All *Hell*, I said, and the Master to tell me what I knew before. What I want to know is *how*?' 'Go and find out,' said the Devil. We turned to the door, and I was aware that my Characters had grouped themselves at the exit. 'They are going to give you an ovation. Think o' that, now!' said the Devil. I shuddered and dropped my eyes, while one-and-fifty voices broke into a wailing song, whereof the words, so far as I recollect, ran:

> But we brought forth and reared in hours
> Of change, alarm, surprise.
> What shelter to grow ripe is ours –
> What leisure to grow wise?[40]

I ran the gauntlet, narrowly missed collision with an impetuous soul (I hoped he liked his Characters when he met them), and flung free into the night, where I should have knocked my head against the stars. But the Devil caught me.

The brain-fever bird was fluting across the grey, dewy lawn, and the punkah had stopped again. 'Go to Jehannum and get another man to pull,' I said drowsily. 'Exactly,' said a voice from the inkpot.

Now the proof that this story is absolutely true lies in the fact that there will be no other to follow it.

Notes

Introduction

1. *contradictory of itself*: Henry James, Introduction to *Mine Own People*, 1891, quoted in *Kipling: The Critical Heritage*, p. 160.
2. *important paper*: Kipling, *Something of Myself*, Penguin, 1987, p. 77.
3. *a vengeance*: *Something of Myself*, pp. 74–5.
4. *tells us*: *Kipling: The Critical Heritage*, p. 104.
5. *sickness*: *Something of Myself*, pp. 76–7.
6. *style*: The advertisement in *Wee Willie Winkie* in 1888 for the other works in the Indian Railway series describes them as 'illustrations of the four main features of Anglo-Indian life, viz., the Military, Domestic, Native and Social'.
7. *English Balzac*: *Kipling: The Critical Heritage*, p. 69.
8. *Wilson pointed out*: *The Strange Ride of Rudyard Kipling*, p. 113. Wilson judges only 'A Wayside Comedy' to be in this category.
9. *Indian Railway series*: Relevant details of original places of publication will be found in the notes to each of the stories.
10. *Indian one*: Charles Carrington, in his biography, p. 44, explains that he uses '"Anglo-Indian" . . . as Kipling and his contemporaries always used it, to signify an Englishman residing in India'.
11. Kim: The stories mentioned are in *Plain Tales from the Hills*, the *In Black and White* sequence in *Soldiers Three* and *Life's Handicap*, respectively. 'The Man who would be King' contains *Wee Willie Winkie*'s one passing reference to a liaison with a local girl, and it precipitates the final tragedy.
12. *Dominant Race*: The idea of the dominant race became an influential, if not a dominant theory in the latter half of the nineteenth century in British India. See the view of Brigadier-General Jacob: 'We hold India . . . by being in reality, as in reputation, a superior race to the Asiatic; and if this natural superiority did not exist, we should not, and could not, hold the country for one week . . . Away, then, with the assumption of equality; and let us accept our true position as a dominant race' (*The Views and Opinions of Brigadier-General John Jacob, CB*, London, 1858, p. 2).

13. *seventh commandment*: For the Preface, see *Under the Deodars*, note 2.
14. *illicit affairs*: Jarrell, *Kipling, Auden & Co*, p. 354.
15. *love affair*: Carrington, *Rudyard Kipling*, p. 142; Jarrell, ibid, p. 351.
16. *economy of implication*: *Something of Myself*, p. 75.
17. *Bovary*: In a letter to Edmonia Hill on 24 April 1888, that is, a couple of months after this story was published, Kipling, in a tone of evident disapproval, mentions having recently read Flaubert's novel (Kipling Collection, Sussex University Library).
18. Divine Comedy: Elsie B. Adams, 'No Exit: an explication of Kipling's "Wayside Comedy"', *English Literature in Transition*, Vol. 11, no. 3, pp. 180–3.
19. *the like*: The newspaper sketch had the same title as this story, and can now be found in one of the scrap-books of Kipling's Indian work in Sussex University Library.
20. *prize tone*: The *Athenaeum* is quoted in *A Kipling Companion*, p. 113; Wilson, *The Strange Ride of Rudyard Kipling*, p. 78.
21. *Kipling had created*: Charles Carrington, *Rudyard Kipling*, p. 152.
22. *I do not know*: *Something of Myself*, p. 71.
23. *another man's skin*: Ibid, p. 157.
24. *the raj*: Cornell, in *Kipling in India*, p. 106, has praised the way Kipling has improved on Poe by making the tale take place in Simla, rather than 'the vaguely Gothic world of the conventional nineteenth-century tale of terror'.
25. *philosophy*: Walter Lawrence, *The India We Served*, London, 1928, p. 42.
26. *twenty years earlier*: Louis Cornell has praised the way Kipling adapts the Poe formula to express a 'genuine Anglo-Indian nightmare', in *Kipling in India*, p. 105, and Angus Wilson discusses it in relation to memories of the Mutiny in *The Strange Ride of Rudyard Kipling*, p. 72, which was, of course, named after this tale. Wilson calls the tale 'one of the most powerful nightmares of the precariousness of a ruling group, in this case a group haunted by memories of the Mutiny not yet twenty years old.'
27. *at its worst*: S. S. Husain, *Kipling and India*, Dacca, 1964, p. 96.
28. *the Mutiny*: This is documented in Eric Stokes' classic study, *The English Utilitarians in India*.
29. *own beliefs*: Kipling expresses views not unlike those of Jukes in his long political letter in defence of British imperialism in India, written to Margaret Burne-Jones on 28 November 1885, now in the Kipling Collection at Sussex University Library.

30. *success*: *Something of Myself*, p. 72.
31. *travelling Masons*: Letter to Margaret Burne-Jones, January 1888, Kipling Collection, Sussex University Library.
32. *King*: *English Literary History*, 25, 1958.
33. *December 1883*: Reprinted in P. E. Howard's *Memoir of W. W. McNair, First Explorer of Kafiristan*, London, 1889.
34. *moral authority*: 'The Kipling that Nobody Read', *The Wound and the Bow*, p. 16.
35. Frontier: C. C. Davies, *The North-West Frontier*, Cambridge University Press, 1932, p. 42.
36. *Tribes of Israel*: See 'The Propagation of Knowledge' (1926), *Debits and Credits*, Penguin, 1987, p. 204.
37. *correctly*: For the Preface, see *Wee Willie Winkie and Other Stories*, note 1.
38. *about them*: Quoted in *A Kipling Companion*, p. 134.
39. Little Lord Fauntleroy: Charles Carrington, *Rudyard Kipling*, p. 141.
40. *Second Afghan War*: Carrington, 'Kipling and the Army in India', *The Reader's Guide to Rudyard Kipling's Work*, ed. R. L. Green, Kipling Society, Vol. 1.
41. Indostan: Published in 1786; Vol. 3, p. 486.
42. *near-disaster*: Wilson, pp. 84–5.
43. *he opposes*: Babel's admiration for Kipling is documented in K. Paustovsky's 'Reminiscences of Babel', cited in Steven Marcus' *Representations: Essays on Literature and Society*, New York, Random House, p. 74.
44. *those days*: Edmonia Hill, 'The Young Kipling', *Rudyard Kipling: Interviews and Recollections*, Vol. 1, pp. 102–3.
45. *forty years later*: See '"Baa Baa, Black Sheep" – Fact or Fiction?', *Kipling Journal*, Vol. 39, no. 182, p. 7ff.
46. Recollections: *Interviews and Recollections*, Vol. 1, pp. 5–14.
47. *Winnicott*: Edmund Wilson, 'The Kipling that Nobody Read', *The Wound and the Bow*. Interestingly, the psychoanalyst Wilfrid Bion describes his own Anglo–Indian childhood in ways that are closely modelled on Kipling's story, in his autobiography, *The Long Week-End, 1897–1919*, Fleetwood, 1982.
48. *should be that*: *Rudyard Kipling: Interviews and Recollections*, Vol. 1, p. 10.
49. *dictatorship*: D. W. Winnicott, *The Child, the Family and the Outside World*, Penguin, 1964.

1. *Under the Deodars*: The title refers to the large cedar trees native
to the western Himalayas, for which the Simla region was famous.
It might call up memories of 'Army Headquarters' in Kipling's
Departmental Ditties, a satire on an Anglo-Indian careerist called
Ahasuerus Jenkins: 'He took two months at Simla when the year
was at the spring, / And underneath the deodars eternally did
sing. / He warbled like a *bul-bul* but particularly at / Cornelia Ag-
gripina, who was musical and fat.' Through Cornelia's patronage
Jenkins leaves his regiment for a plum administrative job, and
becomes 'a Power in the State'.

'Under the Deodars' was originally published with the following
Preface:

Strictly speaking there should be no preface to this, because it deals with things
that are not pretty and ugliness that hurts. But it may be as well to try to assure
the ill-formed that India is not entirely inhabited by men and women playing
tennis with the Seventh Commandment; while it is a fact that many of the lads
in the land can be trusted to bear themselves as bravely on occasion as did my
friend the late Robert Hanna Wick. The drawback of collecting dirt in one
corner is that it gives a false notion of the filth of the room. Folk who understand
and have knowledge of their own, will be able to strike fair averages. The
opinions of people who do not understand are somewhat less valuable.

In regard to the idea of the book, I have no hope that the stories will be
of the least service to any one. They are meant to be read in railway trains
and are arranged and adorned to that end. They ought to explain that there
is no particular profit in going wrong at any time, under any circumstances
or for any consideration. But that is a large text to handle at popular prices;
and if I have made the first rewards of folly seem too inviting, my inability
and not my intention is to blame.

Rudyard Kipling

2. The City of Dreadful Night: The epigraph is from 'The City of
Dreadful Night' by James Thomson (1834–82), a poem that in
adolescence shook Kipling to his 'unformed core' (*Something of Myself*, p. 52). It is slightly misquoted from Section XIII of the poem.

The Education of Otis Yeere

1. *The Education of Otis Yeere*: Originally published in two parts in
the *Week's News*, 10 and 17 March 1888, with the headings, 'Show-

ing how the great idea was born' and 'Showing what was born of the great idea'. The uncollected story, 'A Supplementary Chapter', in the Appendix, is a kind of sequel to it.

2. *In the pleasant . . . degree*: 'The Lost Bower' is by Elizabeth Barrett Browning (1806–61). The lines are from the opening stanza and are quoted again in 'They' (*Traffics and Discoveries*, 1904) where they have a profoundly nostalgic effect on the narrator: '. . . all my early summer came back at the call.'

3. *Fallen Angel . . . Gaiety Theatre*: The New Gaiety Theatre in the Simla Town Hall was completed in 1887, and Kipling played a leading role in an adaptation of a Sardou play in August of that year, one of a cast that included Mrs Burton, the supposed prototype of Mrs Hauksbee. The play's title, however, seems to be fictitious.

4. *Mrs Hauksbee*: First introduced in a story called 'Three and – an Extra', printed in the *Civil and Military Gazette* in November 1886, Mrs Hauksbee plays a leading role in four of the *Plain Tales from the Hills* (1888), as well as this story, 'A Second-Rate Woman' later in the collection, and 'A Supplementary Chapter' and 'Mrs Hauksbee Sits Out', both of which are included in the Appendix. She is described briefly in 'Three and – an Extra': 'Mrs Hauksbee appeared on the horizon; and where she existed was fair chance of trouble. At Simla her by-name was "the Stormy Petrel". She had won that title five times to my own certain knowledge. She was a little, brown, thin, almost skinny, woman, with big, rolling, violet-blue eyes, and the sweetest manners in the world. You had only to mention her name at afternoon teas for every woman in the room to rise up and call her not blessed. She was clever, witty, brilliant, and sparkling beyond most of her kind; but possessed of many devils of malice and mischievousness. She could be nice, though, even to her own sex. But that is another story.'

5. *tiffin*: The standard Anglo-Indian word for 'lunch', probably derived from earlier English slang: Francis Grose in his *Dictionary of the Vulgar Tongue* (1785) has: '*Tiffin*, eating or drinking out of meals.'

6. *chiffons*: *Not* of course French for 'mysteries', but 'lace' or 'rags'. The phrase half-anglicizes the French Phrase, '*causer chiffons*', which means 'to talk dress'.

7. *Hawley Boy*: A young British officer who appears in four other stories involving Mrs Hauksbee in *Plain Tales from the Hills*, and 'Mrs Hauksbee Sits Out'.

8. *Tyrconnel*: An Aide-de-camp at either the Commander-in-Chief's or viceroy's official residence at Simla.

9. *The Mussuck*: 'The leather water-bag, consisting of the entire skin of a large goat, stript of the hair and dressed'; a name derived from Hindustani *mashak*. (Yule and Burnell, *Hobson-Jobson*). The two women use it as a nickname for 'the venerable Indian administrator' mentioned on p. 74.

10. *duff*: A boiled pudding.

11. *the other two things*: i.e., the flesh and the devil: an allusion to the 'deceits of the world, the flesh and the devil,' of the Anglican Book of Common Prayer.

12. *Rome*: i.e., the Roman Catholic Church.

13. *a Power*: Like Ahasuerus Jenkins in the poem 'Army Headquarters', who ends as 'a Power in the State', at Simla.

14. *Baruch*: Advising Lucy Hauksbee to 'turn religious', Mrs Mallowe specializes in twisting biblical allusions to her purposes. This mock-biblical address mixes up 'the Preacher' of Ecclesiastes 1 with 'Baruch the son of Neriah' who 'wrote from the mouth of Jeremiah all the words of the Lord' in Jeremiah 36:4.

15. *convicts*: The idea of Anglo-Indian officials as 'gilded convicts' under a knout is developed in the 1890 poem, 'The Galley Slave'.

16. *Detestable word*: 'Culture' had gained renewed currency by Arnold's *Culture and Anarchy* (1869), but was regarded with suspicion by the assertively 'philistine' ethos of Anglo-India. In *Something of Myself*, Kipling describes the Pre-Raphaelite group that the Burne-Jones' household was part of as 'filled with books, peace, kindliness, patience and what today would be called "culture"' (p. 45).

17. *teapoys*: Small, three-legged tables (from the Hindustani *tipai*, for a 'tripod').

18. darwaza band: 'The door is closed'; the 'formula by which a native servant in an Anglo-Indian household' intimates that his master or mistress is 'not at home' to visitors (*Hobson-Jobson*).

19. *Peliti's*: A famous restaurant and café on the Mall at Simla, described as 'the traditional hotbed of gossip, where an excellent view might be obtained of the current scandal' (James Morris, *Pax Britannica: The Climax of an Empire*, London, 1979, p. 265).

20. khud: A steep hillside or cliff: 'in constant Anglo-Indian colloquial use at Simla and other Himalayan hill-stations' (*Hobson-Jobson*).

21. kala juggahs: Literally, 'dark places'. 'The British in India had a curious convention at all dances, where sitting places known as *kalla juggahs* were constructed. These were cosy, sheltered-off places where you were allowed to disappear with your partner' (*Plain Tales from the Raj*, p. 158).

22. *Conclusion thereof*: An allusion to Ecclesiastes 1:2 ('Vanity of vanities, saith the Preacher . . . all is vanity') and 12:13 ('Let us hear the conclusion of the whole matter: Fear God, and keep his commandments').

23. *Abana and Pharpar*: An allusion to II Kings 5:12: 'Are not Abana and Pharpar, rivers of Damascus, better than all the waters of Israel? may I not wash in them, and become clean?'

24. *Seepee*: According to Sir Edward Buck in *Simla, Past and Present*, 'a small, tea-cup-shaped valley, shaded by magnificent deodars', below the quiet nearby resort of Mashobra.

25. gharri: A carriage, cart or other similar vehicle.

26. Padri: i.e., Padre.

27. *six-eight*: i.e., six rupees, eight annas.

28. *Theosophists*: Adherents of 'Theosophy', and followers of Madame Blavatsky (1831–91) author of *Isis Unveiled* (1875) and founder of the 'Theosophical Society'. Influenced by Buddhist and Brahamanic thinking, theosophy was an 'amalgam of Egyptian, cabalistic, occultist, Indian and modern spiritualistic ideas and formulas' (*Encylopaedia Britannica*, 1902). It was hugely successful in New York and London and, after Madame Blavatsky's visit to India in 1877, also in British India, where she established a Theosophical Temple near Madras in 1879. Kipling recalls its vogue briefly in his autobiography: 'At one time our little world was full of the aftermaths of Theosophy as taught by Madame Blavatsky to her devotees,' she being 'one of the most interesting and unscrupulous imposters' his father had ever met (*Something of Myself* p. 67).

29. *friend*: An allusion to *An Essay on Man* by Alexander Pope (1688–1744), Epistle IV, lines 387–90:

> When statesmen, heroes, kings, in dust repose,
> Whose suns shall blush their fathers were thy foes,
> Shall then this verse to future age pretend
> Thou wert my guide, philosopher and friend?

30. Nursery Rhyme: Kipling makes frequent play with nursery rhymes in his titles and epigraphs to stories (e.g., 'Wee Willie Winkie', and 'Georgie Porgie'), but this one is untraced and may be his own. It is, however, just the kind of jingle recorded in Iona and Peter Opie's *Language and Lore of Schoolchildren*.

31. *Simon Stylites*: A fifth-century Christian hermit who lived on top of a pillar, subject of a famous dramatic monologue of the same name by Tennyson, published in 1842. Tennyson's saint counts

up the years spent in his 'high nest of penance', Mrs Hauksbee prefers to leave the number of years spent 'looking down' on men a tactful blank.

32. *I'll go . . . ironical*: From the contemporary operatic hit, *Patience* (1881), by W. S. Gilbert and Arthur Sullivan. The line is from Act II: 'I'll go to him and say to him with compliment most ironical'.

33. *Monday Pop*: A popular concert – as in W. S. Gilbert's: 'Who thinks suburban hops more fun than Monday Pops.'

34. *Milton Wellings*: A successful popular composer and song-writer of the time.

35. burra-khana: Literally, 'a big dinner'; a formal dinner-party.

36. à la Gibbon: Presumably an allusion to Edward Gibbon (1737–94), the author of *The History of the Decline and Fall of the Roman Empire*. According to Mme de Genlis, Gibbon was too fat to rise from his knees when invited to do so after proposing marriage to Mme de Crousaz, and replied, '*Madame, je ne peux pas.*'

37. *first . . . rapture*: A quotation from 'Home Thoughts from Abroad' by Robert Browning (1812–89).

38. '*Stunt*: A jocular abbreviation of 'Assistant' Collector.

39. *Stars*: Commissioners are senior civil servants with responsibility for a division, each division being made up of several districts supervised by district officers. Stars were the official rewards for high office, like the Companion of the Order of the Star of India awarded to Mr Wick, in 'Only a Subaltern, who'd been a 'Commissioner in his day' (p. 137).

40. ryot: Indian peasant farmer, cultivating tenant, seen by the British after the Mutiny of 1857 as the real backbone of native India, in contrast to educated Indians or effeminate Bengalis.

41. *Punjabis*: Inhabitants of the Punjab, here British civil servants working in the Punjab – in Kipling's day regarded as the cream of the service, unlike poor Yeere's Bengalis.

42. *Ditcher*: A 'disparaging sobriquet' for Calcutta's 'European citizens' (*Hobson–Jobson*). The name derives from the defensive Mahratta ditch, dug in the eighteenth century around the landward-side of Calcutta.

43. *Civilians*: Members of the Civil Service, especially its élite section, the covenanted civil service, staffed almost exclusively by the British.

44. *Member of Council*: After the Indian Councils Act of 1861, the Supreme Government of India was in the hands of the governor-general (or Viceroy) and his council of five or six ordinary mem-

bers, appointed by the crown, with the commander-in-chief as an extraordinary member.

45. *Jeshurun*: An allusion to Deuteronomy 32:15: 'But Jeshurun waxed fat, and kicked ... then he forsook God which made him, and lightly esteemed the Rock of his salvation.'

46. *native pleader*: standard Anglo-Indian term for an Indian lawyer. Native lawyers played an important part in organizing the National Congress, the centre of Indian political consciousness after 1885, and in advocating Indian as against simply government interests. They were generally perceived by the British as suspect, unreliable and potentially subversive.

47. *Gymkhana*: According to *Hobson-Jobson*, 'a factitious' and 'modern' word, 'applied to a place of public resort in a station, where the needful facilities for athletics and games' like tennis and cricket are provided.

48. haramzadas: Bastards, scoundrels; a common term of abuse, of Arabic and Persian provenance.

49. *Providence*: Or, according to Genesis I, 'God'. In *Life's Handicap*, Kipling records the view that the 'control of Providence ceases' east of Suez, 'the Church of England Providence only exercising an occasional and modified supervision in the case of Englishmen'.

50. *Annandale*: The racecourse and sports ground outside Simla.

51. *Mrs Browning*: The first stanza of 'A False Step' from her *Last Poems* (1862). Its last stanza confirms how 'well chosen' it is:

> Thou'lt sigh, very like, on thy part,
> 'Of all I have known or can know,
> I wish I had only that Heart
> I trod upon ages ago!'

At the Pit's Mouth

1. *At the Pit's Mouth*: First published in *Under the Deodars*, though deriving in part from an MS of 1884 now in the Berg Collection in New York. The setting of the story is the New Simla Cemetery, but it may owe something to Kipling's account of the Old Cemetery there, 'Out of Society', written for the *Pioneer*, 14 August 1886 (reprinted in *Kipling's India: Uncollected Sketches 1884–88*).

'The Pit' of the title refers to the open grave encountered in the cemetery (as in Psalm 30:3; 'O Lord, thou hast brought up my soul from the grave . . . that I should not go down to the pit'), but would also seem to recall the punishments of hell (the 'profoundest pit' of *Hamlet*, IV.v.132) and the Old Testament morality of Proverbs 22:14 (see introduction, p. 25).

2. *Men say . . . Enderby*: From 'The High Tide on the Coast of Lincolnshire' by Jean Ingelow (1820–97), rearranged by Kipling.

3. *Tertium Quid*: Latin for 'some third thing', used in philosophical and scientific contexts to represent 'something (indefinite and unknown) related in some way to two (definite and known) things, but distinct from both' (OED).

4. *Plains*: In the summer months, government officials, women and men on leave, took to the hill-resorts in northern India on the fringes of the Himalayas in order to escape from the extreme heat of the burning plains. The opposition of hills and plains, and their alternation in the rhythm of the normal Anglo-Indian year, is crucial to Kipling's Indian work.

5. *Jakko . . . gap*: Names of familiar landmarks and beauty spots round Simla. The Tara Devi gap is about four miles to the south.

6. *banian*: 'An undershirt, originally of muslin . . . resembling the body garment of Hindus'; a vest (*Hobson-Jobson*).

7. *Cantonments*: Permanent military stations, usually located just outside big towns.

8. *Fagoo*: As this is nine miles east of Christ Church, this is the furthest afield they've gone 'out of society'.

9. *Himalayan-Thibet Road*: Described as a 'bridle-road' in *The Imperial Gazetteer*, this led north-east towards Rampur and the Tibet border.

10. *the world*: The Tibetan border is 'the end of the world' of British India (compare with Wee Willie Winkie, who sees the North-West Frontier as 'the end of all the Earth', p. 254).

11. *nine hundred feet below*: Murray's *Handbook for Travellers in India*, published in 1891, warned visitors to Simla that 'a number of people have been killed by falling over precipices at this station, and many more have had narrow escapes of their lives.'

12. *funeral*: The ironic use of the dug grave is also used in a story called 'The Pit that they Digged', included in the Sussex Edition of *Wee Willie Winkie*.

A Wayside Comedy

1. *A Wayside Comedy*: First published in the *Week's News*, 21 January 1888. It is another of those classified in Kipling's autobiography as 'tales of the opposite sex'.
2. *Because . . . upon him*: The preceeding verse from Ecclesiastes 8 is: 'Whoso keepeth the commandment shall feel no evil thing: and a wise man's heart discerneth time and judgment.'
3. jhils: Marshy ponds.
4. *You must remember*: This paragraph was added in the Indian Railway Library edition of 1888 with a further sentence, after 'public opinion', which was cut in 1895. It read: 'If the Israelites had been only a tent camp of gypsies their Headman would never have taken the trouble to climb a hill and bring down a Lithographed edition of the Decalogue, and a great deal of trouble would have been avoided.' Presumably, this was considered too risqué.
5. *immemorial usage*: Francis Hutchins entitled his study of British Imperialism in India *The Illusion of Permanence* (Princeton, 1967). This phrase was added in the 1895 edition, to replace 'etiquette'.
6. dâk: Literally, 'post' or 'mail'; here it means 'journey', below, 'means of transport for a journey'.
7. terai *hat*: A broad-rimmed tropical hat named after the Terai, a region of marshy jungle to the south of the Himalayas.
8. purdah: A curtain, especially a door-curtain.
9. *mashing*: Courting, ogling a woman.
10. sais: Groom.

The Hill of Illusion

1. *The Hill of Illusion*: First published in the *Week's News*, 21 April 1888, headed by the epigraph from Ecclesiastes now used for 'A Wayside Comedy'. For title, see Introduction, p. 27.
2. *What rendered . . . sea*: Slightly misquoted from the last verse of the fifth poem of *Switzerland*, by Matthew Arnold. The verse begins: 'Who order'd that their longing's fire / Should be as soon as kindled, cool'd.'
3. *HE*: The entire story is written as a dramatic dialogue, a method Kipling was to use in a more extended fashion in 'The Story of the Gadsbys' later in 1888 (*Soldiers Three*).
4. jhampanies: Rickshaw coolies.

5. *Tonga*: A small, light, two-wheeled vehicle drawn by a pony.
6. *Kalka*: The names mentioned are stations between Simla and Bombay. The simple arrangements for the honeymoon trip read differently in the original newspaper version. This paragraph then read: 'down straight by night-train to Calcutta, and then the steamer of the 20th for Home, by the long passage. That's my idea. Yokohama and San Francisco – a ten-week honeymoon.' Since this was to be Kipling's itinerary on his way home in 1889, he may have thought it tactful to alter the details of the story to prevent his being identified with the 'He' of the elopement.
7. *Kind ... gown Sir*: From 'My Jo Janet', a Scottish folk-song, collected in Joseph Ritson's *Scotish Song*, 1794.
8. *Keek*: Ibid.
9. kutcha: The opposite of *pukka*, meaning 'crude, raw, rough'; a *kutcha* road would be earthwork only.
10. *matrimony*: A phrase from the Church of England marriage service.
11. *Pendant ... avant*: 'For a whole year / The regiment didn't come back. / It was reported missing / To the Ministry of War. / They had given it up for lost, / When suddenly one morning / It reappeared in the Square / With the Colonel still at its head.' The source of the song is unidentified.
12. *Keene*: Henry G. Keene, a writer who specialized in Indian subjects, the author of *A Sketch of the History of Hindustan* (1885) and an *Oriental Biographical Dictionary* (1881).
13. con molt. exp: 'With great expression'; an Italian musical marking, applied ironically to Mrs Buzgago's rendition of the old nursery-rhyme, 'See-saw! Margery Daw!' 'A Daw' is a 'lazy person, a sluggard', in Scotland 'an untidy woman, slut, slattern' (OED).

A Second-Rate Woman

1. *A Second-Rate Woman*: First published in the *Week's News*, 8 September 1888.
2. Master Hugues of Saxe-Gotha: A poem by Robert Browning.
3. *Stay me ... I am*: An allusion to The Song of Solomon 2.5: 'Stay me with flagons, comfort me with apples: for I am sick of love.' Fondants are soft sweets that melt in the mouth.
4. *Shigramitish*: In the Book of Numbers, an Israelite is found with a 'Midianitish woman' and accused of 'committing whoredom' with

the daughters of Moab; as a result they were both executed (Numbers 25). In Mrs Hauksbee's variant of the word, the women are related to the *shigram*, 'a kind of hack palankin carriage' (*Hobson-Jobson*) often drawn by bullocks, i.e., socially inferior.

5. *Otis Yeere*: 'recorded' in 'The Education of Otis Yeere', pp. 67 to 88.
6. *femme incomprise*: French for a 'misunderstood woman'.
7. *Higher Standard*: An examination taken by army officers.
8. *whom Mrs Hauksbee . . . asunder*: A travesty of the marriage service of the Anglican Church: 'Whom God hath joined together let no man put asunder.' Mrs Hauksbee succeeds in joining this couple together in 'Mrs Hauksbee Sits Out'.
9. *detrimental*: Ineligible suitor; 'A detrimental, in genteel slang, is a lover, who, owing to his poverty, is ineligible as a husband; or one who professes to pay attentions to a lady without serious intention of marriage' (*Household Words*, ed., Charles Dickens, 1886).
10. *sleeping . . . in the sun*: Perhaps a garbled recollection of Prince Hal's remark to Falstaff about 'unbuttoning . . . after supper, and sleeping upon benches after noon' (*Henry IV*, Part I, 1.ii. 2–3).
11. *Elective affinities*: An allusion to the English title of Goethe's novel *Die Wahlverwandtschaften* (1809), describing a married couple's 'elective affinities' for two other people.
12. *in the country*: i.e., in India, though of British parents. The implication is that she has not been sent 'Home' to Britain to be educated, and is therefore definitely lower-caste.
13. *his folly*: An allusion to Proverbs 26:5: 'Answer a fool according to his folly, lest he be wise in his own conceit.'
14. *her dress bewrays her*: An allusion to St Matthew 26:73: 'And after a while came unto him they that stood by, and said to Peter, Surely thou also art one of them; for thy speech bewrayeth thee'.
15. *supplément*: Padding to exaggerate a woman's bust.
16. What shall . . . Deer: a quotation from *As You Like It* (IV.ii.10) where the question receives an answer: 'His leather skin and horns to wear.'
17. *peace with honour*: Alluding to Disraeli's announcement in 1878: 'Lord Salisbury and myself have brought you back peace – but a peace I hope with honour.'
18. *tikka dhurzie*: Hired tailor.
19. *lilies of the field*: An allusion to St Matthew 6:28–9: 'Consider the lilies of the field, how they grow; they toil not, neither do they spin: And yet . . . even Solomon in all his glory was not arrayed like one of these.'

20. tête-fêlée: French for crack-brained.

21. khitmatgars: House-servants.

22. *God gie . . . oorselves*: The phrase is quoted by Burns in a letter of 7 March 1783: 'Lord, send us a gude conceit o' oursel'!'

23. *If in . . . them all*: A travesty of lines from the *Rape of the Lock* by Alexander Pope: 'If to her share some female errors fall, / Look on her face, and you'll forget 'em all' (Canto II, 17–18).

24. *lone, lorn grass-widow*: An allusion to Mrs Gummidge's ceaseless refrain, 'I am a lone lorn creetur'', in Charles Dickens' *David Copperfield* 'Grass-widow' is an Anglo-Indian expression for a 'married woman temporarily away from her husband' (Partridge, *Dictionary of Slang and Unconventional English*).

25. *kanats*: Canvas enclosures.

26. *more quickly . . . presently mad*: The phrase telescopes two Shakespearian quotations, Olivia's 'Even so quickly may one catch the plague?' from *Twelfth Night* (I.v.281) and Beatrice's, 'He is sooner caught than the pestilence, and the taker runs presently mad,' from *Much Ado About Nothing* (I.i.76–7).

27. *Condy's Fluid*: A well-known brand of disinfectant.

28. *Goddess from the Machine*: Translated from the Latin *dea* (more usually *deus*) *ex machina*; a reference to the intervention of some unlikely, usually supernatural, event, or person, originally in classical theatre, to resolve difficulties in the plot. Kipling wrote a story called 'The God from the Machine' (*Soldiers Three*) which had been published in the *Week's News* earlier in 1888.

29. *Valley of Humiliation*: In the *Pilgrim's Progress* by John Bunyan (1628–88), the hero Christian has to confront the 'foule Fiend' Appollyon in the valley of Humiliation: 'it is an hard matter for a man to go down into the valley of Humiliation'.

30. *Paltry*: The anecdote is based upon a real incident, and Kipling wrote it up with relish in a letter, dated 27 June 1888, to his American friend Mrs Edmonia Hill.

31. *Don't ask me*: In the *Week's News* and the Railway Library edition there was another brief sentence after this one, which was cut in 1895: 'She was a woman.'

Only a Subaltern

1. *Only a Subaltern*: First published in the *Week's News*, 25 August 1888. It originally had an epigraph from the German poet Karl Theodore

Korner (1791–1813), 'I had a living comrade', which was replaced by the present epigraph in the Railway Library edition (1888).

2. *Tyneside Tail Twisters*: A fictitious regiment, probably based on the Northumberland Fusiliers who were stationed at Mian Mir near Lahore from 1886 to 1888, and were much frequented by Kipling.

3. *Krab Bokhar*: A fictitious name, derived from the Hindustani for 'bad fever'.

4. *two blades . . . before*: An allusion to the words of the King of Brobdingnag in *Gulliver's Travels* by Jonathan Swift (1667–1745). He said: 'whoever could make two ears of corn or two blades of grass to grow upon a spot of ground where only one grew before, would deserve better of mankind, and do more essential service to his country than the whole race of politicians put together' (Book II, Chapter 7) – Kipling's apologia for a British commissioner of the raj.

5. *stick . . . the Line*: The Line refers to the infantry regiments of the British army. Papa Wicks of course replaces 'the truth' by Regimental Loyalty when he appropriates the oath sworn in British courts to 'speak the truth, the whole truth and nothing but the truth'.

6. *liberty-men*: Sailors on shore-leave.

7. *double-dashed*: Like 'three stars', 'condemned', 'qualified' 'hiatused' and 'foresaken', a euphemistic equivalent of 'expletive deleted', to convey the colonel's grasp of military invective.

8. *markhor-horn snuff-mull*: A snuff-box made of the horn of a wild mountain-goat.

9. *one thousand and eighty*: i.e., full regimental strength.

10. *Hogan-Yale . . . Tick Boileau*: Hogan-Yale also appears in 'The Rout of the White Hussars' in *Plain Tales*; 'Tick' Boileau features in 'The Unlimited Draw of Tick Boileau' (from *Quartette*, 1885) and 'A Conference of Powers' (*Many Inventions*).

11. *Walers*: Cavalry horses named after New South Wales, where they mainly came from.

12. *Sikh Regiment*: One of the native regiments which made up the majority of the Indian army, though rarely portrayed by Kipling.

13. *hortomato*: i.e., automaton.

14. *stoppages*: Sums 'stopped' or deducted from a soldier's pay as punishment.

15. dhoni; A flat-bottomed fishing-boat.

16. *gallantry-show*: More usually 'galanty show', a shadow pantomime or magic-lantern show.

17. *Leave the . . . altar*: A slightly garbled version of the 'Pibroch of Donald Dhu' by Sir Walter Scott (1771–1832): 'Leave untended the herd, / The flock without shelter; / Leave the corpse uninterr'd, / The bride at the altar.'

18. *Doab*: The land between two confluent rivers.

19. *Naini Tal*: A hill-station near the Nepalese border, summer headquarters of the United Provinces Government.

20. *the sickness . . . noonday*: A garbled allusion to Psalm 91:5–6: 'Thou shalt not be afraid for the terror by night . . . Nor for the pestilence that walketh in darkness; nor for the destruction that wasteth at noonday.'

21. *Regulations*: Quoted in the epigraph to the story, the Army Regulations.

22. Tattoo lao: 'Get my pony.'

23. *doolie-bearers*: A doolie is a covered litter, carried by porters.

24. *Is there . . . go*: From 'The Lady Slavey' by Eleanor Robinson.

25. *not unfamiliar tune*: A funeral march, presumably the Dead March from Handel's *Saul*.

The Phantom Rickshaw and Other Tales

1. *The Phantom Rickshaw and Other Tales*: Originally published in 1888 as No. 5 in the Indian Railway Library, with a spookily gothic cover by Lockwood Kipling and the following brief preface:

> This is not exactly a book of real ghost-stories, as the cover makes believe, but is rather a collection of facts that never quite explained themselves. All that the collector can be certain of is that one man insisted upon dying because he believed himself to be haunted; another man either made up a wonderful fiction or visited a very strange place; while the third man was indubitably crucified by some person or persons unknown, and gave an extraordinary account of himself.
>
> Ghost stories are very seldom told at first hand. I have managed with infinite trouble, to secure one exception to this rule. It is not a very good specimen, but you can credit it from beginning to end. The other three stories you must take on trust, as I did.
>
> *Rudyard Kipling*

Two of the stories, 'The Phantom Rickshaw' and 'The Strange Ride of Morrowbie Jukes' first appeared in a Christmas pamphlet produced by the four members of the Kipling family in 1885, called *Quartette*. This means that, with the exception of 'The Gate of the Hundred Sorrows' (in *Plain Tales*, 1888) and 'The Dream of

Duncan Parrenness' and 'The City of Dreadful Night' (in *Life's Handicap*, 1891), they are the earliest stories that Kipling thought worth preserving in his collected editions – certainly the earliest substantial works of fiction – though he revised them significantly for the 1888 Indian Library edition.

The Phantom Rickshaw

1. *The Phantom Rickshaw*: First published in *Quartette*, December 1885; revised for re-publication in *The Phantom Rickshaw and Other Tales* in 1888.

    In *Quartette* it bore the subtitle, 'Being a Record of the Illness of Theobald Jack Pansay, B.C.S.' It was then written throughout in the Poe-like persona of the semi-delirious narrator, and started with what is now the twelfth paragraph: 'My doctor tells me that I need rest and change of air.' A similar kind of story is treated, but from third-person perspective, in a lurid anecdote called 'The Other Man' in *Plain Tales from the Hills*.

2. *May no ill . . . molest*: From the hymn 'Glory to thee, my God, this night', by Bishop Ken (1637–1711).

3. *Globe-trotters*: Tourists; a term of ironic disapprobation used regularly by Kipling and other Anglo-Indians to mark the difference between their own privileged insider's knowledge of India as part of the raj and the spurious impressions of the casual tourist who can never be part of the 'Inner Circle'.

4. *the tale of bricks*: A reference to Pharaoh's response to Moses and Aaron who had come to him with God's message, 'Let my people go': 'And the tale of the bricks, which they did make heretofore, ye shall lay upon them; ye shall not diminish ought thereof: for they be idle . . . Let there more work be laid upon the men, that they may labour therein; and let them not regard vain words' (Exodus 5:8–9).

5. *1885*: The year of the story's original publication. The 1885 version began with the start of the next paragraph.

6. *man born of woman*: A phrase from the Anglican burial service that comes from Job 14:1: 'Man that is born of woman hath but a short time to live, and is full of misery.' In 'The Head of the District' it appears as: 'Man that is born of a woman is small potatoes and few . in the hills' (*Life's Handicap*).

7. *drop-bolts*: A reference to the moment just before hanging, when

the bolts supporting the platform below the victim are about to be pulled away.

8. *from Peshawar to the sea*: Since Peshawar was in the extreme north of British India, on the Afghan border, the phrase is the equivalent of 'from Land's End to John o'Groats', a way of referring to the length and breadth of the land.

9. *visible sign*: An allusion to the Church of England catechism: 'An outward and visible sign of an inward and spiritual grace.'

10. *syce*: Or *sais*, a groom.

11. *from the horrible . . . step*: Playing upon the proverbial expression, 'From the sublime to the ridiculous is but a step,' attributed to Napoleon.

12. *pegs*: Anglo–Indian slang for 'drinks' (especially brandy and soda): '. . . According to the favourite derivation, because each draught is a peg in your coffin' (G. Trevelyan. *The Competition Wallah*, 1864).

13. *There are more . . . earth*: '. . . . Horatio, than are dreamt of in your philosophy'; an allusion to *Hamlet* I.v.166; a favourite quotation of ghost-story writers.

14. *spectral illusion*: The doctor's term suggests a quasi-scientific equation of two senses of 'spectral': 'having the character of a spectre or phantom' and 'produced merely by the action of light on the eye or any sensitive medium' (OED).

15. *Singing . . . senses five*: A quotation from 'The Palace of Art', an early poem, by Alfred Tennyson (1809–92). The speaker in the poem celebrates her blissful 'God-like isolation' in a 'lordly pleasure-house' ('Singing and murmuring in her feastful mirth', lines 177–80), but eventually has to confront 'phantasms' and 'horrible nightmares' which make her wish to purge her 'guilt'.

16. *Syce ghora láo*: 'Groom, get my horse'.

17. *Tennyson's poem*: *The Princess* (1847); the quotation comes from Canto I, line 17–19: 'And while I walk'd and talk'd as heretofore, / I seem'd to move among a world of ghosts, / And feel myself the shadow of a dream.'

My Own True Ghost Story

1. *My Own True Ghost Story*: First published in the *Week's News*, 25 February 1888; then in revised form in *The Phantom Rickshaw* (1888); revised again for publication in *Wee Willie Winkie* (1895).
    The revisions show Kipling tailoring an Indian anecdote for a

wider audience. In the *Week's News* the opening sentence was: 'Over the seas there lives a gentleman who writes the very best stories in the world; and his name is Walter Besant.' In the Indian Railway Library, this became: 'Somewhere in the Other World where there are books and pictures and plays and shop-windows ... lives a gentleman who writes real stories about the real insides of people, and his name is Walter Besant.' In both these versions Kipling contrasted Besant's 'levity' in handling ghosts with a proper reverence 'towards a ghost, and particularly an Indian one'. In the final 1895 version, the anecdote is located from an English rather than Indian angle: 'This story deals entirely with ghosts. There are, in India, ghosts . . .' As usual, in revising his work in 1888, Kipling pruned a proportion of the Hindustani and Anglo-Indian vocabulary away – '*dilmil*' became 'shutter', '*chirag*' an 'oil wick', '*chowkidar*' 'night-watchman' and so on, but it was not until 1895 that he cut the essayistic opening remarks about Walter Besant and the conventions of the ghost story with which he was playing when he wrote it. In fact, in its earlier forms, the story is scarcely distinguishable from the journalistic travel pieces of *The Letters of Marque*, being published in the *Pioneer* at the same time (now collected in *From Sea to Sea*). It also confirms the key role Kipling confers on Besant's influence on him in *Something of Myself*, where he describes Besant's *All in a Garden Fair* as his 'salvation in sore personal need' (p. 71).

2. *As I came ... Desert*: A quotation from 'The City of Dreadful Night' by James Thomson.

3. *pobby*: 'Pobbies' is a nursery word for 'porridge', but this may be a nonce-word derived from Edward Lear's unfortunate 'Pobble who has no toes'.

4. *older Provinces*: Bengal, Bombay and Madras, the earliest areas of British East India Company rule.

5. *changes ... life*: A quotation from the blessing in the Anglican Book of Common Prayer.

6. khansamah: House-steward, cook.

7. *two of them*: In the earlier editions this sentence was followed by two more: 'Up to that hour I had sympathized with Mr Besant's method of handling them, as shown in "The Strange Case of Mr Lucraft and Other Stories". I am now in the Opposition.'

8. *rare*: i.e., bona fide Europeans; 'native' civil servants didn't count.

9. *Memoirs*: These details – the photograph, engraving and Memoirs – were added in the Indian Railway edition, giving a more circum-

stantial sense of the Anglo-Indian traditions upon which the incident depends.

10. *toddy-palms*: Those palm trees (like wild-date, coconut and palmyra) which yield 'toddy', a sap used to make a popular tropical drink.

11. *Sadducee*: A member of a Jewish sect which, according to Josephus, denied the resurrection of the dead.

12. shrab: A drink made of spirits mixed with fruit-juice.

13. *brandy-pani do*: 'Bring me a brandy.'

14. *Society for Psychical Research*: a society founded in 1882 under the presidency of Professor Henry Sidgwick, to introduce scientific method into the study of debatable phenomena such as ghosts, mediums, telepathy and so on.

15. *Kadir Baksh*: The name of Kipling's servant at the time; a sign that Kipling did treat this as very much his 'own ghost story'.

16. Oorias: Natives of Orissa, 'the ancient kingdom and modern province which lies between Bengal and the Coromandel Coast' (*Hobson-Jobson*).

The Strange Ride of Morrowbie Jukes

1. *The Strange Ride of Morrowbie Jukes*: First published in *Quartette* (1885); revised for publication in *The Phantom Rickshaw* (1888). As in the other *Quartette* story, 'The Phantom Rickshaw', Kipling added a prefatory 'frame' to the original Poe-like monologue when he revised the story for the Indian Railway Library edition in 1888. This is the long introductory first paragraph, putting Jukes' strange narrative in context. In 1891 he cut the original concluding paragraph of the Indian editions.

2. *There is no . . . tale*: In 1888 this opening sentence read: 'There is, as the conjurors say, no deception about this tale.'

3. *rich money-lenders*: The British decried the power of the generally Hindu money-lenders or *bunniah* over the Moslem Punjabi peasant-farmers as a consequence of the rising prices of land.

4. *In the beginning*: In the 1885 version, the story began here.

5. *23rd December 1884*: The story was first published in the Christmas supplement of the *Civil and Military Gazette*, 1885, so when it first appeared the date was both 'seasonal' and very contemporary.

6. *hog-spear*: A spear used in the horseback sport of 'pig-sticking', described by Philip Woodruff as 'the game of games' for Anglo-

Indians: 'Ugly lusts for power and revenge melted away and even the lust for women assumed – so it was said – reasonable proportions after a day in pursuit of pig' (*The Men Who Ruled India*, Vol. 2, pp. 180–1).

7. *pickets*: Stakes for tethering horses.

8. *persuaders*: i.e., 'spurs'.

9. *Sutlej*: A river flowing from the upper Himalayas through Lahore and then south-westwards across the Punjab to join the Indus on its way to the sea; it now forms part of the border between India and Pakistan. In March 1887 Kipling wrote a vivid account of the building of 'The Sutlej Bridge' for the *Civil and Military Gazette* (collected in *Kipling's India: Uncollected Sketches 1884–88*), a celebration of the work of engineers like Jukes. There he mentions a visit three years earlier (i.e., in 1884, the year of 'The Strange Ride') to 'an abomination of desolation called Gunda Singh, a few miles on the Raewind side of the Lahore-Ferozepore line', proving 'the nature of the country to be worked on'. No doubt that visit contributed to the atmosphere and setting of 'The Strange Ride'. The two towns Jukes mentions on p. 187 – Pakpattan and Mubarakpur – are situated on the Sutlej River, about 100 miles south-west of Lahore.

10. *ant-lion*: An insect, the larvae of which dig pits to trap ants.

11. *Martini-Henri picket*: The regular rifle used by the British Army in India from 1872 to 1891, named after its Austrian inventor.

12. *local self-government*: After the Mutiny of 1857 the British government thought it politic to foster the self-governing Indian states under their local rajahs and princes, who were subordinate to British influence and protection. Canning saw the native states as 'breakwaters in the storm', and after Victoria assumed the title of empress in 1876, 'the princes were regarded . . . as an order instead of a number of obsolescent survivals', and their states were integrated as quasi-autonomous entities within the Raj (see the *Oxford History of Modern India 1748–1947*, Oxford, 1965, Chapter 7). Kipling's *Letters of Marque* (in *From Sea to Sea*) records his own impressions of the government of the native states.

13. *Deccanee Brahmin*: A member of the highest, priestly Hindu caste from the *Deccan*, a term meaning 'the south'. Khalsia is a term applied by Sikhs to their own communtiy.

14. *continuations*: Slang for 'trousers'.

15. *burnt*: A reference to Hindu cremation sites like the 'burning-ghats by the river' Ganges at Benares, mentioned in *Kim*, Chapter 11.

16. *traveller's tale*: The account of the funeral settlement that follows appears to be based, as suggested by R. Thurston Hopkins in *Rudyard Kipling's World*, 1925, upon *A Journal of a Tour in India* by Captain Egerton, published in 1852:

> We stopped at a ghaut, or landing-place, where they burn the dead bodies of the poorer classes: the very poorest cannot afford to buy the necessary fire-wood, so they merely bring their dead down to the river and literally shove them in, to float down to the sea or to be eaten by vultures, the water of the sacred river, as is well known, conveying them straight off to Paradise. Sometimes they bring down people they choose to fancy to be at the point of death, stuff their mouth, nose, and ears with the sacred mud, and if that does not finish them, leave them there to die, or simply tumble them into the water. Some of these poor wretches have been rescued by charitable Europeans; and there was, perhaps is, a hospital established, and people kept on the look-out for instances of this practice; but it is a thankless office, for the people themselves are not the least obliged to them for their rescue, as they lose caste, if they return to their families, after being voted dead on the banks of the Ganges. There have even been instances of their demanding compensation from their rescuers. The scene at the ghaut is hideous enough. When we saw it, three corpses were burning on separate piles, the half-consumed legs of one, and the head of another, sticking out from the burning wood; the blackened and shrivelled bodies, crackling among the flames, giving out an unctuous and filthy smell. A multitude of dirty adjutants, and disgusting looking vultures, were stalking about close by, hardly getting out of one's way, or else perched on the surrounding huts and houses, waiting for an appetite, or until the meal was sufficiently cooked – whilst some others were in the water, greedily pecking at and devouring what were perhaps human remains; the whole ground around being strewed with carrion, and bones of all kinds – human and animal. It was altogether about as revolting a scene as I ever saw; and is, I suppose, always taking place at low water. The adjutants are, as everybody knows, great cranes, with india-rubber throats, and cast-iron stomachs, which walk about Calcutta, and are extremely useful as scavengers. They eat anything from a thirty-two pounder to a baby.

17. *annas*: An anna is one sixteenth of a rupee in Indian coinage.
18. *pie*: 'Hindu *pa'i*, the smallest copper coin of the Anglo–Indian currency, being 1/12 of an anna, 1/192 of a rupee = about ½ a farthing' (*Hobson-Jobson*).
19. chapatti: Unleavened pancake bread.
20. *European heaven*: Gunga Dass' 'European Heaven' is an allusion to St Matthew 22: 30: 'For in the resurrection they neither marry, nor give in marriage, but are as the angels of God in heaven.'
21. *chase*: This grim method of trapping crows by using another crow

as live bait Kipling probably learned from his father Lockwood
Kipling's book, *Beast and Man in India*, which describes gypsies
catching crows in this way. (pp. 28–9).

22. videlicet: 'that is to say'.

23. *the strongest*: Jukes' words recall those of Thrasymachus in Plato's
Republic: 'I affirm that might is right, justice the interest of the
stronger' (Book 1, Chapter 12).

24. Mignonette: Three survivors of a wrecked boat called the *Mignonette* were brought to trial in Falmouth in September 1884 for murdering and eating the ship's cabin-boy to enable them to survive
their thousand-mile journey in a small dinghy. They were found
guilty and given death sentences, later commuted to six months'
hard labour. (There is an account of this affair in *Cannibalism
and the Common Law*, by A. W. Brian Simpson, Penguin, 1986.)

25. *the dawn*: 25 December, Christmas Day.

26. *greatest number*: Gunga Dass' 'political maxim' is a reflection of
the Utilitarianism of Jeremy Bentham (1748–1832): 'It is the greatest happiness of the greatest number that is the measure of right
and wrong.' English Utilitarians were intimately involved in Indian
affairs, especially after James Mill, the author of a *History of
British India* (1817) (which offered a savage 'philosophical' indict-
ment of the 'hideous state' of native Indian society and religion),
joined the executive government of the East India Company in
1819, followed shortly afterwards by his son John Stuart Mill. In
The English Utilitarians in India (1959), Eric Stokes analyses their
influence on British policy, particularly during the 'progressive'
legal and constitutional reforms of the 1830s and 1840s under
William Bentinck's governorship, as well as their contribution to
the authoritarian administrative character of much British rule in
the nineteenth century.

27. *Vishnu*: One of the three personal manifestations of the one God
Brahm in Hindu mythology; Vishnu is the Preserver.

28. *described*: In its first version as printed in *Quartette* this was followed by an additional final paragraph, cut in 1895:

To cut a long story short, Dunnoo is now my personal servant on a gold-
mohur a month – a sum which I still think far too little for the inestimable
service he has rendered. I have never yet breathed a word to a living soul of
the awful experiences of my strange midnight ride. Even now I expect no
one will believe me, the more so because nothing on earth shall induce me
to go near that devilish spot again, or to reveal its whereabouts more clearly
than I have done. Of Gunga Dass I have never found a trace, nor do I wish

to. My sole motive in publishing this is the hope that some one may
. possibly identify, from the details of the inventory which I have given, the
corpse of the man in the olive-green *shikár* suit'.

The Man who would be King

1. *The Man who would be King*: No magazine publication; first published in *The Phantom Rickshaw* (1888).
2. *Brother . . . worthy*: This unattributed epigraph refers to a Masonic
   tradition and reappears in Kipling's 'Banquet Night', a poem for a
   Masonic Banquet which ends:

   > But once in so often, the messenger brings
   > Solomon's mandate: 'Forget these things!
   > Brother to Beggars and Fellow to Kings,
   > Companion to Princes – forget these things!
   > Fellow-Craftsmen, forget these things!

   (*Rudyard Kipling's Verse*, definitive edition, Hodder & Stoughton, p. 750)

   'The Palace' (1902) develops a comparable Masonic idea:

   > When I was a King and a Mason – a Mason proven and skilled
   > I cleared me ground for a palace such as a King should build.
   > I decreed and dug down to my levels. Presently under the silt
   > I came on the wreck of a Palace such as a King had built.

   > > (*ibid*, p. 385)

   Kipling had become a Mason in Lahore in 1885 (see *Something of
   Myself*, p. 64).
3. *the Law*: Masonic law.
4. *Mhow . . . Ajmir*: Ajmir is both an ancient city and railway centre
   on the Bombay – Delhi line in the middle of Rajputana, about 600
   miles from Bombay. Mhow is a cantonment 320 miles or so south.
   In *Letters of Marque* Kipling wrote: 'From a criminal point of view
   Ajmir is not a pleasant place,' since 'the Native States lie all
   around and about it' and it is 'the headquarters of the banking-
   firms that lend' to them (*From Sea to Sea*, Vol. 1, pp. 42–3).
5. *Loafer*: Compare the *Letters of Marque*: 'Bummers, land-sharks,
   skirmishers for their bread. It would be cruel in a fellow-tramp to
   call them loafers,' Kipling wrote of fellow-travellers in the native
   states, adding: 'A small volume might be written of the ways and
   the tales of Indian loafers of the more brilliant order' (*From Sea to
   Sea*, Vol. 1, pp. 118–19).

6. *Loaferdom*: *Letters of Marque* records the conversation of a character Kipling calls 'the King of Loafers, a grimy scallywag with a
   six-days' beard and an unholy knowledge of native states': 'his
   conversation – he was a great politician, this loafer – . . . turned on
   the poverty of India' (*From Sea to Sea*, Vol. 1, pp. 194–204).

7. *West*: 'Going to the West', 'from the East,' 'on the Square' and
   'for the sake of my Mother' are all Masonic code-phrases.

8. *English newspapers*: Kipling's opinions of the policy of native states
   towards newspapers are developed in *Letters of Marque*: 'With the
   exception of such journals as, occupying a central position in British territory, levy blackmail from the neighbouring states, there
   are no independent papers in Rajputana . . . A 'free' press is not
   allowed, and this the native journalist knows' (*From Sea to Sea*,
   Vol. 1, p. 195).

9. *Harun-al-Raschid*: The powerful Caliph of Baghdad who figures
   in the *Arabian Nights*. 'The shift and play of a man's fortune
   across the Border,' wrote Kipling in *Letters of Marque*, 'is as
   sudden as anything in the days of Harun-al-Raschid's blessed
   memory, and there are stories to be got for the unearthing, as wild
   and improbable as those in the *Thousand and one Nights*' (*From
   Sea to Sea*, Vol. 1, p. 195).

10. *Politicals*: British officials in the native states.

11. *Zenana-mission ladies*: *Zenana* refers to the women's quarters
    behind the *purdah* in Indian houses. Western missionaries tried to
    promote European attitudes towards women within Hindu society
    'by their *zenana* activities which brought new ideas behind the
    purdah (*Oxford History of Modern India*, p. 281).

12. *Gladstone*: William Gladstone (1809–98), Liberal politician and
    Prime Minister of Great Britain, had argued that it was Britain's
    'weakness and . . . calamity' that it had not given India 'the blessing
    of free institutions' (quoted in *Oxford History of Modern India*,
    p. 245). Gladstone's anti-imperialistic brand of Liberalism was ana-
    thema to Kipling.

13. kaa-pi chay-ha-yeh: A mixture of pidgin-English and Urdu.

14. *Modred's shield*: The shield of King Arthur's nephew was left
    blank because he had done no deed worthy to have earned him a
    device (see Tennyson's *Idylls of the King*).

15. *Khuda Janta Khan*: A fictitious name meaning 'God-knows-town'.

16. *Brother*: Masons, like members of earlier guilds and modern
    trades-unions, address each other as 'brother'.

17. *Sar-a-*whack: A nonce-word which seems to combine *sarwat* (mean-

ing 'wealth') and the place-name Sarawak, presumably in reference
to Sir James Brooke, who in 1841 was made Rajah of Sarawak.
Kafiristan: This Persian term, signifying 'The country of the Kafirs
or unbelievers (in Islam)' is 'the name of a mountain tract on the
north of Afghanistan, occupied by tribes which have resisted conversion to the faith which prevails on every side. The country has
never been entered, and even the bordering Muhammadan tracts
have only here or there been touched, by any European, so that we
know hardly anything of its internal geography, and not even the
external geography with any precision' (Col. Henry Yule, *Encyclopaedia Britannica*, 9th edition, 1880, Vol. 13.). This encyclopedia entry was consulted extensively by Kipling in working
out the background of this story.

18. *Roberts' Army*: During the Second Afghan War (1878–80), General
(later Field-Marshal) Roberts led an army of British troops over
300 miles in twenty days from Kabul to Kandahar, where they
won a famous victory over Ayub Khan's Afghan forces and con-
solidated the power of Abdur Rahman as pro-British Amir in
Afghanistan. (See *Oxford History of Modern India*, p. 252 ff.)

19. *English*: Captain John Wood refers to the Kafirs' 'claim of broth-
erhood to Europeans': 'They pride themselves on being, to use
their own words, brothers of the Firingi [foreigner]' (*A Journey to
the Sources of the Oxus*, p. 187). The inhabitants of Kafiristan were
still 'heathens', holding out against the overwhelmingly Muham-
amdan religion of Afghanistan and north-west India. The *Encyclopaedia Britannica* quotes H. W. Bellew's description of a Kafir
officer as 'hardly to be distinguished from an Englishman', and
concludes that 'fairness' was a 'general characteristic.'

20. *Raverty*: Major H. G. Raverty, the author of *Notes on Afghanistan
and Parts of Baluchistan*, 1881. In Section 3, there is a chapter on
'Kafiristan, or Country of the Kafirs'.

21. *Serai*: A *serai* is an inn or rest-house built around a courtyard;
Dravot is referring to the Kumharsen Serai – a place comparable
to the Kashmir Serai, Lahore, described in the opening chapter of
Kim.

22. *draw eye-teeth*: A proverbial expression meaning 'to take the conceit
out of a person; to fleece someone without mercy' (*Brewer's Dictionary of Phrase and Fable*).

23. *priest*: Originally, in the Indian Library edition, Kipling referred
to the priest as 'a *mullah*' throughout this episode and to the
caravan as '*kafila*'.

24. *Roum*: Turkey (*Hobson-Jobson*).
25. *Pir Khan*: The name of a tribal leader. *Pir* is a descendant of a saint, *khan* is a tribal chief, originally a lord or prince (*Hobson-Jobson*).
26. *King of the Roos*: i.e., Tsar of Russia.
27. Huzrut: 'Honoured Sir'; 'a form of address peculiar to the Muslims and applied only to people who enjoy a certain spiritual or religious eminence' (S. S. Husain, *Kipling and India*, p. 109).
28. *Hazar*: 'Get ready'.
29. *Martini*: See 'The Strange Ride of Morrowbie Jukes', note 12.
30. *shall you have*: A possible echo of Herod's promise to Salomé: 'Whatsoever thou shalt ask of me, I will give it thee, unto the half of my kingdom' (St Mark 6:23).
31. *odd and even*: A gambling game.
32. *multiply*: Dravot's words combine God's command, 'Be fruitful, and multiply, and replenish the earth, and subdue it' (Genesis 1:28), with events after the Fall (described in Genesis 3:23): 'Therefore the Lord God sent him forth from the garden of Eden, to till the ground from whence he was taken'.
33. *blooded 'em*: A weird bit of instant anthropological ritual, mixing up the fox-hunting initiation of someone being 'blooded' and perhaps some memory of the sacrificial 'kid' of the Old Testament. They would have read in the *Encyclopaedia Britannica* of the ritual sacrifice of a goat recorded by Biddulph.
34. *Volunteers*: the predecessors of the Territorial Army; therefore somewhat amateurish.
35. *the brown*: A shooting expression, meaning 'to fire into the middle of a covey of game-birds.'
36. *scriptural*: The words are indeed 'scriptural', being quoted from Christ's parable of the talents told in St Luke 19:12–27: '. . . A certain nobleman went into a far country to receive for himself a kingdom, and to return. And he called his ten servants, and delivered them ten pounds, and said unto them, Occupy till I come.'
37. Semiramis: Afghan chiefs have claimed descent from Alexander, who founded a colony in Afghanistan at Charikar; Semiramis was a queen of Assakenoi who bore him a son. (*Oxford History of India*).
38. *the craft*: Freemasons call their organization 'the Craft' and their ceremonies 'the workings'. As some understanding of Masonic hierarchy and terminology is necessary to follow the rest of the story, the following brief account by James Dewar may be useful:

Modern Freemasonry, say the Constitutions of the United Grand Lodge of England, consists of three degrees and no more, those of Entered Apprentice, Fellow Craft, and Master Mason, including the Supreme Order of the Holy Royal Arch ... In each Masonic degree is an initiation rite, and most men who join the movement are content to stop at the symbolic status of Master Mason. The central theme of these ceremonies is the building of King Solomon's temple and the legendary events associated with the work. At the heart of this Masonic mythology is the hero-figure of Hiram Abiff, the principal architect of the temple, murdered by three Fellow-Craft Masons because he refused to part with the secrets of a Master Mason.

(*The Unlocked Secret: Freemasonry Examined*, London, 1966, p. 18.)

Masons are organized in local Craft Lodges headed by a Master, holding warrants from a superior Grand Lodge presided over by a Grand Master. Each of the three degrees of the Mason has a special secret handshake ('the Grip'), code-word ('the word') and type of ceremonial apron. The Fellow-Craft and Master's grips identify those in ranks higher than the basic Apprentice. Billy Fish (p. 230) is a Fellow-Craft. A 'slip' is the technical term for a wrong response to any of the grips. All Masons wear ceremonial aprons, with a different one for each degree. Initiates have a plain white apron, Fellow-Crafts white with two blue rosettes; Masters have sky-blue edging and a third rosette, Past Masters have a device of horizontal and vertical lines plus special ribbons. The layout of Masonic 'Temples' is governed by as strict a protocol as its 'workings' and hierarchy. The Master's chair and pedestal stand in the east, that of the Senior Warden in the west, with those of 'other officers' in fixed positions round the square, the floor of which is black-and-white 'Mosaic pavement' with a star in the centre.

Though modern Freemasonry is a product of the seventeenth and eighteenth centuries, Masons believe that their secret Craft is of profound antiquity and has been passed on clandestinely from generation to generation from the time of King Solomon through the medieval craft-guilds to the present day. They also believe that the secrets of Freemasonry have been revealed to the chosen few in many cultures throughout history – Jews, Muslims, Christians and followers of many other creeds. Kipling would have been familiar with such ideas through reading *The Constitutions of the Freemasons* by James Anderson, first published in 1732.

39. *four-wheel bogie*: A low railway truck or the base of a carriage.
40. *Bazar-master*: Military NCO in charge of policing native

shopping-areas used by the army in a town or cantonment.

41. *by virtue . . . Peachey*: The words are based on actual Masonic formulas used in initiation ceremonies.

42. *raised*: i.e., initiated to the Third Degree.

43. *Kafuzelum*: The name of a character in the racy popular ballad, 'The Daughter of Jerusalem', which begins: 'In Ancient days there liv'd a Turk, / A horrid beast, e'en in the East, / Who did the Prophet's holy work / As barber of Jerusalem. / He had a daughter fair and smirk / Complexion fair, and light brown hair / With naught about her like a Turk / Except her name, Kafoozelum . . . / The harlot of Jerusalem.'

44. *Kohat Jezails*: Old-fashioned Afghan muskets. Compare 'Arithmetic on the Frontier' from *Departmental Ditties*: 'Two thousand pounds of education / Drops to a ten-rupee *jezail*'.

45. *niggers*: In *Cawnpore* (1910) George Trevelyan commented that 'that hateful word "nigger" [was] constantly on the tongues of all Anglo-Indians, except civilians and missionaries', as a way of referring to all Indians indiscriminately. 'On the City Wall' in *Soldiers Three* comments on this practice: 'The Captain was not a nice man. He called all natives "niggers", which, besides being extreme bad form, shows gross ignorance.'

46. *Sniders*: The rifles in general use in the British army before the introduction of the Martini-Henry.

47. *women*: Peachey is referring to Proverbs 31:3 ff: 'Give not thy strength unto women, nor thy ways to that which destroyeth kings. It is not for kings, O Lemuel, it is not for kings to drink wine . . . Lest they drink, and forget the law . . .'

48. *time of answering*: A reference to the Banns read out in the service for the Solemnization of Matrimony in the Anglican Church: 'If any of you know cause or just impediment, why these two persons should not be joined together in holy Matrimony, ye are to declare it. This is the last time of asking.' Dravot wittily 'answers' Carnehan's 'impediments' to his planned marriage by expropriating the words of the prayer book.

49. *daughters of men*: an allusion to Genesis 6:2: 'the sons of God saw the daughters of men that they were fair; and they took them wives of all which they chose.'

50. *Our Fifty-Seven*: A reference to the Indian Mutiny of 1857, as is Ruin and Mutiny earlier. In 'On the City Wall' in *Soldiers Three*, it is said that ''57 is a year that no man, Black or White, cares to speak of'.

51. *as he lived*: An echo of Hamlet's words to his mother about the appearance of his father's ghost: 'My father, in his habit as he lived' (*Hamlet* III. iv. 136).

52. *The Son of Man goes forth*: From the hymn by Reginald Heber (1783–1826), Bishop of Calcutta from 1823–6 and the author of *Narratives of a Journey through the Upper Provinces of India* (1828). Significantly, Peachey mis-remembers the second line, which should read, 'A kingly crown to gain'. Andrew Rutherford, in his *Selected Stories* of Kipling, London, 1987, points out that in earlier editions the first line reads 'The Son of God'.

Wee Willie Winkie and Other Stories

1. *Wee Willie Winkie and Other Stories*: Originally published in 1888 as No. 6 in the Indian Railway Library as *Wee Willie Winkie and Other Child Stories*, with a cover by J. Lockwood Kipling and the following Preface:

This is the last book of the series, and it naturally ends with the little children who always trot after the tail of any procession. Only women understand children thoroughly; but if a mere man keeps very quiet, and humbles himself properly, and refrains from talking down to his superiors, the children will sometimes be good to him and let him see what they think about the world. But, even after patient investigation and the condescension of the nursery, it is hard to draw babies correctly.

Wee Willie Winkie

1. *Wee Willie Winkie*: First published in the *Week's News*, 28 January 1888; revised for publication in the Indian Railway Library, No. 6; separate publication in *New York Tribune*, 24 August 1890. The motto and references within the tale to George MacDonald's *Princess and the Goblin* were added in revision.

2. *nursery-book*: Probably *Johnnykin and the Goblins* (1877), by Charles E. Leland, which has a character named 'Wee Willie Winkie'. The nursery-rhyme 'Wee Willie Winkie' was first published in *Whistle-Binkie: A Collection of Songs* (1841) by William Miller (1810–72), 'the Laureate of the Nursery': 'Wee Willie Winkie runs through the town / Upstairs and downstairs in his night gown, / Rapping at the window, crying through the lock, / Are the children all in bed, for now its eight o'clock.'

3. *marplot*: 'One who mars or defeats a plot or design by officious interference' (OED).

4. 'Hut jao': 'Go away' – one of only eleven complete Hindustani sentences in Kipling's work, according to S. S. Azfar Husain in *The Indianness of Rudyard Kipling* (1983).

5. *Butcha*: Like 'Bell', the name of one of Coppy's dogs.

6. *Old Adam*: An allusion to the baptism service of the Book of Common Prayer: 'Grant that the Old Adam in this child may be so buried, that the new man may be raised up in him.'

7. *the Princess and the Goblin*: A famous children's book by George MacDonald (1824–1902), first published in 1871 when Kipling was six years old – Willie's age. This sentence and the three following it were added in the Indian Railway Library edition.

8. *twelve-two*: i.e., twelve hands, two inches high: four feet, two inches to the shoulder.

9. *for just . . . nurse*: These phrases were added in the Indian Railway Library edition. The illustration Willie remembers is by Arthur Hughes and occurs in Chapter 6 of MacDonald's book.

10. *after all*: This sentence was added in the Indian Library edition.

11. *Sahib* Bahadur: An honorific title: 'brave lord'; *Bahadur* is the Hindustani for 'a hero or champion'.

12. *nullahs*: Watercourses.

13. pulton: 'Regiment'. *Hobson-Jobson* derives the word from Hindustani *paltan*, 'a corruption of battalion', and defines it as 'the usual native word for a regiment of native infantry', adding that 'it is never applied to one of Europeans' (as it appears to be in this story).

Baa Baa, Black Sheep

1. *Baa Baa, Black Sheep*: Published in the *Week's News*, 21 December, 1888 but written for *Wee Willie Winkie*.

2. *When I was . . . place*: A kinked allusion to Shakespeare's *As You Like It* (II.iv.15–16): 'Ay, now I am in Arden, the more fool I. When I was at home, I was in a better place.' It substitutes 'my father's house' from St John 14:2 ('In my Father's house are many mansions') for 'at home', giving a heavenly ring and authority to the idea of being 'at home' with his father.

3. *Punch*: In calling the children in the story Punch and Judy, Kipling makes them palpably fictional, yet archetypal. Punch and Judy

shows were popular children's entertainments at the seaside and elsewhere – and were used by George Cruikshank for his magnificent illustrated puppet-show booklet. It may also be relevant that 'punch' was a popular Indian drink, its name being derived from the Persian *panj* and Hindustani *panch*, meaning 'five', a reference to the five ingredients from which it is composed (*Hobson-Jobson*). There was an Indian as well as British edition of the humorous magazine *Punch* at this time.

4. hamal . . . Surti: A *hamal* is a house-boy or house-servant; a *Surti* is a person from Surat, a city on the west coast of India. Kipling gives the Surti the name of own childhood house-servant, as recorded in *Something of Myself*: 'Meeta, my Hindu bearer, would sometimes go into little Hindu temples where . . . I held his hand and looked at the dimly-seen, friendly Gods' (p. 33).

5. *Ghauts*: A mountain range east of Bombay.

6. Belait: England or Europe; *Belaitee* are natives of England or Europe – hence 'Blighty' for 'Home' in First World War slang.

7. *Roman . . . Parel*: Parel is a suburb of Bombay. Kipling's childhood *ayah* was, according to *Something of Myself*, 'a Portuguese Roman Catholic who would pray – I beside her – at a wayside Cross' (p. 33).

8. *Apollo Bunder*: The main dock at Bombay.

9. *broom*-gharri: The Anglo-Indian term for a 'brougham' carriage, as against a mere '*tikka-gharri*', or hired carriage.

10. second-speech: Kipling tells us that as a child in Bombay he 'spoke English, haltingly translated out of the vernacular idiom that one thought and dreamed in' (*Something of Myself*, p. 34).

11. *Sonny, my soul*: Punch's version of John Keble's 'Evening Hymn' which should read: 'Sun of my soul, thou saviour dear, / It is not night if thou art near.'

12. *Antirosa*: Aunty Rosa is based on the Mrs Holloway (whom Kipling refers to as 'the Woman' in *Something of Myself*) with whom the Kipling children were lodged at Southsea, the fictional Rocklington.

13. *Navarino:* The *Brisk* was one of the boats in the British fleet commanded by Admiral Codrington which defeated the Turkish navy at the Battle of Navarino in 1827. 'Uncleharri' is modelled on Captain Holloway (of the Southsea establishment) who had been a 'midshipman at Navarino' (*Something of Myself.* p. 35).

14. *Ah, well-a-day . . . believed*: This quotation, attributed in early editions to *The City of Dreadful Night* by James Thomson, derives

from 'Easter Day, Naples, 1849' by Arthur Hugh Clough (1819–61). The lines should read: 'Eat, drink, and die, for we are souls bereaved. / Of all the creatures under heaven's wide cope / We are most hopeless, who had once most hope / And most beliefless, that had most believed.' Clough's poem is about the loss of Christian faith, and has as its refrain 'Christ is not risen'.

15. *God*: Compare with *Something of Myself*: 'It was an establishment run with the full vigour of the Evangelical as revealed to the Woman. I had never heard of Hell, so I was introduced to it in all its terrors –I and whatever luckless slavey might be in the house' (p. 36).

16. *fairy tales*: These presumably include Hindu creation-myths and mythological legends from the *Mahabharata* and *Ramayana*. Indian myths and folktales began to be collected and printed by the British in the late nineteenth century, often under the heading of 'fairy tales'. See, for example *Old Deccan Days*, or *Hindoo Fairy Legends* by Mary Frere, published in 1868, and the later *Indian Fairy Tales*, produced by Joseph Jacobs in 1892.

17. *read*: Compare *Something of Myself*: 'I was made to read without explanation, under the usual fear of punishment. And on a day that I remember it came to me that "reading" was not "the Cat lay on the Mat," but a means to everything that would make me happy. So I read all that came within my reach' (p. 36).

18. Sharpe's Magazine: *Sharpe's London Magazine*, a popular children's magazine during the mid nineteenth century.

19. Frank Fairlegh: Originally serialized in *Sharpe's Magazine*, *Frank Fairlegh, or Scenes from the Life of a Private Pupil*, by Frank Smedley, was a popular children's book of the time, first published in book form in 1859, with illustrations by George Cruikshank.

20. *Grimms' . . . Andersen*: The first English translation of the *Märchen* collected by the brothers Grimm, *German Popular Stories*, appeared in 1823, with illustrations by George Cruikshank. The tales of the Danish writer Hans Christian Andersen (1805–75) were an immediate success in Victorian England: Mary Howitt's *Wonderful Stories* for Children (1846) was soon followed by Charles Boner's *A Danish Story-Book* and other translations.

21. *a week*: Compare *Something of Myself*: 'I read all that came within my reach. As soon as my pleasure in this was known, deprivation from reading was added to my punishments. I then read by stealth and more earnestly' (p. 36).

22. *Tilbury*: A horse-trap for two people.

23. *Valley of Humiliation*: See 'A Second-Rate Woman,' note 29.
24. *a lie*: Compare *Something of Myself*: 'If you cross-examine a child of seven or eight on his day's doings (specially when he wants to go to sleep) he will contradict himself very satisfactorily. If each contradiction be set down as a lie and retailed at breakfast, life is not easy. I have known a certain amount of bullying, but this was calculated torture – religious as well as scientific. Yet it made me give attention to the lies I soon found it necessary to tell: and this, I presume, is the foundation of literary effort' (p. 36).
25. Cometh up as a Flower: A novel by Rhoda Broughton (1840–1920), published in 1867 and regarded as rather daring at the time.
26. *Navarino*: Though there are various songs about the battle, this particular ballad has not been traced.
27. *Journeys . . . know*: From Feste's song in Shakespeare's *Twelfth Night*, II.iii.
28. hubshi: The Hindustani word (derived from Arabic *Habashi* and Persian *Habshi*) for a black man or 'nigger'.
29. tout court: i.e., just plain Black Sheep.
30. *nameless terrors*: Compare *Something of Myself*: 'My eyes went wrong, and I could not well see to read . . . Some sort of nervous breakdown followed, for I imagined I saw shadows and things that were not there' (p. 42).
31. *deceive her*: Compare *Something of Myself*: 'One report was so bad that I threw it away and said I had never received it' (p. 42).
32. *on my back*: Compare *Something of Myself*: 'I was well beaten and sent to school through the streets of Southsea with the placard "Liar" between my shoulders' (p. 42). Carrington, who is sceptical about the autobiographical truth of this, notes the similarity to an episode in *David Copperfield*.
33. *blind*: Compare *Something of Myself*: 'a man came down to see me as to my eyes and reported that I was half-blind' (p. 42). Kipling wore spectacles from then on.
34. Andrew Rutherford, in his *Selected Stories*, has suggested the addition of the word 'not',which does not appear in any edition printed in Kipling's lifetime, based on internal evidence and *Something of Myself*.
35. *right arm*: Compare *Something of Myself*: '[My Mother] told me afterwards that when she first came up to my room to kiss me good-night, I flung up an arm to guard off the cuff that I had been trained to expect' (p. 42). Carrington, Kipling's biographer, questions the veracity of this episode.

36. *Fear of the Lord*: an allusion to Psalm 111:10: 'The fear of the Lord is the beginning of wisdom: a good understanding have all they that do his commandments: his praise endureth for ever.'

37. *children away*: Compare *Something of Myself*: 'I was taken at once from the House of Desolation, and for months ran wild in a little farm-house on the edge of Epping Forest, where I was not encouraged to refer to my guilty past. Except for my spectacles, which were uncommon in those days, I was completely happy with my Mother and the local society' (p. 42).

38. pagal: Hindustani for 'fool' or 'idiot'.

His Majesty the King

1. *His Majesty the King*: First published in the *Week's News*, 5 May 1888.

2. *Where the word . . . thou*: Ecclesiastes 8.4.

3. mehter: 'sweeper' (though originally from the Persian, *mihtar*, 'a Prince', according to *Hobson-Jobson*). 'The *mater* or sweeper is considered the lowest menial in every family' (Captain Thomas Williamson, *East India Vade Mecum*, 1810).

4. *cursuffun caps*: i.e., percussion caps.

5. duftar-*room*: 'The office,' from the Arabic, *daftar*, 'a register' or 'public record' (*Hobson-Jobson*).

6. Sirkar: 'The State, the Government, the Supreme authority; also "the Master" or head of the domestic government' (*Hobson-Jobson*).

7. Nautch . . . Burrakhana: *Nautch*, 'a kind of ballet-dance performed by women', was 'in European use all over India' to refer to 'an European ball'; *Burrakhana* means a 'big dinner' or formal dinner-party (*Hobson-Jobson*).

8. *twoofanhonour*: Truth and honour.

9. mahseer: A large fish found in Himalayan rivers, sometimes known as the 'Indian salmon'; H.S. Thomas, the author of *The Rod in India* (1873), gave it as his opinion that 'the Mahseer shows more sport for its size than a salmon'.

10. chu–chu *lizard*: A kind of gecko.

11. chick: A screen-blind or curtain, often made of bamboo.

12. *Mother Bunch*: Originally the name of a legendary Elizabethan alewife; through books like *Mother Bunch's Fairytales*, published in

1785, she became an alternative to Mother Goose as a patron of children's stories.

13. almirah: Wardrobe or chest of drawers.

The Drums of the Fore and Aft

1. *The Drums of the Fore and Aft*: No prior magazine publication; first published in the Indian Railway Library edition of *Wee Willie Winkie*.

2. *Horse Guards*: The War Office, then on Horse Guard Parade, Whitehall.

3. *Sight for three hundred*: i.e., aim for three hundred yards.

4. Pocket-book: The *Field Service Pocket-Book*, the soldier's handbook.

5. *Dr Barnado's*: T. J. Barnado (1845–1905) set up the first of many Dr Barnado's Homes for destitute children in 1867.

6. *Ishmaels*: In Genesis 16:12 it is prophesied that Ishmael, son of Abraham and his wife's maid, 'will be a wild man; his hand will be against every man, and every man's hand against him; and he shall dwell in the presence of his brethren'.

7. jarnwar: Military slang, from the Hindustani *janwar*, for 'animal'.

8. *Mess-nights*: The regimental band would play on guest-nights at the Officers' Mess; afterwards the bandmaster would regularly be invited for a drink with the officers.

9. *hanty-room*: Ante-room, of the officer's mess.

10. *raged furiously together*: An allusion to The Book of Common Prayer Psalms 2:1: 'Why do the heathen rage so furiously together.'

11. *Lost Tribes*: The Second Afghan War; an allusion to the theories of the descent of the Pathan and Afghan tribes of the North-West Frontier from the Lost Tribes of Israel (see Introduction, p. 42).

12. *stories . . . the Colours*: The battle-honours recorded on the Regimental Colours.

13. *territorial idea*: recruited to regiments on a county or city basis.

14. *batta*: An extra allowance made to officers and soldiers in the field.

15. *Paythans*: The standard army form of *Pathan*, the general name for North-West Frontier people speaking the Pakhtu and Pashto languages.

16. *C.B. . . . K.C.B.*: Commander and Knight Commander of the Most Honourable Order of the Bath.

17. *very-close veins*: Malapropism for varicose veins.

18. *housewife*: A small cloth wallet containing a portable sewing-kit, commonly used by members of the armed forces.

19. *Babus*: Native clerks. *Babu*, originally a term of respect, like 'Mr', came to be used 'with a light savour disparagement' to characterize 'a superficially cultivated, but too often effeminate Bengali'; hence used for educated Bengalis in general.

20. *Beni-Israel*: 'Children of Israel'. See Introduction, p. 42.

21. puckrowed: An army word meaning 'to lay hold of (generally of a recalcitrant native)' (*Hobson-Jobson*). *Kiswasti* means 'why'.

22. Khana ... kushy: *Khana* is 'food'; *peenikapanee* 'water'; 'Raja *ke marfik*' means 'like a Rajah'; *bandobust* (literally 'tying and binding') 'discipline' (*Hobson-Jobson*); *kushy* (from *kush*, 'pleasure') means 'easy', and later became First World War slang.

23. *E.P. tent*: European Privates regulation tent.

24. *magnificent ... war*: Translation of the comment by Bosquet on the Charge of the Light Brigade, 1854.

25. *green standards*: Flown by all Muhammadan soldiers.

26. *screw-guns*: Light, dismantlable guns used in mountain warfare.

27. *zymotic disease*: medical term, meaning any infectious disease.

28. *it ... Highlanders*: From Walter Scott's *The Fortunes of Nigel*: 'It's ill taking the breeks off a wild Highland men.'

29. *Ghazis*: a *Ghazi* is 'a Moslem fanatic who believes that he will win Paradise by the slaughter of unbelievers' (W. R. Lawrence, *The India We Served*, 1928). According to the *Encylopaedia Britannica*, 'every other Afghan is a possible Ghazi – a man who has devoted his life to the extinction of other creeds.

30. *I kissed ... Hallelujah*: A negro spiritual. There was a vogue for spirituals in England after the tour of the Jubilee Singers from Fisk University in 1869.

31. *In the ... morning!*: Evidently another negro spiritual, perhaps based on: 'Father Gabriel in that day / He'll take wings and fly away / For to hear the trumpet sound / In that morning.'

32. *kukris*: short-handled, curved knives, used by Gurkhas.

33. *Subadar-Major*: Subadar-Major was the highest-ranking Indian officer; native officers acted as intermediaries between the rank-and-file Indian troops and the British officers who commanded Native Regiments at this time. In the Indian Railway edition he spoke Hindustani: '*Yih* close-order *ki waqt nahin hai. Yih* volley-fire *ki waqt hai.* Ugh!'

34. *Jemadar*: The lowest rank of Indian officer.

35. *cripple-stopper Snider*: Sniders were the standard breech-loading

army rifles before the introduction of Martini-Henrys, apparently still used by the Gurkhas at this time. 'Cripple-stopper' is a shooting term for small guns used to kill wounded birds.

36. *Stung . . . thought*: From *A Death in the Desert*, by Browning.

37. *British Grenadiers*: 'The Old Step', 'the old tune of the Old Line', perhaps the most famous marching-song of the British army.

38. *priest*: Mullah in the Railway Library edition.

39. *Border scuffle*: compare the poem 'Arithmetic on the Frontier' in *Barrack-Room Ballads*.

40. *valley of death*: An allusion to 'The Charge of the Light Brigade' by Alfred Tennyson: 'Into the valley of Death / Rode the six hundred.'

41. *law*: 'in sport, an allowance in time or distance, made to an animal that is to be hunted, or to one of the competitors in a race, in order to ensure equal conditions' (OED).

42. Ressaldar: A native captain of an Indian regiment.

43. *doolies*: Covered litters, 'the usual ambulance of the Indian army'.

A Supplementary Chapter

1. *A Supplementary Chapter*: First published in the *Week's News*, 19 May 1888, and thereafter in *Abaft the Funnel* (1909), Kipling's American edition of uncollected early pieces which was published to assert his copyright after a pirate edition, but was not included in any collected edition. The story is a kind of sequel to 'The Education of Otis Yeere' in *Under the Deodars*.

2. The Song of the Bower: In fact, 'The Lost Bower', a poem by E. B. Browning, also quoted in the epigraph to 'The Education of Otis Yeere' and in 'They' in *Traffics and Discoveries* (1904).

3. *Alice in Wonderland*: In Chapter 6 of Lewis Carroll's book (1865), the Frog Footman sits waiting outside the Duchess' door 'on and off, for days and days'.

4. uninstruite: *Instruite* means 'educated' or 'learned' in French, so this is meant to mean 'ill-educated'. In fact it is merely bad French.

5. *Ouida*: Pen-name of Marie Louise de la Ramée (1839–1908), a popular novelist of the day and author of *Under Two Flags* (1867) and *Moths* (1880).

6. *Collector*: A district official.

7. *Timeo . . . ferentes*: A famous classical tag from Virgil's *Aeneid*, Book II, meaning 'I fear Greeks bearing gifts.'

8. jharun: A coarse cloth; *the scoriac . . . Pole*: A garbled version of lines from the second stanza of 'Ulalume' by Edgar Allan Poe: 'As the scoriac rivers that roll – / As the lavas that restlessly roll / Their sulphurous currents down Yaanek / In the ultimate climes of the pole – / That groan as they roll down Mount Yaanak / In the realms of the boreal pole.'

9. *Théo*: Presumably the heroine of Sardou's play *Théodora* (1884), one of Sarah Bernhardt's most celebrated roles; *Lilith*: The name of Adam's legendary first wife, before the creation of Eve. The Pre-Raphaelite poet and painter D. G. Rossetti (1828–82) adapted the story in 'Eden Bower' and painted a portrait of Lilith as a decadent Pre-Raphaelite Beauty combing her hair.

10. *'98 . . . Récamier*: Madame Récamier was the subject of one of the painter David's most famous portraits and the centre of a *salon* in post-Revolutionary Paris – hence the reference to 1798.

11. *Autolycus*: The 'rogue' and 'snapper-up of unconsidered trifles' in Shakespeare's *The Winter's Tale*.

12. *Main . . . Bashaw*: *Main Girder Boom*: The principle support of a structure such as a bridge. *Kutcha* and *Pukka* are opposites and 'among the most constantly recurring Anglo-Indian colloquial terms' (*Hobson-Jobson*), meaning 'raw, rough, temporary, slipshod' and 'cooked, civilized, permanent, well-made', respectively; *Bundobust*, which literally means 'trying and binding', refers to any system of organization, but in particular to Revenue Assessment. A *Bashaw* or *pasha* is a Turkish title of honour and, according to Brewer, 'a three-tailed bashaw' is a 'prince of princes among the Turks'.

13. *Almirah and Thannicutch*: another mock title. *Almirah* means a wardrobe or chest of drawers or other closed container; *Thannicutch* may refer to a *Thana* or 'police station'.

14. *Uncovenanted*: Members of some departments of the administration who were not under contract and consequently in a less secure position than those in the Indian Civil Service.

15. shaprassi: An orderly or messenger (from *chapras*, a brass belt-buckle).

16. *Meudon*: François Rabelais (1490–1553); see *The Last of the Stories*.

17. *this paper*: the *Pioneer*'s the *Week's News*.

18. *snuffed ... afar*: A garbled version of Job 39:25: 'he smelleth the battle afar off'.
19. daftri: Stationery clerk.
20. *Thug*: From Hindustani *thag*, meaning a 'thief', the term was applied to gangs of robbers and assassins operating in India in the eighteenth century, and was made familiar through the success of *Confessions of a Thug* by Meadows Taylor, first published in 1839.
21. *D.O.*: 'Demi-official' reports.
22. *this trap for him*: Perhaps an allusion to Jeremiah 18:22: 'for they have digged a pit to take me, and hid snares for my feet.'
23. *Paul de Cassagnac*: Paul de Cassagnac (1843–80), formidable French journalist and politician, and a leader of the imperialist cause.
24. salaam bolta: Literally 'she spoke greetings', this means that he has been formally welcomed and invited in.

Mrs Hauksbee Sits Out

1. *Mrs Hauksbee Sits Out*: First published in the *Illustrated London News* Christmas edition, 1890. It subsequently appeared in American editions of *Under the Deodars* under the Scribners' imprint but was not included in the standard English Collected Editions of Kipling, apart from the Edition de Luxe of 1900 and the Sussex Edition of 1938 (Volume V). The text for this edition derives from the Scribners' version. See note to p. 120.
2. puggree: A scarf wound round a sun-hat, turban-style.
3. *Nevermore*: The refrain of Edgar Allan Poe's poem, 'The Raven', first published in 1854 and popular as a song in Mrs Hauksbee's day.
4. *Fair Eve*. This song, 'The Eden Rose', derives from a poem by Susan K. Phillips.
5. *Volunteer ball*: i.e., the Simla Volunteers.
6. *The Hawley Boy*: See 'The Education of Otis Yeere', note 7.
7. *God gie ... ourselves*: See 'A Second-Rate Woman', note 22.
8. *Our King ... Deo Gratias*: From 'The Victory at Agincourt' in Percy's *Reliques of Ancient English Poetry*.
9. *Speak ... peace*: Nature here echoes the words of the marriage service in The Book of Common Prayer: 'Let him now speak, or else hereafter for ever hold his peace.'

10. *hanged . . . lamb*: Proverbial phrase first recorded in Ray's *English Proverbs* in 1670.

11. *Dolly Bobs*: This was the name of one of Kipling's own ponies.

12. *the maid . . . attire*: An allusion to Jeremiah 2:32: 'Can a maid forget her ornaments, or a bride her attire?'

13. *Before me the Deluge*: A variant of 'Après nous le déluge,' a remark attributed to Mme de Pompadour (1721–64).

14. *Mothers in Israel*: A play on II Samuel 20:19: 'thou seekest to destroy a city and a mother in Israel.'

15. *polyandrous*: 'Having more than one, or several, husbands' (OED).

16. *'Now . . . field'*: A quotation from Genesis 3:1.

17. *My heart's in the plains*: A jokey variant of Robert Burns's 'My Heart's in the Highlands': 'My Heart's in the Highlands, my heart is not here; / My heart's in the Highlands a-chasing the deer.'

18. *the feet . . . door without*: Kipling published a poem with this title in 1897.

19. *Si la jeunesse . . . pouvait*: 'If youth knew – if age could' (French). A famous epigram from *Les Prémices* by Henri Estienne (1532–98).

20. *I thought . . . gods*: Another allusion to the serpent's role in the Fall. In Genesis 3:5 it tells Eve of the consequences of eating the apple: 'in the day ye eat thereof, then your eyes shall be opened, and ye shall be as gods, knowing good and evil.'

21. *Alarums and Excursions*: A spoof Shakespearian stage-direction to introduce the National Anthem.

The Last of the Stories

1. *The Last of the Stories*: First published in the *Week's News*, 15 September 1888; reprinted in the unauthorized and authorized editions of *Abaft the Funnel* in 1909. As the title suggests, it was designed as the last of the stories Kipling was to contribute to the *Week's News*. It is a tailpiece to his work for the *Civil and Military Gazette* and the *Pioneer*, and forms a kind of playful, self-conscious coda to the fiction he wrote and published in India.

2. *Wherefore . . . portion*: The verse finishes: 'for who shall bring him to see what shall be after him?'

3. *Kench*: 'Pull' in Hindustani.

4. *Jehannum*: Muslim form of 'Gehenna', the Old Testament equivalent of the Christian Hell.

5. ignis fatuus: Literally a 'foolish fire', it means a will-o'-the-wisp or misleading illusion.

6. *a picture*: An allusion to lines from 'One Word More' in Robert Browning's *Men and Women* (1885): 'Dante once prepared to paint an angel: / Whom to please? You whisper "Beatrice".' It draws on an incident recounted in Dante's *Vita Nuova* and was the inspiration of D. G. Rossetti's painting, *Dante Drawing an Angel on the Anniversary of Beatrice's Death* (1853).

7. *Leopardi*: A reference to the great Italian lyric poet Giacomo Leopardi (1798–1837), 'sainted' in the devil's eyes due to his scandalous pessimism. He was championed in Kipling's time by James Thomson, author of *The City of Dreadful Night*, another infernal poem.

8. *jail*-durrie: *durrie* is a coarse sack-cloth used for mailbags sewn by prisoners, and is also a word for a rough rug or 'floor-cloth' (a word substituted in some early editions).

9. *a book*: An allusion to Job 31:35: 'Oh that one would hear me! Behold, my desire is, that the Almighty would answer me, and that mine adversary had written a book.' The vast 'domed hall' of this Limbo bears a certain resemblance to the Reading Room of the British Museum.

10. *Man of* Us: The Master's joke is an infernal pun on the 'man . . . of Uz' in Job 1:1.

11. *three-volume . . . stage*: At the date of this story most novels were published in small three-volume editions for circulation by lending libraries. Only if they proved successful in this form would they be republished in cheaper, widely available one-volume editions at a price of six shillings or so.

12. *John Ridd . . . characters*: John Ridd and Lorna Doone are the central characters and lovers in the popular historical novel *Lorna Doone* by R. D. Blackmore, published in 1869. Mr Maliphant and the Bormalacks are characters in *All Sorts and Conditions Of Men* (1882), a social novel by Sir Walter Besant (1836–1901).

13. *Oakhurst*: A gambler who appears in a story called 'The Outcasts of Poker Flat' from *The Luck of Roaring Camp and Other Sketches* (1870) by the American short-story writer and poet Bret Harte (1836–1902). The Duchess and Brown of Calaveras are also characters in these stories of life in and around Poker Flat, a mining-camp in the far west, while the Gulches refer to its setting. Kipling

names Hart as one of his earliest literary influences in *Something of Myself* (p. 44).

14. *Doric*: The broad, hard dialect of the natives of Doris in ancient Greece, hence any broad dialect. The paragraph provides an affectionate parody of Harte's play with American dialect from the Gulches.

15. *Caliban*: Here not the 'man monster' of Shakespeare's *The Tempest*, but the speaker in Robert Browning's dramatic monologue based on Shakespeare's play, 'Caliban upon Setebos' in *Dramatis Personae* (1884).

16. *Bishop Blougram . . . no longer*: Another Browning character, the casuistical and epicurean speaker in 'Bishop Blougram's Apology' from *Men and Women* (1855). In the poem, he attempts to justify himself to a certain Mr Gigadibs, to whom he says: 'So, you despise me Mr Gigadibs.'

17. *Robert Elsmere*: The clergyman protagonist of the social novel of that name written by Mrs Humphrey Ward (1851–1920). The novel deals with his crisis of faith in the light of the new biblical criticism, Darwinism and reform; he eventually abandons holy orders to work among the poor in the East End of London.

18. *importations*: Zola's English publisher, Henry Vizetelly, was prosecuted for obscenity after publishing a translation of *La Terre* in 1888 and sentenced to three months' imprisonment.

19. *Black . . . Regiment*: The regiments to which Kipling's Irish soldier Mulvaney in *Soldiers Three* (1888) belongs. The Mulvaney stories first appeared in the *Week's News* earlier in 1888, the same year as the present story and the Zola prosecution.

20. *Coupeau*: The heavy-drinking plumber who marries into the Macquart family in Zola's *L'Assommoir* (1887).

21. *Arthur's Court . . . Fauntleroy*: The legendary court of King Arthur chronicled by Thomas Malory and others was much in vogue in late Victorian England. In 1858 William Morris published his *Defence of Guinevere and Other Poems*, and Tennyson his *Idylls of the King* in 1859. Mr John Wellington-Wells is a character in the comic opera *The Sorcerer* (1877) by W. S. Gilbert and Arthur Sullivan. He sings a song that goes: 'Oh! My name is John Wellington-Wells, / I'm a dealer in magic and spells . . .' Dagonet is King Arthur's court-jester. The tragic love of Tristram and Iseult is told in many medieval romances and retold in such nineteenth-century works as Arnold's *Tristram and Iseult* (1852), Swinburne's *Tristram of Lyonesse* (1882) and Wagner's *Tristan und Isolde*. Allan

Quartermain is the protagonist of the popular African adventures *King Solomon's Mines* (1885) and *Allan Quartermain* (1887). The Impi are a band of African warriors that figure in the novels. *Little Lord Fauntleroy*, published in 1886, had been adapted as a hit play in 1888, the year of this story.

22. *Good . . . Zu-Vendi*: Captain John Good is a character in the Haggard romances, the Zu-Vendi a white African race he and Quartermain encounter.

23. *your make-up*: Presumably a reference to the number of stories Kipling had contributed to the *Pioneer* between January and September of 1888. Appendix I of Louis Cornell's indispensable *Kipling in India* documents his prodigious output during this period.

24. *She began . . . of I*: A quotation from the nursery rhyme 'The Little Woman and the Pedlar'.

25. *Mrs Hauksbee*: The two Mrs Hauksbee stories published in *Under the Deodars* and 'A Supplementary Chapter' were all published in the *Week's News* earlier in 1888. He 'imagined her in the beginning' in the *Civil and Military Gazette*, 17 November 1886. *The Strange Case of Dr Jekyll and Mr Hyde* was published in 1888.

26. *Devil . . . works*: A quotation from the Church of England catechism.

27. Litera scripta manet: Part of a Latin tag, meaning, 'the written letter remains'. It continues *'verbum imbelle perit'*: 'the weak word perishes'. It is included in the 'Delectus', which is a textbook containing passages for translation.

28. *Peterhoff*: The Viceroy's official residence in Simla.

29. *Gilead P. Beck*: A character in *The Golden Butterfly*, a best-selling novel of the 1870s written by Sir Walter Besant and James Rice.

30. *Gunner . . . Shacklock*: Characters in 'The Likes o' Us', a story printed in the *Week's News*, February 4 1888, and only reprinted in *Abaft the Funnel*.

31. *Captain . . . Brigadier-General*: Characters in *The Story of the Gadsbys* from *Soldiers Three* (1888), first published in the *Week's News* earlier that year.

32. *Trewinnard . . . King*: All the names in the paragraph represent characters in Kipling's stories for the *Week's News* in 1888. The following appear in stories which are not included in this volume. Crook O'Neill is from 'With the Main Guard' (*Soldiers Three*); Janki Meah from 'At Twenty-Two' (*Soldiers Three*); Afzul Khan from 'At Howli Thana' (*Soldiers Three*); Durga Dass from 'Gemini' (*Soldiers Three*); Boh Da Thone from 'The Ballad of Boh Da

Thone' (*Barrack-Room Ballads*); Dana Da from 'The Sending of Dana Da' (*Soldiers Three*); the Leander of the Barwhi Ford from 'In Flood Time' (*Soldiers Three*); Peg Barney from 'The Big Drunk Draf' (*Soldiers Three*); Dinah Shadd from 'The Big Drunk Draf' (*Soldiers Three*); Simmons, Slane and Losson from 'In the Matter of a Private' (*Soldiers Three*); Georgie Porgie from the story of that name (*Life's Handicap*). The Tents of Kedar is a story in 'The Story of the Gadsbys' (*Soldiers Three*).

33. *Jackanapes . . . Lollo*: Jackanapes is the child hero of Mrs Ewing's *Jackanapes* (1884) and Lollo is his pony.

34. *Out . . . sucklings*: A quotation from Psalm 8:2, which continues: 'hast thou ordained strength because of Thine enemies, that thou mightest still the enemy and the avenger'.

35. *Musketeers*: Kipling's private soldiers. There were six stories about them in the *Week's News*, collected in *Soldiers Three*. *Helanthami Barracks* is a name used in 'The Three Musketeers' story itself (*Plain Tales*). It may mean 'Hell and the Army'.

36. In saecula saeculorum: 'For ever and ever'.

37. *Entered . . . Sir*: An Entered Apprentice is an initiate in Freemasonry. Kipling is angry to be classed as a raw apprentice having difficulty with his ritual 'ashlar' and his building materials for his House of Fiction. Worshipful Sir is the formal term of address for a Master Mason.

38. *Notre Dame*: The bells were stolen by Rabelais' Gargantua (*Gargantua and Pantagruel*, Book I, Chapter 17).

39. *Trajan . . . frogs*: In Book II, Chapter 30 of Rabelais, satire, Epistemon reports on the occupations of the damned in Hell. There Trajan is reported to be a fisher of frogs, Antoninus a Lackey, and Xerxes a crier of mustard.

40. *But we . . . wise*: From Matthew Arnold's 'Stanzas in Memory of the Author of Obermann,' written in November 1849.